"DELIGHTFUL"
Cosmopolitan

SUSAN ISAACS IS
"A WITTY, WRY OBSERVER
OF THE CONTEMPORARY SCENE."
The New York Times Book Review

"I think that Susan Isaacs is a very wise and funny writer. She knows about the politics of government and those between men and women. *CLOSE RELATIONS* fairly jumps with energy and humor. It is a serious, intelligent book that just happens to be wonderful fun."
Hilma Wolitzer,
Author of *Hearts*

"AN EXHILARATING HIGH . . . Where does one go next to find characters like Marcia, with her endearing, brittle-brave commentaries, with her wit and honest observations?"
Los Angeles Times

"SUPERB, FREQUENTLY HILARIOUS ... A LIVELY DIVERSION."

Kirkus Reviews

"SUSAN ISAACS' SPECTACULARLY WITTY HEROINE COMMITS THE ULTIMATE JEWISH CRIME.
She divorces a full-fledged doctor and sets out on a love odyssey that mortifies her mother and brings despair to Aunt Estelle and the rest of the gang at the mansion. Her eye for the absurdities of life is so genuinely comic and true, I could not get enough of Marcia Green. When she finally meets the love of her life and unsticks herself from the past, I cheered as if it had happened to my best friend."

Consuelo Baehr,
Author of *Report from the Heart*

"HILARIOUS ONE MINUTE ... INTENSELY EROTIC THE NEXT."

The Denver Post

"DELECTABLE"
John Barkham Reviews

"When Rhett swept Scarlett up the stairs, women had their ultimate fantasy. No more. Thanks to Susan Isaacs and *CLOSE RELATIONS*, we now have a wonderful new fantasy to titillate ourselves with. He's smart, funny, rich, handsome and ardently sexy (please underline ardently!)."
Kitty Kelley,
Author of *Jackie Oh!*

"A RISIBLE ROMP THROUGHOUT . . . Delightful . . . witty . . . astringent and candid —the snappy dialogue yielding up laughs on every page, the love story tender and satisfying, the plot pulsing with adrenalin."
Publishers Weekly

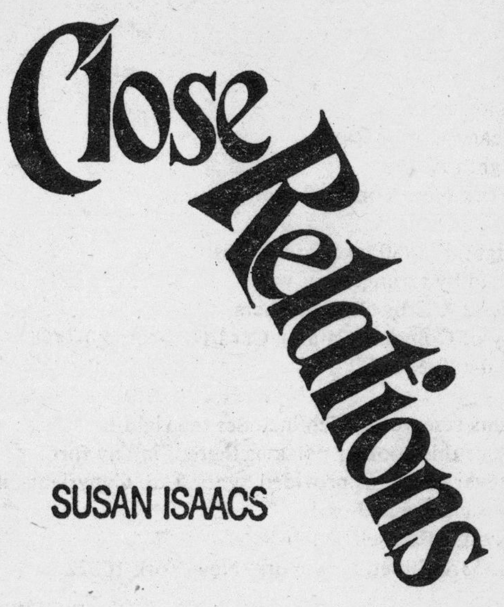

SUSAN ISAACS

AVON
PUBLISHERS OF BARD, CAMELOT, DISCUS AND FLARE BOOKS

AVON BOOKS
A division of
The Hearst Corporation
959 Eighth Avenue
New York New York 10019

Published by arrangement with
Lippincott & Crowell, Publishers
Library of Congress Catalog Card Number: 80-7858
ISBN: 0-380-55681-2

The Lippincott & Crowell, Publishers edition contains the
following Library of Congress Cataloging in Publication
Data:

Isaacs, Susan, 1943–
Close relations.
I. Title.
PZ4.I754Cl [PS3559.S15] 813'.54

First Avon Printing, September, 1981

Printed in the U.S.A.
10 9 8 7 6 5 4 3 2 1

To my parents,
Helen and Morton Isaacs,
with love

Acknowledgments

I sought advice from the people listed below and they gave it freely and cheerfully. I appreciate their generosity.

Janice Asher, Dejon Coffin, Edmond Coller, Ruth Coller, Anne M. Grand, Patricia Hynes, T. Barry Kingham, Edward Lane, Mark BvS Monsky, Bernard Nussbaum, Winston Paley, and Paul K. Rooney.

I would also like to thank my favorite critics—Arnold Abramowitz, Consuelo Saah Baehr, Mary Rooney, Lisa Cronin Wohl, Hilma Wolitzer, and Susan Zises—my agent, Gloria Safier, and my editor, Larry Ashmead, for their wisdom, faith, and unstinting good humor.

And special thanks to Elkan, Andrew, and Elizabeth Abramowitz.

1

My family hated my job. Aunt Estelle had said, "Darling, politics is so unlike you. All those loudmouths and lower-class lawyers. They're beneath you. I know deep down you realize it."

"Roosevelt was a politician. So was Kennedy—Harriman."

"Marcia, sweetheart, they were statesmen. We're talking New York City now, and you know as well as I do that no one you come in contact with is interested in real elegance."

As usual, my mother had let a refined sigh escape through the delicate hole in her pursed lips and then had noted that I seemed to spend a lot of time catering to people in slums.

Uncle Julius had muttered that politicians wouldn't know a nice girl if they fell over her.

Cousin Barbara was thrilled that I was fulfilled but hinted I might combine my career with marriage and children for even deeper fulfillment.

It was a situation from which half-hour television comedies are made. "*Marcia!* In tonight's episode, Marcia Green's warm and winning and wise and wonderful Jewish family reminds her that she is thirty-five, divorced, and childless."

It would have been a veritable laff riot except that it was

my life they were criticizing. They belittled every choice I had made by myself.

That job. Who does she think she is, Miss Last Hurrah, chasing around with all those Democrats, getting older and older and her uterus shriveling to the size of a walnut so she can be guaranteed not to have a family and live a normal life? And her apartment, up four flights of stairs like she was an immigrant, in the middle of Greenwich Village, with weirdos and women who don't shave under their arms for neighbors.

And him. Can you believe what she's involved with? There would be howls of laughter on the sound track as they schemed to drag still another eligible man across my life, trying to pry me away from *him*. Can you believe her, divorcing a very fine third-year medical student, running around Manhattan like she was a wild Indian, and then winding up living with an Irishman from the Bronx old enough to be a lot older than she is? We'll find her a real boyfriend. The camera would pan to a smiling Aunt Estelle. Before the commercial, there would be an ethnic joke about beer cans and perhaps a line or two about blood-shot eyes.

Ha! Such a life our girl Marcia is living.

Jerry Morrissey's eyes were not bloodshot. They were clear, framed with a heavy fringe of dark lashes. And while he sipped an occasional beer, he was quite elegant. Late on that morning when everything began happening, a lock of his thick black hair fell over his forehead and it looked tasteful and quite wonderful, as if styled by a Hollywood hairdresser for a fast take of vulnerable dishevelment. He brushed it away gracefully.

He spoke nicely too. "Listen, if you're hungry, you can grab a hot dog at the stand over there. The governor probably won't be here for another fifteen minutes."

"I'll wait till after the rally." I remained close to Jerry. "Anyway, I saw those hot dogs and they're really an unhealthy-looking pink. They look like they'd bite back."

"Well, it's a tough city, sweetheart."

Across from us, a handbill stuck under the windshield wiper of a parked car flapped in an unusually gentle winter wind. I couldn't read it, but I could guess what it said: THE BOROUGH OF QUEENS SALUTES GOVERNOR GRESHAM!

There would be fifteen sentences about the rally, fourteen followed by exclamation points.

"Morrissey! Marcia!" William Paterno, President of the Council of the City of New York, climbed from the leather softness of his official car and hurried toward us. His legs were short and his feet small, but he moved fast, doing two steps for a longer-limbed man's one. "Gresham's motorcade just went through Long Island City. He should be here in ten–fifteen minutes. Paterno's expression was sour. "Crazy," he went on, "the governor calling a rally outdoors in the middle of February, just to say hello to people. You'll see, five thousand people will come, a third catch cold and blame it on him and vote Republican next November. Gresham's nuts."

Jerry offered him a diplomatic shrug. I offered the truth: "They love him. Did you see the crowd? It's huge." Jerry glanced away while Paterno glanced at me, dyspeptic. Then I added, "He's unbeatable."

Well, he was.

If James d'Avonne Gresham had only listened to his nanny's lectures on table manners, he would still be governor of New York. Small bites, James. Chew thoroughly. Slow-ly. We're in no hurry. But he was, after all, a politician, so someplace between his first meeting of the New York County Independent Democrats—where he quickly made his mark as the only person in the room not shrieking—and his first race for State Assembly, James d'A. Gresham began tear-assing around. His nanny would have deemed it highly unseemly. Members of the leisure class do not dash from a Fifth Avenue penthouse to inappropriate parts of Brooklyn to lunch with Negroes. Nor do they seek the counsel of Jews who have not yet learned to lower their voices. Rather, they sit in law firms and banks and nod to each other. They remain calm. And despite the occasional deviant, the aberrant Roosevelt, they do not become Democrats.

I could be nothing but a Democrat, although my mother attempted to instill good breeding in me post partum: "Marcia, a lady dips her soup spoon *away* from her." While Governor Gresham's grandfather began crewing at Princeton, mine spent twenty dollars to change his name from Isadore Greenbaum to I. S. Green. Alas, by the time

Grandpa Gresham entered Harvard Law School, Grandpa Green had been rolling hems on ladies' better coats for three years; two years later, he moved up to finishing collars, and that was as high as he got.

But this was America, so things got better. In the next generation, when Gresham's father took up the oars for Princeton, my father, the optimistically named Victor Green, was in his third year of night school at Brooklyn College. Papa Gresham became an investment banker, Papa Green an accountant. However, the Greens lacked the Greshams' intuitive grasp of the spirit of capitalism. So while d'Avonne Gresham moved on to become Secretary of Commerce, my father remained an employee of Nathan L. Fingerhut, C.P.A., until his death. But as my aunt told my newly widowed mother, "You can always hold your head up. You were married to a professional."

The sirens from Gresham's motorcade grew from a nearly subliminal hum into a shrill scream. I groped through my handbag for my pen and pad. Paterno would be up on the platform with Gresham, and he liked me, his speech writer, to take notes. If, unconsciously, he scratched his nose or blinked too much or allowed his mouth to hang open, he wanted to know about it so he could control it the next time. He recognized that appearing with a relaxed and Protestant Gresham made him especially uneasy.

I found it exciting. I was the last Green, the only member of the third generation, but much closer to the Greshams. Both the governor and I earned our living in the same way—from New York Democratic politics. That he supplemented his salary with a twenty-five-million-dollar trust is not the point.

In fact, Gresham is not the point either. His soon-to-be-famous Rego Park rally is simply a convenient place to begin. And he provides a nice contrast to everyone else in my life. James d'A. was profoundly Episcopalian, his pure WASP-hood muddied only by a tinge of Huguenot blood.

The rest of us were real New Yorkers: ethnics, minorities. Our roots were mainly in the working class. Paterno's father had been a gravedigger. Jerry's had been a cop. Although we never got to Princeton because the subway didn't go to New Jersey, we got to college, we got away from our old neighborhoods, we got to run the city that aristocrats like Gresham conceded was the most exciting in the world.

We were assimilating into the Great Washed, the rest of the country. We were moving up. Of course, Gresham remained tantalizingly remote. We minded our manners; he scratched his crotch at the April in Paris Ball and forgot to write thank-you notes.

But Gresham wasn't too remote. He loved New York City and we loved him back, joining with the rest of the state to put him in the governor's mansion. Governor Gresham alliterated well, looked well, and performed magnificently.

Jerry called, "Marcia, over here." He had returned from escorting Paterno up to the flatbed truck that would serve as a stage during the rally. Normally, he did not follow Paterno about. He was Paterno's most important aide, his Chief of Administration, and as such remained at City Hall and performed important chiefly duties. But a rally for the governor required special attention.

"Is Bill nervous?" I asked.

"El Wrecko," Jerry answered. Paterno had been hoping this was the day he could pull the governor aside and search him for clues as to whether Gresham planned to drop his present lieutenant governor and select someone worthier—like Paterno. "He keeps complaining that his mouth is too dry so he gives a fast spray with that blue mouthwash he carries and his mouth smells like a disinfected bathroom. And he's cranky. Edgy as hell."

So were we. Jerry's career and mine were tied to Paterno's. His success became ours. Our prestige and power derived from his. In that sense, Jerry and I were like children—or serfs.

"How are you doing?" I asked.

"Me? I'm fine."

"I mean, how's your back?" Jerry had exited from the official car at a bad angle.

"Just a pull." His back was fragile. He had a wooden board under his side of the mattress. "You'll give me a nice soft massage tonight."

"I promised to have dinner . . ."

"That's right. I forgot."

"But I'll call my Aunt Estelle and—"

"No, go ahead. I'll get into bed with the heating pad. It's a good opportunity to catch up with some paperwork."

"Jerry, I really don't mind."

"No, you haven't seen them for a while. Anyway, whenever you get back from a family dinner you're so happy to see me that I can get you to do whatever I want."

"What do you want?" I whispered, waiting for him to whisper back something hot and sexual, or something tender and long-range.

"What?" he demanded loudly, as though I had interrupted a conversation he was having with someone else. He looked annoyed. "Come on. No funny stuff during working hours. I thought we agreed on that."

Embarrassed, afraid he knew how I wanted my own question answered, I glanced away, but he threw me a fast wink before I could completely avert my eyes. Jerry gave gifts and then snatched them away and handed back different ones. His presents were more than enough to keep me with him, yet he never bestowed so much that I might be tempted to cut all my other ties and irritate him with my demands for more winks, more sex, more companionship. "Sorry," I murmured. He reached out to me and traced my lips with his index and middle finger: a consolation prize to keep me happy for the next twenty-four hours, so I would not surrender under the combined Green/Lindenbaum barrage of guilt and hope at dinner and consent to meet the latest anesthesiologist or raincoat manufacturer.

"Don't apologize," he said. "It's just that I have to keep a clear head during daylight hours." And he even gave me a bonus, a grin.

Jerry Morrissey was a very good politician.

The crowd in the parking lot surrounding Alexander's Department Store grew thicker, waiting for Gresham. They were people I considered of my ilk. There were women a decade younger than I, in their mid-twenties, placating toddlers with a pretzel or a bottle of orange juice; pairs of middle-aged women in synthetic furs, fifty-year-old tigresses and leopards, pawing in their shopping bags to retrieve and display a polyester sweater, unbelievably discounted; a sprinkling of older men, retired, faces blank and ashen after forty-five years of shuffling paper under the fluorescent lights of Metropolitan Life.

The crowd grew even heavier, responding to the come-on of Gresham's advance team, young men with electronic bullhorns. "Ladies and gentlemen, in just a very few minutes, the governor of this great state will make an appearance right here! In Alexander's parking lot! Don't miss this opportunity, ladies and gentlemen!" Two sound-equipped trucks cruised the streets, luring the patrons of boutiques, delicatessens, beauty salons, and furniture stores with the same pitch. "Governor Gresham is coming! Come see him, ladies and gentlemen!"

Jerry shifted around, switching his weight from one foot to the other. He did not complain that his back ached, although it obviously did. He grew angry at frailty, even though he was discovering, at forty-seven, that he was increasingly susceptible to viruses, pains, allergies. He equated illness with weakness. For Jerry, a person was either fit or dying.

He lifted his cleft chin toward the truck, pointing it at Paterno. "Look at him. He has his hand around his wrist. I bet he's taking his goddamn pulse again." Paterno's mild hypochondria annoyed Jerry terribly. It made him feel he was working for someone who was less than a man.

"Come on," I said, believing he took Paterno's weakness too seriously. "He's just sitting there quietly, waiting for things to get moving. When he's worried about his health, he twitches—you know, feeling for lumps under his arms or palpating his stomach."

"Marcia, he was complaining about chest pains again last night, right before I dropped him off. We went to that German-American cultural thing, and he must have put away about ten pounds of bratwurst. Then, on the way home, he puts his hand against his chest and kind of looks away, out the window. So I say, 'Anything wrong, Bill?' and he says, 'No. Nothing, A little tightness in my chest. It must be gas.' So I agreed with him."

"You could have been a little more sympathetic."

"Sure. Right. Then I could have had the fun of spending the night at the emergency room at New York Hospital while he gets another EKG. Do you know how many man-hours have gone into giving that guy cardiograms? It's crazy. I'm not going to play his game."

"But he's been lonely since Terri died, living in that big house all by himself. He wants attention."

"So let him get married again. We could use a good wife in the next campaign."

I turned away from Jerry, partially because I didn't want to argue with him. I knew he'd be in a testy mood if his back was bothering him. And also, I still had trouble—even after two years of living with him—in fighting with him and looking at him at the same time. His handsomeness was glaring enough to be distracting.

Generally, handsome is an easy word, casually bestowed. It is withheld only when a man possesses a major flaw, like inch-thick glasses or a forehead studded with blackheads. Any man with reasonably even features is called handsome by someone, as long as he keeps his weight under an eighth of a ton and doesn't drool.

Beautiful is a more exacting adjective saved for special occasions. Women with pleasant features can be attractive, cute, nice-looking, or pretty. My mother told me I looked pretty on my wedding day, although there were mitigating factors: I had had my hair straightened and I was marrying a future physician. Jerry now and then said I was pretty, but I think he was simply declaring his preference for women with my coloring. He could have said "I like blue-eyed blonds" instead. For I am not really pretty. I get my eyes from my Grandma Malke, who, as a girl, stood by the family pushcart twelve hours a day peddling herring. They are quite ordinary pale blue eyes, washed with the same gray as Grandma's herring. As for the blond hair, every humid New York summer it contracts from a smooth yellow cap into a crazed kink. And I am short, so overall I look like a stunted Scandinavian. But I'm pretty enough for politics, where women routinely look intense and blotchy, like the "before" picture in a magazine makeover.

But Jerry was objectively, truly, and irrevocably handsome. His looks were so classically lovely they were dazzling. They startled people who met him for the first time, for such looks do not normally appear in mundane contexts. They seem to demand at least a tuxedo and a microphone, not a rumpled blue suit and the I.R.T. subway.

Jerry, at the height of middle age, was a joy, a treat. His chin was still rugged, magnificently, squarely carved and then, miraculously, cleft dead center, giving the glorious strength of his jaw just a quarter inch of vulnerability.

And the thick, straight, soft black hair, now shot with sparks of silver at the temples. It called out to fingers for a run-through. It curled into teeny o's at the nape of his neck.

The nose? It goes without saying. Perfect and straight. None of that Boston Irish thickness around the nostrils or that crude County Limerick pug. It was a nose to make the chief of plastic surgery at Mount Sinai Hospital eat his heart out.

But the eyes were the best, the Oscar winner in a face of nominees. Blue. Real blue, not drained by gray like mine. Not flecked with brown or pushed around by the threat of green. Jerry's eyes were true blue, deep and so soft that you wished you could stroke their color, lick them.

Such a face.

The crowd pressured us, growing, taking up space. The cops set up wooden barriers and began herding everyone behind them.

It was an unnaturally warm February day. Several people, coats hanging open, faces damp, glanced around, perhaps fearful of being seduced by Gresham into forgetting their dentist's appointments. But most stayed and more joined them, attracted by the tumult, by the blast of "Happy Days Are Here Again" and "East Side, West Side" booming from the huge round speakers atop the cab of the truck.

"You know," said Jerry, "I once tap-danced to 'East Side, West Side' in the fifth grade, in the school talent show."

"You? Really? You tap-danced?"

"Yeah. My mother made me take all these lessons. She thought I'd be the male Shirley Temple. But I lost to this redheaded kid, Paul Rooney, who sang 'Anchors Aweigh.' Little bastard wore a sailor suit."

Gresham's advance team was putting on the pressure, whipping up the crowd. "In just a brief moment or two, ladies and gentlemen, Governor Jim Gresham will appear right here. . . ."

The crowd waited. They wanted to see their governor. It was more than the hoopla, more than curiosity. They loved him. Gresham was perfect for New York: an aristocrat with dirty hands. He played sea chanteys on his harmonica. His doctoral dissertation at Princeton had concerned his great-grandfather's diplomatic missions during World War I. He had given up an assistant professorship at Columbia to live in East Harlem, where he had instituted a successful consumer mathematics program. And he was good-looking, with great Paul Bunyan shoulders and a thick blond lumberjack mustache.

"They have a great ad campaign," said Jerry, a little bitterly. "No slogans, no copy at all, just pictures of Gresham at work. All candid shots: at his desk, talking to people on the subway, having dinner. There's this picture of him sitting down with an Italian family. He's got this monster loaf of bread in his hands and he's tearing off a piece and you see ten smiling Dago faces around the table. He's the only one with a blond mustache."

"Jerry, be quiet."

Gresham was so much the aristocrat that he was beyond class, so secure in his position that he could comprehend the needs of all the people. He was Gresham the Good, Gresham the Invincible. Paterno, who probably began coveting the governorship the day he learned the office existed, had, after a few perfunctory conversations with supporters, decided that challenging Jim Gresham in a primary was faster suicide than a revolver to the temple. He took Jerry's advice, which was that if Gresham, in his second term, decided to try for the Presidency, he would rather bestow the governorship on a man who would not embarrass him, like Paterno. The current lieutenant governor, Lawrence Parker, né Piatagowski, had been one of Gresham's few public mistakes.

"Okay, get back, everyone," a cop ordered, stretching out his arms to herd the last few strays behind the barricade. On the platform of the flatbed truck, Paterno sat stiffly on a gray metal folding chair, three seats away from where Gresham would be.

"He's sweating," I commented. "Why is he so nervous?" Paterno's high, furrowed forehead was shiny with perspiration. With his sallow complexion, it gave him a sickly look. "Do you think it's because he's with Gresham, that he feels so much is riding on their relationship?" Paterno's dark eyes darted about the crowd, as if he were searching for someone who loved him. He was a small man, about five feet six inches, and beside the mayor, the borough president, and the city comptroller, he looked quite fragile. The only things big about Paterno were his eyes, huge and a little protuberant, his great forehead, and his stomach. He had a huge appetite, and all the food he ate seemed to settle in his belly, as if the rest of his small body was not equipped to assimilate it. If a frog who'd been kissed by a princess turned into a man, he would look like Paterno and not like the prince in fairy tales.

"Sure he's sweating," Jerry conceded. "He's wearing long johns."

"Why? It's warm today, for God's sake."

The sound equipment shrieked a wild, high-pitched cry and then calmed down, emitting only intermittent crackles, random pops. "And seated next to the Mayor of this great City, ladies and gentlemen, the President of the great Borough of Queens!" The reflexive booing of the mayor subsided, and the crowd, responding a little to the manic joy in the advance man's voice, applauded lightly.

"I know it's warm today," said Jerry, sounding peeved. "But it's February. And you know Bill. If it's February it's winter and if it's winter it's cold and if it's cold he needs long underwear, so he won't get the chills and die." Even in frigid weather, politicians do not like to be seen in overcoats. They feel it makes them look weak, vulnerable, old.

We watched Paterno lift the back of his hand to his face, ostensibly to massage the tip of his nose. He wiped some perspiration off his upper lip.

"And, ladies and gentlemen," the advance man continued, his voice soaring to new height of ecstasy, "the President of City Council, the man from this wonderful Borough of Queens who almost single-handedly settled the police strike *and* the great garbage strike, ladies and gentlemen, the son of immigrant parents who rose to become a great New Yorker, a truly great American, William Paterno!"

Shoving my handbag under my right arm, I applauded furiously, accidentally poking the woman next to me with my left elbow. Reflexively, she started clapping, a gold crucifix bopping rhythmically each time her upper arms crashed into her huge balloon breasts. Jerry, on my right, stuck two fingers between his lips and gave a piercing, practiced whistle. It was not the sort of sound people anticipate from an adult. Several glanced around, looking for the acne-ridden fifteen-year-old responsible; unsuccessful, they applauded anyway, not without enthusiasm.

"Hear that?" Jerry demanded, his eyes moist, sparkling. "They love him."

"They *like* Bill. They love Gresham."

"Marcia you're wrong. They just know Gresham better. He's been more visible, that's all. If Bill had as much coverage . . ."

"If he had as much coverage, he'd be better known, period. He's not the sort to inspire love. Respect, sure. But he can't—"

"Bullshit," Jerry snapped. "You're talking defeatist bullshit. No wonder . . ."

A woman stood on the other side of Jerry, an ordinary, upwardly mobile Puerto Rican woman in a subdued beige coat. She was in no way remarkable except that she was staring at Jerry, her eyes traveling the circuit, her jaw drooping, so that I, on his left, could peer past him and look inside her mouth, where a reservoir of saliva had accumulated around her bottom teeth. She did not, of course, notice me, even when I rubbed against him familiarly.

Jerry sensed her glance and turned his head to look at her. Most women, upon being discovered, would have averted their heads or pretended to be searching for a friend just past Jerry. That always happened on the subways and at parties. But this one kept staring, examining him unself-consciously, as though he existed in another sphere and could not sense her presence.

He leaned down and whispered into my ear, "Weird lady," and grasped my arm, maneuvering me a few feet closer to the flatbed truck.

"And now, ladies and gentlemen," the advance man said, his tone growing calmer, almost reverential, "the man who needs no introduction. Ladies and gentlemen of Queens, Governor James d'Avonne Gresham!"

From where he had been secluded, Jim Gresham strode around the side of the truck and leaped up onto the stage. The crowd bellowed its delight, the roar bouncing off the storefronts on Queens Boulevard and returning to the parking lot, refueling the excitement. Whistles, screams, squeaks, sighs, and gulps of suppressed desire, surreptitious peeks at the bulge, probably visible at ten yards, under the fly of the gubernatorial jeans. This brave new man, this radiant leader, this easy, self-assured great guy beside whom all other politicians seemed as attractive as Quasimodo, sauntered up to the microphone.

"Hey," Gresham began, "I'm glad to be here. But I've got to tell you something. I didn't come here because I was in the mood for a drive through Queens. You know why I'm here." Pause. Grin. Swivel head slowly. "Pretty soon I'll be asking you for another four years."

The blast of noise was even stronger than that following his introduction. Shouts and applause, the thunder of approval, indicated that another four years were his, no need to ask. "Thanks," Pause. "Thanks a lot." Another grin. Wait until noise dies down. "I'd like to tell you a few of my ideas."

"Listen," I said to Jerry, "do you think Bill could inspire that sort of reaction? That exuberance? That love?"

"No." Jerry ran his fingers through the gray part of his hair. "But that sort of love isn't necessary. It's too volatile. It can't last."

Jab a finger at audience. "The rights of the middle class have to be protected," Gresham was explaining, "because if the majority cannot live in peace, there will be no peace for rich or poor." The majority seemed to agree, because the tumult began again.

"It's lasted three years," I said.

"What?" Jerry yelled over the applause. "I can't hear you."

"I said it's lasted three years!" I stood on tiptoe, my hands forming a megaphone around my mouth, aiming my voice at Jerry's ear. "They're as wild about him now as they were during his last campaign."

"Horse shit!" The crowd's excitement had waned somewhat, so Jerry's "horse shit" was heard by quite a few people standing near us. Even a cop turned, eyed Jerry suspiciously for an instant, and then, assured that he was not dealing with a potential rat-faced assassin, an Oswald or a Ray, turned away.

"Not horse shit," I murmured. "Look."

Gresham bent over, reaching out to a woman in the crowd who had maneuvered near the edge of the flatbed truck. She offered him something. He took it and held it aloft. It was a pale brown square, a knish, half wrapped in a rectangle of flimsy white paper.

"This is why I like campaigning in Queens," Gresham enthused. "A knish. Real food!" The crowd beamed as the Ultimate WASP, their Beloved Non-Ethnic, smiled and inhaled, seeming to savor the greatness of the knish. The dignitaries seated behind him put smiles on their faces, showing they too were enjoying this moment. Paterno's eyes were wide open; he was probably hungry and, could he have gotten away with it, would have grabbed the knish from Gresham's hand and stuffed it into his mouth. "Fantastic!" Gresham took a large bite. Too large, his nanny would have said. The clapping began again, the crowd expressing its pleasure at the communion of candidate and knish.

The applause ebbed, and then it ceased.

Gresham's face turned red, then purple. His grin contorted into a grimace. His long, muscular arms flailed about, as if he were doing some crazy boogie for the folks.

"Je-sus," said Jerry.

Paterno was up first, reaching Gresham at the same time as his advance man and his state trooper bodyguard. The governor's mouth had dropped open, his tongue flopped out, and he would have fallen if the state trooper hadn't grabbed him around the waist and held him up. But Gresham was too big for one man, and the trooper would have keeled over had not Paterno and the advance man propped him up. Within seconds, two cops were on the stage, followed by a News Alert cameraman.

'My God," said a wizened little man standing near us. "Something is wrong up there."

One of the cops, a huge black man who looked like a defensive blocker for a successful team, moved behind Gresham and instituted the Heimlich maneuver. He held his hands under Gresham's diaphragm and squeezed, attempting to push the air up and out of the governor and, with it, the offending glob of knish that was choking him.

But the giant bit of knish did not fly out of Gresham's mouth. Paterno grabbed the microphone that had fallen to the floor and yelled into it, "Is there a doctor? Is there a doctor anywhere?"

Seconds later, a man pushed past us. "I'm a doctor," he

kept calling, all the way up to the truck. Later reports in the Post indicated that he was Steven H. Greenlick, a dermatologist.

I heard whimpering around me, fearful bleats, moans of "God" repeated over and over. Gresham could be held up no longer. He pitched forward and crashed to the floor. The police, politicians, state troopers, and Dr. Greenlick pushed and shoved each other as they moved around, trying to save the governor.

I swallowed guiltily, great gulps of saliva. The air felt colder and seemed to solidify around me, pierced only by the crazed, atonal moan of an ambulance that must have been summoned. It screamed up Queens Boulevard, racing toward Gresham.

"Why can't they do anything?" I whispered.

Jerry shrugged and continued to stare at the truck. I closed my eyes. "Marcia," he said a moment later, poking my arm. "Look."

I opened my eyes, half expecting to see Gresham leap off the floor and wave. But he lay there still, and the police and troopers and pols and Greenlick backed away.

"Christ," Jerry muttered.

A *Daily News* photographer scooted around the stage and stopped in front of Paterno; she focused on him and began shooting. He had begun crying as she approached.

A cop pushed back against the crowd saying, "Get back. Get back." It wasn't necessary. Everyone remained motionless, even after the ambulance arrived, even after Gresham's once-powerful six-foot-six-inch body was squished onto a stretcher made for lesser men. The crowd started to shuffle only as the ambulance drove out of sight.

I whispered, "My God." The air grew icy, numbing me. Then I sensed, more than felt, Jerry wrapping his arm around my shoulder. "It's awful," I added, realizing that the strange feeling on my face was the frosty path made by tears running along my cold skin. I sniffled. "It's like a nightmare, Jerry."

"Well, it's going to put quite a crimp into the knish business," he observed.

2

My uncle, Julius Lindenbaum, furrier and family man, yanked open the door a second after my pressing the lighted button that set off a four-note chime. "Marcia honey," he boomed. "Did you hear about it?"

"You mean about the governor?" I mumbled the last two syllables into his blue alligator as he gave me one of his specialties, a crushing hug, squeezing my arms to my sides and squashing my face against his shirt.

"Terrible," he said, leading me into the house. "Ever wonder how come it's Democrats who always die?"

My mother's sister, Aunt Estelle, and her husband, my Uncle Julius, lived in Jamaica Estates in the borough of Queens, one of those upper-middle-class areas of New York City so greenly landscaped, so secure with its oak doors and brass knockers, that if you clapped your hands over your ears and refused to listen to the residents' accents, you could imagine yourself in Shaker Heights or Bellaire.

Their house was a colonial, red-brick, two-story, with a large central hall. On the left of the hall was a beige living room; my aunt had determined that monotones were quietly rich-looking. On the right was the dining room, filled with brilliantly waxed dark furniture: table and chairs, of course, and a huge breakfront displaying the Lindenbaum Collection of Extremely Fine China, and a buffet—with a marble top for serving and long thin drawers underneath—for holding Aunt Estelle's sizable stock of ecru tablecloths.

"Hello, Marcia." As I walked into the living room, I saw my mother.

"Hi, Mom." Observing her sister's dictum on monotones, my mother wore a brown dress. However, since she was the poor relation, she looked fittingly ill-clothed. The dress clung to her everywhere except the waist, like a late-fifties chemise with static. "How are you?" I asked.

"All right," she answered. "I saw your employer on the news. Did he say anything to you about having seen . . .?"

"I was there." I said it simply, knowing I had scored so many points with those three little words that I could afford to toss them off. My Uncle Julius even waved his hairy arm graciously, offering me a seat anywhere on their couch.

"Oh?" she murmured.

"I'll tell Aunt Estelle you're here," Uncle Julius said. "She's in the kitchen, but don't say anything till she comes, so it's still fresh in your mind." He lumbered out of the living room, anxious to find my aunt and, I think, relieved to get away from my mother and me. Uncle Julius did not seem comfortable with people who could not afford fur.

"Well," my mother said, "you picked an exciting career." Her voice was thin, weary. It sounded about five minutes from dead.

She spoke a little like she looked. My mother is plain-looking, short—like me—and dried out like a parched, neglected houseplant. It's as if the routine of living—pouring orange juice, applying deodorant—sapped her strength. Even when I was a child thirty years ago she was the same, sighing after tying each shoelace, silently serving me peanut butter sandwiches which she never had enough energy to cut into halves. Nothing I did, knock-knock jokes, making perfect hospital corners on my bed, graduating number six in my high school class, made her perk up.

As a young woman, she must have possessed some élan, an aspiration or two, because as a child I heard stories about Hilda saving up to buy a Packard, Hilda keeping company with a Columbia boy and making plans to go to Hunter College, Hilda forgoing the movies so she could buy fresh flowers every day to pin on her lapel.

But after high school she spent four years typing up tax

returns for an accountant with offices on Kings Highway in Brooklyn. Then she met my father, Victor Green, certified public accountant, when he was hired to fill the opening left by another accountant, who had suffered a paralytic stroke during tax season.

My father was not a Columbia boy. He had five years of night school at Brooklyn College and, from their wedding picture, appears as pale and ordinary looking as I remember him. Definitely not the Ivory League type, as my Grandma Yetta would have said. So Hilda Shochet Green traded her dream of a Packard for the reality of a Toastmaster. They moved to a tiny apartment on Ocean Avenue in Brooklyn. Instead of buying a sprig of sweet lilacs, she bought waxed apples and bananas for the green glass bowl on their dinette table.

"How has the television coverage been?" I asked her. "Did they have any footage . . . ?"

"Uncle Julius asked us not to discuss it until he and Estelle can hear it together." She did not look at me as she spoke.

I shifted around on Aunt Estelle's beige couch. I don't think my mother trusted me. She seemed to suspect that I was perpetually on the verge of doing something crass that would further decrease her status in the family, like passing gas or mocking a cousin's choice of stemware. "How have you been feeling?" I asked.

"All right. Oh, I was reading *Reader's Digest.*"

"Any good articles?"

"Let me think. Oh, they had one about the wives of the ones who aren't circumcised."

"What?" I asked, momentarily more confused than curious.

"These women have a very high rate of it." She stretched her short arm across my aunt's long coffee table and took a cashew from a crystal bowl.

"A high rate of what?" I demanded.

"You know what I mean, Marcia." She held the nut between her thumb and index finger and nibbled it delicately with her front teeth.

"No. I don't know what you mean."

"Cancer," she hissed. "Cancer of the vagina."

"You mean cervical cancer?"

"Whatever." Her next selection was an almond, which

she examined closely, as if it were a new and fascinating species.

"Mom." She turned to me, her weakly colored brown eyes trying to fix on mine. "Why did you bring up the subject?" Her eyes returned to the almond.

"I was just making conversation."

"Come on, Mom. You're thinking about me and Jerry."

"I most certainly was not," she countered.

"Mom," I said, "he's a decent person. He's clean. Cleaner than I am. He takes two showers a day."

"That's not funny."

"Who said it was funny? I wasn't trying to be funny."

"My girls having a good time?" Uncle Julius loomed on the threshold of the living room.

My mother and I both smiled and nodded at Uncle Julius.

"Good. Good. Estelle will be in in just a minute. You didn't cheat, did you, Marcia? I hope not a word—"

"I'm saving it all for you and Aunt Estelle."

"Wonderful. Well, just make yourself comfortable." He stalked the living room and sat at the other end of the couch. It was a leviathan of a sofa, a sectional that wound its eighteen feet around two sides of the living room. "You want a drink, Marcia?"

"A drink?" my mother muttered. Our family, of course, did not drink before dinner, although once at the table, a glass of tomato juice with an overhanging lemon wedge was de rigueur.

Uncle Julius spoke fast. "I got some Cherry Heering and some Dubonnet. Or do you want something harder? Scotch?"

"Nothing, thanks."

Uncle Julius shot my mother a fast glance: See, Hilda, at least Irish isn't contagious.

"But if you want something, don't let me stop you."

I could not imagine anyone stopping Uncle Julius. He combined a massive, czarlike presence with unwavering self-assurance. The resulting force was so powerful it seemed elemental. I could no more deflect his hugs and prolonged cheek kisses than I could order a hurricane to leave New York and go blow on New Jersey.

Because he never questioned himself, no one ever questioned him. Women accepted his suffocating embraces, pulling their lips inside their mouths so as not to smear lipstick on his shirt. Men fought not to wince as Uncle Julius shook their hands and squashed their knuckles. Did you ring his bell, collecting for Cystic Fibrosis or the Heart Fund? He'd bellow a "hi, sweetheart" and tear off a fast twenty or two from his roll of bills and stuff it into your hand. Was your son having trouble getting into medical school? Don't worry, Dave, I'll speak to a couple of people. Uncle Julius, apolitical, not even registered to vote, understood power. In Jamaica Estates, he was a mover, a doer. And he demanded no quid pro quo, although obviously, if he had managed to get your semiliterate daughter a summer job at the local library, you bought your lynx at Julius Lindenbaum Fine Furs Ltd. when the leaves began to fall.

"How is Barbara?" I asked him. His daughter, my cousin, was six months older than I.

My Aunt Estelle glided up behind me and answered. "She's fine, darling. Just finishing a diet with a special metabolism doctor on Fifth Avenue, near the Guggenheim Museum. How are you?" Like my mother, she wore brown, but hers was a tissuey wool, finely tailored with a soft pleated skirt and high collar. It flattered her short body; she looked rich and well turned out, like an expensive roast.

"I'm fine, thanks." My aunt leaned her head to the left, offering me her right cheek to kiss. I did so.

"Now," she said, lowering herself into a straight-backed chair that was upholstered in a creamy silk, "tell me what happened today." Her pale, fleshy arms rested on the carved mahogany ones of the chair. She was a queen granting an audience.

"Well, some woman offered him a knish—"

"And he took it, just like that?"

"Yes. I mean, it was an impulsive gesture."

"It never occurred to him that she could be a Red China spy with poison?" My mother and uncle simultaneously pursed their lips in thoughtful expressions and, separately, nodded at my aunt's sophisticated insight.

"Well, the woman looked ordinary."

"How did they know it's a knish? You turn on the radio in the kitchen and all you hear is knish, knish. It was probably one of those square cocktail egg rolls, full of shrimp and all those vegetables they use and God knows what other dreck."

"Aunt Estelle, it looked like a knish to me."

"Darling, have you ever heard of anyone choking to death on a knish?"

In my family, caprice always triumphed over logic, opinion slaughtered fact. Normal conversation was impossible because all rules of reasonable discourse were suspended. I found a five-minute discussion of my vacation plans more exhausting than a month's worth of intense political campaigning.

Maybe it's universal and there's dementia released whenever two people from the same gene pool meet. I've rarely seen anyone who didn't look paler returning from a family gathering than leaving for it.

"Aunt Estelle, let me explain what I saw."

"Later, Marcia darling. It's so upsetting. Come over here and let me see that necklace."

I walked across the thick, spongy carpet and bent toward her.

"What a sweet locket," she said, peering closely for a thorough inspection. "Is it new?"

"Jerry gave it to me. For Christmas."

Silence. Sorry, my fault. My mother glanced down at the buff-colored carpet, ashamed. Uncle Julius stuck his paws in his pockets.

"Would you like to hear some more about this afternoon?" I offered. "About Gresham? I was only about ten feet . . ."

But Aunt Estelle endured. "Let me see it," she cooed, lifting the dainty heart. "How nice. Did he pick it out himself?"

"Yes," I snapped. I didn't know what she had planned, but sensed it couldn't be good.

"Real gold?"

"Yes."

"I don't think so, darling. I mean, I'm sure he paid for real gold but I think it's electroplated." She rubbed it between her fingers and let it drop back to my neck. I stood upright. "He probably just walked in off the street. I mean, he doesn't have a relationship with a jeweler, does he?"

"I don't know."

"Probably not," she said, smiling again. She turned her

head toward my mother. "They leave themselves wide open, unless they can afford to go to Tiffany's, and then they pay for the name."

"Aunt Estelle—"

"I'm sure he means well, Marcia."

"He does mean well."

"Good, good," enthused my Uncle Julius, who began pacing the room, trying to escape the inevitable clash.

"He more than means well. He makes me happy."

My aunt looked at my mother and demanded, "What is happiness?" My mother shrugged.

"Look," I snapped, "every time we get together it's the same thing. Can't you just accept that I'm content?"

"A minute ago it was happy," my mother observed.

"Goddamn it, you refuse even to meet him, to give him the chance—"

"He wouldn't feel comfortable here," my Aunt Estelle said. "Anyway, Marcia, before you lose your temper again, just remember that we don't like these scenes any more than you do. But you say you're happy and what do we see in your life? Nothing. What does this man have to offer you? Marriage? Children?"

"Where will you be five–ten years from now?" my mother chimed in.

"Let me do it, Hilda," my aunt said. "Marcia, he may be very sweet for all I know, but he could wander off to a bar and grill one night and never come back. Did you ever think of that? What would happen to you then?"

"Nothing would happen. Listen to me, try to understand. I can take care of myself. I'm doing that now. I have a wonderful job, friends—"

"Friends? Your friends are political people who stab friends in the back for a living."

"Aunt Estelle, please—"

"Taking care of yourself! In an apartment without a doorman where any rapist could walk right in."

Uncle Julius refereed. He pulled out an exceedingly large handkerchief and blew his nose *Honk!* Aunt Estelle rose, said "Dinner," and gave my cheek two light pats.

The big rectangular dining room table was covered with a pale linen cloth trimmed with brown lace at each of its four corners. It was nearly obscured by the place settings and the platters and bowls of gold-leafed china, silver, and cut crystal. These serving pieces, as my mother and aunt called them, were filled with the usual Lindenbaum cuisine: rolls and white and rye bread, pot roast and tiny potatoes, kasha and varnishkas. Four thick slabs of stuffed derma steamed under a heavy blanket of flour-thickened pot-roast gravy. My family may have moved up to English bone china, French crystal, and Belgian linen, but in food, good taste remained strictly Eastern European.

Someone once described Jewish food as a brown cuisine, which is essentially true, although that definition did not allow for the ruby red of borscht or the deep forest green of sour pickles. That night, the table was further accented with a shimmery orange ring—a gelatin mold—and a crimson blaze of pickled peppers on Florentined Wedgwood.

"Hilda darling, another piece of meat," my aunt urged. My mother only took one slice of meat at a time, although she'd invariably make two or three return trips. "'What will happen now that he's passed away, Marcia?"

"Gresham? Well, there will definitely be a primary. You see, the lieutenant governor really has a very narrow political base."

"That should be exciting," my aunt remarked. "Hilda, you've hardly eaten anything."

"All right, one more," my mother said, accepting the platter of meat my uncle placed on her uplifted palms.

"Do you want to hear about what happened this afternoon?" I asked.

"Later, Marcia," Aunt Estelle said soothingly. "Not at the dinner table."

Conversation did not cease, of course. Uncle Julius volunteered that I was too "petite" for a long-haired fur like fox or coyote. Aunt Estelle explained that in my case "petite" meant short. My mother asked if I wanted my copy of *The Complete Poems and Plays of T. S. Eliot* or should she donate it to the library because I hadn't looked at it since college and she needed the space on the bookshelves. Aunt Estelle whispered that her friend Miriam Zackheim's sister had had a mastectomy and, lowering her voice even more, that a girl who was my age who also went to Queens College was a homosexual and she wouldn't mention names because she had sworn not to but this had been a nice girl, a sorority girl who had never had any problems meeting boys.

And two cups of tea and a slice of jelly roll.

"No fruit, Marcia?"

"No, thanks, Aunt Estelle."

"I ripened the peaches myself. They're not hard." I took a peach and was about to bite into it when I heard: "There's a fruit knife right next to your plate, darling. That little knife with the mother-of-pearl handle."

I took a few stabs at the peach and then excused myself, walking back through the central hall toward the bathroom. But on my way I was drawn by Aunt Estelle's wall of pictures, a floor-to-ceiling gallery of photographs of every relative born since the invention of the camera. Each photo was matted and framed, whether it was a snapshot or a full-fledged portrait, like the one of my cousin Kenny, the littlest Lindenbaum, taken when he received his doctorate from M.I.T. The photographer had airbrushed out Kenny's acne scars, so he looked quite handsome, like a fat-faced Montgomery Clift. Kenny lived in New Mexico, where he worked as a biophysicist for the army, doing some research that made him terribly nervous. During his annual Passover visit, his left cheek twitched and his hands trembled so that he could barely break a piece of matzoh. He was not his parents' favorite.

There were other pictures too: Grandma Yetta cuddling baby Estelle while three-year-old Hilda stared at the floor, her toddler shoulders slumping wearily; Uncle Julius as a boy in Bensonhurst, slouching, trying to look cool and American. And Cousin Helen in her middy blouse, waving; Great-aunt Bertha, whose breasts were so huge, like two giant knackwursts, that her belt fit over them; Cousins Morty and Harold, grinning, their eyes obscured by the shadow from the peaks of their Brooklyn Dodger caps. There was even a picture of my parents pushing me in my carriage; I was sitting up but kept in place by a harness that attached to the carriage. I must have been less than a year old. I was bald and unsmiling.

But most of the photographs were of my cousin Barbara, the finest flowering of the family tree. There was Barbara as a child, pudgy-cheeked, in her Brownie uniform. Barbara on roller skates. Barbara dressed in a pink, gauzy strapless prom gown, a corsage of orchids on her wrist. With a tennis racket. With a bridal gown. With Buckingham Palace behind her. With Philip, her husband, beside her. With Michael and Peter, her sons. And again with tennis racket, this time on her private court.

On her wedding day, Barbara had turned to me, her matron of honor, and whispered, "Isn't life wonderful?" I found myself smiling instead of gagging. She had seemed sincere. Barbara had been born happy and lucky. When she smiled, the world beamed back.

Aunt Estelle somehow wafted into the hallway, landing right beside me. I did not realize she was there until she touched my arm.

"Marcia," she said, taking my hand into hers. Her hand was padded and soft, like the softest part of a baby. "Don't be depressed, darling." I turned to meet her eyes, but they were gazing at a silver framed snapshot of her grandsons, dressed in identical blazers and slacks, the uniform of their country day school. "You'll meet someone right. Your time will come too."

It wasn't until later, on the way home, that I realized I had been so upset with my aunt that I had forgotten to go to the bathroom.

My mother and I took the same subway. Her ride was only minutes long, and I had another three quarters of an hour to Greenwich Village, but our short time together was more frightening and silent than the rest of my ride, alone in the subway. Full-bladdered, I twitched about in my seat. She sat beside me for those few minutes, her legs pressed tightly together, her hands, clenched into hard fists, resting on unyielding thighs. I listened to the gut-churning screech of the train's wheels, read a poster advising victims of violent crimes to telephone a Manhattan number for counseling, and learned from the writing on the wall that Carmen sucks cocks and Susan loves Jay 4-ever.

My mother's silence felt stifling. I sensed she was hard at her wordless work, raking over her resentments. Her squat, thick trunk, seemingly detached from her mind and rigid legs, swayed and shook with the subway's motion. First, of course, was her weekly humiliation by my aunt Estelle. My mother saw herself forced to sit at a dinner table covered with meats and starches and condiments that cost more than she spent on food for an entire week. She saw herself accepting the castoff cashmere cardigan, the outmoded handbag, the dross of a wealthy woman's life, the passé luxuries Aunt Estelle concluded were too good for her maid.

My mother ran her fingers over her cheek; both hand and face were covered with a veil of wrinkles. Her sister's face was lubricated by the queen bee, colored with powders and gels so expensive that a half-ounce jar of night cream cost what my mother might spend on a new spring coat. To have such a sister as Estelle, to yearn to buy, despite shrugged disclaimers, nightgowns with hand embroidery and to be visited weekly by a little Polish lady who creams your cuticles, to go to a Florida health spa to lose five pounds, to gain it back at catered luncheons and restaurant dinners. To realize that while she cut coupons for 10¢ off Fab, her sister was cutting them from City of Utica bonds, 6.1 percent, due 1996.

It wasn't right. My mother was smarter than her sister. While my Aunt Estelle skimmed the label of a blouse, searching for assurance that it was truly one hundred percent silk, my mother read books. Each Saturday afternoon she would visit the library, leaving an hour later with a shopping bag of ten or twelve books that would last her until the next weekend. She read everything, from ponderous translations of German allegories to modern gothic romances, where the heroine is ravished once every thirty pages. She read biographies of musicians, accounts of demonic possession, ghosted autobiographies of politicians and starlets, and every book that dealt, even peripherally, with American and Western European aristocracy.

So unfair, said my mother's tight mouth, with dry little lines radiating from her lips. To have had only one child and then, at age sixty, to discover an inexorable law of nature: Losers beget losers. Her daughter was not dependable. She was not married. She was not elegant. Her humor was suspect. Hilda couldn't even have the pleasure of a few warm chuckles with a bright, delicious daughter, a fair-haired Barbara who would invite her to lunch in Manhattan and tell her frothy tales of her joyous marital life.

"Good-bye," she said as the train pulled into her stop.

I returned to an empty apartment. Jerry, I knew, was with Paterno, holding his hand and fielding telephone calls from cronies and reporters who wanted an eyewitness account of Gresham's death.

The apartment we shared in Greenwich Village was about two blocks away from the charming section and a half block from where the old Women's House of Detention used to be, until it had been razed when someone decided it was unfit even for whores and junkies. Our building, a five-story walk-up, was constructed from the same sort of dank brick that the jail had been, and it looked gloomy. If Emily Brontë had written about apartment houses, she might have seen the façade of ours in her imagination.

But inside, the rooms were spacious, the ceilings high, and the rent not outrageous. I opened the refrigerator and took out the only thing we had to drink—a can of presweetened iced tea. After work, I was generally too tired to market and Jerry never considered it; he could thrive on year-old saltines.

Since we had no dining room, I sat at a small round butcher-block table in the end of the living room near the kitchen. The chairs, made from bentwood, were not ungraceful, but they were uncomfortable. The woman who had lived with Jerry before me, a demographer who worked for the Harris polling organization, had had an unerring eye for the decorating cliché. Kathye Baron, for that was her name, had built her dream house for Jerry, furnishing the living room with an ersatz Tiffany lamp, an oak umbrella stand, several floor pillows fashioned from midget-sized Oriental rugs, and a huge bronze jar that sprouted tall stalks—dried wheat or swamp grass.

The scale of the furniture would have gotten a first-year interior design student an unequivocal B minus, but Kathye Baron's sense of color was off. The room irritated people. The couch was not a true red, but a cherry so dull it was almost maroon. The carpet, probably intended to be a neutral pale brown, had so much yellow that it looked stained by some unhealthy secretion. Even an impulsive purchase, a small mohair blanket she had bought for Jerry's birthday, was jarring. It was thrown over the arm of the couch. She had probably thought she was selecting a soft pink to harmonize with the red fabric. Instead, the blanket was the color of human flesh and guests made certain not to lean against its hairy softness. Then, just two weeks after Jerry's birthday, in the cold end of January, Kathye Baron had moved out.

I traipsed across the rug and turned on the television. Channel Five featured a man pointing to a piece of oak tag with a diagram featuring a red esophagus and a blue trachea. Channel Four was running a head shot of Gresham along with Verdi's *Requiem* for background music. Channel Two, finally, had a newscaster, a young woman in her mid-twenties with thick swirls of blue-black hair, luscious garnet lips, and a heavy midwestern accent.

". . . according to New York City Medical Examiner Irwin Robinson, the cause of death was a piece of liver knish. A knish"—and she blinked at the teleprompter—"is a fried or baked turnover of dough with a filling like potato or kasha or, in this case, liver. The knish lodged in Governor Gresham's—" She pronounced "knish" with a silent k; I changed channels.

Channel Seven showed the same few hunded feet of film that I was to see over and over that night, film taken by the stations' pool camera. Gresham smiling. Gresham not smiling. Gresham falling. Gresham dead.

"How," asked Dr. Donald Finkelberg, dean of commentators, later that night on Channel Five again, "how could such a thing like this happen?"

And a panel of experts on Channel Thirteen, to a person, could not answer him. Dr. Hazel Bennett, identified as "thoracic surgeon" in small letters that hid part of her chin, was able to offer several theories. "But bottom line, Mel," she informed the program's moderator, "bottom line is that the Heimlich maneuver should have worked." She adjusted her microphone with long, flexible surgeon's fingers. She wore no nail polish.

Dr. Bennett was right. As we learned several days later, the reason Officer John Baker failed in his first-aid attempt was because access to Gresham's diaphragm had been blocked, cut off by the hip-to-chest corset the governor had been wearing until he lost the forty pounds ordered by his media director.

I watched Gresham die, again and again, until it was nearly ten o'clock. By then, it had become so familiar that it was almost comforting to watch. I knew Gresham would fall sideways and would lie on his left side, jerking his legs about as if he were having a dream about running. The left half of his big blond stand-out mustache would be squashed against the floor of the truck, leaving the right half sticking up in the air like a hairy question mark.

"Marcia?" Jerry had a gift for smooth, silent movement. He would have made a superb burglar, sneaking in on cat feet. I hadn't even heard him opening the locks.

"Here. By the TV." The room was dim, lit only by the glow of the television. I was somewhat obscured by the darkness and Kathye Baron's dry, dusty stalks.

"Come on. You're still watching that?"

I nodded, noting that the governor's shoelace on his right work boot had become untied. I didn't turn to look at Jerry.

"Would you please turn the damned thing off? It's morbid, you sitting here in the dark, watching that."

"It's not morbid. It's news." The camera panned quickly, but there was an excellent shot of Paterno looking appropriately shattered.

"It's not news," Jerry said. "It hasn't been news since lunchtime."

"How's Bill?" I asked.

"Impossible. Blabbing away and then all of a sudden sitting back stricken, like *he* had choked. I finally called his sister and got her to take him for the night; otherwise he'd talk himself into something fatal and I'd have to bail him out of the hospital at three in the morning. Now would you please turn that goddamned thing off?"

"How's your back?"

Jerry moved gracefully through the darkened living room without tripping and turned off the television. Then he came, leaned over me, and said, "Let's go inside."

"Did you have dinner?" I asked, rising from the chair.

"Three pretzels. They were delicious."

"And a drink too. Right?"

"I see," he remarked. "You're going to be the poor, long-suffering woman, staying home and mourning while the old Irish sot gets himself pissed. Well, I had two drinks. Scotch. Very tasty."

"Don't be so hypersensitive. I didn't say you were a sot."

"No, but in your heart you felt it. Nasty goyim drinking whiskey instead of a thimbleful of Manischewitz."

"Goyim' is plural."

"So are two scotches. But they're not enough to make me drunk, Marcia. Not even enough to get a mild buzz on."

"I know."

"I know you know. But every time you come home from your aunt's house you need a little reminding. They weaken your resolve."

"They weaken more than that. Listen, I'm really tired."

"Then let's get into the bedroom."

"Jerry, it's been such a long day. . . ." He walked ahead of me into the bedroom, switched on the light, and began undressing, stage center, before I could finish my lines.

Jerry's skin was very light, but without that dead New York pallor. Instead, it was opalescent, almost white and shimmery, and it contrasted with his straight black chest hair, making the hair look thickly luxurious, like a black flower on a white satin sheet. The stem of the flower ran down his belly and then rooted itself in the curlier hair around his penis. I moved in a little closer.

"Come on. All the way over here," he said. With one hand he grasped my wrist while the other reached around the back of my neck, pulling me up to him.

"Oh, God." His hands were so hot that, reflexively, I stiffened and then, almost instantaneously, softened. Each time he touched me, my skin startled to Jerry's heat.

His temperature was always a degree or two above mine, but I never seemed to remember it until the moment I felt him. He was lighter in spirit than I, easier-going, so I anticipated coolness. Calm, pale people should be cold to the touch, chilled by eons of exposure to icy winds off the North Sea. But temperate, tranquil Jerry always burned.

As his hand slipped over my neck to my throat and down past the open collar button on my shirt, it flamed the skin in its path. His fingers slid inside my bra and moved around in electric arcs. I moaned. I felt invisible, downy hairs standing on end, tiny capillaries dilating to rush blood in, compensating for the sudden fire that burned slowly across my breast.

His tongue and lips and saliva were hotter too. Even the prickles of his beard seemed heated; as we kissed, turning and maneuvering our heads, his roughness seared and abraded the soft skin of my face.

"Jerry, please." He kept kissing and feeling me, so I pulled off my own clothes with shaking, clumsy fingers, letting everything fall around me on the floor. "Now. Please."

Our thighs pressed together, breasts and chests and bellies rubbing hard. All at once, I had his whole body suffocating mine, his mouth and tongue infecting my openings with hot licks and kisses, his teeth nibbling away at my flesh. And at that moment, like always, I caught his fever.

3

"What do you actually get from him?" my cousin Barbara demanded.

"Three guesses."

"No, seriously, Marcia." Her voice was muffled because she was inside her closet, debating which pair of gray shoes to wear with her gray and violet tweed suit. "You can get *that* any place, apparently. From what I've been reading, people are having relationships with mechanical devices. Ridiculous, going out for D batteries instead of cocktails." She emerged from her closet with a pair of spike-heeled shoes with pointed toes, the sort that must have been worn to country club luncheons in the mid-fifties. They looked dated. "Do you like these? I bought them last week. Horrendously expensive, but I loved their lines." She turned a shoe to show off its profile. I nodded. "Now, what was I saying?" she asked.

"You were teetering on the brink between vibrators and Jerry."

"Oh," she murmured. Barbara sat on an antique ivory satin chaise longue near a window in her bedroom. This bedroom, in the Drexlers' ten-room Manhattan pied-à-terre, was less elaborate than the one on their Long Island estate. There, she and her husband glided over rugs fit for a Chinese emperor and slept in an ornate canopied bed reputed to have belonged to Louis XIV's second-favorite mistress. "Sometimes I blather on, don't I?"

"Well," I muttered, "I was kind of intrigued with the vibrators."

"Have you ever seen one?"

"No." She seemed disappointed. "Have you?" I inquired politely, knowing the answer.

"No. Of course not." She paused and brushed a thick lock of her dark hair behind her ear. "Could we talk seriously, Marcia?"

"Aren't we?"

"No. Come on, don't be intentionally difficult. You're bad enough without trying. Really, whenever we have lunch, you're only relaxed when we're discussing my life—or politics. The minute I steer the conversation to you personally, you gulp down your coffee to make a fast getaway or glare at me as if I were going to beat you into submission: force you to wear eyeliner, or sell you into marriage to an Orthodox computer programmer." She slipped her new shoes over her pearly-gray-stockinged feet. "Trust me, Marcia. You know I've always been on your side."

"I know."

"How are they?"

"What?"

"My new shoes."

"Fine. Lovely. Very chic."

"You don't like them."

"I do."

"You don't. You said they were chic. Chic isn't one of your words. What don't you like about them?"

"I don't know. Aren't they kind of nineteen fiftyish?"

"Of course. They're supposed to be." She lifted her eyebrows and added, "They're very chic."

Except for carrying around her father's lush, dark eyebrows, my cousin Barbara showed few signs of having sprung from five minutes of heaven between Aunt Estelle and Uncle Julius on some blacked-out night during World War II.

She was much taller than the rest of us—her mother, my mother, and me—about five feet seven inches, and big, but in an entirely different way. Barbara's figure was giving and generous. Her shoulders were wide, her breasts heavy and round, her hips wide, like two parentheses enclosing important information.

For six months of each year, she remained Aunt Estelle's girl, going to fashionable diet doctors, even though, as on that day, she suffered under the regimen, looking pale and drawn from deprivation. But, like the rest of her mother's friends' daughters, she carried little plastic bags of carrots and celery sticks to crunch, to drown out her silent screams for ice cream. But for the rest of the year, she was herself, comfortable, full, and at peace. To look at her, you sensed she was content. Hot fudge fills deep needs. You could almost hear her purr.

Women loved her. She was relaxed. She was friendly. There were no hard edges to Barbara, just round warmth.

Men loved her too. For many, her size signaled sex; it was padding to cushion and comfort them during long nights of bed work and, later, for mornings of cozy pleasure.

Not that Barbara had a past. She was no Lady Bountiful, spreading her ample thighs for the boys at Syracuse. On the contrary, being the child of Julius and Estelle, she was far more level-headed than lustful. I visited her once, during our sophomore year at college, and saw how she cooled the fires burning inside the cuffless pants of the brothers of ZBT.

"Barbara!" they'd call, trotting up to her on campus, throwing a ski-jacketed arm around her raccoon-covered shoulder. "Hey, Barbara." And she saw, as I did—because it couldn't be missed—that heavy-lidded stare of nearly crazed need, saw how they wanted to fling off her Lindenbaum fur, pull up her pleated skirt, and roll her right into the nearest snowdrift, sensing that having her would make their world feel like Fort Lauderdale. "Barbara," they'd murmur. But Barbara was schooled to be patient.

"Larry," she'd say, or "Vic, how *are* you?" her voice pitched just high enough to shatter their desire. But her dark brown eyes held theirs for just long enough to suggest that—well, maybe next time. "This is my cousin, Marcia. She's a sophomore at Queens." They would glance at me, startled, as though I'd just been blown before them by a whoosh of February wind.

"Hi," they would mumble.

"Hi," I'd reply, although by that time a response would be superfluous. Their eyes would be back on Barbara, on the thick black hair that framed her creamy, full-cheeked face.

But Barbara could wait. She touched my arm and said, "Let's go get some hot chocolate, Mar," leaving the boys from Syracuse behind.

A month after her graduation, at a friend's wedding, she met Philip Drexler, just back from Oxford, where he had spent two years reading British jurisprudence after graduating from Brown and Harvard Law School. Barbara stood close to Philip, the only son of what the other guests were whispering was the second richest Jewish family in America. She smiled. "Tell me, Philip," she asked, "what are the *real* differences between the English and the American systems? Not the superficial ones." He told her, at length.

Three months later, they spent their honeymoon touring Great Britain, visiting Old Bailey and the Inns of Court, buying cashmere sweaters and melton bathrobes and mohair stoles to cover Barbara Lindenbaum Drexler's soft, generous, and finally compliant body.

"Why don't you take the afternoon off?" Barbara suggested from her chaise. "Come on. We'll visit a gallery or two. Have tea at the Palm Court. It would do you good."

"I can't. Paterno's giving a big Veterans of Foreign Wars speech tonight, and I have to write something bellicose. And then I have a pile of sympathy letters—"

"Sympathy letters?"

"You know. We check the obituary page every day to see if anyone Paterno knows has died. Then we get out our file card on the person, find the name of the wife or child or whatever, and write a touchingly sympathetic personal letter. 'Dear Mary-Louise: I was deeply saddened to hear of your loss. Big Jim was a fine man, a credit to the trade union movement. Blah, blah, blah. Please extend my condolences to Little Jim and Peg.' They're on our file card too. 'With warmest personal regards, Bill Paterno.' "

"Really? You really do that?"

"Sure. If, God forbid, anything happened to you, Philip would get a letter—"

"Marcia!"

"It's true. He contributed five hundred to the last campaign. If he'd contributed a thousand, he'd get a handwritten letter. Come on, Barbara. Don't look so shocked. I was kidding."

"About the whole thing?"

"No. About the handwritten letter. Anyway, I have a pile of work. But lunch was fabulous. The chicken salad! Are you sure it's dietetic?"

"Yes. What I want to know is, why won't you allow yourself any fun?"

"What are you talking about?"

"You won't go to an art gallery. You won't go—"

"Barbara, I told you. I have a lot of responsibilities. There's going to be a primary campaign soon, and I have to start revving up for it."

Barbara rose from the chaise longue and paced across her beige and blue and rose Persian rug. She rubbed her upper arms with her hands, as though she was chilled. "I'm not talking just about today. You know that. But the only thing in your life seems to be politics. And that man. No. Wait. Let me talk. And the only thing I hear about him is that he's an Irish Apollo and ninety percent of the women in New York are panting for him and—just wait—and that you have not only hooked him but hold onto him by not letting him out of bed except to go to work."

"You have no right to do this, Barbara."

"I have every right. You're one of the most intelligent women I know. Or were. I remember, no matter what we talked about—literature, art, music—you always had an original comment. All through college, all during the time you were married to Barry, you were so alive. I'd call you up and first thing, you'd say, 'Hey, you've got to read so-and-so's book. It's brilliant. It's witty.' I mean, you'd get excited, passionate. And now—"

"Now I'm not a twenty-year-old kid with a goddamn library card. I'm thirty-five and have a demanding job, and as for Jerry . . ."

Barbara stopped in front of the small chair I was sitting in. Her shoes, added to her height, made her loom over me like a giant threatening shadow in a horror movie. "You are a thirty-five-year-old woman who is cheating herself. I know you're going to say I sound foolish, but sex and politics aren't enough. Even for you, Marcia. Look at you. You dress in the drabbest colors!"

"What would you like me to do, Barbara? Go on a shopping spree to Dior with you? Spend a month's salary on a scarf? I didn't marry a—"

"Marcia, you're making a decent living. There's no reason in this world why you can't afford nice-looking clothes, clothes that will emphasize what you are—a wonderful-looking woman. You dress like a beatnik, with those black tights. You never do anything anymore. When was the last time you went to the theater? When?"

"I'll answer when you stop badgering me, damn it."

"I'll tell you when. It's when I threatened never to speak to you again unless you saw *The Iceman Cometh* with me. When Philip had the flu. And before that? Probably something in Washington with Barry. Listen, if you were some philistine, I wouldn't be saying anything. But I was with you. I saw how excited you got, how involved you were in the performance. But you've cut yourself off from that pleasure. Anything beautiful, anything fine, is no good to you."

"What do you want me to do? Tell me."

"Allow yourself to enjoy things, feel things."

"Barbara, I do. It's just that my interests aren't what yours are. I don't want marriage. I don't want an estate on Long Island. I don't want an apartment in Paris."

"Why not?"

"Because I'm not you. Understand that, Barbara. We're cousins, we're close friends, but we're very different people. I don't just work for money, because I have to. I work because I love to. And I don't live with Jerry Morrissey because no one will marry me."

"You're living with him to ensure no one will marry you."

"Barbara, first you give me this gorgeous lunch with the most perfect chicken salad I've ever tasted and then you follow it up with out-of-season raspberries that must cost the same as a pint of rubies and then you give me indigestion with this glib analysis that sounds like you stopped off and picked it up at your mother's house on your way into the city. Come on, now. You were raised to marry, to be a wife, and you do it better than anyone else I know. But I wasn't raised the same way. Really."

"Of course you were. You were raised with the same goals, the same aspirations I was."

I stood. "But I put them aside when I divorced Barry. I've found other things that mean more to me."

"No you haven't."

"Yes I have. I really have. But I'm not going to try to persuade you of that. I don't have to justify myself. If it comforts all of you to think I'm walking around unhappy, incomplete just because I don't wear fancy shoes—"

"Marcia, it's not the shoes. It's what will make you truly happy. Being married to someone fine, someone caring . . ."

"Someone rich. Go ahead. Say it."

"You know, that's a very cruel thing you just said."

"Well, how do you think I feel, Barbara? You call me, tell me how much you miss me, how you can't wait to see me, and then when you see me, you tell me that my life is sterile."

"All right. I'm sorry. All I'm saying is that you can have sex and politics and everything *with* marriage. You want what I want, Mar. It's just that . . ." Barbara paused and adjusted the strap of her thin, elegant gold watch. "Okay. No more. I promise. Really. I'm sorry if I overstepped the bounds of cousinhood and friendship."

I sighed, weary from our argument, from wielding her heavy sterling knives and forks and minding my manners while her maid served us. "Okay. Listen, I have to go now. I'll speak to you next week."

"Are you sure you don't have time for just one gallery?"

"I'm sure. Positive."

An hour and a quarter later, I stood before Paterno's desk, listening to him read the speech on civil defense I had just written. "Preparedness doesn't stop at the Pentagon," he intoned. "We must push—"

"Wait," I interrupted. "Too many p's. Take out 'push' and put in 'move.' "

"I'm not looking forward to tonight," Paterno said. He put both elbows on his desk and rubbed his big forehead in his hands. "I'd rather rest up. It's been a rough week, and these guys are an awful audience. Remember last year? Half of them were soused and kept calling out questions."

"Yes. Oh, God, now I remember. They were awful. That guy who got up to ask you about where you had stood on Vietnam and then started yelling about getting it in the hip in Normandy. What finally happened? You just stopped, didn't you?"

"Yes. Sure. Especially after that idiot with the medals started arguing with the guy about Normandy. What was it?"

"Trenches, I think. Whether the trenches were deep enough. Anyway, you'll sound like a tough militarist tonight. They'll probably salute instead of applauding."

"Why do I have to go through this? Speaking to all these jerks about things I don't know about. Why a city official has to jabber on and on about defense posture, I'll never know. Even a candidate for governor. What the hell—excuse me—can the governor of New York do about West Africa or East Asia? Why can't I just shut up and work?"

"Because I need the job, Bill."

"Well, I guess that's as good a reason as any. Where was I?"

"Getting rid of 'push.' "

Paterno marked his copy of the speech. He sighed. "I should have listened to my mother, been a tenor."

"What stopped you?"

"No talent. Did you ever think of doing something different?"

"No," I replied. "Never."

4

William Paterno's lawyer suggested that he get an electroencephalogram.

"You really think so?" Paterno demanded, his large head bent forward intently, his slender shoulders hunched up around his ears.

"Well," Eileen Gerrity said, "it could rule out a brain tumor."

"Dammit, Eileen!" Jerry, from the chair nearest Paterno's desk, glared across the room at the couch where Eileen and I were sitting. "This is no time—"

"I mean," Paterno said, ignoring Jerry, "I'm not really worried that it's a brain tumor. It's just that I've been getting these headaches for the last few weeks. All of a sudden. I've never been headache-prone, and now, every morning, I wake up with this tightness around my forehead, and by the time I get dressed and downstairs for breakfast it's developed into a—"

"Look," soothed Eileen, smoothing out a crease in her gray flannel skirt, "you're under a lot of pressure. Why give yourself something else to worry about? I'll make a few calls, get the number of a good neurologist, and you can go have yourself checked out."

"Does this kind of thing, I mean, around the forehead, have any—um, significance?" Paterno asked, talking to a pile of papers on his desk.

"Yes," Jerry hissed. "It means you're a marked man, Bill. You'll be dead before sunrise tomorrow."

"Jerry," Eileen said softly, glancing up at the ceiling.

"Eileen," Jerry crooned, matching her voice in softness, "if you cater to that kind of crap, he'll be in a wheelchair by the time Marcia drafts his declaration. Just ignore him."

Her voice grew a little sharper. "You don't just ignore something like that. If he's on edge, doesn't it make more sense to reassure him?"

"No," said Jerry, "no, no, no." He slammed his fist on the edge of the desk. "Once you start playing his hypochondriac games . . ."

Paterno still leaned forward, listening intently, his dark eyes darting from chair to couch to chair. It was not clear whose side he was on, although he seemed to nod more when Jerry spoke. I shifted around, trying to find a perfect niche for myself, somewhere between the back and the armrest of the sofa, debating whether or not to direct the meeting back to its purpose: deciding the best time for Paterno to declare his candidacy for governor.

Eileen stretched a long thin finger at Jerry and suggested he was insensitive. Jerry countercharged with an accusation of mollycoddling. Paterno remained aloof, although an expression of contentment that seemed nearly a smile played about his mouth. He glanced across the room, finally focusing on a gleaming brass log basket that sat by the mahogany mantel of his massive nonworking fireplace.

The three top officials of New York City, Paterno, the mayor, and the comptroller, all worked in surroundings that would have been appropriate only for an Anglican bishop. In Paterno's office, the chairs and couch were all of a worn oxblood leather, except for the chair Jerry sat on. That was a pull-up of glossy mahogany, upholstered in a faded blue brocade. It looked as if it had been dragged in from some dining room, an extra seat for a visiting vicar.

"Listen, you two," Paterno began slowly, "we really ought to get down to the business of planning a campaign." He rubbed his hands together, not in glee but in a kind of awed respect, as if conscious of touching the hand of the future governor of New York. But none of us spoke. We peered out the window, down to our shoes, over at the painting of Giovanni da Verrazano Discovering the Narrows. We looked everywhere except at William Paterno.

"Let's get started," he finally ordered. "You three are the core of any campaign organization I'm going to have, and you're just sitting here like you've got sunstroke. Wake up! That's better. Now, Eileen and Morrissey, no more bickering, okay?" They nodded. "Good. Marcia, you have to speak up more. There won't be time to write memos. All right?" I nodded. "Good. Now, the first thing we have to come to grips with is timing. Now, today is . . ."

"March tenth," I offered eagerly.

"Good. Thanks. Okay, it's March tenth. We have a few weeks of enforced grace, at least till the end of the month, when the official state mourning period is over. It would not look good if I declared my candidacy and the TV cameras picked up a flag still flying half mast for Gresham. Right? By the way, does anyone have to go to the bathroom or anything before we really get started? No? Okay, now, when are petitions due?"

"Not till June fifteenth," Eileen said.

"Hmmm." Many men, when thinking, rub their foreheads. Paterno massaged his nose between his thumb and index finger. "So if we figure six weeks for a decent petition drive, we can wait to declare till the beginning of May, which should—"

"That's too late," Jerry said.

"No it's not," Paterno argued. "Not if we have everything ready to go. Not if—"

"By that time, do you know how many deadheads will have declared? Six thousand radicals, five thousand one-issue jerks who told their mommies to watch for them on television, and three or four viable candidates. And you'll be viewed as just another one of them." Jerry caressed the cleft in his chin with the knuckle of his index finger.

Paterno looked at Jerry and stopped rubbing his nose. "But if we declare too soon—" Paterno began.

"Bill, listen to me," Jerry continued. "If you come out soon, right in the beginning of April, you'll get all the coverage you want. They'll treat you like a statesman, a gentleman. Every other candidate who declares after that will automatically be compared to you."

"I don't know," Paterno muttered, shaking his head slowly back and forth. "It's so soon."

"Jerry's right," Eileen said. "And it would give us an

extra month to fund-raise, to approach a lot of heavy contributors before everybody else does." Although she and Jerry routinely sniped at each other, their political judgment was remarkably compatible. According to Jerry, they didn't dislike each other at all; they were simply too much alike, coming from similar lower-middle-class Irish backgrounds, to find each other interesting. Bickering, he explained, helped them to keep awake in each other's company.

Eileen acknowledged that their outlooks were very similar but felt obliged to inform me that men like Jerry were, beneath a thin layer of charm, sexist, narcissistic, and anti-intellectual. When we were alone, she teased me about being a sucker for a pretty face and called him names like Heartthrob. She had suggested that men like Jerry were a dime a dozen in her old neighborhood in Jackson Heights.

"Thank you for your support, counselor," Jerry said, flashing her a wide, bright-toothed smile.

And it did seem that she avoided men like Jerry, selecting soft, quiet, bookish men to date, men whose pale lips matched their eyeglass frames, men who called to discuss the body politic.

Eileen turned from Jerry back to Paterno. I felt bad that they couldn't enjoy each other, because I wanted the three of us to be friends. But each said they had enough of the other in the office, so my friendship with Eileen was limited to long lunches and to evenings when Jerry was busy. She came to our apartment only once, when Jerry was safely in Houston at the Democratic Convention. She had gazed around the living room and asked, "Kathye Baron?" I had nodded. "Well, she certainly tried, poor thing."

Eileen was five years younger than I, thirty, but I thought of her as more than my peer. She never acted uncertain. She maintained a dignified distance from the raucous, boorish, political world she worked in. She could ignore the crass and smile at the grotesque. People felt calmer in her company; she exercised a kind of tranquilizing charisma: Our Lady of the Law.

She even looked a little like a madonna, full of pastel composure. She had placid green eyes and pink cheeks and light hair. Her hair was her best feature, a blond so pale it barely missed looking white. It was not very thick, but she had let it grow and piled it on top of her head with combs or barrettes, so it looked heavy, opulent. My mother would have pointed out her sharp nose and thin lips.

But I felt Eileen's was the most congenial expression in the room, so I addressed my remarks to her. "It's not too soon," I suggested. Although I never minded attending meetings, I didn't like to speak at them. Invariably I'd be challenged or interrupted or snapped at, and I'd stutter, turn red-faced, and wind up addressing clumsy remarks to the carpet. I preferred taking notes, so afterward, alone with my typewriter, I could declaim in an incisive, assertive fashion.

"Good. Glad you're speaking up," Paterno said. I smiled at him, then lowered my head. "Wonderful," he enthused. I looked up at him and he said softly, "You were talking kind of low. What did you say?"

"I said, it's not too soon to declare your candidacy. I can understand your wanting to wait for the end of the mourning period, but you really should do it very soon."

"Why soon? Why not wait until May?"

"Because of the poll," I murmured, wishing now that Jerry and Eileen would leave the room. My articulateness is inversely proportional to the number of people in a meeting. With just one I can be dynamic. With two I can hold my own. I fade with three and with five or more become indistiguishable from the furniture.

"Marcia, what do you mean by the poll?" Jerry asked in the gentle, patient voice people use when dealing with a retardate. He knew I didn't excel in public speaking.

"I mean . . ."

"Which poll?" Paterno demanded. "Our poll? The *News* poll?"

"Well . . ."

"Marcia," Eileen said, "would it be easier if we cut open your gut and read your entrails?"

"Yes," I answered. "What I mean is, I'm referring to our poll, the one Victor Chang took." The three others nodded. "Your upstate recognition factor is only twenty-two percent, and you need time to build that up."

"Hmmm," Jerry said.

"Ummm," said Eileen.

"And that twenty-two percent isn't a solid figure. Remember what Victor said, Bill?" Paterno blinked his black, bulgy eyes and caressed a liver spot on his right hand.

Victor Chang was the newest polling star in the political firmament, although he twinkled on a limited wavelength. He told the *New York Times* that he felt "morally obligated" to work only for "decent Democrats." For a fast ten thousand dollars, he had done a quickie poll upstate the week before which showed Paterno with a "fluid twenty-two" percent of the respondents claiming to recognize his name. Apparently, ten percent of these voters approved of Paterno's skills as a negotiator and "urban manager." Another eight percent knew him but disapproved of him, believing that he had usurped the mayor's role during the police and sanitation strikes, this despite the fact that the mayor's only recognizable asset was his ability to keep his ears clean.

Of the remaining four percent, half had him confused with Fiorello LaGuardia, although Chang insisted that this was a plus; people still held the late LaGuardia in high esteem. The other two percent thought Paterno was someone outside of politics; a nightclub singer, a football coach, and a Mafia don were suggested identities.

"Well," I said to my shoes, "what do you think?"

Eileen, who would never address her feet, cleared her throat and eyed Paterno. "Marcia's right," she announced. "We have a good, solid base down here, but we can throw the whole thing if we just concentrate in the metropolitan area. You've got to start calling in your upstate cards, Bill. And don't forget, with the new campaign finance statutes . . ."

"I know," Paterno said, inserting his upper lip between his teeth and gnawing on it.

"Now that Parker's in," Jerry said, referring to Gresham's lieutenant governor, who had risen to the number-one position on a bite of knish, "you can't just sit back and be Catholic. You're going to have to woo a lot of people you don't particularly like."

"I know, I know," Paterno declared. His mouth grew tight, giving him a grim expression. "What kind of support do I really have up there?" he asked Jerry.

"You really want to go through this again?" Jerry gave Paterno a cool, blue patient stare.

"I want to go through it again."

"Mother of God," Eileen whispered.

"What? What did you say, Eileen?" Paterno demanded.

"I said, 'Mother of God,' " she responded forcefully.

"Oh." As usual, Paterno backed down. He even offered her a small, conciliatory smile. Eileen was convinced that Paterno put up with her because of her legal expertise and because he secretly, passionately desired her. She was as romantic as a Victorian maiden. Professionally she may have fought with frigid logic and cold sarcasm, but privately she placed monogrammed packets of sachet in each drawer and interpreted men's glances according to their degree of significance. Paterno's bulgy eyes gave him an almost perpetually significant look. I agreed that he admired her—no one knew New York election law better than she—but thought his glances quite insignificant.

Politicians have a reputation as insatiable studs, continually tumescent. They are rumored to go through aides and secretaries like an electric drill through a wooden plank. But many of them aren't sexual at all. Their energies and interests are focused on personalities, on plots, on simply recollecting the name of the district leader's spouse. Some grow weary because they work hard. Paterno's appetites were huge, but they were not sexual. Not that he behaved like a castrato. He appeared to be a normal man. He had had two children, and his late wife, Terri, had seemed reasonably content; at least she never had a hungry, crazed, Anna Magnani look. But I never saw him breathe hard for any woman. Paterno was solicitous of Eileen because he valued her expertise. Also, he probably had visions of feminist hellions who would spring to her defense and tear his limbs off if he fired her.

But Paterno's gentility could go only so far. He was less patient with Jerry. "What the hell do you know about anything?" he'd often snap, or "Who's feeding you your information, Morrissey? Boss Tweed?" Jerry, in turn, treated Paterno as though he were not completely *compos mentis*, explaining political maneuvers in a maddeningly slow, simplistic fashion or giving Paterno a list of phone calls to make, people to cajole or soothe on some particular issue. "Now don't forget, Bill," he'd say, "if they're not there, leave word you called."

They seemed like opposites: tall/short, handsome/

homely, calculating/emotional, and in many ways they were. But, at work, the opposites attracted and merged, forming a complete political being.

"All right," Jerry said, uncrossing his legs, leaning forward toward Paterno's desk. "I'll go through the names again, the county leaders, assemblymen, and senators who owe you. Some owe you from years ago, when you were up in Albany. Those are—" and he reeled off a list of six or seven names. Paterno, who had lifted up a pen as Jerry began to speak, put it back on his desk after the third name. "Now, the next group are people who owe you from when you were chairman of the constitutional convention. Are you ready?" Paterno nodded seriously, then looked annoyed. This time Jerry whizzed through a dozen names, five of whom I had never even heard of. I was tempted to ask who they were but didn't want to embarrass Jerry by making his list sound less than the definitive one of New York State Movers and Doers. "Anything else?" he asked Paterno.

"I don't know."

"What's the matter, Bill?"

"How solid are they?"

"What do you mean?"

"Just what I said. How solid? Can we really rely on these guys?"

"I've spoken to them all within the last week. They're with you. They just need a signal that you're going to run. Look, you're popular and they think you've got a good shot at beating whoever the Republicans put up. But you have to get through the primary before you can go after Republicans." Paterno nodded his head up and down, very slowly, as if he were suddenly privy to a long-kept secret. "They know and we know that Parker is such a jerk it takes all his concentration to hit the urinal, but he has one thing you don't."

"He's governor now," Paterno said mechanically.

"Right. And in any political contest, there's an automatic prejudice in favor of the incumbent."

I found my voice again. "But the incumbent is excruciatingly stupid. I mean, Parker is publicly dumb."

"As long as he keeps his clothes on and speaks something that people believe is English, the incumbent has an advantage," Jerry said, still eyeing Paterno. His voice was strong, sure, without a single doubt. "But we're not dealing with unsophisticated idiots. These upstate guys are not a bunch of dumb farmers." Paterno was peering at Jerry, intrigued with his notion. "They know that Parker has an excellent chance of making an ass of himself in a general election. And they would very much like a strong candidate. Therefore, they will go to the man"—Jerry's eyes moved to me and Eileen for a second, and he exhaled loudly—"or the woman who shows some strength and popularity. They know your clout here in the city. They know all about your—uh, sterling character and abilities. But they're sophisticated enough to know that you're not a known factor upstate. They want someone who will appeal to the dairy industry, the winegrowers, the apple farmers."

"My grandfather was a farmer," Paterno muttered.

"What did he grow?" Jerry demanded.

"I don't know. Olives, I think."

"What the hell good is your grandfather if you don't know what kind of farming he did? And do you think it's going to impress some megafarmer with fifty thousand cows that your grandfather grew a fig tree outside of Palermo?"

"We didn't come from Palermo. We came from a little town—"

"Bill, save it for the Sons of Sicily breakfast. Look, they like you, but they want some assurance you're in this thing seriously. They're not going to put their asses on the line for you without a real commitment on your part. They don't like Parker, they certainly won't go for the rest of those cabbageheads. You've got to declare, though, go up there and make some sort of impact before they'll risk offending the incumbent. And we've got to get a petition drive going if you want to get more than three signatures in Herkimer County."

"I know," Paterno said. He picked up a ball-point pen and rolled it between his palms. "But are you sure?" He seemed to be riding Jerry harder than usual. I glanced at Jerry: his eyes had narrowed, but he seemed more irritated than angry or defensive. I felt a little uneasy, though, because in trying times Paterno usually abandoned his normal querulousness; he would hang on every word Jerry uttered with the fervor of a young animal clinging to its mother. "Morrissey, I was just thinking that if—"

"Jesus H. Particular Christ," Jerry snapped. "I'm telling you, Bill, you can't sit around playing Hamlet. You've got to build an effective organization upstate."

"Okay," Paterno said, pointing the pen at Jerry, as though it were a long metal finger. "Let's get into that."

"Into what?" Jerry's voice sounded cool, but his face began to flush.

"Into an organization. Who do we have?"

"Where? What do you mean? Upstate?"

"Anywhere." Paterno's voice had grown cooler than Jerry's.

"All right. Down here, we have Brooklyn, Queens, Nassau, Suffolk, Westchester, and probably Manhattan. The Bronx is iffy because Bob Aponte keeps thinking he's emperor instead of county chairman, but voter turnout has been so low for the last two years that it probably—"

"I'm not talking about backing. I know who's supporting me, for Christ's sake. I'm talking about staff."

"Staff?"

"Staff." Paterno and Jerry were now into their high-gear, man-to-man politician dialogue. This happened frequently. Eileen and I were useful for specific functions, for legal counsel, for writing, but deep down I don't think either man trusted our general judgment. They would ask us to meetings, consult us, listen to us, but when the conversation ranged a few inches beyond the specific, they behaved as though we had faded away. They could only hear each other.

"Okay," said Jerry cautiously. "We've been through this —what, ten, twenty times? But we'll make it twenty-one. You have me. Joe Cole for blacks. Mary LaRosa for petitions. Carl Obst and Linda Freeman for fund-raising. Eileen here for counsel. Marcia for speeches. Consuelo Fuentes for Hispanics and women. Eileen can also help out on women if necessary—"

"Think, goddamn it. Will you think? Who have you got, Morrissey?"

"I've got a fucking good group of people for you, that's who I've got, and if you don't stop these guessing games, you can take them all and ram them up your Italian ass because I'm not going to take this crap."

Paterno's voice went soft. "Morrissey, where are all these people from?"

"I told you, I'm not going to play guessing games."

"They come from New York!"

"So what? Who doesn't?"

"I mean, they come from here, the city. Not one person is from upstate. You haven't got a single goddamned Protestant in that whole crew."

"I think Joe Cole is Protestant."

"He's black as midnight."

"So?"

"So are you going to trot Joe Cole up to Plattsburg to have tea with the Lutheran minister's wife?"

Jerry swiveled his head slightly, just enough to glimpse Eileen and me, the audience on the couch. When he turned back to Paterno—the entire movement took less than a second—the flush had spread to his ears. I felt his embarrassment. "I have got," he said in a monotone, "a good campaign staff lined up. If you want to take advantage of it, that's just dandy. If you're not pleased with what I've been doing, you can find someone else."

"Look, I'm not criticizing you, Jerry." Paterno's tone was controlled and sincere as Nixon's.

"Bullshit."

"No. I mean it. I think you have the makings of a great staff. I was only wondering if maybe we need someone with some upstate experience."

"I have upstate experience," said Jerry. "If you remember, I've only been working for you for eight years. I had a life before that."

"I'm not saying you didn't."

Jerry had had a nice life: Special Assistant to Bernard Merkin, Attorney General for the State of New York. Bernard Merkin, the Mafia's nemesis, the consumer's champion, the—who knows?—maybe the first Jewish candidate for Vice-President of these United States. Gerald Michael Morrissey had a good life. How would he know that his employer, his friend, his creation, his Merkin would take up with one Floria Garcia, a twenty-one-year-old summer interne, and that Mrs. Bernard Merkin, the previously loving Bernice, would object, especially when September came and went and Bernard's infatuation with the young Floria did not die? And not even so close a friend of the Merkins as Jerry Morrissey, a friend who came to dinner every single Thursday night, would dream that sweet Bernice,

Bernice of a thousand fund-raisers, would bundle up a tote bag full of family papers and trot down to Foley Square in Manhattan and share with the Chief of the Criminal Division of the United States Attorney's Office the secret that had been hers and Bernard's—that for five years the Attorney General of the State of New York had forgotten to report his outside income, which amounted to about $100,000 per annum. And even an ace forecaster like Jerry Morrissey couldn't have predicted that, eleven months later, Bernard's attorneys would be working on his appeal from conviction while Bernice got her divorce in Mexico and Floria went to law school in Brooklyn.

And Jerry Morrissey was out of a job.

"Well." Jerry confronted Paterno. "Just what are you saying?"

"Why are you so angry? I'm not trying to undercut you or anything. But you haven't had *recent* upstate experience."

Jerry was not out of a job for long. As Merkin began his trip down the tubes, Jerry waved him a saddened bon voyage and cast about for a new politician. After just a few weeks of floundering, he joined Paterno, recognizing in him two key qualities: promise and need.

William Paterno, on the verge of running for the Presidency of New York's City Council, had great potential. He was bright, ambitious, and popular. He was also in trouble because, until he hired Jerry, his advisers' vision did not extend beyond his assembly district in Little Neck, Queens. His lawyer pals and his clubhouse cronies knew Bill had the stuff, but they didn't know how to package and transport it over the 59th Street Bridge to Manhattan.

But Jerry Morrissey knew. For years he had lived behind his blazing blue eyes, observing, calculating, registering the moves of the wrinkled, the pockmarked and birthmarked, the plain; watching as they schemed and sneaked and screamed and whispered. Jerry had grown from a mere employee, a paid adviser, into an artist, a creator. He knew, and he stepped in, taking William Paterno's life and shaping it, giving it form and a purposeful design.

By that election night eight years before, Paterno was no longer viewed as just another shrewd pol. He was special. Jerry had exploited Paterno's extraordinary capacity for work, giving him position papers, reports, articles to study, until Paterno became the city's greatest expert on sewage conversion, expense budgeting, and public education. Jerry had manipulated Paterno's instinctive, politically dangerous tendency to say whatever was on his mind into a reputation for amazing honesty: in East Harlem, they called Paterno "el honorable". And Jerry had channeled Paterno's huffy self-righteousness into a career as a labor negotiator: no one could talk down the municipal unions on behalf of the city as well as a puffed-up Paterno.

"Don't jerk me off, Bill. I mean it."

"I'm not." Paterno thrust out his lower lip, offended.

"All right. Then just what do you want?"

"Nothing. Nothing at all."

"Good."

"I was just wondering. You know. Whether if we picked up a little extra help, if it would help any."

"Help helps, Bill."

"Yes. Right. I mean, maybe one of Gresham's people. I mean, they know upstate like—well, like you know the Bronx. I mean, some of them have really been way up there, visited those people. Do you know they make cheddar cheese up there?"

"Who did you have in mind?"

"What? Oh, I don't know."

Jerry leaned back in his chair, forcing himself to look casual, putting too much weight on his weak lower back. "Just any old Gresham aide? You don't have anyone in mind?"

"Maybe—um"—Paterno gazed at the ceiling, trying to appear thoughtful—"maybe someone like Lyle LoBello."

My fists clenched in protest. Eileen, beside me, took in a fast gulp of air. Paterno looked at Jerry and attempted an ingenuous smile. He failed, managing only to display a lot of teeth.

"Someone *like* Lyle LoBello," Jerry said. "Tell me, Bill, who is like LoBello?"

Lyle LoBello was unique, at least in Gresham's organization. He had been the governor's appointments officer, his closest adviser, dearest pal, big-ass buddy, and, thus, the second most powerful man in New York State. He and the guv had even double-dated, and it was rumored that they frequently switched girls mid-evening. "What do you mean?" Paterno said. "No one is like LoBello. He knows upstate and—"

"Where does he come from? Syracuse? Watertown?" Jerry demanded, letting his chair return to all four legs.

"Brooklyn," Paterno mumbled. "Red Hook, I think."

"Red Hook," said Jerry. "Perfect. Go get him, Bill. He's just what you need—an upstate Protestant who just happens to look and act and sound like a Neapolitan pimp and who comes from Red Hook. Really a shrewd political move, Bill. Ace."

"Are you nuts, Morrissey? Jesus, I've never seen anyone so touchy. All I did was mention LoBello and—"

"Where are you going to put him in a campaign? On the mimeograph machine? Collating petitions? Or are you going to stick him in as something like—well, like campaign manager when I step out for a second to take a leak?"

"Of course not!"

"Do you think he'd take a secondary role? I mean, old Lyle's used to being a mover."

"I don't know. I mean, he's out of a job."

"And he needs the money?"

"No. It isn't that. But—I mean, he offered to help. It was really nice of him, especially since he's so down in the dumps about Gresham. It was just decency on his part."

"For which he expects nothing in return."

"All right. I'll call him. Right now." Paterno's hand stretched for the intercom box, to jingle one of his secretaries. "I'll tell him no thanks, that you feel you can handle upstate and that we don't need him. Is that what you want?"

"That's what I want," Jerry answered.

Paterno pulled his glance away from Jerry's glare and looked toward the sofa. "Excuse me, ladies," he muttered. Eileen and I shuffled our feet, unsure whether we had received a courtesy or a dismissal.

Jerry interpreted for us. "Out," he said, never taking his eyes off Paterno.

And that night, he would not take them off the ceiling. "Jerry, talk to me."

"What?" he mumbled, trying to will me far away, where

he would not have to listen to my analyses of Paterno's motives.

Lying beside him on the bed, I propped myself up and leaned over, putting my face near his, interrupting his examination of the ceiling. "You'd be happier if you talked about it."

"No, you'd be happier. Come on, Marcia. I need some quiet."

"Jerry," I murmured and leaned over to kiss his one flaw, a chicken-pox scar right below his eybrow.

"Marcia, just leave me alone."

I rolled back to my side of the bed and opened a paperback that seemed to be about a young American doctor uncovering a huge cryogenic facility with thousands of icy Nazis about to be defrosted. The cover assured me the book would not only be a breathtaking thriller but be spellbinding as well. For the third time that week I put it down. I watched Jerry watch the ceiling.

I wanted to cradle him in my arms, pacify him with deep, humming noises. Jerry wanted silence. I wanted to lie on top of him, a shield between his heat and the cold community we worked in. Jerry wanted his own side of the bed. I wanted to recite the lines from *Othello* I had been saving since college: "Perdition catch my soul, but I do love thee; and if I love thee not, chaos is come again." Jerry wanted to listen to the ten o'clock news.

"Listen," he had said, about three days after I had moved into his apartment. I was sitting on top of the toilet seat, watching him shave. "There's something I want to make clear."

"Perfectly clear?" I had demanded.

"Yes. I'm serious."

"Nobody with a huge gob of shaving cream on his chin can be taken seriously."

"Marcia, I hope this arrangement lasts for a long time." I had nodded, swallowed. "But I don't want to get married. It has nothing to do with you. It's just a decision I made a long time ago, about what's best for a guy like me."

"Fine. Sure."

"Okay. I just don't want any misunderstandings."

"No. Of course not. There won't be."

"No hurt feelings. No pressure a year from now."

"Absolutely not," I had vowed, watching his jawline emerge in the razor's wake. "I value my independence as much as you value yours."

"Good," he had said, nodding his approval to the bathroom mirror.

I never tried to tie Jerry's life into a knot, and that was probably my chief attraction. I was company at breakfast, company in bed, but I restrained any word or gesture that might interfere with his privacy. He continued to cherish his independence. I allowed myself only an occasional quiet thought about having him always, about a bright-eyed baby with a lilting cry, so perfect my family's hearts would collectively melt. But most of the time, I remained a realist.

I leaned across the bed and stroked his cheek. "You don't have to talk," I said softly. "I didn't mean to pressure you."

A moment passed and then Jerry turned onto his side, facing me, and stretched out his arm toward me. The black hair stopped at his wrist, making a neat, natural cuff. I reached to stroke it but he slid his hand under my nightgown, working it up slowly between my thighs "What can I do for you tonight?" he asked, his voice slow and silky. "What would make you happy, Marcia?"

5

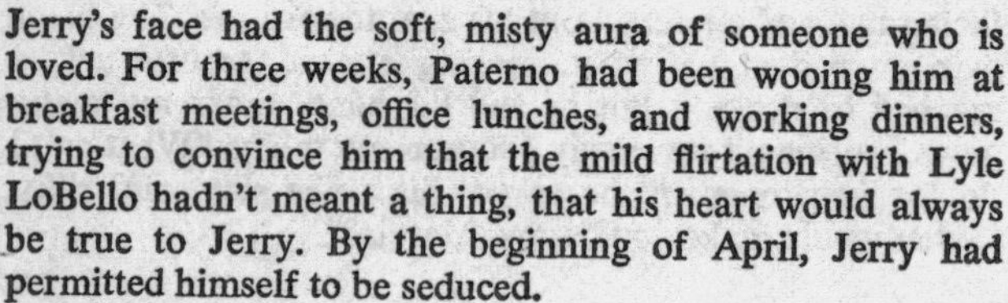

Jerry's face had the soft, misty aura of someone who is loved. For three weeks, Paterno had been wooing him at breakfast meetings, office lunches, and working dinners, trying to convince him that the mild flirtation with Lyle LoBello hadn't meant a thing, that his heart would always be true to Jerry. By the beginning of April, Jerry had permitted himself to be seduced.

"Jerry."

He gazed out of the grimy taxi window into the foggy, chilly night.

"Jerry?"

"What?"

"Nothing." On behalf of Paterno, we were heading uptown to a political affair, something called Dollars for Dick, a fund-raising dinner for Richard Krasnoff, who had retired gracefully from the House of Representatives after twenty-two years of selfless service and was now, sadly, the subject of a very intense and doubtless grossly unfair investigation by the Securities and Exchange Commission. "You look wonderful tonight," I murmured.

"Thanks," he said, abruptly. Jerry did not take compliments very gracefully, nor did he tolerate discussions about his appearance.

His response to his extraordinary looks was largely denial. When we were first getting to know each other outside of the office, sitting over coffee and trading vignettes of our childhood, exchanging dead father stories, I had asked him about his handsomeness.

"Were you a beautiful child?"

"Cut it out, Marcia."

"I mean it. Did the little girls lust for you in the sandbox? What was it like, growing up knowing people loved to look at you?"

"This is a ridiculous conversation. I was a normal kid. I went to school, played ball—"

"But didn't you have an abiding sense that you were different?"

"Nope."

He knew though. He dressed neatly but unimaginatively, ignoring changes in style. When he heard that my ex-husband, Barry, had used hair spray, he had laughed with surprise. But his casualness was just an attempt to downplay his dazzle. He wanted to be one of the guys, trusted, relied on, and he sensed that other men distrusted beauty.

So he muted his flash, except when it became a political weapon. Fund-raising for Paterno, he'd slowly lower his black lashes and give a long, easy grin to a short, tense, rich widow. Inevitably, she'd cough up a few hundred more for Paterno. Talking to a woman reporter or a gay banquet manager, he'd lean back in his chair with his legs spread slightly, so the healthy swelling between his thighs was just barely evident.

The taxi stopped for a light. Jerry turned from Sixth Avenue to me. "You okay, sweetheart?"

I nodded.

"It's not so bad. Just think of it as three hours of continual smiling. You can handle it."

"Don't you hate it, glad-handing and buttering up all sorts of awful people?"

"No. It's fun."

Jerry would never concede that he despised political dinners. How could any decent person possibly enjoy a roomful of pols and building contractors and hungry lawyers all drinking whiskey of unknown origin and nervously gobbling egg salad canapés? I would demand.

"So I don't discuss the meaning of life," he would say.

"So what? I walk around, say hello to a few of the boys I haven't seen for a while, pick up some interesting gossip. I enjoy it."

I would explain, patiently, that the room was very hot and it was hard to talk standing up. And some criminal court judge from Queens who looked like an Easter Island statue would sidle up and mumble a few damp sentences that I could not understand because of the noise but sensed were disgusting. And Jerry would say, "Marcia, you have two feet. Put one in front of the other and take a walk." And then I would remind him that even after cocktail hour, when we were seated at Table 137, with a brash band playing "Tie a Yellow Ribbon," he would carry on a yelling conversation with some clubhouse Neanderthal at Table 135 rather than talk to me. "Marcia, we don't go to these things to be together. We're supposed to be out there smiling, making friends for Bill, patting asses. But the minute we get there, you grab my arm and start to discuss your childhood or tell me your College Board scores."

Then I'd sniff and tell him that if this kind of part was the sort of thing that he, Gerald Morrissey, a graduate of Fordham University who had been on full scholarship, found appealing, well, he had my pity. He would sigh and I would pout and together we'd enter Spanelli for Congress or the Cardiac Infarction Fund Honors Esther and Selwyn Litwak dinner and part. I would seek a potential wallflower, an electorally doomed assemblyman or another speech writer, and ask how they were and then listen.

Jerry would work the room, laughing, drinking, standing with his arm around a crucial state senator and whispering bright ideas, breaking into smiles of gladness as the women came up: wives and secretaries and officeholders who would pass him and then say "Jerry!" as though they had only accidentally noticed him. And he would beam at them, a special smile as though—just between him and her—she had made his evening by noticing him.

With his intelligence and courtesy added to his fine looks, he was nearly irresistible in a world of the glib and the cruel. There seemed no reason why he couldn't have any woman at all. There was simply no reason to deny him.

Women bolted from their escorts to greet him. They

phoned him at the office and at home. He'd empty his jacket pockets at night and discover odd pieces of paper with phone numbers written on them that women had slipped in, women he could barely remember meeting. Twice he found a key.

Except among women who had specific requirements of men—wealth, knowledge of nineteenth-century American literature—Jerry's appeal was nearly universal. I think he realized it and was secretly a little sad about it. Since he could charm just about any woman he met, since he knew the inevitability of his attractiveness, he lost some of his interest in women. Their value decreased because the supply so grossly exceeded the demand.

The taxi pulled up to the Hilton and I paid the driver. "Now Marcia," he said, as we shared a quadrant within the revolving door, "this isn't a date."

"I know." Still, I liked to think of him as my escort. People could say, "There's Marcia Green," and automatically look for Jerry Morrissey.

Ever since I began working in politics, right after I was graduated from Queens College, I had an even chance of meeting him. We could have said hi at the annual fund raiser for the Queens Symphony Orchestra, shaking hands over a silver bowl of chopped liver while our employers dashed about, kissing cheeks and pounding backs and proclaiming their passion for the orchestral form, or at least mumbling that they thought music was a wonderful idea.

We could have been introduced at the Rathskeller, a bar not far from City Hall. We could even have crossed paths when I was living in Washington. Bernard Merkin had testified before a House subcommittee that my boss, the Honorable Dave Flaherty, chaired.

"Marcia Plotnick, Jerry Morrissey," someone could have said.

"Hi." He would have offered me a hand and a flash of blue eyelight.

"Hi." I would have lowered my head and addressed his loafers, trying at the same time to conjure up a picture of my husband, whitecoated Barry Plotnick, his stethoscope twinkling in silver, his wedding band gleaming in gold.

I had heard of Jerry, of course. Rumors, ruminations, remarks about him had drifted through my life for years.

Even when he was in his mid-thirties, he was considered one of the grand old men of New York City politics, the pro's pro.

A health-care lobbyist, cooling her heels waiting for Flaherty, her behind spread over a third of my Washington desk, had demanded, "Y'ever see Jerry Morrissey?"

"No."

"Oh. Well, he's gorgeous. A living dream."

"I think you may be sitting on my pencil."

"Not that he's not smart too," she added.

We finally met by appointment. "Hi, Marcia."

"Hi." I was looking for a job.

"Well, let's see. You were with Dave Flaherty. . . ." His voice faded but his finger continued the probe, moving slowly down the page of my résumé. "What made you leave Washington?" he asked.

"Oh, I got a divorce. . . ."

"I see."

Six months later we began having dinner together, at first every couple of weeks, eventually most nights. I assumed we were friends; we always split the check and he never tried to kiss me. We probed each other's histories and discovered we both correlated our private lives with public events: my Grandma Yetta died on the same day as Jack Benny and Jerry first had intercourse the night before Eisenhower was inaugurated. We discovered mutually a passion for nasty Mayor Lindsay stories, a near mastery of the city's bus and subway routes, and a strong disinclination to see foreign movies.

I fell in love with him but forced myself to act casual, afraid of having him think me just another eager lady. But after a month of intense camaraderie, I wanted more. I spent my mornings plotting ways to make him seduce me in the evenings. By the afternoons, I was overwrought from the excitement of my fantasies, from planning traps, and from guilt at neglecting my work. I began to fear that Jerry would not only not desire me but might fire me as well. So I'd bang the typewriter passionately, until he would knock at my office door. Ready? he'd ask. I'd begin each dinner with him feeling frazzled, exhausted, and decidedly unseductive. But our conversations were fun, and by dessert, I felt so happy, so at ease, that my morning plot—to drop my coffee spoon and let my hand brush his thigh while reaching for it—was forgotten.

We slipped into bed casually one evening when we stopped at his apartment to check the movie listings and found only Clint Eastwood in the neighborhood. We were sitting on the bed, and Jerry leaned across the *Village Voice* and gave me a cautious kiss. I responded, far less cautiously. An hour later he said softly, "I can't believe I wasted all that time thinking you just wanted to be friends." The next night I moved in.

I never totally understood why he chose me. It was clear he enjoyed me in bed, but it was also clear that I wasn't some hotsy-totsy lover, a dynamite dolly who could make a man crazed with lust. I had no secret tricks and my muscle tone was such that I could assume only the most conventional positions.

I never cooked for him except once, to make him a grilled cheese sandwich when he had bronchitis; he admired the sandwich, but not so much that it would bind him to me forever. Even if I had prepared the sort of nightly feasts that I had spread before Barry—home-baked rolls, succulent stews, piquant salads: meals that I'd dash from my office on Capitol Hill during lunch hour to prepare—Jerry would not have been influenced. His interest in food was minimal. He could be satisfied by any cuisine, from Hunan to Hungarian, as long as he was allowed to sprinkle a dram or two of salt over his entrée.

His taste in women was equally broad and accepting. From what I could ascertain—and I tried to ascertain a lot—he had a preference for blonds, but blonds come in many packages. Kathye Baron, who preceded me, was half Jewish, half Irish, the latter being dominant after four years at Manhattanville College of the Sacred Heart. Before her were a couple of WASP ladies—out-of-towners who had been drawn by stories about the Algonquin Round Table—a few pure-bred Irish ladies, and I think one Pole. They lived both in and out, but they were all on the light side, although there had been a hot affair with Felicity Weiner, a dark, not-too-handsome assistant to the deputy mayor for intergovernmental affairs, and an earlier college romance with Laura Aldarissio, which ended during their senior year when she tossed her black locks at Phil Savelli, the son of the city's most prominent cement contractor. I noticed when they saw each other at political affairs, Jerry would redden and Laura, now Mrs. Savelli, would lower her now-gray head and breathe, "Hello, Gerald"—though Jerry swore he had never slept with her and had, at most, gotten a meager handful of bare tit the night after finals in their junior year.

"Why did you ask me to live with you?" I once asked him.

"I was desperate."

"Jerry, I'm serious."

"So am I. They just raised the rent and it was either move or find a roommate."

"Is that the truth?" I asked, feigning lightness but feeling heavy with the dread certainty that Catholics never really lie.

"Why do you have to analyze everything to death? I like you. You're a great girl. I wanted to live with you."

Like me, he may have been very lonely. So out of all the women, he chose me. I was nice. I was interesting. I was there at the moment he decided he wanted company.

A voice boomed down to us as we rode the escalator to the Hilton's banquet floor. "Hey, Morrissey, you old bastard. I should've known you'd be here," John McConachie bellowed. Jerry, ahead of me, stepped off the escalator and was immediately swept up in a handshake and a backslap. McConachie was second in command of the Electricians' Union. He was in his early sixties and despite his nearly perpetual grin, he had the quick, darting, pale eyes of the easily annoyed; he had waited nearly seventeen years for Herbert Stutzermann, the union's president, to die so he could take over, but Herbert had just celebrated his happy, healthy, eightieth birthday. However, everyone still treated grinning John with great seriousness.

"John," Jerry said, as the escalator delivered me up to them, "have you met Marcia Green, Bill's speech writer?"

"I haven't had the pleasure," he replied. McConachie prided himself on never forgetting a face. "I never forget a face," he told me.

"Oh," I said, smiling. "Well, very nice meeting you."

"My pleasure, young lady," he said. Then, turning back to Jerry, he asked, "Can you still call them 'ladies' or does it have to be 'women' nowadays?" Jerry began to chuckle at McConachie's wit and I flashed a final smile, waved, and walked toward the room where cocktails were being served.

"Marcia!" someone called, giving it the not-unusual New York pronunciation *Mah-sher*. "Over here, babe." I peered at the crowd backed two deep at the bar and saw Wendy Friedman, the Deputy Commissioner for Cultural Affairs. "How's everything?"

"Fine, Wendy."

"Jerry? The two of you still together? Huh? Doing okay?" The nostrils of her large, splayed nose flared with interest.

"Yes. We're fine. And you?"

"What can I tell you? Who has time for anything anymore? I can't remember the last time I got laid. I should have it bronzed and keep it as a memento. Anyhow, that's neither here nor there, is it? I hear Bill's announcing tomorrow. You write him a good, socko speech, hon?" I nodded. "He coming tonight?" I shook my head. "I didn't think he would," she went on, "because if he's declaring tomorrow he has to go into the high-class business, and being seen here with scutzy Dick Krasnoff and all his vermin friends wouldn't be smart, would it? So, by the next time I see you, you might be packing your bags, heading up for Albany with a fancy title, Special Assistant to the Governor for Rhetorical Affairs or something. What kind of opposition do you expect in the primary?" Wendy moved into this question casually. At twenty-four, she was already on her way to becoming one of the keenest politicians in New York. Although loud and coarse, she attacked and killed with grace.

"You mean, who do we think will enter besides Parker?"

"Yeah, sure, besides Parker. Once everybody decides Parker's vulnerable—and let me tell you something, my mother's poodle has the brains to figure that out—do you think they're going to let Paterno have it gratis, for the asking, you know, without putting up some kind of major stink? Huh?"

"Well, so far the only opposition that's surfaced isn't really very threatening. I mean it, Wendy. They're people with small constituencies—"

"Sweets, you're jerking my chain. Don't tell me Bill Paterno thinks he can just walk into the governor's mansion without having some kind of positively lethal hand-to-hand combat."

"Of course not. We're prepared for a rough primary."

"Well, we'll see," she said offhandedly. She was smiling now, grinning over my head. When I turned around, I saw Charles Basile, the mayor's press secretary, pressing through the crowd, waving at Wendy. He waved a little less energetically when he saw me, although he managed to whip up enough enthusiasm to give her a large, chirpy cheek kiss and an exuberant "Hi, Wendy!"

"Cómo está, Charlie?" she replied.

"Bueno, bueno," he rumbled, still smiling, suave. "And you, Wendy?"

"Terrífico," Wendy said.

"How are you, Marcia?" he asked, sounding bored.

"Fine."

"Good. Glad to hear it."

"Where do you two know each other from?" Wendy demanded.

I answered quickly. "The '73 mayoral primary."

"Gotcha," said Wendy. "And you two were waging your own sweet campaign. Oh, come on, Charlie, stop looking at me like I brought out some new and fascinating aspect of your personality. What do they say? If you laid your girl friends end to end. . . . Oh, sorry, Marcia. But listen, it's no big deal and there's been a lot of water under everyone's bridge since 1973. Right? God, I was just out of high school in June of '73. Now tell, Charlie, when's the great Mayor Dip Shit going to decide about the goddamn Shakespeare festival?"

I was able to continue smiling for another fifteen seconds. By that time it was Charlie's turn to talk, and I proclaimed my need for a drink and got away. I tried to mingle with people at the bar, but as usual at parties where the socializing is vertical, my height proved a disadvantage. Being short, I could not spot allies in a crowd. And strangers reflexively treated me as a child, patting my shoulder as I passed, tousling my hair. Even though I was over five feet tall and had crow's feet, bartenders often viewed my request for wine with suspicion.

People pressed against me, pushing me aside to get closer to the liquor. I was trod on, elbowed, felt up. I retreated, finally, to the ladies' lounge and sat in a small pink chair with my eyes closed, so everyone would think I was being brave, suffering in silence from a tension headache or cramps. There was a strong but not unpleasant odor of floral room deodorant; it was like being smothered in bougainvillaea.

But at least I was safe from the pushers and the gropers and as far away from Charlie Basile as I could get without leaving the hotel entirely. He had, I observed, dropped his Spanish accent completely, now that there were few points for originality being handed out for being Puerto Rican. He no longer had to be friendly to everyone either, now that he was Mayoral Spokesman. And he didn't have to play the exotic to get laid, as he once had.

"Mar-see-ah," he had murmured, rolling my "r" and then running his teeth along the palm of my hand. "What you doin' tonight after the Brooklyn debate? You goin' home?"

"Yes."

"No, you comin' with me." Then he bent down and kissed the nape of my neck, his thin dark lips warm and moist enough to send chills down my back and arms. "Hey, we'll have some fun, Mar-see-ah." As a preview, his hand reached in front of me and tweaked my nipple. "Lots of fun."

But before we got to the fun, we spent over a half hour in the corridor of campaign headquarters, debating where to establish our pleasure palace. Each time someone passed, we'd stop whispering and emit a few loud sentences about "projecting an image of warm responsibility" before calming down to talk of our impending passion once again.

"Your place?" he asked.

I had to say no because I shared an apartment with two other women, both also divorced, who stayed in every night to wash their hair. Charlie's apartment was unavailable too, because his wife was there.

"I didn't know you were married," I said.

"Yeah. But it's not workin'."

"I'm sorry."

We agreed to meet back at campaign headquarters after the Brooklyn debate, around ten. A few minutes after midnight, I dashed in, having taken a rather frightening subway ride back to Manhattan because the candidates were still screaming at each other at eleven fifteen. Charlie jumped from the couch in the petition coordinator's office and greeted me. "Hey, you know what time it is? Where the fuck you been?"

We did it on the couch. Charlie spread some mimeographed copies of the previous day's schedule underneath me "so we don't get come all over." But Charlie couldn't come. He pumped and grinded till after two in the morning. The schedule disintegrated with my perspiration, shreds of wet paper clung to my back and legs. At last, to my relief, he pulled out. "You're too dry," he complained. "No guy could come inside that."

"Sorry."

"S'all right. Just suck me off. Come on. I don' have all night."

Charlie was the twelfth man I slept with after my divorce. I'm not certain how many men there actually were before Jerry, since I stopped counting with Sheldon Glantz, number twenty-three, when it occurred to me that keeping score of lovers might be neither sophisticated nor amusing. Sheldon, who was counsel to the New York State Department of Mental Hygiene, became passionate only post-coitally, when we couldn't find my underpants.

"It's all right, Sheldon. They weren't such good ones."

"Have you looked in the bathroom?"

"I wasn't in the bathroom."

"Let me check. Maybe they caught on my toe or something and I dragged them in when I went to wash off."

"Sheldon, I'll go home without them. Really, it's okay. If you find them, you can just throw them out."

His breathing was shallow and rapid, and his tongue kept darting back and forth. "I can't have your underpants here."

"Maybe you'll find them in the morning, Sheldon. They'd just be here overnight," I pleaded. I had put on my coat after a half hour of searching proved fruitless, and I felt dirty and sticky from perspiration and the residue of Glantz semen. "Maybe if you shake out the sheets." I glanced at his tousled single bed.

"Oh, my God." And then he wheeled around to glare at me, his Black Watch plaid bathrobe pulled tight around his lumpy body. "What kind of person loses their underpants?" he hissed.

Like Charlie, like Sheldon, my men were all government subsidized. This shtup has been made possible by a grant from the Department of the Interior. I was never forced into singles bars, into reliance on cousins to fix me up with their friend Harvey who had just gotten a divorce which wasn't his fault. I met many men. Politics made bedfellows.

Barry and I separated in 1968, and after that, after having known nearly every whim and crevice of one man all my sexual life, I found myself ricocheting all over Washington, from bed to bed, then shooting up to New York, where I thought I'd find a comfortable, familiar world. Instead, there were more beds, more men. In one week, I slept with three different men named Norman. All were inept.

I exited marriage into a very different world from which I entered. In 1968, I found out, women were no longer wooed or seduced or flirted with or even whispered to suggestively. They were asked: You wanna? I suppose I did, for I often found my legs wrapped around a pair of meaty hips before I even had time to conjure up a compensating fantasy. You wanna? I guess so, for I became the easiest of lays, kissing and licking and stroking men so homely or boorish or dull that I would never have introduced them to even my most distant relative.

Some of the men, mainly the older ones, still observed the amenities. They would pledge a love that would last till eternity but which usually succumbed on the first Wednesday in November. "I know I said I loved you, Marcia, and I did—do—but I have to go back to my (1) family (2) law firm (3) old mistress who's been threatening suicide and would leave a note. Look, you know I don't want to hurt you," explained (1) Vinnie Pinello (2) Bob Figueroa (3) Hal Moskowitz (4) Timothy Francis Xavier Driscoll.

A few saw little reason for even superficial gentility. Post fellatio, an assistant district attorney called me "Marion" several times and seemed annoyed when I insisted my name was Marcia. A vice-president of the Health and Hospitals Corporation said, "Boy, kiddo, do you ever got pudgy legs!" the first time I undressed. Oliver Murray, studying hunger in Manhattan on a luscious H.E.W. grant, began our evening by informing me how fortunate I was to be on the brink of a shattering sexual experience with a black man at the height of Afro-American Consciousness Season. In bed, though, he merely played piston to my cylinder, in-out, in-out. "I'm really not attracted to white girls." Five more minutes of friction elapsed. "If I do go for white girls, it's not for little blonds. But you looked so sad. You depressed or something?" In-out.

No one wanted to go to the movies anymore. Gentlemen callers no longer dined you, although they might wine you or offer a joint of marijuana as a kind of pregame warm-up. Hardly anyone told me I was cute, and few asked where I had gone to college.

I sensed a more comfortable, conventional world existed, but I didn't know how to break into it. Cut off, alone, I saw men and women strolling through Georgetown, holding hands or carrying home a pizza made for two. But none of the men I met at work had time for these indulgences. Together, we would race along M Street, past the pizza carriers, and rush up to an empty apartment to have a quick half hour of sex before he would have to dash out for a cocktail party or dinner with a reporter or an evening of television with his family in Chevy Chase.

I had no real friends, because when I moved to Washington, my life had centered only on my job and Barry. Women did not flock to my side to be pals when I became separated. In fact, since most of the women I met had the same sort of professional and social life I had, all us spent our late evenings plugged into hot rollers and douche bags; we were too tired, too frightened, and probably too competitive for confidences.

When I moved back to New York after my divorce in 1969, I saw my cousin Barbara, but she could manage only lunches. Her evenings were spent with her husband and sons. She offered to arrange dates for me with her husband's colleagues, but for some reason I considered accepting a blind date with a professor of law more humiliating than going to bed with a wall-eyed, buck-toothed, second-string politician whose underwear was suspiciously gray.

Not all men were vile, of course, Arthur Golden, Deputy Police Commissioner for Public Information, was actually nice. He proposed on our first evening together. We were in his parents' double bed in Flatbush. They were in Fort Lauderdale, looking at condominiums. "Let's get married," he said, as we lay side by side, the mahogany headboard having finally stopped its rhythmic slapping against the wall.

"No. No thank you, Arthur."

"You didn't like it?"

"It was fine. Wonderful. You were terrific."

"So?"

"I just don't want to get married again."

"Why not?"

I wanted Jerry. I strode out of the ladies' room and over to the small, horseshoe-shaped table which held the place cards. Jerry, I discovered, had taken care of himself, because only Morvillo and Magill remained under the M's. I found myself, Ms. M. Green, Table 74, half buried by Mr. & Mrs. Stanley Golub. I tossed them aside and then, conscience-stricken, reached to retrieve their card. But I was unable to because a hand covered my eyes.

"Guess who?"

I knew the voice, naturally. "I can't," I lied. The hand pressed harder on my eyes, pulling me until my back leaned hard against a firm body. I smelled a strong musk cologne.

"Sure you can." And he gave my a friendly reminder too; he leaned down and began to suck my earlobe.

"Stop it." I leaned far to the left, but my lobe remained captive in his mouth. The suction hurt. "Please."

Surprisingly, he let go, like a vacuum cleaner suddenly shut off, and my lobe, sore and wet, fell back into place. But my eyes remained masked. "I'll let you go if you tell me my name." Even Rumpelstiltskin had more class. "Who am I? I know you know."

Partially because I knew the inevitability of my defeat and partially because I was curious to see how many people had witnessed my public earlobe assault, I said, "Lyle." The hand drew away from my eyes slowly, traveled gently over my forehead, and laconically passed through the thick of my hair.

"I knew you knew," he said, his voice silky with triumph. "I didn't think you'd forget me so fast." I turned and faced him. Lyle Lo-Bello had learned a lot from James D'Avonne Gresham. He had learned to abjure polyester shirts. He understood that gentlemen do not wear tie clips. He no doubt bequeathed his gold link bracelet to his cousin Sal in Red Hook. But he was too neat, too well-packaged; he lacked the governor's scruffy appeal. "Well, say something, Marcia," he commanded, looking properly authoritative but a little indecently muscular in a perfectly tailored navy suit. "You're the speech writer." Even the black mole under his left (brown) eye gleamed at me, as though he had remembered to keep it polished.

"I'm sorry about the governor, Lyle. I know how close—"

"Thanks," he said quickly. "So, tell me what you've been up to, smart lady. Life treating you okay?"

"Yes. Well, you know I'm still working for—"

"Marcia, you're talking abc's to me. Come on. The real stuff. Is Morrissey making you happy?"

I swallowed noisily, a little stunned that Lyle had been interested enough to keep track of me. "How did you know about me and—?" I began.

"Are you kidding? Jerry Morrissey's an important guy. But you know that. Half the city owes him. Meantime, you didn't answer my question." He smiled. Lyle's lips were heavy, the sort unimaginatively referred to as sensuous, and when he smiled his lips did not flatten entirely, but remained a little loose. Were he to have jumped and smiled at the same time, his lips would have jiggled.

"What was your question?" I asked, gazing at his mouth.

"Is the old mick treating you okay?" Lyle was good. He got in a good dig about Jerry's age, thus spotlighting his own comparative youth; Lyle must have been a couple of years younger than I, maybe thirty-two or -three. And the question also showed how urbane he was by using the pejorative "mick" that the Irish sometimes use with each other and that anyone else but a very close friend is careful to avoid.

"Yes, thanks. We're managing pretty well."

"Pretty well?"

"Very well, Lyle." He raised one eyebrow, skeptically, as though he had studied Charles Boyer movies. "Really."

"Good. I'm glad." We smiled at each other. I shot my eyes over his shoulder to see if I could spot a familiar face to rescue me. "He's one hell of a guy," Lyle said. I let my hand glide over my throat, nervously smoothing my skin. "One terrific mick," he added, watching my hand.

I'm not sure why the Italians have it in for the Irish. Maybe it has something to do with the preponderance of Irish priests and nuns who do something to incur the wrath of small Italian children. Maybe it's a resentment of the acceptance of the Irish. All men wear emerald bow ties on St. Paddy's Day, but who besides the Italians breaks out the fettucini on October 12? Maybe it's because the Irish, of all ethnic groups, look so American: they appear clean even before their showers, and they generally have neither shaky lips nor shiny black moles.

"I'd better go find my table," I said, still smiling cheerily.

"Okay. Great," said Lyle, smiling broadly at a point someplace behind me. He had obviously caught sight of an individual worthy of a display of intense charm.

"Bye. See you," I said. I gave my dress a sturdy tug just below my hips, preparatory to walking away from him. But Lyle hadn't finished with me; I felt his hand on my back.

"Marcia," he said. As I turned back to him, I saw him wink and hold up an index finger to Larry Woodward, attorney for the diocese of Brooklyn, signaling that he would be with him after a few more words to this broad. Woodward waited for Lyle, a small smile on his mottled pig face as he watched Lyle put his arm around my shoulder, draw me tight beside him, and whisper. "Listen, Marcia, you and I are going to be seeing a lot of each other." Anticipating my stiffening, he continued quickly, "I'll probably be giving Bill some help on the campaign. Now I know you might feel awkward about it. You know what I mean. Because you and I have—well, let's call it a past."

Sweat began to form. I felt it particularly under my arms but sensed it behind my knees, under my breasts, along my back. I was terrified for Jerry. Paterno had not merely lied to him, he—

"Don't worry," soothed Lyle, sensing my panic, "you can rely on me not to say a word about what went on between us. I wouldn't hurt you or Jer for the world." I force myself into casualness, lifting my shoulders in a shrug, glancing around. Woodward, having witnessed this prolonged consultation, had let his smile broaden into a leer. "And listen, Marcia, I'm sure we can work together. Hell, I read the declaration speech you wrote for Bill and it's really great. I only had a couple of fact changes to add."

"Lyle, listen," I began, but before I could continue, Lyle ruffled my hair, gave me a loud kiss on the cheek, and moved over to Woodward, leaving me alone to find Jerry.

As I walked, analyzing LoBello's words, I noticed former United States Representative Richard Krasnoff, hopping from table to table, thanking all his good friends who had made this wonderful evening possible and in addition had made his continued retention of a law firm of four former assistant United States Attorneys possible. Thinking I was moving toward him, Krasnoff raced over to greet me. "How're ya doing, sweetheart?" he demanded, grabbing my hand, shaking it with the vigor of the righteous, the as-yet-unindicted. But he dropped it quickly. My hands were drippy with cold sweat. I wiped them on my dress and hurried to the table.

Our host, Mike Mazer, was a second-rate real estate tycoon who had purchased a table—for two thousand dollars—and had given tickets for two of the ten seats to Paterno. Paterno, naturally, could not appear at a dinner honoring a man under heavy federal scrutiny, but by the same token he wanted his presence there, so he sent Jerry. And since Jerry's eyes and ears and mouth were sufficient for a simple Dollars for Dick dinner, the second ticket went to the person in the office who most wanted to trail after Jerry Morrissey and/or have a free prime ribs dinner.

"Marcia." Jerry stood about ten feet away, waving, blocking the numbered sign on our table. "Over here." I waved back and weaved through the crowd of people who had not yet sat down to their scooped-out pineapple half heaped with fruit. As I got closer to him, I saw his coloring was high, bright, indicating he had managed four or five scotches between conversations. He looked loose and happy, his waving hand so relaxed it almost drooped. I smiled at him. I had just finished the final draft of Paterno's declaration that afternoon and had dropped it on his desk at five thirty, right before Jerry and I left the office to go home and change. That meant LoBello had read the speech probably minutes after we left. Paterno must have called him to tell him the coast was clear—Morrissey had gone.

"Marcia," Jerry said as I reached the table, reaching out for my hand. "Let me introduce you to everyone." Like the paterfamilias, he motioned everyone at Table 74 to sit, and they did so. In fact, nearly everyone at Tables 72, 73, 75, and 76 did so also.

"This is Mike Mazer," he began, nodding toward the

mini-mogul. "Of course you've heard of him." I beamed and nodded, as though a day did not pass without someone singing hosannas to Mazer Enterprises. Mazer was small, dark, compact, and wrinkled, like a human cigar. He smiled back. "And his wife, Francine Mazer," Jerry continued, directing my attention to a woman in her late twenties who was scratching a minute reconstructed nose with a clawlike, dark-painted nail. "Francine manages a belt boutique," Jerry added, sounding as though he thought it was a marvelous idea. Francine barely glanced at me before returning her bronze-lidded eyes to Jerry, gazing with an intensity bred of a desire to take her dark nails and rake them hard down his back. "And Tom Fitzpatrick," Jerry continued, as he gave me a tour around the table, remembering each name, reciting everyone's station as though each were vital to the nation's peace and security.

"Jerry," I whispered nervously. Maybe there was no problem. Maybe he had told Paterno to speak with LoBello. Jerry took his maraschino cherry and placed it next to the one on my fruit salad.

"Having a good time, hon?" he asked, giving me a slow glance and a thick-lashed blink and a warm smile—in short, giving me a strong hint that I should be having a delightful evening, just as he was.

"Fine," I answered. I could hear him exhale gently, in gratitude. I reached for my spoon and shoveled in a few ounces of tart fruit. Jerry rearranged a pineapple chunk, moving it in front of a grape, while he astutely ignored Francine Mazer's significant looks. "Guess who I saw?" I added.

"Who?"

"Lyle LoBello."

"No shit. When did he slither into town?" Jerry's voice contained no concern.

"I don't know," I mumbled.

"Well, I guess I'd better say hello to him at some point, just to show I don't resent his trying to pull a fast one with Bill. I mean, Jesus, he's such a two-bit little snake. But so obvious." He stopped and turned his attention to Mike Mazer's analysis of the problems of the city's capital budget structure. He nodded several times, seeming awed at Mazer's profundity.

"Jerry," I whispered a few minutes later. Beneath the

heavy yellow tablecloth, he took my hand and placed it between his legs and gave it an initiatory push. "Jerry, please listen."

"Make nice to the man," he murmured. "Don't worry. The man will make nice to you later on." His hands were on top of the table now, one relaxed, one grasping his drink.

"Jerry, Lyle read the draft of my declaration speech. The one I just gave to Bill this afternoon."

For a moment he didn't move. Jerry was a total politician. He knew he had been betrayed. He could read the signs and knew they forecast evil days for him. Then he stood and, clutching his glass very tight, beamed down at the table and said, "Would you people excuse me for a minute? I'm just going to get a refill."

6

Jerry and I were raised by widows, neither of them merry. But at least he had a pocketful of glad Daddy memories, stories he could whip out, family snapshots. There's handsome Jim Morrissey, bouncing Jerry and brother Denny on his knees, singing, for some reason, "Nothing Could Be Finer Than to Be in Carolina" in an off-key but obviously endearing baritone. Or Jim at the Bronx Zoo, roaring, terrifying the lion that frightened baby Annie. Once again, broad-shouldered and serious in his policeman's uniform, the day the whole family turned out to see him sworn in as sergeant. Even in his last year, age thirty-three, as he lay in bed weak from the leukemia that was killing him, he kept his eight-year-old son enthralled for hours, reading Tarzan stories. Every half hour or so, Jerry would let his father close his eyes for a few minutes. Then the tales would continue.

I had two years more. A month after my tenth birthday, my father walked into a Glickman Pillow Company truck that was rumbling down Avenue M in Brooklyn.

"Well, what was he like?" Jerry would ask. We'd study our history on weekends as we hiked for miles through Central Park or the Lower East Side or across the Brooklyn Bridge into the Heights.

"I really don't remember him," I'd answer, generally a little breathless from keeping up with Jerry's longer strides.

"Oh, come on. He didn't die till you were ten."

"Really, I hardly have any memories." Victor Green certainly never sang "Nothing Could Be Finer Than to Be in Carolina." I'd try to look Jerry straight in the eye, and he'd peer back, skeptical. "He must have been quiet," I'd try to explain.

He must have been. His footsteps are certainly not etched in my memory, but perhaps that's because he glided through the house in his socks. Thin white socks, sagging around his slender, pale ankles. Our conversations were somewhat terse.

"Hi, Daddy."

"Hello, little girl."

He'd pat me on the head. He wasn't being condescending. Patting heads was simply an acceptable adult-to-child gesture. He had probably seen it in a Shirley Temple movie.

My mother and my Aunt Estelle would often recount, with sad little smiles and sighs and nods of the head, tales of my papa, who left his little sweetheart half an orphan. "Remember, Marcia, how he taught you long division when you were only in second grade?" Actually I didn't.

"Remember when you dislocated your thumb, Marcia? You were about six, and for weeks he'd cut your meat for you. Remember?" I do remember the splinted thumb. I can even recall the adhesive tape that turned a sooty gray and curled up at the edges. But I cannot—although I wish I could—recall any role my father had in my thumb crisis.

I sensed that he loved me, but he must have thought it inappropriate to tell me so, although occasionally he tried to show me. In a burst of fellowship, he once tried to teach me pinochle, but I didn't catch on; he said we'd wait a few years and try again. He seemed annoyed when I cried to watch "Captain Video" instead of a kinescope of the day's McCarthy harangue and patiently explained why the senator was more important than the captain. But although I agreed to watch the politician, I remained unconvinced, and I knew he realized it. Each bedtime he kissed me good night, but his kisses were dry and pecky. And a couple of times he called me his little towhead, but as I assumed he was calling me a toe-head, my response probably wasn't encouraging.

"That's it?" Jerry demanded, raising a doubting eyebrow.

"Honestly, that's all." I recall feeling that my father was the pleasanter parent and assumed we could share a father-daughter relationship like Nancy and Mr. Drew as we both grew older and less shy.

I don't remember hearing about his death, but a few days afterward I overheard some of the details. My mother had sent me outside our apartment building to play, but since it was January I was bundled in a storm coat, gloves, muffler, and pom-pom hat and therefore not easily recognizable. Coming inside after five minutes of solitary fresh air, I waited, wrapped in wool, for the elevator. Two neighbors waited also.

"You heard?" The fatter one asked.

"Horrible," her companion answered.

"I mean, about what happened after. The truck stopped so fast the back opened up and the pillows fell out. It was a pillow truck. A truck from a pillow company."

"I didn't know that."

"Oh, well, better you shouldn't know from such things." The blubbery lady's voice grew softer, not because she realized I was there but out of awe of her terrible insider's knowledge. "I heard," she murmured, "the body went flying and when it fell, the head"—she paused—"landed on a pillow."

"Oy."

Indeed, Inside the elevator, I pressed 4 and slowly unwrapped my muffler from my face.

Jerry asked, "You don't even remember the funeral?"

"No. They didn't take me. They thought it would be traumatic."

Jerry, naturally, could recall the entire requiem mass, enumerate the number of tears shed both inside the church and at the cemetery, and how his sister Ann had peed in the limousine after the burial.

I do remember my Aunt Estelle whispering to Uncle Julius, "Nothing's wrong with Marcia. The whole world doesn't have to cry and carry on the way your family does. She's in a state of shock."

But I wasn't in shock, merely a little frightened about living alone with my mother. I knew she found me an onerous obligation even when my father was alive. But the week of shiva went by quite pleasantly, with lots of neighbors and relatives dropping in, bringing pecan coffee cake and chocolate cookies and prune danish. Mr. Fingerhut, my father's boss, actually sent over a turkey, carved and put back on the skeleton—the frame, as the caterer called it—the meat held in place with judiciously placed wooden toothpicks.

"The cheap momser," Aunt Estelle commented to my mother, as she transferred the remaining shreds of turkey onto a small plate and covered it with two layers of waxed paper. "He couldn't break down and send a roast beef after all those years Victor practically killed himself for him. How much more would a roast beet have cost him?"

A few months later, she sat across our kitchen table from my mother, her rosy index fingernail picking at a chip in the white enamel. "Why are you worrying about a few extra dollars, Hilda?" she demanded.

"Because I don't have a few extra dollars," my mother replied. There were no tears in her eyes; even then, she was too dried out to cry. Her sister, opposite her, was fuller and plumper and juicier even than the catered turkey had been. Compared with her, my mother looked dehydrated. Look, the ad would proclaim, a fresh morsel of woman, showing a picture of Aunt Estelle. And beside it, the unappetizing freeze-dried variety. But their features were the same: small noses with oddly rounded nostrils, slightly receding chins, milky brown eyes. But Aunt Estelle's face was a soft white with pudgy pink-rouged cheeks; my mother's had yellowed and cracked.

"You have to live somewhere," Aunt Estelle countered. "And in Queens, you'd be much closer to us, and Marcia would have a much better class of friends. I mean it, Hilda, look at Barbara's friends. A lovely bunch of girls. And almost all their fathers are professionals."

I wanted to point out, from the foyer in which I was lurking, eavesdropping, that my father was a professional, an accountant, albeit a dead one, whereas Julius Lindenbaum was a furrier with a mere two years of high school, a man who said "erl" for "oil," a man who always smelled a little like a fox pelt. My mother must have known that too, but she merely sighed. She could never summon the energy to confront her sister.

"And before you know it," Estelle continued, "she'll be

ready for college. Right? Look, I don't have to tell you what her I.Q. is."

"I know," my mother breathed.

"And do you think boys from the fine families will want to hear she's from Brooklyn?" Hardly. "Hilda, look at your face. Don't worry. Would Julius and I let anything happen to you?"

Of course not. So we moved to Queens, to a dank rent-controlled apartment in Forest Hills. "Very good schools," Aunt Estelle noted, and my mother gratefully bent her head, as though about to receive a pat or a benediction. The apartment had one small bedroom which my mother let me have, while she slept on a couch in the living room. This arrangement suited me, although when I got older, her snoring often disconcerted my dates when they brought me to the door to say good night.

"What's that?" they would whisper, their eyes darting about the hallway, as they heard my mother's regular, chesty snores, interrupted occasionally by a moan or frightened dream whimper.

"Oh, that. It's my mother. She sleeps in the living room."

Aunt Estelle and Uncle Julius took care of us. They invited us to their house for dinner every Wednesday night. Often, there would be enough food left over for my mother to take home, a packet of brisket or chicken. And, living in Queens, it was only a ten-minute subway ride back to our apartment, so the meat was often still warm by the time we'd return home. Wordlessly, we could wolf it down in our kitchenette.

I received the cream of my cousin Barbara's wardrobe: camel's-hair coats and lamb's-wool sweater sets and ruffled blouses only one year out of style and three sizes too large. And each Chanukah, there would be a box of white handkerchiefs with pastel "M's" for me and a stiff new hundred-dollar bill for my mother.

"Look, Hilda, I took care of the funeral, didn't I?" Uncle Julius demanded when my mother finally came to him, seeking more help. "But I don't want you to be dependent on us. It would affect our relationship, wouldn't it? I mean, you and Estelle are sisters, and it wouldn't be healthy."

"What did your mother say to him?" Jerry demanded. We were walking through the Central Park Zoo, past the yak with its mangy brown fur—not the sort of line my Uncle Julius would carry.

"What could she say?"

"She could tell him to go fuck himself. She could tell him that they were the hotshots, the ones who got her to uproot you and move to Queens, so they goddamn better get up some of the rent money."

"Right. Sure." It was a warm afternoon and the air was full of rank animal odors. "And then what would have happened?" Jerry moved his jaw, began to reply, but at these conversations I was much quicker. "I'll tell you. She would have been left alone. She would have had no one, nobody, zilch."

"Wrong, Marcia. They would have respected her."

"You're wrong. She had no money, no friends, no power. If they couldn't pity her, they didn't need her."

Jerry wiped the back of his neck with his hand. "I don't know," he said slowly.

"Well, I know," I snapped. His demands for fresh confidences made me edgy; I had to balance my ravenous need for understanding with a vague sense of obligation to protect my family's good name.

As usual, Jerry allowed time out for crankiness but then persisted toward his goal of knowing all there was to know. He took my hand, kissed it lightly, and demanded, "Did your mother ever have any boyfriends?"

"No." After my father died, she showed no interest in men. Her manner never changed when a man came into a room. She never flirted, never reached up to stroke her hair, never even smiled. Men did not interest her. Actually, I don't think they interested her before my father died. I don't recall my parents ever touching, kissing, whispering, or even exchanging knowing looks.

"Any women friends?"

"Not really. She'd say hello to a few ladies in the building, but I think she lost touch with all her old acquaintances once we moved to Queens. So there was just my aunt. And a few cousins, but she only spoke to them about once a month. Most of them lived in New Jersey, and it was too expensive for her to call."

"But didn't she try to meet people? Join a club or—"

"No. She was more interested in what was going on in a book than in what was going on around her—unless she was at her sister's. But in our apartment she'd sit in this old, lumpy green chair in a corner of the living room with just one small light focused on whatever she was reading." It was as if it were a spotlight. The book was the real show, the action; everything else was shadowy. I knew I was. I'd wander into the living room and ask her a question and she'd startle, as though I'd shocked her by demonstrating there was another world besides the one on the page she was reading. "Sometimes I'd walk in after school, and even before I had a chance to close the door she'd say 'shhh' instead of 'hello,' like she was irritated that I insisted on breaking into her perfect world." Jerry shrugged. "It's true. Books were her only passion."

"Didn't she play Mah-Jongg?"

I began to laugh. "That's not funny."

"Of course it's not funny," Jerry concurred. "Four or five little old Jewish ladies sitting around a table is serious business."

"Don't little old Irish ladies play Mah-Jongg?"

"If you had any idea how absurd that idea is, Marcia—"

"What do they do with themselves? I mean, once you're finished with mass, you have a whole day in front of you."

"They don't spend it playing Mah-Jongg."

"Canasta?"

"No."

"Filling up the ice cube tray for happy hour?"

"Marcia, come on."

"I will not come on. You know, I really resent your remarks about Mah-Jongg and all that. Just because you see your mother as Saint Agnes . . ."

"I do not."

". . . the patron saint of widows . . ."

Agnes Morrissey was a truly noble soul, a fine lady, a good Catholic with a grand heart. I hated her. We never met.

"Hello," I'd answer our phone.

"Is Gerald Morrissey there?" this twinkly little Emerald Isle voice would say. Never How are you. Never Oh, I've heard about you, Marcia, and I look forward to meeting you even though you're a Jew.

"I'm sorry, Mrs. Morrissey, he's not in right now."

"Thank you," she'd say briskly, as though I were Jerry's answering service. "Please tell him I called."

I would ask him, "Why can't your mother say hello to me?"

He would answer, "Beats me. Why don't you ask her?"

After her husband's death, Saint Agnes rolled up her sleeves and went right to work, refusing to condemn her three darlings to subsistence on her widow's dole. She taught herself to type and got a job as a secretary to the owner of a local funeral parlor. And after an eight-hour day, she'd dash home to cook the three darlings a good hot meal—probably oatmeal—and bathe them and sing to them and make sure they knew their catechism.

"Jesus, Marcia, she's a nice lady. Why are you so hostile? Because she doesn't say hello? Maybe she's shy," Jerry would say. "Anyhow, I'd think you'd respect her. I mean, she was a working woman and all that."

"Boring."

"What do you mean?"

"Boring. I find saints boring."

"Come on, she wasn't a saint. She was always so ambitious for me, wanting me to be somebody—a priest, a lawyer. And she always let me know she was just a little disappointed. But she was a good mother. She worked so hard at it. You're just upset because your mother didn't—"

"You better stop it, Jerry."

Every so often, I kept myself busy wondering why my mother never got a job. Unlike Saint Agnes, she had worked before her marriage and had what she called secretarial skills. A couple of times she mentioned being able to do something at seventy words per minute, but I'm not sure if she was referring to typing or shorthand. She certainly didn't talk at that speed. Her voice came out slow and weary, and generally her conversation was limited to "Do you want milk in your tea?" or "Well-bred people wear gloves when they go to the city."

But back to work. We had a little insurance money, a small allotment from Social Security, and Uncle Julius's annual hundred. We padded our food budget with a lot of potatoes and twice a week ate something my mother called "fish stew," which she concocted from the bones and heads of fish—which the fish man bestowed upon her gratis—and a carrot and a can of tomatoes. It was horrible, and while I ate it, I breathed through my mouth.

"More?" She held the chipped china ladle carefully, so none of the thin, reddish liquid would dribble on the table.

"No thanks."

There was no money for college, but I was offered partial scholarships to Goucher and Cornell. I was offered a full scholarship to Pembroke.

My quiet mother became crazed. "How do you expect to get from here to Providence?" she yelled. "Sprout wings and fly? Do you have any idea how much bus fare costs? And clothes! The clothes you'd need there, at an Ivy League school." Our apartment was not used to such loud noises. I was afraid the walls might crack from sympathetic tremors to her screaming.

"But why—" I began.

"You just be quiet! And what would you pack your fancy college clothes in? Shopping bags? You'd need suitcases or a trunk. Do you have that kind of money, to buy matched luggage?"

As she yelled that last one, I imagined with unusual clarity a set of red leather luggage: pullman, two-suiter, round hatbox, even a cute little makeup case. All in rich-to-the-touch leather. And I shrieked back, "Then why the hell did you let me apply? You sat there, with me and the guidance counselor, and you said it was okay if I got financial aid. I heard you, damn it, and now I have it." I picked up the letter with the Pembroke seal and shook it in front of her face. "This is it. This is the most money they give to anybody! They say they think I'll be an asset to the student body—"

"Get out." Her voice was normal again, thin and lifeless.

"What do you mean?"

"Get out of this house right now."

I didn't know quite what to do. People in our family never shouted; we knew only lower-class people did that. We made neither scenes nor idle threats. I stomped to the closet, grabbed cousin Barbara's ex-oden coat, and bellowed, "Fuck!" It frightened me nearly as much as it did my mother, since I had never heard it said aloud before. It was a killer word.

And then I left and walked up and down Queens Boulevard for a couple of hours before wandering over and ringing the chimes at my boyfriend Barry's house—the same Barry I was later to marry. I told him what had happened, and after a heated, whispered discussion with his mother in their kitchen he emerged with a dinner invitation. And while his mother, Sheri, wore her tightest mouth during the meal, I dined on veal chops and asparagus and heaps of salad and rice casserole and raisin cake and baked apple. Sheri managed to part her lips after dessert to ask, "Had enough, sweetie?" Barry, when he walked me back to the apartment later that evening, squeezed my hand and said, "Don't be angry with your mother. She means well."

When I returned home my mother nodded at Barry. When he left, she said nothing, not even to express mild curiosity at what I'd been doing for five hours, although I suspect she thought I was doing something dreadful with Barry, something that would make him lose his respect for me. And him going to Columbia, premed. Actually, she never said another word about higher education until my first day at Queens the following September, when she murmured, "Good luck at college." Queens College was free to New York City residents. Queens College was a fifteen-minute bus ride from our apartment. I did not need suitcases.

But I still wonder why she didn't work. Had I bus fare and luggage for Pembroke, I could have met a boy from even a finer family than Barry's. But she stayed home.

Of course, in those days, the nineteen fifties and sixties, most people's mothers did not work. They were housewives. But my mother had only a three-room apartment to clean, and while she did it well—rubbing the faucets until they gleamed silver, washing the floors and covering them with newspapers so they would not get dirty immediately—it could not have taken all day. She chatted with my Aunt Estelle each morning, but for no more than ten minutes. She shopped for the cheapest toilet paper, the least extravagant bag of onions, but she was never gone for more than an hour. She had no friends, suitors, hairdressers, manicurists, tailors, or stockbrokers to spend time with.

I do not believe my mother rejected the notion of working because of her desire to care for me. At ten, I required little care, being able to bathe and dress myself and prepare hard-boiled eggs. She did not need to hover about, urging me to study, because I was a natural grind, highly motivated to prove to my classmates that beauty and wealth weren't everything.

Nor was she mad for me, calling me her ootsie-wootsie lambie and pleading with me to keep her company. Rather, I sensed she found me a little unappealing, although I'm not sure why. While no young lovely, I was at least prettier than she, but that was hardly a contest. I had no vile habits on public display except for cuticle chewing, and she broke me of that long before my father died, by slapping my hand down from my mouth and saying "Stop it." And since I was nearly as quiet as she, I can't think that she found my personality offensive. But perhaps she wanted a jollier child, like my cousin Barbara, who could win an extra Mallomar by merely grinning at the adult nearest the cookie jar.

Jerry could not accept this. "Marcia, she had to have loved you."

"Nope." I was operating on a piece of corned beef, trying to separate the lean from the fat. We were having lunch in an overpriced, non-kosher delicatessen in Brooklyn Heights where they were willing to comply with Jerry's disgusting request for a roast beef sandwich with butter and lettuce.

"But you're lovable. I mean, when you're not being a pain in the ass, you're fun and pretty and smart." But clearly not lovable enough to get him to tell me he actually loved me.

"But she didn't think so. If it had been socially acceptable, she would have exposed me on a mountaintop."

"That can't be true," he remarked and took a bite of his sandwich.

"That is the most disgusting goyishe thing I've ever seen you eat. I'll bet you'll want to follow it up with a Twinkie."

"What's a Twinkie?"

"Oh, it's this kind of sickeningly sweet cake with . . ." He was smiling broadly. "You son of a bitch, you know what a Twinkie is."

"Damned straight."

I almost joined him in a smile, but instead I said, "My mother was very cold."

"Tell me."

"When she would help me with a zipper, she would hold that little tab of the zipper very carefully, between her thumb and index finger, so her hand wouldn't touch my back or my hair or anything."

My mother did not like touching of any sort. When receiving change from a shopkeeper, she never extended her hand but waited until he put the coins on the counter.

She kissed me, with less fervor than an actress kisses a talk-show host, twice after my father died: the day I graduated college and on my wedding day. Actually, she kissed me twice on my wedding day, but the second time she was ordered to by the photographer.

"But look," Jerry began. He spoke slowly, the way he often did in strategy sessions, so he could think fast. "Isn't it possible that she wasn't—what would you call it?—a demonstrative person?" He blinked, waiting for my answer. Because his lashes were so thick and dark, his mere lowering of them seemed the initiation of a sexual act. I swallowed. "Well?"

"You know, Jerry, you're such a politician. Everything has to be explained away, so there's always the appearance of fairness. The whole world has to be happy."

"You're so fair with everybody else and so tough on your family. Christ, why won't you give them the benefit of the doubt?"

"Why should I?"

"Come on. Your mother obviously cared about you."

"All right. Do you want to hear the good or the bad news first?"

Grinning, he said, "The good news. Come on. Let's see if you can say one positive sentence about her without gagging."

"The good news is," I announced softly, "she told me to watch out for speeding trucks."

"Marcia, you are an unbelievable shit."

It's an inherited characteristic. But perhaps I am being unfair. In certain contexts, she cared about me deeply. Those contexts were always potentially public.

"When you're having soup," she explained, just after reading a biography of Jenny Jerome Churchill, "you must sip silently, like this." She would demonstrate, using her fish stew in lieu of the cream of truffle soup I would one day be having. "It's one of those small details that speaks volumes about a person's breeding."

Or, "You can never go wrong with basic black and pearls." She said that the day I came home carrying a rather bright pink blouse. Since I had to split my baby-sitting earnings with her, it had taken me four months to save up for it. "It may be unfair," she continued, "but people do judge you by your clothes."

"Everybody is wearing blouses like this." Some had it in lime green and purple, too.

"Not 'everybody,' Marcia. Many people prefer simple, classic clothes that you can wear year in and year out."

My mother's standards of deportment and taste came from her reading and were modified by her sister's pronouncements. But they were so grandiose, so unyielding, that in my mother's judgment, half of any graduating class of Miss Porter's would be deemed schlumps. She and my Aunt Estelle could discourse on the correct placement of fish forks, how to publicly blow your nose, what to say to a bride on a receiving line ("I'm so pleased for you").

Oddly, I never even had the opportunity to say "I'm so pleased for you" until my cousin Barbara got married, because most people in our family were too hungry after a long ceremony to wait around to shake hands and shoved their way straight to the smorgasbord. But Aunt Estelle insisted on a receiving line. "I'm paying for the finest room at the St. Regis, and for once, people in this family are going to behave like mensches." When my turn came to tell her of my pleasure, Barbara flashed one of her zippy love smiles and grabbed and hugged me. I think I mumbled "Congratulations" into her veil.

I always wondered where my mother and my aunt first got it, their fanatic snobbism, their fascination with the mores and the manners of the aristocracy. Their own mother had ironed pleats into skirts in a sweatshop until she was married at seventeen by a terribly unchic-looking Orthodox rabbi. Their father, Herschl Shochet, a house painter, had rainbow-speckled hair and, I remember vaguely, used to spit into the street quite a bit.

Yet they knew all about Gracious Living. My Aunt Estelle could give an account of Brenda Frazier's debut as though she had been cavorting at the table next to Madcap

Brenda's. My mother's most cherished tidbit was about one of those dear Baronesses de Rothschild, although she never wasted it on me alone. Only Aunt Estelle could bring it out.

"Hilda, tell Barbara and Marcia how the Baroness de Rothschild coordinates her dinner parties."

"Jesus," I breathed.

"Marcia," my aunt said patiently, "right now you're a newlywed and Barry is in medical school, but once he graduates you're going to be called upon to function as his hostess. You're not going to keep on working forever." She gave me her most genteel smile. "Go ahead, Hilda," she ordered.

"Well," my mother would begin, glancing around Estelle's beige living room as if checking that none of the Baroness's social competitors were hiding behind the brocade drapes, listening to this gem, "she keeps a system of filing cards. Each time someone comes for dinner, she writes down the date and what she served."

"So that next time," Estelle carried on, "she won't repeat the same menu!"

God forbid that should happen. Barbara, recently engaged to Philip, leaned back on her mother's beige sectional sofa, picking at a thread on a white silk pillow and nodding. She seemed fascinated. Sitting next to her, I heard the low-pitched choking noise meant for me, as though Barbara were about to heave. "How clever," she told them.

"And there's more, Barbara," her mother said, leaning forward.

My mother leaned forward too. "She writes down the name of the china pattern she's using, and the sterling too. She has more than a hundred sets of dishes!"

Later, Barbara and I sat in her bedroom, dangling our feet over the edge of her narrow bed onto her white shag rug. "And what do you serve the viscomte when he comes to dine?" she asked.

"Pork."

"But of course."

Yet right beside this idiot infatuation with the elite, the two sisters had a different set of values which admitted a little more reality. Under this system, Roz Weinberg, wife of Lou the Podiatrist, had compensated for her husband's lack of an M.D. degree by wearing Kimberly knits and having an apartment in Palm Beach, as opposed to Miami Beach. Norma Klein, who had grown up with my mother and aunt, had married well—her husband was a lawyer for what Estelle called "corporate interests"—but her house!

"Hilda, let me tell you," said Estelle. "Unbelievable." Estelle had been invited to a reunion. My mother had not. "Custom-made plastic seat covers. I mean, if she's not going to take them off for us, who is she going to take them off for?"

"I didn't think she was that lower class," my mother observed.

"That's nothing. You know what her color scheme was? Purple."

"No."

"Purple, I mean it. All right, I'll be fair. She mixed it with a little lavender." And they both shook their heads, filled with awe and pity for the tragedy of Norma Klein. "And you should see her. Hilda, you wouldn't believe the change. Remember that sweet, lovely Norma? So understated? Well, she wore bright orange lipstick and iridescent green eyeshadow. I mean, she looked like a kurveh." Kurveh is Yiddish for whore.

The two sisters dropped bits of Yiddish all around them, apparently never considering that it littered their refined landscape, that Brenda Frazier would call last year's dress "that old thing" rather than a shmateh. The mother tongue was as much a part of them as their receding chins.

But that was the extent of my ethnic heritage, unless prejudices were counted. In that case, I scored quite high, having learned early (Jews being both precocious and brilliant) that: (1) If anything is missing, its disappearance can be blamed on a black maid or the most recent black to pass through the neighborhood, (2) Irish men are alcoholics and Irish women have thick ankles and somehow, despite their lack of discernible sexuality, they have large families, (3) Italians comprehend the importance of a meal and are almost as good parents as Jews, except they smack their kids and don't worry about higher education, (4) Poles are stupid and anti-Semitic, (5) Puerto Ricans carry knives, and (6) WASPS feed their children TV dinners and won't let Jews work in their banks.

"What did they used to say about Jews in the Bronx?" I asked Jerry. "Come on, tell me."

"Nothing much."

"Really, you can tell me."

"They used to say, 'Give a Jew a quarter and he'll make a dollar.' Stuff like that. About Jews being pushy and greedy and loud."

"Did they really?" He nodded, looking quite cheerful. "Come on, what else?" I urged.

"That's it."

"That can't be it."

"That's it, Marcia. What do you think we did, hung around the corner talking about Jews all day?"

"No, but I'll bet they just didn't say that Jews were pushy and leave it at that. It must have been a lot nastier."

"And what did you say about us?"

"Just about the drinking and stuff."

"What stuff?"

"You know. Smacking your wives around and having those tenor voices because you don't have enough sex hormones. But it's just an attitude. No one really discussed it or even thought much about it."

"Why is it, when anyone makes a derogatory comment about Jews, that you interpret it as meaning they want to drag you off to Auschwitz, but when you talk like that about other people, you call it just an attitude? How come?"

I responded, "Because there was an Auschwitz."

"But there's not one now—and don't give me that crap about how it could happen here, when you people have done better here than any other goddamn group and you know it."

"See? You just lump us all together and call us 'you people.'"

"And you? For your information, Marcia, my father never got drunk, and for your further information, he never laid a hand on my mother—"

"Who'd want to lay a hand on a saint?"

"Eat shit."

"It's not kosher. *You* eat shit."

But aside from the little exercises in ethnic awareness

that Jerry and I had, I was generally of little use as a Jew.

My old boss Dave Flaherty asked, "Jesus, kid, why did you try and shake hands with Mrs. Wolk?" We were emerging from a small brick house in Kew Gardens, part of Flaherty's district, where I had accompanied him on a condolence call.

"What was wrong—"

"When you pay a shiva call at an Orthodox house," Flaherty explained, "it's a custom not to shake hands with the mourners, so they don't communicate their sorrow."

I grew up knowing that some Jews lit candles every Friday night and mumbled something after they did this, but I had no idea of what the substance of the mumbling was, for I knew no prayers—in Hebrew, at least. A friend in third grade had taught me the Paternoster, but I sensed somehow that it was best left unsaid. Better no prayers.

"What are you wearing?" my mother demanded.

"What?"

"Slacks. You're wearing slacks."

"So?"

"So, it's Yom Kippur and you don't go outside wearing slacks. If you're going out, wear a skirt." I should have known it was a holiday because there was no school and because the small radio in the kitchen had just emitted a wish for its Jewish friends to have a peaceful and healthy New Year. "This is the most important holiday of the year. A very serious one," my mother added. And skirts are far more serious than slacks. The radio began playing "Let's Call the Whole Thing Off," by George Gershwin, one of its dearest Jewish friends. "You say pajamas and I say pajamas. . . ." I knew nothing about Jewish liturgy and law until I took a college course in comparative religion.

"We have to be married by a rabbi," Barry said. We were lying together in his dorm room at Columbia. It was May, so we weren't cold, even though we were naked.

"Why? Why go all through that? You know you're an agnostic."

"But that's an intellectual position, Marcia. Look, it's a nice tradition and it'll make our families happy." Furnald Hall had been built in the days of gentlemen. Its walls were thin. Down the hall, another couple was coming; she made long, high *aaaah* sounds and he staccato grunts. "Come on," Barry whispered and moved down the bed so his mouth would be nearer to my breast. "Come on." So we began again. He took my nipple between his teeth and slowly began to bite it, harder and harder.

"Okay, Barry," I agreed. "Okay. Whatever you want."

7

Barry was smarter than I was. When we met, in our senior year at Forest Hills High School, he was already initiated into mysteries that would forever remain obscure to me. For the entire first marking period of Mr. Pforzheimer's honors English class, I was so intimidated by Barry's brilliance that I was afraid to speak in class. And I developed such a crush on Barry that I was afraid to speak to him after class.

I had no idea what to say to a boy who dropped terms like "objective correlative." I wondered if someone who could make offhand references to John Ruskin would want to go to a prom.

Barry was so appealing. In a school full of boys with loud voices and purple mohair sweaters, he spoke softly and wore pale crew necks. And once, when he stood to read a short biography of Thomas Hardy he had compiled, an erection rose beneath his khaki slacks.

After the fourth week of school, after endless conversations with girl friends on the subject of How to Get a Boy to Notice You Without Seeming Too Obvious, I returned to class and smiled. He didn't notice. I made myself read a book of essays by Edmund Wilson and spent a week with my hand raised, trying to get the teacher to recognize me so I could work Wilson's name into the class discussion and wow Barry with my culture. Mr. Pforzheimer did not call on me; he did not care what I thought about *Hamlet*.

Instead, Barry was chosen. "What do you think, Barry? Is it 'solid flesh' or 'sullied flesh'?"

"You can make a good case for either one, Mr. Pforzheimer."

"Well, what case would you make for 'solid'?" Mr. Pforzheimer leaned forward and licked his lips, hungry for Barry's analysis.

"Melt is the key word." Barry Plotnick stood by his desk one row away from me and several desks behind; between us were the alphabetical interlopers: Kaplan, McCann, Nussbaum, and Obermaier. As usual, he spoke enthusiastically, stopping only once or twice to gaze up at the ceiling and gather his thoughts and let the tip of his tongue make a quick pass over his lips.

"Fine, Barry," said Mr. Pforzheimer. "And what about 'sullied'?"

Barry spoke of nausea, of sickness unto death, and mentioned something about teetering on the brink of an existential abyss. He pronounced "Sartre" beautifully, and even Heidi Gold, who had gotten early acceptance to Radcliffe, peered at him with interest.

He was cute, even while proclaiming that hell is other people. Barry had a moon face, round brown eyes, and a short broad-bridged nose dotted with endearing freckles. The corners of his mouth turned up slightly and he generally looked pleased, even when grim. In fact, I later realized he looked a little like Howdy Doody, friendly and approachable, and indeed, most people, without knowing him, assumed he was a real regular guy.

I decided to act fast. I got to him after class, successfully blocking Heidi, whose tactics were refined and scholarly. "Hey," I said, "you were very incisive."

"Thank you."

I could not tell if he was shy or was used to being complimented. But Heidi seemed about to come up on his left so I asked, "Have you ever thought about applying that same sort of existential analysis to *Lear*? I mean, dealing with an absurd universe and . . ." I let my voice trail off, hoping that I was making sense; I was not sure what I was talking about.

"Hey, that's interesting," Barry said. His round eyes

seemed to grow in circumference, widening enough to accept me as well as Shakespeare.

We met after school that day and on most other days. At first, we talked about Shakespeare, then Proust, then about the 1960 Presidential election which was a few weeks away. Naturally, I wanted Kennedy. Barry thought J.F.K. a "fake intellectual" and Nixon miles beneath contempt.

"How can you not care?" I demanded. "Don't you have any idea how important this election is?"

Fastidiously, Barry lifted a piece of lint from his gray sweater. "Ultimately," he said, "politics has nothing to do with the human condition."

But mostly we made out, progressing from excruciatingly extended kisses—exploring each other's mouth till we nearly drowned in saliva—to Barry touching me on top, to me touching Barry below. By the time Kennedy picked his cabinet, Barry was touching me, with astounding expertise, below.

"Oh, boy," I said, upon achieving my first male-induced orgasm.

"Like it?" he asked.

Loved it. By that time I was carrying about a purse pack of Kleenex, to mop up his semen.

By Valentine's Day, I used them to wipe off my Cherries in the Snow lipstick before going down on him. On George Washington's Birthday weekend, he knelt on the tiled floor of his finished basement, prepared to oblige me.

"No, Barry."

"Why not?"

"I don't know. It's not necessary." I sat primly on an icy leather chair, trying to put my knees together so my thighs would look thinner. He pried my legs apart. "Barry, no, please. Come on, Barry. Stop. This is like sixty-nine." Not quite, since he remained on the floor, which must have been as cold as the chair. Soon, though, I closed my eyes. "Oh, my God," I whispered.

The first Tuesday in March, when Sheri had her canasta game in her living room, Barry and I had intercourse for the first time in the Plotnicks' 1960 Chrysler Imperial. First, we wrapped ourselves in a beautiful, heavy blue quilt we found on the floor of the garage, a quilt Sheri had determined was perfect for the Salvation Army when she redecorated the master bedroom in what she called "peaches and cream."

I was trembling. "It's freezing." I could feel the goose bumps on my upper arms as Barry rubbed me briskly. But his massage only made me shiver more because his hands were freezing. "Maybe not today."

"But we talked about it," Barry said. "We discussed the whole thing and we both agreed—"

"I know. Okay, let's do it."

Barry maneuvered on top and put his cold hands under me, causing me to arch my back. This got him quite excited and he started thrusting, although he was closer to my navel than to his goal.

"Barry, please, your hands are so cold," I commented lightly, turning my head away from his, toward the driver's seat; I had been panting a lot that afternoon—from fear and desire—and was afraid my dry mouth was a breeding ground for virulent bad-breath germs. "Barry, what if I bleed? Barry?"

What if Barry's father, Dr. Plotnick, found blood on his green leather seat? "Don't worry, Marcia." His father was an obstetrician with a very busy practice; he had no time for unessential spotting. "We have the quilt."

"But what if your mother changes her mind about it? What if she . . . ?" Barry found his way inside. "It hurts. Barry, please stop for just a minute. It hurts so much."

He stopped. "Uh-oh, I forgot the rubber," he remarked. He reached down to the floor of the car and picked up a foil packet. "Just a second." It took nearly a minute, actually, with Barry balancing his weight on his right hand and reaching under the quilt with his left, to roll up the condom.

"Barry," I tried again, as he finished his contraceptive ordeal.

"I'll be careful," he whispered, finding his place again quite quickly. I writhed a little, trying to displace him, but he moved with me. "God, oh, God, it's so hot inside there," he said.

Unlike seventeen-year-old boys of fiction, Barry was not easy come. Within a month I would appreciate this attribute, but that first time I was not pleased.

"Marcia," he said, "stop crying. Please."

I did not bleed. We wrapped the condom in Kleenex.

Later, we put it directly in the next-door neighbor's outdoor trash can, under a neatly brown-bagged package of garbage.

We walked into the Plotnick living room. The canasta ladies lifted their matching heads—they all wore a hairdo called a beehive—and stared at us. Barry grinned at them. I stared at the dark-red velvety rug. Sheri asked, "Did you have a nice walk, Barry?"

"Yes. Great, wasn't it, Marcia?" I think I mumbled yes.

It became the greatest thing in my life. I felt so valued. We had sex daily; neither cold nor rain nor menstruation nor fear of parents stopped us. We did it in every room in Barry's house. We did it in the basement of my apartment building, in the laundry room, where we switched off the lights and humped to the easy rhythm of the wash cycle. We went to the city and did it in a dressing room in the men's department at Macy's. We did it in a smelly little room that said "Employees Only" at the Donnell Library.

We still talked at other times, of course. We discussed Mozart's life. We debated whether George Bernard Shaw was a great dramatist or just a good one. We decided that since Barry was a Renaissance man anyway, he might as well go to medical school and make his parents happy. But naturally, Barry would have to break the news to his father that he was not only going to be a doctor, he would be a writer too.

"Look at William Carlos Williams," he said.

"Chekov," I added.

"And who else?"

"I'm not sure, but I know I've heard of others. Anyway, if you want it, Barry, you'll make it. No one can stop you."

"I know that, Marcia."

It never occurred to me that the above was our warmest, most personal discussion. I never considered that all our talks could have taken place between two very bright students at some college's freshman orientation program.

I never realized that we only had fun with our clothes off. We were grand together then, enthusiastic and inventive and nearly indefatigable. And since we were also able to find things to say to each other when dressed, I believed we were chosen by heaven, a stellar match. "We can screw or discuss Hegel," I boasted to my cousin Barbara the following year. She paled, both at my hymeneal loss and at my language, but still nodded respectfully. It did not dawn on me until long after our divorce that Barry and I were merely compatible. We were two very bright people who loved to fuck. We certainly never fucked to love.

But we were proficient. In college, when Barry's fraternity brothers bragged about making a girl hot by high-pressure ear blowing, Barry would slowly draw his tongue over me, from my heels all the way up to the nape of my neck, where later, between nips, he whispered, "This is your cervical vetebra."

Afterward I said, "I would have thought the cervical vetebra would be much, much lower. I mean—"

"No," he explained. "Not that cervix." He paused. "Let me put it in layman's terms. . . ."

From his first day at Columbia, Barry embraced his premedical studies with a passion even greater than that which he brought to bed. He was a gifted student, a natural scientist.

But he continued to take English courses. We each wrote a paper on Blake; his was more subtle, profound, and better written than mine.

And he would glance at me sideways, his heavy lids half closed over his large brown eyes, and sigh, "Please, Marcia, not E. E. Cummings."

"But I like E. E. Cummings."

"And I suppose next it will be Ogden Nash?"

It already was. By the end of freshman year, I sensed I would not be the scholar Barry was expecting. After college, we would not strut up to Cambridge, arm in arm, Mr. and Mrs. Barry Plotnick, and emerge from Harvard four years later as Dr. and Dr. Barry Plotnick, he from the medical school, me from the university's English department. I did not enjoy research. I was sloppy. I lost index cards with bibliographical information. I cared mainly for expedience. I learned to choose my subject with an eye to my professor's prejudices; one look at Professor Prager and my term paper in nineteenth-century English literature became "The Genius of Oscar Wilde."

Our meetings would be called to order. Any old business? Not really, although as we undressed he showed me how the bite marks I had made the previous weekend had cleared up. New business? "I don't think I want to go to graduate school, Barry." It had taken me a year and a half to find courage to say this.

"Then what are you going to do while I'm in medical school? Marcia, we discussed it. I'll have very long hours, and I can't take responsibility for amusing you."

"I'll work."

"As what?"

"I don't know. Maybe as a reporter."

Barry lay back on a filthy, green-draped couch in his fraternity house. The only light in the room, coming from a red bulb screwed into an unshaded lamp, causing his freckles to look purple.

"Or maybe something in politics."

"What?" I had said the last sentence very fast.

"Politics," I repeated. "I don't know, maybe something else. But I'll get a job and—"

"I can't believe you'd want to make a career of hanging around those people. I mean, you're the only one in that club who doesn't have acne."

Barry did not like my friends, the members of the Queens College Young Democrats. He claimed they would have me chomping on Juicy Fruit gum within six months.

"They happen to be very interesting," I said. "I mean, they may not win the best-dressed award, but they're very involved."

"In what?"

"Politics."

"Wouldn't Metternich be surprised. Look, Marcia, they're involved because no sorority or fraternity would have them. I mean it. Try to be objective."

I tried. Barry was a brilliant student, the most popular pledge in his fraternity, and an increasingly natty dresser; only during our admittedly frequent beddings was he without his Harris tweed jacket and meerschaum pipe.

On the other hand, I looked decidedly shabby. My cousin Barbara had departed for Syracuse University with a trunk full of clothes so fine they would not wear out, and thus, after high school, no hand-me-downs came my way. And objectivity, those lovely sorority girls my mother kept murmuring I should meet did not find my baggy gray skirt and chestful of campaign buttons alluring enough to want to call me sister.

But having heard Kennedy's call, I didn't mind. I was

doing for my country, eking out a B-plus average and working with the college's Young Democrats, which served as a kind of Kiddie Korps for the regular Democratic political clubs in Queens.

Unable to vote or tote petitions until we were twenty-one, the other club members and I did what we were asked, sticking leaflets under windshield wipers, driving voters to the polls, running to the library to return a city councilman's wife's overdue books. For an hour a day I read Milton and for another six hours I stuck handbills onto lampposts, handbills which touted the virtues of a Democratic candidate who could barely utter a simple declarative sentence.

"They're loud," Barry observed, not too softly, at the Young Dems annual dinner, which took place in Wang's Chi-Am restaurant in Kew Gardens.

They were, at least some of them. They were nineteen-year-old boys like Robert Lombardo, who boomed instead of spoke, smoked stinky cigars, and sported Carmine De-Sapio dark glasses. They were girls like Susan Wolf who wore black tights because she couldn't remember to shave her legs and who made caustic, nasal remarks about fuzzy-minded liberals. My friends were the heirs to Tammany Hall. Their grandparents had never learned English. Their parents did not seem to care that they wore garish prints and didn't know the serving secrets of the Baroness de Rothschild. They were a noisy group, aggressive, sometimes crude, occasionally embarrassing to be seen with.

But they were content. They were enthusiastic. They were nice. Robert saved me his *Times* each morning, so I wouldn't have to buy one. Susan taught me to drive. Several of them invited me for dinner on weekends when Barry was studying, informing their parents that "Marcia's going with an Ivy League guy, from Columbia." Their parents would smile with their too-bright dentures and offer me more pea soup or tortellini. They did not seem to care that I was seeing a prospective professional from a very fine family while their own child was dating a future civil servant. "Hey," they would say as we would leave for the movies, "button up. It's freezing outside."

But my mother and Barry must have sensed a threat because they suddenly became allies. She had always been polite, almost deferential, when he came to the apartment, standing in the kitchen doorway and wiping her hands over and over on a dish towel, hardly daring to speak. He, in turn, had been almost ridiculously polite, calling her "ma'am" like he was from Ohio and telling her how nice it was to see her again. Actually, I think he was repelled by her pasty, wrinkled skin and her hunched shoulders.

But like two magnets of opposing polarities, they drew together and clicked on the issue of my political friends. "Ill-bred," said my mother. "Tasteless," Barry responded. "So brash." "They belong in vocational school, not a four-year college." They seemed afraid that I carried some genetic anomaly, some downwardly mobile chromosome that forced me to seek out the inelegant and the churlish.

I would come home, after an exhausting evening of debating how Queens College Young Dems could stop Goldwater, and find my mother waiting up, wrapped in a ratty flannel bathrobe.

"Your sweater. It's stained."

"We had pizza. It'll come out."

"I'm sure Barry and his friends from Columbia would love to see you looking like that."

Or Barry would examine my fingers and discover purple mimeograph ink. "Making a better world, I see." I'd pull my hand away. "Look, Marcia, do what you have to do. But I think these—uh, associations of yours are disturbing to your mother. That's it. I'm not going to say any more." And he would begin sucking each of my fingers, to show how the purple ink didn't bother him.

I began mumbling to my mother I was going to a friend's house to study. I made sure I kept my hands clean. But I continued my involvement in politics because, like sex, it was completely enthralling. It excited me, exhausted me, amused me, and linked me to other people. My course work only involved me in a remote sense. Unlike Barry, who reported he wept each time he read *Lear*, I would close the book, thinking that Cordelia was something of a fool, and reach for a newspaper.

On the other hand, I threw up for three days after Kennedy was assassinated. Barry said it was very sad.

Less than a year after that, Goldwater was defeated and Dave Flaherty got swept into Congress in the Johnson landslide. That fall semester of my senior year—taking courses like creative writing and modern American poetry so I would have lots of free time—I put in a full eight hours for Flaherty each day. I began by typing envelopes and making phone calls, but by early October I was bored. Flaherty was due to speak on NATO, not his best subject.

"What the hell am I supposed to say?" he demanded of an aide.

I overheard and offered to write a speech. He peered at me, a little suspiciously because I looked nothing like Ted Sorensen, but agreed, probably because he didn't want to offend such a proficient envelope stuffer.

"Hey, this is really good," he said later, thwacking me on the back. "You're a really smart kid, kid. Wanna do more?" I did. I began to travel around the district, cutting classes, listening to Flaherty mouth my words. I learned to write in his voice, essentially monosyllabic and direct. "Kid," he remarked, rejecting my third or fourth effort, "I'm no Kennedy. Take out this Yeats stuff."

We got on fine. I liked Flaherty because he was friendly, hardworking, and funny. He liked me because I was quiet. A few weeks after the election he suggested I work for him in Washington.

"I can't, Dave. I'm getting married in June."

"Too bad, kid. All right, let me know if you have a change of heart."

It was not my heart that changed, but Barry's plans. He failed to get into Harvard Medical School. He also was rejected by Yale, Columbia, University of Pennsylvania, and Cornell. Sheri said they were letting too many colored in and had re-established their Jewish quota. Barry claimed, a little ex post facto, that he had had a stomach virus when he took the medical boards and had spent the morning fighting off spasms *and* griping pains.

"But you got accepted at Georgetown," I protested. "If you went there, I'd have a ready-made job on Capitol Hill."

"I've also been accepted at University of Cincinnati and Penn State. I mean, I'm building the basis for a career . . .

I finally convinced him by handing him over to Flaherty at a Heart Fund dinner dance I had dragged him to. "Kid," Flaherty said to him, "I'll be paying her a big ten. Can she make that in Cleveland?"

"Cincinnati," Barry said, trying to pull his bicep out of Flaherty's hand.

"Wherever. She'll wind up with six thou a year and you'll have a pile of debts when you graduate. And," he continued, noticing Barry preparing to speak again, "think of the connections you'll make down in the District. I mean, all those N.I.H. doctors, those fancy professors hanging around for federal grants. I requested Health Care as one of my committee assignments. . . ."

That night, Barry said he'd go to Georgetown. We'd live in Washington. He understood that marriage meant compromises. If I wanted to work for Flaherty, that was my decision.

"Barry, when you get to know him, you'll really like him. He's honest and very sincere about—"

"Marcia, he is no philosopher-king."

We married in an elaborate ceremony at the Forest Hills Jewish Center, which Barry's parents paid for. They allowed my mother to invite twenty people. They invited a hundred fifty-five of their closest relatives and dearest friends. The chuppa—the bridal canopy—was decorated in Plotnick peach, covered with hundreds of peach-dyed carnations and peach roses. In the banquet hall, the cloths and napkins were peach, as were centerpieces of some unrecognizable but clearly peach flowers combined with peach-dyed feathers. The mother of the groom wore peach chiffon. The rabbi, somehow, escaped color coordination and wore a black robe.

My Uncle Julius walked me down the aisle and parted with a "Love ya, sweetheart." My Aunt Estelle told everyone at the table how she had paid over two hundred dollars for my wedding dress. It was one hundred sixty-seven fifty, including tax. Sheri Plotnick put a manicured hand on at least ninety arms and explained that they felt for me because I was a poor girl so that they had paid for the wedding. "Even the monogrammed fingertip towels in the bathroom," she confided. Dr. Plotnick, whom even Barry called the invisible man, actually stayed through the entire affair, having arranged with a colleague to cover for him. We danced and he squeezed me against his hard, mountainous stomach and told me he knew I would make Barry very happy—although if there were any problems I could give him a call and he would keep it strictly entre nous. My mother's Cousin Nettie from New Jersey announced in an easily audible screech that she had broken a cap on the gristle in the prime ribs. Barry's Aunt Gussie sat for four hours with a see-through plastic raincoat protecting her dress because she was afraid of gravy stains. My mother took me aside as the waiters began serving coffee.

"You're going to have to be a wife to Barry tonight." Naturally, she did not look at me as she imparted this embarrassing information.

"I know," I said, perhaps snapping a bit.

"Well, mazel tov," she said. "Aunt Estelle said don't forget to give her back the pearls before you leave."

We had a grand wedding night at a motel near the airport, a rather sleazy place that smelled of disinfectant. "Hardly the Georges Cinq," Barry remarked, although he had never been to Paris. I had been anticipating that night because I was certain that Barry would tell me he loved me. I had imagined him saying something like, "I've been so horribly negligent. I've never told you how much I love you." He said, "Try pulling your legs up higher and spreading them more."

Our honeymoon—seven days and six nights on a small Caribbean island named for an obscure saint—was a predictably enjoyable sexual marathon. By the end of a week, our own throbbing soreness and sensitivity was itself a stimulus.

For the rest of the summer, we furnished our Washington apartment, using our wedding gift money to buy what was probably the year 1846's entire output of oak furniture, and visiting the museums and historical sites we wouldn't have time for once medical school began. We dashed about, as if trying to fill some arbitrary aesthetic quota. And naturally we had sex, making the national weekly average our daily minimum; by August, though, my pleasure was so inevitable that I looked forward to our joinings with only mild fervor. Barry's passion was unflagging, however, although he seemed to have to construct more and more elaborate precoital scenarios. I did not mind this, except when he insisted I play a character with a different name.

And then September came, with great promise. Flaherty was delighted to have me in the office; my co-workers were nice; I got an electric typewriter and a phone number at the Library of Congress where my most arcane question would be answered in minutes. Barry would come home from school about nine thirty, and over a late dinner of blanquettes de veau or carbonnade à la flambande, we'd chat about how best to lift the skin off the face of a cadaver or how Flaherty was being pressured by the left-wingers to vote against military expenditures in Vietnam. Our sexual activity slowed to a staid once a night, which ended in intercourse only about half the time. When I asked Barry about this, he said, "Do you want to have children now?"

"Of course not. We discussed it and—"

"And," he said laconically, "that means there's no reason to limit ourselves. Anyway, you have better orgasms the other way.

I guess I did, but by late December, when we visited New York, my orgasmic activity was largely self-induced. Barry would return from the lab or library after eleven at night, too exhausted to even speak, so tired that he couldn't even undress until the next morning. "It's very competitive," he once managed to whisper. On weekends, he aroused himself by having me recount the sexual fantasies I had as I masturbated.

"How is everything?" my mother-in-law asked, as we three Plotnicks sat around the dinner table on Christmas Eve, eating Sheri's ecumenically colored salad greens with cherry tomatoes. Dr. Plotnick had been called away during the tomato soup to do something fast to someone's Fallopian tubes.

"Fine," I answered.

Sheri, looking elegant and almost seductive in a garnet velvet hostess gown, her tight features eased by the candlelight, said, "Good. I was worried about you. You look tired."

"Barry and I have been working very hard."

"I'm not tired," Barry said, summoning the energy to utter his first complete sentence in two months.

And that was it. It never got any better. Periodically, we'd have bouts of intense sex, but it was a hot body need, as though we had to flush our systems of excess fluid. But we never talked as though anything was wrong. We often talked of the future.

Barry was told that he had fantastic fingers and that he was destined for surgery. He decided to become an otorhinolaryngologist, dedicating his genius of a right hand to salvaging teeny ear bones. His appreciably talented left would be saved for tonsillectomies and diddling me, easier work requiring a certain aptitude, but not brilliance.

"We haven't had intercourse in two months," I said one Sunday in May 1967.

"Oh, all right." Most times, we did not speak as much as whine at each other: "Hurry up. Get undressed."

"Barry!" I called, about three months later. "I'm bleeding. Barry!"

"Stop getting hysterical," he called from the bedroom. "A little spotting is normal during the first trimester." I looked at the toilet paper in my hand, soaked with blood. "You'll call Dr. Susskind in the morning," he added.

"It's not just spotting, Barry. Please." He called Dr. Susskind.

We drove from our apartment on the outskirts of Georgetown to the hospital. I kept wanting him to tell me that it would be fine, that they'd put in a few stitches or a wad of cotton and stop the bleeding. Or at least reassure me that such quantities of blood did not necessarily mean a miscarriage. But all he did was turn off the car's air conditioner when I began shaking. And when we pulled up to the entrance of the hospital, he said, "Go straight to the admitting office."

"Can't you take me?"

"I have to park. You'll be all right. I wouldn't take unnecessary chances."

I opened the door of the car gingerly, afraid that any unsettling movement would prove the coup de grace for the fetus, that tiny humanoid sea horse floating inside me. "Marcia," he called, as I began to shuffle to the entrance, "you forgot your suitcase." So I came back and bent down, taking the overnight bag from the floor of the car near the passenger's seat. Slowly, I straightened up, but not so slowly as to avoid a stab of agony that knifed through my lower back down to my vagina. "See you," he said. Later, after listening to Dr. Susskind explain to me that I would lose the baby, that it was probably already dead, Barry said softly and compassionately, "Look, you didn't really want it anyway."

When I got back to the office, Flaherty, who had never done more than thump my back with glee, kissed my forehead and held my hands between his. "You don't know how sorry I am, kid. It's a real loss. You deserve a hell of a lot better." I hadn't written those lines.

Eight o'clock on an ugly, slushy February night in 1968. "Barry? I have to work tonight." No sound, but the telephone seemed to tremble with his unexhaled sigh. "Look, I'm really sorry, but Flaherty wants me to go over the language on the aid-to-digestive-diseases bill. I wish I could get out of it, but it was to be on the Speaker's desk tomorrow and—"

"Couldn't you have called earlier?"

"I wasn't sure whether I'd have to stay late."

"Okay. I'll go out for a bite."

"There's some chicken left over from last night." It wasn't much, just half a poitrine from a somewhat desiccated coq au vin rouge, but perhaps enough to satisfy him, although it was the first night in our almost three-year marriage that I had not prepared at least four courses for him. "Or I can stop on my way home. . . ."

"That's all right. Don't put too much pressure on yourself. I'll run downstairs, see if the deli has any decent canned pâté." He added, "When will you be home?"

"I'm not sure. It depends if Flaherty wants any revisions. Ten thirty, eleven. Midnight at the latest."

"I'll try to wait up."

And that night, when I knew Barry was agonizing over the semicircular canals, I had my first postnuptial proposition. The administrative assistant of the Honorable Quincy Dade of Little Rock, Arkansas, came into our office, which was next to his, to use our electric pencil sharpener. He leaned over my desk, blinked a pair of green eyes at me, and asked me out. "Wan' go out?"

"I'm married," I explained.

"Me too!" he said, sounding pleased that we had something in common.

I was not even tempted. With a hearty "No thank you" I arose and strode into Flaherty's office, proclaiming that the bill's language was both literate and precise.

"Good. Thanks for staying, kid," he muttered, not looking up from the Knights of Columbus newsletter he was reading.

It had begun to sleet, but I drove as fast as I could, stopping first at the French market for Genoa salami and Swiss cheese for two, and made it home by nine o'clock.

My hair was soaked, hanging in strings, dripping icily down the back of my neck. Through the door I heard *Don Giovanni* blasting. I think I smiled. If Barry was playing Mozart, he was in a good mood. In any case he liked Genoa salami.

He was not in the living room, stretched in his usual place on the rug between the two stereo speakers. I marched into the bedroom, paper bag in hand. And there, of course, was Barry.

The future Dr. Plotnick was lying on the bed, naked, fully and awesomely tumescent. And not inches away, chin resting on the mattress, probably catching a quick breath between slurps, was Noreen Ostermann.

"Remember Noreen Ostermann?" he had asked a few weeks before. "That nice little speech therapist? Let's invite her over for dinner."

"Okay." She had brought a bottle of Beaujolais.

Noreen saw me first. Perhaps she hadn't been as excited as Barry. Perhaps she was not as much a music lover. She let out an off-pitch scream, capturing Barry's attention. Following her stare to me, his mouth went slack, rapidly followed by his member. I dropped the bag and ran out of the apartment and spent the night driving over the icy, twisted roads of the Virginia hunt country.

I often wondered if Barry and Noreen ate the salami and cheese. I had a couple of Danish beers in the refrigerator. Also some Dijon mustard.

8

I was frightened for Jerry, for I knew he would suffer badly. Born to elicit joy, he would reel at a slap in the face. Pain would shock his system. Fury could mutate him.

And if he changed, what would happen to me?

Everyone on Paterno's staff knew something was wrong. Whispers slipped along the corridors of the office, rumors skitted about in closed rooms, and innuendos wafted up, only to be obscured by frosted glass doors. A few words reached me anyway: "Morrissey gave Paterno one last chance" and "Jerry said it was either him or LoBello, and if Bill didn't make up his mind soon . . ." and "There was such geshreiing and carrying on" and even "Morrissey threw a chair across the room, but Bill ducked" and, of course, "Shhh, here comes Marcia."

I asked Jerry later, "Did you really throw a chair at Bill?"

His face brightened for an instant. A grin emerged. "Is that what they're saying?" I nodded energetically, pleased at any sign of animation on his part. "No," he said. "Of course I didn't throw a chair. Do you think I'd risk throwing out my back again for that double-dealing bastard?" I smiled, prepared to remain in lighter times with him, but his face fell back into seriousness.

"What happened then?" I asked, more subdued. "I mean, someone obviously heard something."

"I really don't remember. I probably pounded my fist on his desk a few times. Anyway, it's not important."

"Of course it's important. It's your entire life, your job."

"I'm going for a walk. Don't wait up."

But that was later. The night of the Dollars for Dick dinner, when I told Jerry that Lyle LoBello was going to be involved in the campaign, Jerry's anger worked itself up into such a fever of rage that he was nearly struck dumb. He turned, marched away from the table, and returned a few minutes later, his eyes moist from a few belts of scotch, although that was not sufficient anesthetic. But he remained in control; he mumbled a few words to our host, Mike Mazer, that he had an extremely hush-hush municipal emergency, and Mazer, extracting the stub of an unfiltered cigarette from his mouth, said, "Gotcha, Jer." Jerry gave the rest of the table a fast wave and a wink and left. I received no special signal.

"Well, honey," Mazer said, turning his attention to me, "tell me about yourself."

"I'm Bill Paterno's speech writer," I explained, and offered him a smile. It did not suffice. Mazer wanted a speech. "Let's see," I began. When not actually writing, my value to Paterno was as an observer. The others—Jerry, Eileen Gerrity—talked. I watched. But after Jerry left I became his surrogate, so I offered my repertoire of Dave-Flaherty-Unforgettable-Character stories, tossing about phrases like "on the Hill" and "standing committees" which nearly always capture the interest and respect of New Yorkers.

But my conversation was mechanical, and by the time it was Mike Mazer's turn to reciprocate, I felt nauseated with tension.

Mazer fancied himself a raconteur, chortling at his own mots, creating dramatic tension by smoking at least a quarter of a cigarette between sentences. *Puff.* ". . . and this pimple-face fucker from the Senate . . ." *Puff, puff.* Finally, the conversation turned to bond ratings. I didn't have to seem interested. I could excuse myself, return to the apartment. But as I began to inch my chair back, I felt a hand on mine.

Mrs. Mazer, young and so perfectly coiffed and made up that she seemed to have been dipped in Plexiglas, talked out of the side of her mouth, like a convict. "Tell me, you work with that Jerry Morrissey?" Her hand was cool over mine. Her long slender fingers were heavy with twisted gold rings. Although she was a brunette, she hadn't a trace of hair on her arms.

"Yes, he and I—"

"Shhh," she said. "Not so loud." She motioned me closer. "Have you known him long?" Her voice was low enough that the murmur that arose implied girl talk; we could be discussing leg waxing, menstrual cycles.

"Yes."

"Tell me, hon, is he married?"

"No." I tried to pull my hand from hers, but she pressed mine onto the table.

Francine Mazer continued, "Is he straight? Not gay or anything?"

"No."

"No what?"

"No, Jerry isn't gay," I replied, tempted to raise my voice and let her husband in on the conversation. But I had been in politics too long. I recalled Mazer's lavish potential as a campaign contributor and realized he would not be generous if threatened.

"Now, hon," Francine said, "tell me. Is he living with anyone?" She licked her darkly glazed lips. Her words came faster as she grew closer to her goal.

"Yes."

"What's she like, the one he's living with? Decent looking?"

"He's living with me, Mrs. Mazer." She pulled her hand away. "We have an apartment in the Village. We've been together for years. . . ."

"But you're not married. Right, hon?" Several minutes later, as I left, she was clinging to her husband's arm, her glossy black hair flowing over his sagging shoulder.

She had her man, I had an empty apartment. Jerry was either drinking or walking. For a minute I imagined him on a suicidal solo hike, trudging through the South Bronx until stopped by a machete across his face or a bullet in his spine. That forced the inevitable: I dashed into the bathroom and got sick.

But the storm of garlicky roast beef and three cups of

coffee still raged. I had gobbled dinner as Mazer orated, gnashing the mealy meat between my teeth as though it were Paterno's heart. And then I got sick again.

My mother would demand: Would he make himself sick over you? And my Aunt Estelle would second the motion: You bring him rain instead of sunshine, darling, and in two minutes flat he'd find himself a sweet little shiksa, the kind that doesn't have moods.

"Jerry? What time is it?" He lowered himself down slowly and sat on the edge of the bed.

"Are you okay? Where did you go?"

"Just leave me alone. I feel sick."

"Me too. I got sick twice. The whole thing is literally disgusting. Listen, Jerry, I'll make some tea and we'll talk about it and—"

"No!" he bellowed, and put his head into his hands, but not before a gust of whiskey breath nearly toppled me.

"You don't want to talk?" Obviously not, because he didn't reply. "Let me get you something for your stomach," I suggested.

"No," he whispered from between his hands.

"It's no trouble," I said sweetly, shimmying up from under the blanket.

"I don't want any goddamn medicine, Marcia!" he shouted. Then, in a lower voice, as though the shout had exhausted his last reserve of energy, he murmured, "Just leave me alone. Please."

But I trotted into the bathroom, closing the door tight behind me. I made a show of turning on the light and rummaging through the medicine cabinet, but after a few seconds, dazed by the brightness, I lowered the toilet seat and sat. I forced myself to breathe quietly. I wanted to be able to hear any threatening noise Jerry might make.

I was, after all, my mother's daughter. Out there, in the bedroom, was no friend or lover who had overimbibed, no decent middle-aged man feeling frightened, vulnerable, depressed. Hilda's daughter saw that, of course, but she also saw with her mother's eyes: beyond the bathroom door was a beefy Irish brute with whiskey slopping down his filthy undershirt. She saw him leaping from the bed, ripping open the door, and smashing a thick, calloused hand across her gentle Jewish jaw.

They are suspect when sober. When drunk, dangerous.

Ridiculous.

Read history. They kill.

"Marcia," he called. I swallowed, stiffened, but remained rigidly on my sanctuary. "Hey, Marcia, get finished in there, okay?" I rose, opening the door enough to let one eye peer out. He was still sitting on the edge of the bed, hunched over. "Do me a favor," he called softly. "Come here and rub my head. It hurts like anything." I emerged. When I reached the bed, he grabbed my arm.

"Ow!" I nearly screamed.

"Sorry. Look, Marcia, I just want quiet. No discussions now." Having delivered his message, he let go of my arm. I glanced at it; there were no bruise marks.

"Lie down," I said quietly. I eased him down, placing a pillow under his head. I massaged his temples and shoulders, feeling his skin hot and damp under the soft cotton fabric of his shirt. Ten minutes later he whispered thanks and fell asleep, so deeply that when I curled up right beside him he didn't even move. I reached over him and loosened his tie. He made a short humming sound.

But when I woke the next morning, he was in no mood for tenderness. Clean, showered, wearing a banker's-gray suit, he spoke brusquely. "See you around six tonight. Maybe we'll go to a movie."

"Are you all right?" I slid over to his side of the bed, but it was already cold.

"Yes. Leave me alone."

Jerry spent the day in Paterno's office. I could only gather the mistiest rumors about what was going on. I sought counsel from Eileen Gerrity; analytical, curious, she was the person most likely to possess at least a tidbit of inside information. She would sit behind her desk, relaxed and reassuring, and people would enter her office, close the door, and drop off confidences.

But all she was able to report was that at one thirty someone in Paterno's office had ordered sandwiches. "One Swiss cheese on whole wheat and one bologna with mayo," she reported. "Does that tell you anything?" I shrugged. "I gather you don't want to be amused," she observed.

"No. I'm really worried about this, Eileen."

A strand of her pale, silky hair drooped over her forehead. She pushed it back with a pencil. "Well, let's be serious, then. What did Jerry say?"

"Nothing. That's the worst part of it. He won't confide in me at all. He just keeps telling me to leave him alone, so naturally I keep imagining the worst."

"Well, he's had quite a shock."

"I know that. But I can help him. I mean, even if we can't get Bill to change his mind, I can still be there for Jerry. I can offer—you know, support. But he's so afraid of anything smacking of commitment—"

"Marcia, in fairness to Pretty Boy, he's had a major kick in the pants and it's hardly the time to expect him to cement your relationship."

"I know that. I know exactly what he's capable of giving."

'Do you? Then why do you keep expecting him to bare his soul to you when he's never seen it himself?"

"I don't know," I said quietly.

Eileen began tapping her pencil on the desk, concentrating on its rhythm. "Look, let's try to analyze what's happening here." I glanced at her. "No, not with you and Jerry. I mean this Lyle LoBello intrigue. Now, is Bill Paterno smart?" I nodded. "Is he an astute politician?" My mother would have corrected Eileen's pronunciation. Not *as-toot, as-tyut*.

"Yes."

"Then why would he get rid of Jerry, the very man who made him? And why now, at the beginning of the most important campaign of his career?"

"Because he wants to be remade in the Gresham image, by LoBello. Eileen, he wants the governorship desperately, and he knows this may be his only shot. He's scared. He's looking for upstate magic—"

"Nonsense, Marcia." She tossed her head in an imperious gesture, the sort she used when dealing with the hyper-emotional and the silly. I will not deal with irrationality, her head announced. Behave! I settled back in my chair. "All right. Would Bill Paterno risk offending his supporters, his biggest contributors, by firing Jerry? Would he risk alienating the staff by bringing in Lyle LoBello? Would he risk alienating you?"

"Why not? I mean, he could hire someone else."

"Marcia, think about it. One day he rents space for headquarters and the next morning fires his chief of staff. And by doing that, he mortally offends his writer. Would he risk that, leaving himself actually speechless at a time like this?"

"Yes. He absolutely would, if he thought it was part of the price to win. Anyhow, LoBello would get another writer for him in a minute. He wouldn't know the difference."

"Stop that," Eileen snapped, shaking her pencil at me. "Modesty doesn't become you. You know you're the best there is. Now, let's think. Analyze. Yes, Bill could conceivably find another speech writer, and for the next two months he'd go around sounding like an Alabama senator or a Cambridge don, and you know and I know how that would play in—wherever, Plattsburg. He needs you and he needs Jerry. Anyway, you know Bill. He's very insecure. He needs people who have proved themselves, people who he can trust. He knows what a slippery fish LoBello is supposed to be. When push comes to shove, do you think he'd rely on someone like that?"

I found out later. Jerry pushed open my office door a few minutes before six thirty.

"Look, I want you to get your things together." I'm sure my jaw dropped. I must have stared. But Jerry was ticking off a list in his mind and simply didn't focus on me. He continued impersonally. "As of next Monday you're off the city payroll and on the campaign payroll. You'll be uptown at headquarters, and Bill expects—"

"Jerry?"

"What?"

"What happened?" His eyes had puffed from the effects of a hangover and fatigue and he squinted at me through two slits, not quite comprehending what I wanted from him. "What happened?" I repeated. "With Bill. You were in his office all day and—"

"Oh, that. I'll tell you later." He studied his watch as if just learning to tell time. Finally, he said, "If you can wait till seven thirty, we can go for dinner. Okay?"

"Jerry . . ."

"Not now, Marcia." Under the fluorescent lights, his end-of-day stubble of beard shone gray, giving his face an ashen cast. With his color drained, bright eyes obscured, I felt I was seeing a Technicolor extravaganza that had inexplicably turned a bleak black and white.

"All right. I'll leave you alone. But are you all right?"

"I'm fine. See you for dinner."

"If you're too tired . . ." He turned and left, not even bothering to mutter under his breath.

Later we shared a silent subway ride uptown. Jerry stared at an ad for suppositories, probably not even seeing it. I stared at him.

But when we came up to street level, he revived for a few minutes, recapturing a trace of his usual flash. Jerry seemed to thrive in midtown Manhattan. He'd nod benevolently at limousines idling in front of restaurants. He'd smile as a couple swathed in fur—like a pair of urbane foxes—glided by. He had self-confidence enough to feel such style was a mere matter of money; if he took a different job, made a hundred thousand or two a year, he could fit in. I don't think he questioned his right to belong anywhere.

Of course I did. I never felt at ease in sleek Manhattan. My country was the outer boroughs, where ethnics huddled in tight little groups to insulate themselves from assimilation and rebuffs. Down at City Hall, working with my kind of people, I felt at ease. Sometimes I shone. Uptown, I always felt frumpy, out of place, but didn't know how to remedy the situation. That night, I wore a blue dress and a beige raincoat. I had thought I looked all right. But we passed women who were so flawlessly groomed they made me look naked. They dressed every part of themselves; they wore textured stockings, armloads of bracelets, intricately knotted scarves, hats that were themselves accessorized with pins or plumes or nets.

Jerry exchanged the hand he had been holding for my elbow and guided me eastward on Fifty-eighth Street as I tried to make conversation. "Do you want French food? Because if you do, we'd be better off downtown. The prices around here are—"

"You know, the thing that first attracted me to you was that you were quiet. You didn't blab all the time."

We continued toward the river until Jerry discovered a restaurant whose facade unaccountably beckoned him. It was a tiny, seedy place, an Indian restaurant, with an almost palpable fog of garlic and curry hanging about. The maître d' / owner / waiter sat us at an uncomfortably large square table covered with a blue vinyl cloth. Only one other table was occupied, by two Indian men, probably relatives of the owner commandeered to give the place the appearance of authenticity. They were neither drinking nor dining.

Jerry didn't even smile at the waiter. He was not looking for votes that night. "Johnnie Walker red, straight up," he said.

"You want?" the waiter asked me.

"Nothing, thank you."

"Good," said Jerry. "You wouldn't want to become an alcoholic."

"Your fight isn't with me, Jerry."

" 'Your fight isn't with me,' " he mimicked. "All right, all right," he added. "Just leave me alone."

"You were the one who asked me out to dinner."

"Everyone makes mistakes."

I turned away from him and watched the waiter, who was standing behind a small bar, pouring scotch as though it were his own blood he was donating. He brought it to the table and Jerry drained it and demanded another before he spoke.

"Sorry if I was a little rough."

"It's okay."

"I'm out of sorts."

"I know. You should be. Do you want to talk now?"

"I'm campaign manager," he said.

"Jerry! That's wonderful. I mean, that's what you wanted, isn't it?" He didn't reply, but ran his finger hard along the tablecloth, making deep x's. "Okay. Listen, Jerry, let's just have a quiet dinner and we'll talk later."

"There's nothing to talk about. We had a few words at the beginning that must have lasted about two, three hours. Then, when the dust settled, he said I was campaign manager, and so we spent the rest of the afternoon mapping strategy. We're opening headquarters next Monday, and about half the City Hall staff will go up there. Then—"

"What about Lyle LoBello?"

"Lyle LoBello. Well, Bill told me not to worry, that he couldn't rely on Lyle because he's still in mourning for his dear buddy, Jim Gresham. Crazed with grief, old Lyle is. And according to Bill, anyone that emotional isn't much good to us. Of course, there's no reason why we can't avail ourselves of Lyle's upstate expertise those times that he can manage to stop crying. But—"

"You want curry?" the waiter demanded.

Jerry began to wave him away, but I asked, "What kind do you have?"

"Good curry."

"What sort? Chicken?" The waiter shook his head. I requested shrimp or lamb, but the waiter said no and intoned: veg-e-table. "I don't care for vegetable," I said.

"Jesus, Marcia, would you take the goddamn vegetable thing and be done with it? It all tastes the same." The waiter nodded, apparently agreeing with Jerry, and trotted into the kitchen. "Where was I?" Jerry demanded.

"You were saying how Bill might use Lyle on an occasional basis."

"Well, read between the lines."

"I'm not quite sure what you mean."

"Really? You, the great intellectual, don't know what a simple guy like me means? I should be flattered. I'm so subtle that the resident thinker can't follow my line of reasoning. Jesus, this is an important moment in our lives."

"It may be," I said softly.

"Don't threaten me, Marcia."

There followed about ten minutes of silence. The waiter deposited two bowls on the table. I put a small mound of curry on the side of my plate, then dumped a globe of gelatinous rice into the middle. Jerry waved aside my offer of help and ordered another drink.

The food was vile, sharp, just on the edge of rancidity. I considered getting up and leaving but realized I had no place to go. The waiter sneezed, covering his mouth with his hand. I watched him for a while, but he did not go to the bathroom to wash it off. I decided not to order dessert. I turned back to the table and looked at Jerry's hand on his glass, his index finger rising and falling, teasing the little beads of moisture. If I left, he might decide all of a sudden that he needed solace and then where would he find it? All over. Anywhere.

"Jerry, please talk to me. I'm sorry if I pushed too hard. But you need someone to talk to, someone you can trust."

"Can I trust you? Completely?"

"How can you even ask that?"

"If I asked you to do something, would you go along with whatever I asked, on faith?"

"What do you mean?"

"See? You start drawing up amendments before I even start. If you were on my side completely—"

"Jerry, what do you want from me?" He didn't answer. "Jerry, please. Don't you think I'd do anything . . . ?"

"Sure. Sure I do. Anyway, I'll tell you what's happening. I'm campaign manager." I nodded. "Bill says he's behind me one hundred percent but that's crap." He held up a hand as I was about to protest. "I know that's crap because he's sending me out of town."

"What?"

"Sending me up to Sullivan County. I'll explain some other time. You know at the beginning of a campaign—Christ, in any part of a campaign—you need a warm body here, running things. But he's telling me he needs me more in the boonies. That's the essence of crap. He claims it'll just be for a few days, that Eileen Gerrity can run things till I get back, but you know and I know that's bullshit. He'd never trust a woman in that role." I hadn't known that. It was interesting. "You know what he's going to do? He's going to bring in LoBello. He'll talk him into accepting some temporary half-assed title until he can figure out how to handle me, but he'll give LoBello the reins. He's screwing me, Marcia. He's giving me the biggest screwing of my life, and I can't do anything about it. 'Morrissey,' he says, 'you're my man. You're campaign manager.' And he's right. I'm his man. I'm forty-fucking-seven years old and he's sending me out of town like a kid to camp. What the hell am I going to do?"

I didn't know. His hands were trembling slightly, as though the ground was vibrating under his feet. "Jerry, are you sure?"

"Yes."

"Can I do anything?"

"No. Just let me be."

"What are you going to do?"

"Go. Go up to Sullivan County."

I paid the bill and we left the restaurant.

Sullivan County is in the Catskill Mountains. It is sometimes referred to as the borscht belt. Sometimes as Solomon County. Its big industry is tourism, and many of its residents work at the hotels. Others raise chickens. It is, on balance, a nice place to visit.

And that, as he later explained, was why Jerry was going

there. Not for a vacation, of course. But the rumors were traveling fast down the Quickway to the city: Sidney Appel, the nouveau premier hotelier of Sullivan County, was making gubernatorial noises.

The next day I heard the details from Joe Cole, Paterno's coordinator of minority affairs. Joe had gone to Paterno and Jerry with a riddle: What does it mean when a rich white businessman shows up at the Abyssinian Baptist Church on West 138th Street on a Sunday morning?

It meant, Jerry had told him, that the aforementioned businessman is running for something. But governor? Sidney Appel?

He knew about Appel, of course. Everyone in New York politics did. He was a tiny man, Bronx-born, who looked like a bulbous-nosed elf. He had parlayed a chunk of his wife's hefty inheritance from her father's cat-food business into even bigger money by opening a health oriented hotel built mainly from pine logs and spit. He called it the "Family Farm," using a smiling chicken as his logo and advertising "Clean Air Like Grandma Used to Make." For some reason, people found that appealing, and Family Farms were ganged together in the Adirondacks, the Poconos, and the not-too-depressed areas of the Appalachians.

He made millions charging deluxe prices for vegetable cutlets, bunk beds, and several miles of overworked hiking trails. He pitched to parents: "When was the last time you saw your child climb a tree?" His ad pictured a small, brown-haired, genderless child embracing a huge but safe-looking oak. "We're people people!" another ad announced, and its picture was a campfire surrounded by weenie roasters of every race and creed, all smiling beatifically, looking like shills from the National Conference of Christians and Jews.

But despite the red bandanna he always wore around his neck, Sidney Appel retained the heart of a city boy. He loved the Democratic party more than the 4-H Club. Instead of collecting rifles, he bought politicans. Not an unheard-of hobby, certainly not an impractical one. But why would the hunter choose to become the animal he preyed upon?

"He thinks he can be governor?" I had asked Joe Cole.

"Sure. He has the money." For a black man, Joe Cole

had an unusually Semitic face: an opulent hooked nose and a big chin that called out to be rubbed in deep thought. Maybe we were distant cousins. "Listen, Marcia, he'll go out and do some token fund-raising to conform to the law, but he could take five million out of his pockets—or his wife's pocketbook—and not feel the difference."

"But, Joe: governor? What experience does he have?"

Cole cleared his throat and orated in a forced basso: "What New York needs, ladies and gentlemen, is a businessman! We need a governor who knows what it means to meet a payroll, who has *never* had an unbalanced budget, who—"

"Come on. What kind of organization does he have? What kind of support?"

"Money, honey. He can buy all the support he needs. Ask your boyfriend."

But my boyfriend was not in shape to give an advanced civics lesson. That night, riding downtown after work, I asked him if he thought Joe Cole was right about Appel. "Well," he began, "I've known Joe for years and his instincts—" Jerry's voice broke then, as if cut by the recollection of Paterno's perfidy. His normal, consuming interest in anything political had been replaced by something else. Maybe fury. Maybe horror at finding himself in the midst of a maneuver he had not manufactured. We sat and swayed silently on the subway.

When we reached our stop, Jerry exited first, not even checking to see if I was behind him. I was, though, scurrying to keep after him as he strode to the first flight of stairs as if he had an urgent appointment. But on the staircase he slowed, climbing them wearily, pausing before putting a foot down on each new step, leaning heavily on the railing.

"Jerry." I just called his name. I had no idea about what to say to him. How was your day? would have been pointless; it had obviously been as awful as the previous one.

"Yes?" We stood before the second flight of steps that led up to the street. He was eyeing it as if it were too much for him to manage, although it was plain he was not out of breath.

I asked him the same question I had been asking him. "Jerry, can I do anything?"

"You're trying to push me, Marcia. You're trying to get me to lean on you so I'll be a cripple without you. I told you once, you've got to give me room."

"I'm not trying to crowd you, Jerry. I swear. I just want—"

"Why don't you find yourself some new doctor or something and quit bugging my ass?"

I rushed away from him. Where else would I go? To bask in the warmth of my friends? I had two: Eileen, who spoke of privacy with religious reverence; Barbara, with a husband, two sons, five servants, three cars, and four charities.

Back to my mother? To one of the men who wouldn't even remember whether he had just propositioned me or actually slept with me?

Or maybe out on my own? I could find a cheap walk-up on the West Side and spend my nights sniffling into damp tissues and listening to cockroaches walk across the floor. I sensed that Jerry was giving me all I could ever get. I had been alone for a long time after Barry. I was not a woman who valued her independence.

Jerry caught up with me. His arm slid around my shoulder. "Okay, you can come upstate."

"What?" My throat dried, then tightened up.

"You can take Friday afternoon off and be back late Sunday."

"Oh. Of course. Sure."

"Listen, who knows, I may be in a decent mood by then. We could even have some fun."

He met me Friday evening at the bus depot in a town called Liberty. He waited in front, leaning against a car and waving, looking like one of the local boys in a dark green army parka. I saw him mouth "hi." He had acclimated himself to the town in the thirty-six hours he'd been there; if he hadn't been meeting me, he probably would have played a few hands of poker at the firehouse or met a couple of new pals for a few beers.

"Hi," I said, climbing off the bus. April in Liberty could never inspire a song; it was bitterly cold, and I pushed my hands into my pockets. It kept them warm and kept my approach casual. "Where did you get that parka? You look like a USO ad for our boys in Korea."

"How are you?" he asked, and bent over to kiss my lips.

"Wanna dance, sarge?"

"No. Listen, I'm sorry if I was a shit this week."

"That's okay."

"You're not mad at me?" I shook my head. "Look at me and tell me you're not mad at me."

I looked. His cheeks were burnished by the icy air. The cold had brought tears to his eyes, and a few of the tears rested on his lashes, which glistened a deep, solid black. The white light from the street-lamp illuminated only the upper part of his face, so the bottom was in shadows, emphasizing the pouty fullness of his lower lip, deepening the cleft in his chin. "Of course I'm not mad at you."

Jerry led me across the street to the rented Chevrolet he was driving and held the door open for me. "See how mannerly I am?" he demanded.

"Wonderful. Do you chew with your mouth closed too?"

"Most of the time. Listen, call your mother and tell her I'm very well bred, very refined."

"Of course. She'll be so pleased. Listen, maybe we could invite her to spend the weekend with us. Give her her own room, her own six-pack."

"I'd like that, Marcia."

He drove carefully along a well-paved but very narrow mountain road. The car smelled of years of stale cigarettes; its heater didn't work. "Do you think the car can make it up the mountain?" I asked him.

"No."

But we arrived alive at the Pineview Inn. It was an ordinary cheap motel, with nailed-to-the-wall pictures of kittens and a mousetrap baited with a petrified piece of yellow cheese shoved between the toilet and the sink. The Pineview Inn was notable only because it offered just a bed and bath in an area of resorts where, minimally, guests were given the choice between indoor or alfresco swimming, matjes or Bismarck herring as a breakfast appetizer. The Pineview aspired to nothing.

"I'm just curious," I said, still in my coat. "How come you picked this place?" The room was a mite warmer than the car but did not offer sufficient comfort for me to even take my hands from my pockets.

"Because it has a kind of raunchy, illicit atmosphere. I

thought that would appeal to you." Having hung his jacket over a metal pipe, Jerry flashed me a practiced smile and began unbuttoning my coat.

"Really?" I asked. "Does it have any of those X-rated movies?"

"No, but for an extra five bucks the owner will throw in his nubile twin daughters. Actually, I picked this place because it was sort of anonymous. I mean, I know maybe ten, fifteen people up here, and the way my luck is going, I'd run into the one or two who shouldn't know I'm up here poking around."

"What have you found out?" Jerry threw my coat beside his jacket. Then he sat on the yellowed white bedspread and motioned me over.

"Appel's running. He'll probably announce the end of the week after next."

"What else?" He unzipped my jeans slowly, so I would have time enough to contemplate what was going to happen. He inched them off, together with my underpants, easing them over my hips, kissing me along the way.

"Want to hear about Appel's media director?" he whispered.

"No." I left my pants in a mound on the floor and lay on the bedspread, feeling its stiff cotton bumps press into the small of my back. Jerry spread my legs apart and sat between them. Then he leaned over, using his tongue first, then his mouth. Only there did my body heat match his. He kept it up for more than an hour, lifting me up on pillows, taking the pillows away, sometimes blowing cool air on me softly, sometimes pressing roughly with his fingers. I was so satisfied I could have spent the rest of my life on the bedspread, lying on my back, lowing stupidly, like a cow. "Oh, Jerry."

"Happy, sweetheart?"

We got out of bed the next day only because the owner's wife knocked on the door, whimpering that her husband would kill her if she didn't make up the room. "We'll go for a hike in the woods," Jerry announced, as I pulled on a heavy sweater.

"In the woods? Are you kidding? Didn't you ever read 'Hansel and Gretel'?"

The day was cold but full of beaming sunshine. We walked, pausing to examine the branches of trees: their tight little buds, a few weeks away from splitting open and putting out, seemed ungenerous. I gave Jerry a big, wet, open-mouthed kiss.

But I felt a little uncomfortable. My kind of nature was controlled. Like Central Park, it had perimeters. I demanded to know what would happen if a hunter thought I was a deer. I confessed to being afraid of getting lost and suggested we mark our path with my dental floss. Jerry shook his head, promising no harm would come if we stuck to the trail. And no harm came. After a half hour, we found a clearing, a nearly perfect circle of pale new grass surrounded by a ring of dark evergreens.

Jerry lay down, letting his body ease out onto the cold earth, as comfortable in the Catskill forest as on the East Side of Manhattan.

"It smells nice here. Like room deodorant," I said.

We spent the afternoon there, splitting a jar of peanut butter we had bought in a general store across from the motel; the proprietor was neither friendly nor homespun but sat hunched on a stool behind the counter, his legs crossed, reading a magazine that displayed a lot of unnaturally pink female genitalia. But Jerry and I were quite friendly and, if not homespun, at least warm and cuddly. We rubbed noses. We played Name That Tune. As usual, I stumped Jerry. "It's 'Long Before I Knew You' from *Bells Are Ringing*. You really didn't know that?"

"No. Never heard it."

I bellowed the entire song. "Now do you recognize it?"

"No, but maybe somebody three mountains away will. You are *loud*."

"I am not. I'm subdued and elegant."

"Come here. I'll show you what I do to elegant ladies."

We had pizza and chianti. We saw a monster movie. We made love. We read the Sunday paper together in bed. We could have been featured in a *Newsweek* cover story on The Great Middle-Class Weekend.

"Have a good trip home." We stood before the window of Katz's bakery, watching cheese danish, waiting for the bus to pull into Liberty. "I'll call you during the week."

"Jerry?"

"What?"

"Do you know when you'll come back to the city?"

"Soon. I'll spend another couple of days pretending to be

busy and then I'll be home." His voice seemed to get clearer and louder. Saint Agnes had sent him for elocution lessons, then acting lessons. Jerry was her baby Barrymore. He gave me his self-assured public smile. "Don't worry."

"I'm not worried."

"You are. But it will be all right, I promise you, Marcia. I'm in control of this thing." Again the smile. "What can happen?"

—

9

My new office at campaign headquarters did not make me happy. The William Paterno for Governor Committee had rented the fourth floor of a medium-sized midtown hotel that had stumbled over the brink from shabby gentility into seediness. Mildew perfumed the corridors. The elevator creaked as it rose, and when the wind blew across the air shaft it made long low noises, like the moans of the ghosts of dead guests.

Normally, the beginning of a campaign was like the arrival of a perfect spring. Vigor and joy welled up. People smiled. I'd feel clean and bright and capable of writing speeches so brilliant that millions of fingers would twitch in anticipation of pulling my candidate's lever. With each new campaign, I became a virgin again. Hope abounded.

But not this time. Everything looked ugly. My office had an ominous dark-red stain on the carpet. And it was right across the hall from Lyle LoBello's office, so two or three times a day I had to endure his greeting; he'd say "hi" and wink simultaneously and then let his eyes gaze below my waist while he added, "How're you doing?" If my pubis could have talked, it would have answered, Not very well.

I couldn't sleep with Jerry away. He was a pacifier. Each night I would curl myself around him and be lulled by his smell and his warmth. Without him, cars crashed, women screamed in the streets, bottles smashed down onto the pavement.

Even though we rarely had sex more than three times a week, I felt the need for him every night and every morning. I didn't like walking around in a state of unfulfilled desire; I was afraid strange men would sniff it out, the way a dog can scent fear.

Instead of coming home from Sullivan County, Jerry had been ordered even farther upstate. Paterno declared that Jerry's information on Appel had been so valuable that he needed Jerry to dig up dirt on his chief opponent, Governor Parker. "Any smart college kid could find out this stuff," Jerry fumed. He called me collect at the office each day, to hear what was happening at headquarters. We'd talk for at least an hour; the phone bills were certain to annoy Paterno.

"What did you find out?" I asked when he called from Buffalo. Parker had been born there, attended law school there at night, and then had made a routine climb up the ladder of the city's elective offices. "Anything extraordinary about him?"

"No, of course not. He's a decent, ordinary hack," Jerry reported. In the first days of exile, Jerry's voice had weakened; he talked with difficulty, as though he had emphysema. But then it had grown icy with control. "He heard that Gresham wanted an upstate Catholic on the ticket, so every time he had a free minute he genuflected like crazy and Gresham picked him. No big deal. Parker's plan seems to have been to take it easy for four years in Albany, then go back to Buffalo and open up a hotshot law practice. He saw the lieutenant governorship as his pinnacle of success. If he had thought anything would happen to Gresham, he probably would have stayed in Buffalo."

"But he's going to run now?"

"Sure. He's a politician, isn't he?"

"But he's so unqualified. Isn't he afraid people will—"

"Marcia, he's a politician. He thinks he can win, the jerk."

"But do you think—"

"I don't think. I don't give a shit what happens."

"Jerry, that doesn't sound like you."

"Are you starting again, Marcia?"

"No. Really I'm not."

"Just leave me alone. Everything's fine."

It wasn't. It was terrible, and of course Jerry knew it. But he seemed unable or afraid to come back down to the city and confront Paterno.

Jerry might have won. Paterno was nervous and guilty. Instead of his usual three-minute warm-up chitchat with me before each new project, he'd grab a handful of notes and say, "Okay, let's get the show on the road." He didn't look at me. Because he was a direct man—for a politician—and because he had a conscience, his treatment of Jerry made him jittery. He seemed to be waiting for retribution. As I would begin to outline my ideas, Paterno's small hands would clench a little, as though he were expecting a verbal attack or a punch in the mouth.

Once, in the midst of preparing a speech on agriculture he would be making in Ithaca, he looked at me over a page of notes on recycling animal waste into fertilizer and murmured, "I bet you miss your friend. Morrissey, I mean."

"Yes."

"Well, he'll be back soon. Boy, I could really use him around here."

I asked whether we could use the term "feces" just to break the monotony or if we should stick to "waste" throughout the speech.

"I hope you're not angry at me about this. I mean, it's just a routine administrative detail. He'll be back soon."

" 'Waste' or 'feces,' Bill?"

"Waste, for God's sake. This whole speech is disgusting. I don't know why I have to talk about stuff like this."

Besides Jerry's absence, I was driving too hard at work, pushing out six or seven speeches a day and—at Paterno's request—reviewing everything the ad agency produced, from scripts to memos. I didn't enjoy that. A copywriter, tall and uptown-chic, dressed in what looked like an ivory cashmere shroud, told me I was "an utter ass" when I rejected her plan to film Paterno walking through Little Italy, his footsteps in sync to a tarantella.

"You cannot walk to a tarantella," I told her.

"You can if you walk fast. It's a thirty-second spot. Anyway, you said you want to appeal to ethnic—"

"Subtly."

"Listen," she said, "I won't be condescended to."

"Then don't give me tarantellas. And no large family groups. No spaghetti. Get it?"

"And you expect me to do my job? Let me tell you a thing or two about advertising. You could stand to learn something." I told her to get out of my office. Paterno made me call and apologize, but at least there were neither tarantella nor pasta commercials.

"I hear you were snippy to Margo Blythe" LoBello snapped. I stood before his desk.

"Who?"

"The copywriter, goddamn it."

"Sure I was snippy. She's a dope."

"She's a lovely woman."

"You sleeping with her, Lyle?"

"What's with you? You're acting crazy, Marcia. Everybody's saying 'What's with Marcia Green? She used to shut up and do her work and now she's acting crazy.' "

"Fire me, Lyle."

"Get out of here. But you better watch yourself, Marcia. Watch your step. I'm keeping an eye on you." He realigned the French cuffs on his shirt. "Your future may depend on me," he added softly. "You better be nice."

But my description of Lyle is too limited. He was no mere manipulator, no Neapolitan Sammy Glick, no slimy run-of-the-mill pol. He was all those things, of course, but he had a dynamism that fuzzed his less attractive attributes. Years before, when we were both free-lance political operatives working on a mayoral campaign, he had pursued me with a monomaniacal intensity that was irresistible. Marcia, you are one adorable girl. You want coffee? A doughnut? Two doughnuts? Would you keep me company while I check over the Queens petitions? Would you do me a great favor and rub my neck? Did you know you had fantastic, gentle hands? That was the first hour we knew each other.

During the second, he grabbed my wrist, pulled me into a supply closet, and pushed me up against the mimeograph forms. To my surprise, he used none of the ass-kneading, breast-grabbing techniques politicians employ in closets. Instead, he talked. "Listen, Marcia, you're driving me crazy. Nuts. No, don't interrupt. I mean it. I have to have you. I've got to have you or I'll quit the campaign. I can't walk around like this for three months, with a case of blue balls. Jesus, I don't want you to feel I'm putting pressure on you. You make your own decision, but I want you to know what's on my mind."

I stood in the closet, stunned. To be desired so strongly, just a month after the final papers of my divorce went through without a word of protest from Barry. Lyle insisted, swore he had to have me. No one else I had slept with seemed to have had such a need. In fact, I sensed several of them would have preferred a pastrami sandwich, had the deli been closer.

"Lyle," I had said, with the intention of going no further. My mouth opened enough to signal I wanted his over it. He obliged. And he groaned and then invoked two of the three members of the Trinity. He rubbed up and down against me, and his body was so hard it felt superhuman; Lois Lane would run her hands over such a physique.

"Tonight," he said. "It's gonna be so good."

He undressed first that night, slowly, as if I were an audience deserving of a careful performance. He stood barefoot on the blue shag carpet of his apartment. The carpet, an unmade bed, and an elaborate set of weights and barbells were the sole furnishings. But I saw only Lyle.

He was astoundingly muscular. His upper arms were divided into swollen biceps and triceps, and his chest was so full he seemed to be holding his breath. His thigh muscles bulged extravagantly. His penis looked small, probably because it was overwhelmed by his enlarged other parts.

"Wow," I said. Then I waited, prepared for his attack. After all, he said he had to have me. But Lyle was able to postpone his pleasure.

"Come on," he said. "Come over here. You can touch me. I know you want to." I did. I ran my hands all over him. There was not a trace of flaccidity; his entire being was transcendentally firm. And he was used to being stroked; he even pivoted around for me. I had never realized the human back had so many muscles. "I knew you'd like it," he said.

But my response was awe, not passion. I wanted to run my hands from his swollen chest down his unyielding stomach over and over; caress his magnificent shoulders for hours. I didn't particularly care about sleeping with him.

But Lyle finally had enough adoration. He was ready for me, although I didn't realize it until he pulled off my turtleneck with such vigor that my nose nearly came off with it. "Bed," he said.

After a moment or two of polite foreplay, Lyle climbed on top of me. Actually, I was grateful, because I did not like seeing my body next to his; I was mushy, covered in spongy flesh, with mounds of undisciplined tissue that would often travel in a direction opposite from the one in which I was moving.

Lyle entered me and remained busy for a time, without gasping or groaning with the effort. He was, after all, in superb shape. When it was over, I was neither sore nor satisfied, merely sleepier than I had been before and grateful that in a few minutes I could dress and go home.

The next morning at work I found a note in my typewriter: "I want you so bad I can't stand it. L.LB." So I returned to his apartment that night, curious to see if his A.M. desire could last till P.M. It didn't. But he gave me the opportunity to admire him again and nearly equal time to receive him. His technique never varied. During the day he'd be a brilliant advance man for himself; at night, having rounded up his crowd, he performed the way he pleased.

We spent every evening together for the next couple of months, except every other Sunday, when he went to visit his parents. He seemed satisfied with me, although he once expressed disappointment that my pubic hair was darker than the hair on my head. "You're sure you don't dye your hair?"

"I'm sure, Lyle."

"Then how come the colors are different?"

That was our most profound discussion. But I made no move to get rid of him, for I sensed the next man would offer little improvement. Certainly he would not be as pretty. And leaving Lyle—or any of the others—would mean leaving a hole in my life which would remain until I could find another man to come and plug it up.

But two nights after that mayoral election, Lyle told me, as I was buttoning up my blouse, that though he didn't want to hurt me, he didn't think we were compatible.

"All right," I said.

"So don't bother coming around tomorrow night."

A week later, I heard he was seeing a woman named Laura Crane, a stupid socialite who wafted about, floating from one noble cause to another. Presumably she and Lyle were compatible, because I saw them wrapped around each other at a few parties. She called him "Lylie."

Since the number of people whose constitutions thrive on New York Democratic politics is not large, I often saw old bedfellows in new campaigns. Most were polite. A few tried to rekindle the old flame. But only Lyle leered, salivated over our past, as he called it, and used it to try to keep me in line.

Several days after my run-in with him over the advertising campaign, he came into my office and shut the door. "Does Morrissey know?"

"What?"

"Does he know?"

"Know what, Lyle?"

"You know."

"You mean . . ."

"Yeah. About us. You and I. I mean, he called to report in from Buffalo and I felt real hostility on his part."

"Maybe he just doesn't like you, Lyle."

"Marcia, I'm going to forgive you for that remark. I know you're not yourself. You're on edge, right? Come on, don't feel you have to have a snotty answer for everything I say. I know what's going on with you, with him being away. Now listen, just between us, if you need a man—well, you know what I've got."

"Get out of here."

"Honey, come on. You're so horny."

Eileen Gerrity told me to calm down. "Come on, Marcia. Have another sip of wine." I sat on the edge of her couch, recounting that afternoon's confrontation with Lyle LoBello. "He is horrendous, though. How could you ever have been able to . . . ?"

"You should see his muscles."

"You're joking. Surely you're joking, Marcia."

"I'm not. He lifts weights."

"That should be sufficient deterrent." Eileen sat curled up on the far end of her couch, waiting for our TV dinners to heat. Her concept of entertaining guests was to serve a great deal of white wine. Dinner was an icy Salisbury steak which she sprinkled with red wine; when it was cooked, she transferred it from the aluminum tray to a plate. She scattered small flowers of parsley over it and surrounded it with small bombs of congealed starch called potato puffs which came with the meat.

I shrugged, finished my wine, and poured myself another glass. And then another.

"Marcia, stop watching the rug. It doesn't need too much attention. Now talk to me. I'm a decent person. I'm making you a fancy dinner, which is more than you've ever done for me, despite all that boasting about what a grand gourmet cook you were and how you used to make your husband pheasant cutlets every night."

"Well, it's not really Lyle who's bothering me."

"Of course it's not Lyle. He's a pest, but you're shooing him away adequately. It's Jerry, right?"

"Yes."

"Well?"

"What do you want me to say, Eileen? Everyone knows what's happening. He's being screwed."

"Indeed he is."

"So do you think it's fun for me to watch him being screwed—long distance? When I'm helpless to do anything?"

"But you're not the one who should be doing anything. It's Jerry I don't understand. Why is he toddling around upstate when he should be down here, sabotaging LoBello?"

"Because Bill Paterno is standing right behind LoBello. What can Jerry do?"

"Are you kidding? He can fight. And if he loses, he can quit. But it's madness for him to be off like a good little boy on some meaningless expedition now. It's going to kill him politically. Everybody is going to see he's vulnerable, that LoBello was able to finesse him out of the picture. He's got to get to Paterno. He's got to come back and fight."

"And if he loses? What happens then?"

"He gets another job."

"Where? For God's sake, where? Eileen, what can he do? He's forty-seven years old."

"That's not dead, Marcia."

"I know. But what can he do besides be a political adviser? Retire and sit on a park bench?"

"You have a real flair for hyperbole."

"Sell shoes like his brother Dennis?"

"I'll tell you one thing. I'd rather be playing with people's feet all day than playing games with Bill and LoBello. It's much more honorable."

"Honor has nothing to do with it. Who has honor in politics? Paterno? Jerry? Me? I write speeches about Bill Paterno's passionate commitment to women's rights, and then fifty calls come in that another day-care center was shut down. And Bill goes on TV and says 'I'm passionately committed to the working poor,' and calls you and tells you to draft some new legislation—"

"Will you calm down?"

"No. So you draw up a couple of new regulations, and then he has Joe Cole and a couple of the others trot it around, singing hallelujah. And then what happens? He calls another press conference to say he has the problem licked, that all those women can keep their jobs and not go on welfare because their kids are taken care of and—"

"Marcia, we're all trying. You're not the only one who cares. We all work very hard."

"We're working for ourselves."

"But that's politics. Even when we act in our own self-interest, we benefit others. We have to be responsive to the public to succeed."

"We have to *seem* responsive to the public."

"Well, if it's such an abhorrent business, why aren't you glad Jerry's on his way out? In fact, why are you still around, making all this dirty dealing sound so pretty, making a slippery pol like Bill sound like Saint Francis of Assisi? Why don't you go up to Harlem and offer to baby-sit?"

"This is all I know how to do, Eileen, Jerry too."

"I don't believe that for a minute. You could be working for a newspaper or making up jingles to sell floral douches. And Gorgeous could sell real estate or lobby for the insurance industry or squire around a rich widow."

"Listen to me, Eileen. I've only known politics. That's it. The only person I know who isn't involved in running for some office is my mother, but she's congenitally unelectable. Look, who else do I know outside of politics?"

"I don't know, but—"

"Who do you know on the outside? Come on."

"Well, my sister Elizabeth is a teacher."

"Not family."

"All right."

"So?"

"Just a second. All right, there's my friend Joan. We've been friends since fourth grade. She's a housewife with two kids."

"When was the last time you saw her?"

"New Year's Day. But that's not fair, Marcia, because we've been extra busy, and since Gresham died I've been—"

"When was the last time you saw her before New Year's Day? Come on."

Eileen examined her short but perfectly manicured nails. "The New Year's Day before that. But what does that prove? If you worked for a newspaper you'd have lunch with journalists. And if you were a teacher, your best pal would be an academic."

"But political people are the only people I know. I've been with them since college. I have nowhere else to go. God, the only man I ever slept with who wasn't on or about to be on the public tit was Barry. Every other man was employed—"

"Marcia, be rational. There are men all over the city who have other jobs. Really. I've met them. You can too."

"I don't want to meet them. I have Jerry."

"Let's have dinner."

We sat at the table, a circle of glass set on a truncated tree trunk. I peered through the glass, wondering whether Eileen had ever counted the age rings of the tree. Her apartment, a tight studio in an expensive cooperative building, was jammed full of objects that had nothing to do with each other. What's her decorating concept? my Aunt Estelle would demand. Does she think it's elegant to live in the middle of a rummage sale?

A Lucite footstool was pushed against the wall. Above it hung a Navajo blanket. Under the window, a line of green glass jars and ceramic pots were filled with pussy willows. The couch was as padded and prim as Queen Victoria at her Diamond Jubilee. Beside it, there was a rocking chair made of leather and chrome. But Eileen loved each of her objects; sitting at the table, she ran her hand around the rim of her cut crystal wineglass, over the surface of the ceramic salt and pepper shakers, shaped like black and white poodles.

"You said you have Jerry," she said, "but you really can't *have* him, not in any conventional sense. You need more than he can give you."

"You sound like my family."

"Well, maybe they have a point you should be listening to. You're clinging to him because you need security, continuity. But Marcia, the minute he feels you're depending on him too much, he'll bolt."

"That's not true."

"Of course it's true. I know so many like him. Don't you understand? To you he's an exotic. To me—well, he's just another good-looking Irish bachelor. I have an uncle just like him, and a couple of cousins too. The point is, they're a type. I can predict exactly how Jerry will behave because I've seen the pattern dozens of times."

"So?"

"So, they never marry. They pick up the scent of intimacy in the air and they run. Look, you can think the two of you are so close your lives have merged, but he won't think the same way. My Uncle Bob saw the same woman for seventeen years. Seventeen! And one evening he just decided he'd rather be doing something else and he shook her hand and wished her a nice life."

"I still don't see the point."

"Then you're not looking. Maybe what your family wants for you isn't so awful. They want to see you married because they want you protected, loved."

"Let me tell you something, Eileen. In the twenty-one years I lived with her, my mother never told me she loved me. She never protected me; I would ask her permission to go someplace and she'd give me a wave of her hand and say, 'Do whatever you want'. She barely talked to me. I kept interrupting her reading. All my family cares about is that I do the correct thing: marry the right sort of man—rich, Jewish—have a couple of children, and be on a first-name basis with an interior decorator."

"Well, at least your mother cares enough to want something for you. Anyway, if you look at it, none of their aspirations for you are intrinsically terrible."

"They're all superficial. There's no love there."

"You supply the love. Your family is just giving you the outline."

"Look, my family is spiritually and emotionally deficient."

"But you're not."

"The point is—"

"The point is, Marcia, that the Jerry Morrissey you're defending may be spiritually and emotionally deficient too. He can't give you—"

"The point is, Eileen, that I love him."

"Well," she said softly, spearing a potato puff with her fork, "that won't admit to rational analysis, will it?"

But neither would anything else in my life. When I got home, I called my mother. She sounded pleased to hear from me. I sat on the bed, stunned.

"Marcia, I'm so glad you called."

"Oh. Well, good. How are you, Mom?"

"Not too bad. I was going to call you."

"What's new?"

"Nothing much. What's new with you?"

"Well, I'm working uptown now, at campaign headquarters. I'll give you my number there."

"I just spoke to Aunt Estelle."

"That's nice."

"Well, it wasn't so nice."

"What happened?"

"Remember her next-door neighbor, Lydia Leventhal?"

"No."

"You know her. Well, her husband passed away yesterday afternoon. Lung cancer. Inoperable. They opened him and sewed him right back up."

"I'm sorry to hear that. Anything else new?"

"No. In any case, Marcia, I discussed it with Aunt Estelle and she thinks it would be nice if you went with us to pay a shiva call."

"Look, Mom, that's out of the question. Completely out of the question. I'm swamped at headquarters, and I don't even know Mrs. Lowenstein."

"Leventhal. Of course you know her. She's lived next door to Julius and Estelle for over twenty years. In the English Tudor house with the wrought-iron bench in the front. And," she continued, speaking with a verve she generally reserved for the Rothschilds, "I know how much it would mean to Uncle Julius if you came. He says Mr. Leventhal was very active in politics, so it could be worthwhile for you to show up." I could pass out Paterno for Governor buttons. "Uncle Julius says the Leventhals always thought highly of you."

"What was his first name?"

"Mr. Leventhal's? Ira. He was a very fine man. An attorney."

"Never heard of him. He probably just belonged to the local club in Jamaica Estates and—"

"No. He was very important, according to Uncle Julius."

"Uncle Julius may know mink, but he doesn't know beans about politics. Listen, Paterno's from Queens, and if someone's a big Democrat I know who they are. No Ira Leventhal was ever a factor."

My mother's voice remained calm and took on pearly, cultured overtones. "Mr. Leventhal was a Republican, Marcia. A very fine man. He always dressed in three-piece suits. But I can't force you to pay a condolence call. If you don't want to go because he belonged to another political party, that's entirely up to you."

"It has nothing to do with that. It's just that I'm so swamped."

"Sometimes I don't understand you."

"What?"

"You're liberal enough to mingle with all sorts of people, but for a Republican—"

"Look, I like Republicans. Okay? They're wonderful. My second favorite political party."

"All right, Marcia. I'll let you get your sleep."

"All right, I'll go to Mrs. Leventhal's. I'm not sure which night I can make it, though."

"Aunt Estelle wanted you to come tomorrow night for dinner. If you and"—pause, swallow—"your friend don't have plans. Not that he needs to come. I mean, since he didn't know the Leventhals, it wouldn't be appropriate."

"Too bad. He loves Jewish mourning practices."

"All right, Marcia. Forget the whole thing."

"Stop it. I was joking. Look, he's out of town anyway."

"Oh."

"I'll go. I'll meet you at Aunt Estelle's tomorrow night."

"I'm sure Mrs. Leventhal will appreciate it." She paused. "And the rest of her family."

"How many Leventhals are there?"

"Just the son, Butch. Aunt Estelle says he's probably shattered, first with his divorce, now with his father's death."

"Mom."

My mother was no fool. "I'll meet you at six at Aunt Estelle's. She asked that you don't wear slacks. It's inappropriate, and you have a tendency to be bottom-heavy." Then she got off the phone fast.

10

"Who puts dill into lentil soup?" my Aunt Estelle demanded.

"I do," I said, sprinkling a spoonful of the herb into my aunt's soup pot. It was large enough for Macbeth's witches. "It's nice. Adds a kind of Russian flavor."

"Who wants Russian flavor? All they know is beets."

"They know more than beets."

"All right. Cabbage too." She supervised my peppering the soup. "Not too much. Uncle Julius doesn't like things too spicy."

I had left work early, mainly to escape Lyle LoBello. He had sauntered into my office, leaned against a wall Bogart-fashion, and murmured, "How're you getting through the nights, little Marcia?"

"Do you use parsley?" I asked my aunt.

"Of course I use parsley. What do you think, I'm one of those old fashioned Jewish cooks who only knows onions and garlic?" She retreated from the stove and sat at her kitchen table, where she began to peel a small pyramid of potatoes. "Do you get to do much cooking in Greenwich Village?" she inquired.

"No. I don't think I've ever even opened the oven there."

"Really?"

"Well, by the time I get home, six–seven at night, I'm really too tired to cook."

"And your friend doesn't cook?"

"No."

"I asked because men are cooking these days. Barbara says Philip makes bread. Can you imagine that? And he doesn't even have to, with a cook. You wouldn't believe what kind of a salary that woman gets. And that's including two days off a week and sometimes they just have a plain steak and baked potato for dinner. Not that she's not a fine cook. She used to work for the Whitneys, but they never made her feel part of the family, the way Barbara does. She's colored, you know."

"Black."

"So he doesn't like to cook?"

"Who? Oh, Jerry. No."

"Well, they're not exactly experts when it comes to food."

"Come on, Aunt Estelle."

"All right, he's a great gourmet."

"Actually, you're right. He eats things like luncheon meat. You know, those squares of bologna with sliced olives and things stuck in them."

"I've seen them in the supermarket. I always wondered who bought that chozzerai. Does he make you eat it?"

"No. Of course not. Look, he's a lovely, civilized person, Aunt Estelle. What do you think, he ties me to a chair and forces me to eat luncheon meat? I don't want to start another argument when my mother and Uncle Julius are here, but if you'd just give him a chance, I think you'd like him. He's bright, handsome—"

"Of course he's handsome. You ever go past a firehouse? They're all Irish, and one after another they look like movie stars. It's like Errol Flynn coming over and squirting a hose in your window."

"Aunt Estelle, if you'd—"

"Marcia, has he asked to come here? Has he said to you, 'Please introduce me to your family?' Well?"

"No."

"And he's not going to. Don't give me one of your looks. I'm just being realistic. You share the same apartment, share the same telephone and everything else, why should he want to meet your family? Things are perfect for him just the way they are. If he started coming here, it would add a whole new aspect to your relationship, and let me tell you something, he doesn't want that any more than we do."

I covered the soup pot and sat across from my aunt.

"You're not fighting me because you know what I'm saying is true," she said.

"But he's the only person who ever made me happy. Doesn't that count for anything?"

"It counts if you can count on him. Barbara looks across the dinner table and sees Philip, sees a husband, someone who'll be there ten–twenty years from now."

"Well, I was married."

"Marcia, please."

"Well, I was. You all approved of Barry. You all thought he was a brilliant catch. But he didn't make me happy. I couldn't count on him. Look, it's more than ten years and I look across the dinner table and he's not there."

"Marcia, darling, I'm not saying every husband is right for every wife. Maybe we were wrong in thinking he was such a catch. Who knows? I met his mother at Loehmann's a couple of months ago. That Sheri, that phony. Everyone knows her name is Sadie. I took a good look at her. And you know what? Beneath that surface polish, there's no real refinement. She wears costume jewelry earrings and has that hard cigarette voice. You know what I mean? She may set a nice table, but she's one tough cookie. By the way, she told me Barry's wife is pregnant with twins, but I got the impression things weren't going too well with them. Here, take the potatoes and cut them into very thin slices. No, that's too thin."

My Aunt Estelle made my crazy, but she helped me keep my sanity. In the years after my father died, when my mother drifted around the apartment like someone half dead, it was my aunt, with her nagging and nosiness and nearly intolerable manipulativeness, who gave me the feeling I was alive and worth fussing over.

Some major human component was missing in my mother. She echoed her sister's prejudices, snobberies, and idiocies, but she had none of my aunt's compensating vigor, competence, and charisma.

My mother would never attempt to browbeat me over a pot of lentil soup. She didn't care enough. Something had happened to her. In her universe, where smothering mothers were considered merely devoted, she never questioned where I was going, what I was doing, or with whom I was doing it. She never even bought me a birthday present, but instead gave me two or five or ten dollars to buy my own gift. Her loyalties remained with her own family, with her sister; she had no maternal feelings. But at least she cared enough to offer me up as a human sacrifice to my Aunt Estelle. My aunt then told her what to do: "Hilda, Marcia needs new shoes," or "If she's having dinner at the Plotnicks', let her bring flowers. Candy is too lower class." My mother would nod, and I'd get new shoes or money for a bouquet of flowers.

When I came up to New York to tell my family I had left Barry, my mother paled and shrugged. My aunt shrieked, demanded smelling salts, and spent an entire three days—until I fled back to Washington—trying to discover what had happened. "What's wrong, darling?" she had said. "He's not paying enough attention to you? He's fooling around a little? He didn't hit you, did he? Marcia, listen to me. Give him another chance. He'll come to his senses. You don't throw out a husband like he was an old crust of bread." But at least she ensconced me in Barbara's old bedroom and donated three days of her life to tormenting me. My mother had gone home by nine fifteen the first night, saying she didn't like taking the subway after ten o'clock.

"Go get a pot of cold water," my aunt said. "Put the potatoes in after you peel them and they won't turn gray. That's from the starch."

My aunt loved to run things. She had taken charge of her daughter's life and turned Barbara into a woman so showered by blessings that other mothers might have blushed at the audacity of accepting such good fortune. Aunt Estelle felt her success with Barbara was merely the result of planning and hard work. She had not done as well with her son, Kenny, but then she hadn't tried very hard. Kenny was nervous and inarticulate and hadn't interested her too much, so she only bothered getting him through Yale and M.I.T. He showed no interest in fine English worsteds or girls, but my aunt was able to ignore these defects because he lived out of town.

I could never understand why my aunt wasn't president of General Motors or chairman of the Federal Reserve. There was no doubt that she could have governed New

York City; she was smarter than the mayor, more resourceful than the comptroller, more energetic than Paterno. Mere sexism could not have kept her in the kitchen. She was so formidable that I could not imagine anyone stupid or courageous enough to try and discriminate against her.

But she limited her sphere of influence to Jamaica Estates. There, she was queen. And had I been willing to accept her patronage, she would have ruled my life completely, taking me to her manicurist for porcelain nails, arranging dates for me with orthodontists and restauranteurs and third-generation garment-center moguls. She would have redecorated Barbara's all-white bedroom in pearly beiges suitable for a thirty-five-year-old career girl and laid out my clothes for me each night.

"Do you ever speak to him?" she asked.

"To whom?"

"I'm glad to see you're still grammatical. To Barry. I mean, he's living in Philadelphia, so I thought you might have been in touch."

"No. I have nothing to say to him. Why should I be in touch?"

"I'm not saying you should. I was just wondering. He never called you?"

"No."

"I hear his wife comes from a very impressive family. On the Main Line."

"Come on, Aunt Estelle. Their name is Goldfarb or Goldblatt or something."

"You don't think there are Jews on the Main Line?" She finished her last potato and wrapped the peels in a paper towel to throw into the garbage. "Grandma Yetta used to save the peels. She used them to thicken soups and gravies."

"Was Grandma Yetta from the Main Line?"

"You know that's in Philadelphia and stop being fresh, Marcia. Anyway, you haven't told me a thing about your campaign. I hope you're writing good speeches, so he wins. That Governor Parker is such a bulvon, with that fat nose. And how he spits when he talks. James Gresham must be turning over in his grave when he sees Parker. Did you know he went to the same prep school as Philip? Gresham, I mean."

My mother arrived an hour later, as my Aunt Estelle

was beginning to move in on me, unsheathing her fairy godmother wand. "Hilda," she said, "I was just trying to persuade Marcia to try a little makeup."

"I don't like makeup," I said.

"I'm not talking about heavy pancake makeup so you look cheap. If it's done with a light touch it can enhance your features." She turned to my mother. "Look at Marcia's eyes. Gorgeous. Aren't they gorgeous?" My mother barely glanced at me but nodded enthusiastically to her sister. "See, Marcia?" my aunt continued. "You should emphasize them. You could look like Grace Kelly."

"Please, Aunt Estelle," I said.

"Your eyelashes are very pale," my mother observed.

"I think I hear Julius at the door," my aunt said. "Marcia, go upstairs to Barbara's bathroom and wash up."

At dinner, Uncle Julius agreed with his wife that I should wear eye makeup. Fortunately, the conversation then turned to Uncle Julius's bookkeeper, Nadine Silverstein, who wore cheap false eyelashes and too much rouge, and from there, to Nadine's daughter Tammy, who could not decide between secretarial school and a junior college. Aunt Estelle decided for her and, after she had swallowed the last of her cherry strudel, announced she would speak to Nadine in the morning and tell her what Tammy should do. "Leave the dishes," she said. "I'll take care of them when we get back from the Leventhals'. Marcia, a little lipstick?"

"No."

"Ready?" Uncle Julius boomed. He held the front door for us and we scurried by him, three short, slightly broad-beamed Goldilocks past the Papa Bear. The early spring air was chilly and moist.

My mother sniffed and looked back at her sister's house and sighed. Aunt Estelle sighed back, misinterpreting, perhaps, her sister's melancholia. "Hilda, darling, I know shiva calls are painful for you, but . . ."

"It has to be done, Estelle," my mother responded, in the family tradition of noblesse oblige. We walked over to present our condolences to the bereaved Leventhals, mourning a hundred feet down the block in a miniature Tudor manor house.

"I'm sorry," I managed to say to Mrs. Leventhal. She was a big woman, but not overly fat. Her size seemed derived from large bones covered with solid tissue, not from sloppy flab. Naturally, she wore black, a severe dress in a stiff fabric, relieved only by a slightly scoop neck. Big Mrs. Leventhal's appropriately large breasts, pushed together by a hard-working bra, made a long, thin furrow that continued beyond ordinary cleavage territory and on up to a couple of inches below her neck. One of the pearls from her necklace had caught in the furrow; it looked like an egg being devoured by a large-mouthed monster.

"Thank you, Marcia," she murmured, acknowledging my sympathy. "So sweet of you to come. Ira would have appreciated it." Mrs. Leventhal was seated on an avocado-colored cut velvet couch, obviously not aware that monotones were elegant. I stood before her with Aunt Estelle's arm around my waist, so everyone would know that I was under my relative's noble chaperonage. My mother had been left behind near the threshold of the living room.

Whether by chance or some subliminal caste recognition, my mother had paired off with the only other woman in the room who did not meet even the fairly flexible standards of northern Queens chic—wrinkles were acceptable, overweight in the second generation countenanced as long as it was neat and solid and swathed in expensive clothes. But my mother's companion, chattering a little too gaily, was stupendously obese, with a bagel-sized roll of fat about her ankles that hung over the edge of her tan laced shoes. She was encased in a yellow dress with fat white polka dots, so she looked like a great slab of Swiss cheese.

"Marcia's terribly busy with her politics right now," Aunt Estelle was saying. Her grip around my waist had tightened when she noticed me glancing away from Mrs. Leventhal. "She goes everywhere with him, you know." Mrs. Leventhal nodded. I smiled and tried to break from my aunt's control, but failed. "He wouldn't be running for governor if it wasn't for her." Of course, "he" was Paterno. I wasn't sure if Aunt Estelle was avoiding his name because she had forgotten it or because she thought it bad form to utter the name of a Democrat before the soul of a Republican had a chance to rest in peace.

"He's running for governor?" Mrs. Leventhal asked. "I've been"—and her voice fell—"well, preoccupied lately." My aunt's hand left my waist and reached out to her neighbor. "I used to follow all the news before Ira . . ." Mrs. Leventhal's voice faded into silence.

"Oh, Lydia," Aunt Estelle said fervently. "I know. I know. And you've been a pillar. An absolute tower of strength." She turned to me. "Taking him for radiation treatments. Do you have any idea?"

"I used to read the *Times* every day," Mrs. Leventhal continued, "all four sections, before . . ." A large tear slipped from her left eye.

"I'm sorry," I said once more.

"That's all right." Mrs. Leventhal sighed. Then she looked at Aunt Estelle. "She's such a sweet girl."

"Very," my aunt agreed. "Lydia, darling, there are so many people here, I don't want to monopolize your time. I'll drop in again tomorrow, with some lentil soup. Marcia made it. She's a fine cook. Is Butch here? I want to extend my condolences to him. Such a good boy." Thirty-seven years old.

"A wonderful son," Mrs. Leventhal concurred. She gazed at me, a momentarily grief-free, clear-eyed gaze. "He's a graduate of the Wharton School." I nodded. "That's a part of the University of Pennsylvania." I nodded again.

"Is he around, Lydia?" My aunt was not impatient, but she wanted to get on with it, before Lydia Leventhal began her hymn to Butchie's major in management, her ode on a Master of Business Administration.

"I think he's in the kitchen with a few of his associates."

"Come, Marcia." I managed a quick good-bye before Aunt Estelle led me off, past my mother, now alone—deserted even by the fat lady—through the hall, into the dining room, and up to the double door of the kitchen.

"Please, Aunt Estelle. I don't know him. There's really no point—"

"What do you mean, no point?" Her whisper was so harsh it could have been a scream. "His father died."

"But I don't know him."

"Of course you do. You met him several times. I was there. I introduced you myself."

"But I don't even remember him. It must have been years ago."

"So?" she demanded. "Do you need another introduction? Are you going to stand on ceremony in a house of mourning?"

"If it's a house of mourning," I hissed, "it's a hell of a time to be playing matchmaker."

"Don't think you can get out of this with a temper tantrum, Marcia. I happen to know for a fact that your mother told you that Butch would be here, and if you didn't want to see him you wouldn't have come, so let's go. Or do you want to spend the rest of your life with that shikker? Is that your ambition? He's too old for you. You'll be taking care of him when his liver gets yellow. Is that what you want? Because if it is I'll just leave you alone. Now come on. Be nice to Butch." And with one hand pushing my back and the other opening the door, Aunt Estelle propelled me into the kitchen. And there, sitting at a tiny glass table on a wrought-iron pedestal, apparently abandoned by his associates, was Butch Leventhal.

It would be pleasant to report that under the fluorescent fixture was Butch the Beautiful, that beneath his white shirt were powerful shoulders straining to break through the polyester blend, that compared with him, Jerry paled to a small-potatoes Celt. Or it might be comforting had it been Butch the Crass, a drooling, thick-lipped oaf, a Semitic Stanley Kowalski without the sexuality. Or that he was Butch the Blessed, a gentle soul who scribbled sonnets on ledger paper. Or Brainy Butch, the Wizard of Wall Street.

But of course when Ira's and Lydia's Republican genes intermingled, the product was predictable. Nice. Balding, with a few limp hairs still growing on the top of his shiny scalp. Stood up when introduced to me by Aunt Estelle. Said thank you when I said I was sorry about his father. Nodded when Aunt Estelle told him I was a very important speech writer to a very powerful politician—so powerful that his name, like Yahweh's, could not be invoked. Responded with a short list of Anglo-Saxon surnames when asked by my aunt what management consulting firm he belonged to. And shook my hand after I offered mine and told him, "Nice meeting you."

This time I led, followed by Aunt Estelle, Uncle Julius, and my mother, all the way out the front door. They scurried behind me for the ten seconds it took to get back on Lindenbaum turf.

"Something wrong?" Uncle Julius asked.

"Of course not," his wife answered quickly.

"Well," my mother began.

"Well," I said, trying to sound lighthearted, "when they hand out the awards for great love stories that shook the Borough of Queens, the tale of Marcia Green and Butch Leventhal will not be among them." But I was no Noel Coward.

My mother looked beyond me, at her sister. "How can you tell after just two minutes?" Aunt Estelle demanded. She pursed her lips and glanced up at the streetlight, which I assumed stood for heavenward. "And you certainly didn't go out of your way to make conversation."

"How could I make conversation with Butchie? It would be like talking to a pot roast. He has as much vivacity as—"

"Boy-oh-boy," crooned Uncle Julius, singing Aunt Estelle's song. "My little niece is a tough cookie. Such high standards, Marcia. Seriously, sweetie, don't you think you're demanding a little too much? I mean, you're an adult now, not a kid like the first time."

"I am demanding," I began, "just a touch of understanding from my family." Off to the side, I could see my mother's anticipatory shudder. I raised my voice. "I am demanding not to be trotted out—in the middle of a primary campaign—to meet some semi-comatose conservative who's in mourning!"

"Marcia!" my mother's voice broke out, snapping at me in anger and humiliation.

"And while I'm demanding a little too much, I'll also demand that you remember that I am living with Jerry Morrissey and that you cannot make it go away by parading a bunch of jerks who have the I.Q.s of parakeets and whose only attribute seems to be that they're Jewish and have a natural sense of compound interest."

"Marcia." That was my mother again.

"You've become a Jewish anti-Semite," my aunt announced coldly. "The lowest of the low. I hope you realize that."

"Estelle, don't be so hard on the kid," Uncle Julius interceded. "What has she got? Huh?"

My mother could not look at me. But Aunt Estelle swallowed saliva and pride simultaneously. "All right," she said. "It's my fault. I'm sorry. I didn't know. Maybe I shouldn't have pushed." Her voice grew softer, caressing. "Marcia, I just want for you the happiness Barbara has." She spoke to my mother. "Maybe Butch Leventhal isn't right for her, Hilda. I don't know. His real name is Cyril. Maybe it had some effect on his personality."

My mother shrugged. "I'll help you with the dishes," she said.

"Then you won't need me," I murmured. "I've got some work to do at home." My mother shrugged again. I looked away.

"Don't be discouraged, Marcia," my aunt said. "We'll find something for you. Don't worry."

"I've got to get home," I said.

Less than an hour later, I leaned against the cold metal door of the apartment as if it were a treasure discovered after a long hunt. I put a key into the lowest lock.

Suddenly I heard a tiny voice. "Hello." Heart banging, mouth dry, I froze. The ultimate irony, to be killed in the hallway of the house my family had tried to save me from. "Marcia?" The voice was thin and distant but finally recognizable. I rushed and fumbled to open the rest of the locks. "In the bedroom."

I threw my handbag and key ring on the floor and dashed inside, prepared to leap onto the bed and do anything I could to enchant Jerry sufficiently to make him announce that this would always be my home. "Jerry!" I shouted, rushing in.

"Muscle spasm," he barked. "I called headquarters from Buffalo and then here from LaGuardia, but you weren't in. Joe Cole had to drive out to the airport. He got me upstairs and waited for the doctor. Where the hell were you?"

"At my Aunt Estelle's."

"Jesus!" Jerry cried out in pain. He tried to move, to ease himself, but he could only wince. "I'm a goddamn mess."

I waited for his agony to subside. "Jerry . . ."

"Wait a second." It took several, but finally he spoke. "How are you? You look tired." He spent a moment settling into a comfortable position. His body relaxed. "Your family work you over again?"

"A little."

"Figures. Come here. Give me a kiss, but do it lightly. No pressure on the back. I have to stay flat with a pillow under my legs for a minimum of four or five days, and the doctor says I can only get up once a day, to take a crap. I'll have to pee into a bottle or jar or something. Is that okay? It's up to you. Otherwise, I'll have to go to the hospital. My mother offered to take me in, but she's crippled with her arthritis, and my sister has the five kids. So it's your decision." He exhaled and smiled. "How d' you like that for a greeting?"

"I think I'll go back to my Aunt Estelle's."

"That bad? Well, come on now. Bend down and kiss me hello."

I knelt down on one knee, like Al Jolson about to deliver a mammoth "Mammy." I was afraid of falling over, of putting too much weight on him, of collapsing and immobilizing him for life. I brushed my lips against his.

"More," he ordered. "Come on. Open your mouth and close your eyes." We kissed such a prolonged, warm kiss that I nearly fell onto the floor with exhausted contentment. "I wish we could do more," he whispered. "Maybe by tomorrow we'll figure something out." I took his hand and planted small kisses on the pads of each finger. "Marcia, listen to me. I know you're going full steam with the campaign, and if you want me to check into a hospital, I will. No problem. No guilt trips."

"This is your home."

"You're great, sweetheart. A real trouper. Come on. One more kiss before lights out."

11

Lyle LoBello wore a musk cologne to the meeting, and the entire staff seemed dazed by its heaviness. People slumped in folding chairs with half-closed eyes. Not a single person moaned in dismay as Paterno's daily schedule was read.

"Any new business before I go on?" LoBello demanded. He took off his suit jacket and rolled up his shirt sleeves, displaying both sides of each impressive forearm: the solid upper and the bulging veins and muscles of the lower. "Any new business?" Most of the women and two of the men stared at his arms.

Before the campaign, when Jerry had run staff meetings, he had been stared at too. But people had noticed more than one part of him, more than arms, voices, cleft chin. Eyes glistened at his charm, jaws drooped at his entire countenance, toes curled with each movement of his body, and minds leaped with excitement over his ideas. Jerry was more than just a sum of parts.

LoBello sat on the edge of his desk, his hand resting on his powerful thigh. "Come on, people. Now is the time to speak up." The key members of Paterno's campaign staff—about twelve of us—remained silent. We had not meshed. Half of us were from Paterno's City Hall staff, but the others were strangers, LoBello's hired guns, people who knew the rest of New York State the way we knew New York City.

"All right," LoBello continued, loosening his tie and opening his top collar button. "Let me make my announcements, and then we can all get to work. First and foremost, you probably know by now that our friend and colleague, Jerry Morrissey, injured his back upstate—working for the cause—and he'll be out of commission for a while. Anyhow, we all hope he gets better fast. Would you give him our regards, Marcia?" I nodded. "Marcia?"

"All right."

"Good. For those of you who are new, Marcia and Jerry are—um, close personal friends. Am I right, Marcia?" He stood and strolled toward my chair. The odor of his cologne was so powerful and animal that for a second I forgot not merely who Jerry was but who Lyle was also. But then he spoke again. "Marcia? Huh?"

"I'm sorry, Lyle. I wasn't paying attention. What did you say?" Since he had begun working on the campaign, I found myself resisting his authority in the most adolescent ways possible. I'd yawn while he spoke, declare in front of Paterno that an idea LoBello had just presented was unworkable and amateurish. Every time Lyle remonstrated with me, I'd threaten to quit. After witnessing one of these skirmishes, Paterno had muttered that I seemed a little "testy," but he did not seem interested in refereeing any conflict between LoBello and me.

"Forget it," LoBello said, trying to unclench his teeth enough to appear casual. He reacted to my challenges in different ways. Sometimes he'd ignore them. Several times he hissed "bitch" at me, and once he screamed at me to shut up. In a crowded elevator he stood behind me and pressed against me, rubbing his pelvis up and down, whispering, "You need to get laid, baby. Look at how tight you are."

He strolled to the front of the room. "All right, everybody. Let's get down to serious business: Sidney Appel."

I peered at my watch. It was a few minutes after eleven, and I had promised Jerry I'd be home by noon to empty his urine jar and give him lunch.

"Are you interested in this campaign, Ms. Green?" LoBello called out.

I continued to study my watch. Jerry had protested, of course, telling me I needn't miss work, especially during a campaign, but he also managed to grit his teeth with pain once and to turn white as he reached across the bed for the metropolitan section of the *Times*, so I knew he wanted me with him.

"All right," LoBello said. "Where was I?"

"You were going to say something about Sidney Appel," Eileen said. Her voice was slow and patient, like a teacher helping a slow but hard-working student. "Remember, Lyle?"

"Thank you, Eileen." But he glanced at me as he spoke, as though suspecting we had plotted to undermine and emasculate him. "Okay, let's get going. Sidney Appel is going to be a problem. No two ways about it. Now you may be wondering why I'm talking to you guys about Appel now. I mean, it's before the weekend, Bill's upstate, what can happen, right? Well, what I'm going to say will explain it all."

A huge sigh followed LoBello's sentence, a sigh of ennui so explosive that it commanded the attention of the entire staff. It had come from Joe Cole, Paterno's minority affairs expert, one of Jerry's oldest cronies.

"Anything wrong, Joe?" LoBello asked. He sensed insurrection. His voice was tight trying to transform his anger into nonchalance for the benefit of his upstate audience.

"Come on, man," Joe urged in a slow, impatient ghetto voice. "It's almost eleven fucking thirty." Joe usually wore Brooks Brothers tones in the office, but he donned an uptown cadence when he wanted to intimidate whites. "I got things to do."

"All right," LoBello said, almost apologetically. Then he became brusque. "We're all busy, you know. Now, Sidney Appel. Sidney Appel is going to declare his candidacy on Monday. Try to comprehend the importance of that. That's a week before we thought he'd be ready." He peered at me and said, "Our Sullivan County intelligence was faulty." Then he cleared his throat. "Okay, how are we going to counter him? How are we going to direct our energies?"

"I'm going," I announced, standing up.

"What the hell do you think you're doing, Marcia?"

"I'm going to work at home. I have too much to do and I need quiet." I left, my exit embellished by LoBello's speechless rage and calls of "bye" and "see you Monday" and "best to Jerry" from Joe and Eileen and the rest of the City Hall contingent.

"I give it seven on a scale of ten," said Jerry, rating the insurrection. Lying flat on his back, addressing the ceiling, he applauded Joe's sigh, smiled at the unexpected backup from a snide Eileen, but was irate that no one had challenged LoBello's remark that the intelligence on the Appel campaign was faulty. "You realize that that was a direct criticism of me, that he's saying I didn't do my job, that son-of-a-bitch muscle-bound jerk."

"No one was taking him very seriously. Now, can we please talk about what's happening to you? You just can't pretend—"

"Enough. It's not necessary. Listen to me for a minute, Marcia. I told Bill that Appel would be announcing before May first. I couldn't say when because before I could get any more information, he sent me up to goddamn Buffalo. But my source was good."

"Who was it?"

"Appel's wife's best friend."

"A woman?"

"Sure. She hangs out at this bar in Monticello. The county chairman introduced me to her. Her husband's a big real-estate guy up there and a buddy of Appel's."

"Doesn't he mind that she hangs around in a bar?"

"How the hell should I know? Maybe he's glad to be rid of her. She's a real hard drinker. But she is a lot of fun, and I guess she keeps Appel's wife amused with her stories about the men she scores with. Anyhow, I bought her a few rounds and it turns out she's one of these smart alcoholics. You know, half whacko, never sober, but doesn't miss a move. Well, turns out she hates Appel, thinks he's the meanest son-of-a-bitch on wheels. Anyway, she knows that Appel's been cheating for years and using her friend's inheritance not just to bankroll his own projects but to buy trinkets for his little cuties. He seems to like high school girls who like sports cars. He never touches anyone over seventeen. So just to even the score for Mrs. Appel, she's reporting everything she can find out."

"Does Mrs. Appel know she's talking to you?"

"No. Of course not."

"So theoretically she—"

"Marcia, you know there's nothing theoretical about a Democratic primary."

"Did she make a play for you?" I was standing next to the bed and leaned over to gaze directly at him. "How come she was so willing to confide in you? I mean, you were a near stranger, a man—"

"Stop it," he said sharply. I averted my head. "Marcia, it was the kind of knee-jerk flirtation that type goes through whenever she meets someone new, just to keep in practice." I glanced back in time to see him passing his tongue over his lips.

Jerry lived in a tempting world, a universe of candy and cookies and ice cream, and although he seemed content with the sweets he got from me, he could, at any time, grab an extra little yummy without a thought: a bite from a rum-soaked bonbon in the Catskills. Every once in a while, I'd suspect he took such a nibble; but then I'd shrug off my suspicions. I had no proof, no clue, not even a hint. It could be my own fears projected onto him. Besides. what could I do about it? So much sex was offered to Jerry that he could—at least theoretically—take on a woman with no more thought than he would give to accepting a stick of gum. Tasty. Thank you.

Naturally, sex was available to me too. There was always a Jack to play to my Jill, at least for a night. But the men I met were interested in mere coupling, a woman to provide the requisite friction. I knew from experience how tempting it would seem and how trivial or how humiliating it could be.

But with Jerry, the ladies wanted more than mere sex. They wanted to play and please. They wanted to poke their fingertips into the cleft in his chin and giggle. They wanted to feel his heat and see how much hair he had on his chest. They wanted to chat. They would present themselves forward or backward or upside down to get his attention. For a wink they would iron his shirts. For a smile and an afterwork hug, they would schlepp his groceries a mile. They might kill for a serious conversation.

He reached for my hand. "I hate to tell you this."

"What?"

"The jar is full. It got boring here alone so I spent the whole morning peeing."

"That's okay." I lifted the jar, recently for mayonnaise,

and took it into the bathroom. I emptied it and then stood still, a little uncertain about how to handle the problem of jar, hands, and lunch.

Jerry called, "Bring the jar here, then go back and wash your hands."

I did and then returned to the side of the bed. "You're a born executive, Jerry." I brushed the hair off his forehead. "Want lunch?"

"Sure. It'll be the high point of my day. What's on the menu?"

"Anything. I have to run out to the store, so I can get whatever you want. And don't worry, I still remember how to cook."

"Anything?"

"Well, I'm not going to make beef Wellington."

"What's that?" he asked suspiciously.

"Never mind. What do you want."

"Scrambled eggs and sausages."

"For lunch?"

"Okay. Peanut butter and jelly."

"Don't you want something more interesting? A salade niçoise? A nice roast beef sandwich?"

"Marcia, what do you want to make me for lunch?"

"A fines herbes omelet?"

"I can just hear your little domesticated motor humming."

"Then you're hallucinating. Listen, how about some cheese and pâté and I'll get a French bread and some wine. Red or white?"

"Red. And I want you back soon." I leaned over and kissed his mouth. "Before my jar fills up again."

I dashed down the stairs and outside, clutching my keys and money in my fist, and strode over to Sixth Avenue with the anticipation and enthusiasm of a Washington hostess about to fete a British duke. "That brie is overripe," I accused one shopkeeper. I rejected another's selection of wine as uninspired. I wound up in a cold tiled store where the Greenwich Village rich shop and bought two pâtés—coarse and fine—two rich cream-logged cheeses from France, and a pale, thin blond one from Denmark. I picked out a long elegant French bread.

I went three blocks farther and finally found a store that sold me a blue-and-white checkered tablecloth. I would have bought daisies to strew on the bed, but, sensing that Jerry might construe any overtly romantic act as pressure, I scurried back to the apartment, the spring chill nipping at my arms and legs.

"A picnic!" I announced, spreading the cloth over the blanket that covered Jerry.

"Hey, this is really nice. What a fuss! I love it. I may become a professional invalid." I tucked a soft paper napkin under his chin and combed his hair back with my fingers. "Will you darn my socks for me too?" he asked.

"Invalids don't need socks. But I'll buy you coloring books and Hershey bars." I dragged two chairs in from the dining area, one for me, the other for the wineglasses.

"Marcia," he said, "this is inspired."

"Thank you." I sat on the chair next to him and reached over for a fast stroke of his hand.

"Do I get lunch too?" he asked.

"Yes, of course. You're just too distracting, lying there like that."

"Helpless."

"Stop it." I hurried into the kitchen and returned with the cheeses and pâtés on a cutting board. I discovered a pear in the refrigerator and placed it there, water-beaded and glistening, and tucked the French bread under my arm.

"You're trying to weaken my defenses with this homemaker routine," he said.

"Right. Pretty soon I'll make lace curtains for the living room, and maybe I'll buy a pair of his and her madonnas for our dressers. You'll be totally besotted, putty in my hands."

"You really wouldn't want that?"

"The only thing I want is lunch," I remarked, and tore off a piece of bread for him. "Watch out for the crumbs. Now, do you want me to fix up a plate for you?"

"Sure. I'm going to milk this thing for all it's worth." I cut small wedges of cheese, little squares of pâté, even broke his bread into bite-sized bits. Then, tilting the wineglass, I let him take tiny sips. "This has to be one of the best lunches of my life," he said. I leaned over and licked a crumb from his lip.

"Stand up," he said, a few minutes later. "Take off your clothes."

"It's too bright in here."

"Off." I did, but turned my back to him as I unhooked my bra.

"Come on. Turn around." I did, but with my arms hugged in front of me, as though I were cradling a litter of kittens. "Marcia, put your hands down." I felt the warm flush on my face seeping into my neck and shoulders. I was embarrassed. I knew Jerry knew my breasts were small, but I didn't want them viewed in bright afternoon sunlight. "Sweetheart, come on. Hands down."

I complied, but looked away from him while he studied me. He examined me for a long time, not speaking, not breathing hard, and I felt stiff with anxiety over whether I would pass his test, but also soft inside, moist and receptive to the helpless man in the bed who was controlling me.

"Come closer," he said at last. I stepped nearer, to the edge of the bed. I looked at him finally, but only at his hand; I could not meet his glance. His fingers reached out and began a feathery massage of my stomach. My muscles contracted in response. I placed my hand over his and tried to push it lower. "No, Marcia. Just stand there. Don't do anything." His light touch continued and finally his hand moved lower, but it was only to touch my legs, to run from my ankles slowly up my calves and all around my thighs. Each time I moved or tried to maneuver him, every time I moaned, he pulled his hand away.

He reached up, but the stretching made him wince. "Kneel on the floor," he ordered. He traced my midriff and chest and neck over and over, until my breasts began to ache from not being touched. Finally he caressed them too, but lightly, as though he were immune from the roughness of passion. His fingers then reached for my face, probing my ears, moving around and around my lips and inside my mouth, over my tongue. "Stand up now. Come on, Marcia." My knees wobbled and my legs shook a little, but I stood. "Open your eyes. That's right. Now look at me. Not down at the blanket. At me." I met his eyes, hard, cold, blue stars. He ran his hand across my hip but then withdrew it. "Keep looking at me. What are you going to do now?"

"What?" I whispered.

"My arm is tired. What are you going to do with yourself? Don't move. Stand there. What are you going to do?"

"What should I do?"

He didn't answer. His face remained somber, almost sullen.

"What do you want me to do?"

"Make yourself come, Marcia. That's it. Slower. Much slower. And keep looking at me." I watched him staring as my fingers worked. "Very nice." Then he looked up and merely blinked as he saw the tears in my eyes. "Come on. Finish up. Finish up. That's it." I continued, his eyes holding mine, until the final releasing shudder that let me close my eyes. But still I stood there, waiting for him to tell me what to do. "That was fine, wasn't it?" I nodded and began to turn away. "Come on now, sweetheart. Come into bed, under the covers. I want you next to me."

"Jerry," I said as I felt his warmth across the sheet.

"Touch me now. . . . Oh, that's wonderful."

Later I said "Jerry" again, after I had touched him to his satisfaction.

"Shhh. Close your eyes now. We'll have a nice long afternoon nap."

He slept until evening, occasionally letting his hand drift lightly over my bare skin in his sleep. "I love you," I whispered when I was certain he was in a deep dream.

Jerry wanted everything light. Just as he would not commit himself to marriage, so he would not enter into a liaison where he might be pushed out of control, even for only a half hour. Maybe it was his latent Catholicism, his sense of sin, his feeling that great sweats and orgasmic shrieks and purple teeth marks would not benefit his immortal soul. He may have held back from me, specifically, because he knew all about me. Jerry was a politician; it was his business to know people. I have no doubt that when I visited his office for my job interview, he knew with nearly as much precision as I the number of men I had slept with. It was not that he was inquisitive and loved gossip, although almost all politicians do. If he was hiring a speech writer for Paterno, he wanted to know about any potential kinks that might interfere with her work, any entangling alliances that might divide her loyalties. He had not been forced to ferret out the information. No doubt he knew about me just as I knew about him before I met him, by sitting back and letting late-afternoon chatter flow around him.

He was too sophisticated to be shocked by my level of post-Plotnick promiscuity, for it was certainly not unusual among the women he dealt with. And I don't think he recoiled at the thought of his friends, colleagues and adversaries who preceded him. I'd been around, and he took comfort in my ability to care for myself. We coupled casually. With me he had no fears about permanence or paternity. After three nights of drinking with the boys he would return to a receptive woman, diaphragm perpetually in place, always welcoming. He appreciated a woman who knew very well what other men had to offer.

But Jerry was conventional too. Even if he suddenly had dreams of picket fences and babies, he would have trouble trying to fulfill them with a fast woman by his side. He was too Irish to go the whole route with a divorced Jew with a racy past.

Perhaps he did not trust me. Why, indeed, should he give me his all when I might take up with a state assemblyman from Chinatown on a whim? Or when my family might finally succeed and convince me to run off with the first circumcised pharmacist who proposed?

But that evening was fine, and so was the next day. I lay beside him, talking, gazing at the black hairs rooted in the satiny white skin of his chest, making him meals and snacks, emptying his jar. He refused to discuss current events; Paterno, LoBello, his status in the campaign were classified objects. He wouldn't contemplate his future.

"We're not going to talk about any political shit," he announced.

"Do you think that by ignoring the problem it will go away?" I demanded, smoothing the blanket.

"No."

But since Jerry's definition of "political shit' 'applied only to the current campaign, we chatted about old battles and old flames. Since we both reckoned our personal history by public events, we thought of the two together. For me, 1969 had been a horror: Procaccino ran for mayor against Lindsay and I had run through Mitchell Rosten, Harlan Falkowitz, and Michael Smiley; all four campaigns were disastrous.

For Jerry, the campaigns were far more memorable than the cuties. He could report how each election district in Queens had voted in the 1968 Humphrey-Nixon contest, but all he really recalled about 1968's Joan O'Day was that she got sleepy by ten at night—a serious defect for a political operative—and that her sister had been a nun.

"Was she bright?" I asked, as if she were dead.

"Yes."

"Pretty?"

"Yes. But I think she was too short."

I, on the other hand, knew that Harlan Falkowitz was six foot two and three quarters, that Mitchell Rosten had the hairiest backside I'd ever seen, and that Michael Smiley was morose and hated his last name. If encouraged, I might have quoted entire conversations with Harlan or Mitchell or Michael—insipid as they were. But I wasn't encouraged. Jerry wanted to know Procaccino's media budget.

"Who remembers things like that?" I huffed.

"How could you forget something like that?" Jerry demanded.

"How could you forget whether Joan O'Day was short?"

"I said she was too short."

"You said you thought she was too short, not that she definitely was. And what is your definition of too short?"

"Shorter than you. Anyhow, why is Joan O'Day's height so important?"

"Because you were sleeping with her."

"We were lying down, for Christ's sake."

Jerry had had brief encounters and long love affairs. As far as I could gather, his ladies were all reasonably intelligent and passably pretty. There were no stars; he chose a councilman's clever secretary, a mayor's deputy assistant, a pollster's junior statistician. He kept away from the rare high achiever as he kept away from the nice girls Saint Agnes had been wanting him to meet for the last thirty years: sweet Moira or darling Maureen or lovely Mary who lived with her dear old mum in an apartment in the Bronx.

But his women seemed to be a frame around his life; the real picture for him was politics. And now the picture was out of focus.

By Sunday, he grew weary of proclaiming old triumphs.

The present was intolerable. And he couldn't look forward to anything. "I don't feel like talking," he said. But he was able to get out of bed by himself, although this was accomplished with complex, minute twists and low staccato grunts. He shaved, losing the rakish air that had been increasing proportionately with the length of his beard. He took a hot shower. I dried him.

"You smell like a lilac," I said softly, patting the backs of his legs.

"You're the one who buys this goddamn faggot soap," he barked.

I put the towel back on the rack. "What's wrong with you?"

"Nothing," he snapped again, reaching for the towel, folding it in half vertically, and placing it back on the rack. "Can't you do anything properly?"

"I'm going to get bagels."

"Aren't you going to help me back to bed?"

"Not if you talk that way."

"Oh, excuse me, princess. Believe me, I'd bow if I could."

"I know you're depressed, but you don't have to take it out on me."

"I'm not depressed."

"Of course you are. Admit it. You'd be abnormal if you weren't."

"All right. I'm abnormal. Does that make you happy? Or would you feel better if I was depressed?"

"Of course not. I'd feel better if you were happy."

"I'll be happy if you just lay off. I can manage by myself now." Naked, he shuffled toward the bed, his torso twisted, so in stance he resembled a comma. "All weekend you were hovering over me, playing nurse. Or mother. That's what you're really after, isn't it? I told you—"

"You were flat on your back, for God's sake! What should I have done, left you alone to starve and mess the sheets? You have no right to make those kinds of accusations when it was you—*you*, Jerry—who asked me to take care of you."

"Well, I can take care of myself now," he shouted, bracing himself with one hand on the night table. "When you go back to work tomorrow, you don't have to come home for lunch. I can manage myself."

"Is that what's bothering you? My going back to work tomorrow? Look, let's talk things over."

"Let's not talk things over. Is that the way you think problems are solved? By talk? Maybe it's your writing all those goddamn speeches, that you think problems can be solved with words. Let me tell you something, it's actions that count with me. If you think things will get better just by having a good heart-to-heart, you're living in a dream world, sister."

"Don't you think it would be more constructive to deal with your problems instead of attacking me?"

"You think I'm not dealing with them?"

"Well, Jerry, you haven't exactly confronted anyone."

"Well, Marcia, maybe I'm a little more knowledgeable about handling these things than you are. Did that ever occur to you? You sit playing with a typewriter all day while I'm managing people, making hard decisions. Do you think you could give me a little credit for being able to run my own life? Just a little, sweetheart? I don't ask for much. I know how much better at these things you are, but I like to try."

I slammed the bedroom door as I marched out, then strode around the living room several times. Finally, I sat on a floor pillow picking at my cuticles, waiting for him to call out an apology. I waited about ten minutes. There was only silence. I opened the bedroom door and asked, in a haughty Duchess of Windsor voice, "Do you want bagels?"

"No. Come in here, will you? I want to talk."

"What is it?"

"Come on. Sit down. I know you're mad at me."

"Of course I'm mad at you. I'm under control of your whims. One minute I'm taking my clothes off, the next minute you're throwing me out. I'm trying to help and you call me a princess and—"

"Let's have a proper talk."

"What do you want?"

He remained silent. His hands were folded prayer-fashion on his chest and he gazed at them.

"Look," I muttered, "I'll go out for the papers and bagels and maybe when I get back—"

"Have you given any thought to your—what's the best way to put it?—your status?"

"My status?"

"It seems to me it deserves some thought," he added.

"Yes," I said.

"Marcia, you've been with me long enough to understand these things. I just want to know where you stand."

"Jerry, I'm not sure I do understand. Please, what are you talking about?"

"Look, you know it's over." I stood immobile. "It can never be the same again. Not after Bill has gone the full route, publicly humiliated me."

"Oh."

"Even if he doesn't win the primary—and with Appel definitely in he may not—there would be no question of my ever going back. The basic trust is gone. I mean, even if LoBello leaves—and he will if Bill loses—I wouldn't consider going back."

"I see. You hadn't said anything."

"What was there to say? I knew you knew what my only alternative was. Why belabor the issue by talking about it?"

"Jerry, what are you going to do?"

"I'm going to lie here and rest my back, all the while collecting a salary. Then, when I don't look like a pretzel anymore, I'll get another job."

"What?"

"I don't know." He sounded bland, bored, as if contemplating switching to a new brand of toothpaste. His face, framed by the pillow, was pale, but now it was the pallor of the convalescent, not the anxious. "No more politics, that's for sure."

"What are you going to do? Jerry, I'm sorry, I don't want to sound a sour note, but you're forty-seven years old and you've been in politics all your life. What else—"

"I can sell insurance, real estate. I've got connections over the whole damn city. I can represent a union, some contractors' association. I can set myself up as an urban affairs expert, for Christ's sake, and get funded by one of those diddly-poop foundations. That's not the problem." He glanced from his hands over to me. "It's you I'm worried about."

"Me?"

"Yes, you. Look, for better or worse, you're associated with me. How long do you think LoBello's going to let you hang around?"

"What do you mean?"

"You know damn well what I mean. Do you think he's going to trust you?"

"Yes."

"Come on. You're talking like a kid, some wide-eyed, asshole reformer."

I sat on the edge of the bed. "I am talking," I said, finally starting to understand him, "like the professional I am."

"Okay."

"Okay, what?"

"Okay, if you have faith in your job security, let me be the first to congratulate you."

"You don't have to be sarcastic."

"I'm not being sarcastic, Marcia. I'm being realistic. Do you think LoBello and Bill are going to trust you, let you listen in when they're having a conference over some legislative matter, or—"

"Yes, goddamn it."

"Yes, if you start sleeping with little old Lyle again. Don't look surprised. The whole world knows."

I shifted my position on the bed. The mattress sank enough to cause Jerry some discomfort.

"All right," he said, seconds later. "I'm sorry."

I stared at the fuzz balls on the blanket and gave a sigh I could have learned only at my mother's knee.

"I said I'm sorry, Marcia. I can't crawl on the floor to beg your forgiveness or I would, okay?"

"You don't trust me," I said. "I don't believe it. You think I would . . ."

"Come on, sweetheart, You didn't come to bed with me dressed in white."

"Neither did you, Jerry, you goddamn hypocrite bastard. But that was your damn business and I don't go throwing it up in your face—"

"Look—"

"Just let me finish. Never, never one single time since the first time I slept with you have I even thought of sleeping with anyone else. I have been loyal. I have been true. I have been faithful. And I assumed you were the same. I never—"

"There are other kinds of loyalty, Marcia." He was using his noble Christian voice, patient and compassionate.

"Up yours."

"I said I apologize for the remark about the sex business. But you stay there, day after day, not saying a word to me."

"What kind of word do you want?" I yelled ."You refuse to discuss anything."

"You don't have to shout. I just want a word you're on my side."

"Whose side do you think I'm on?" I demanded.

"Your own."

"Oh, come on. Do you honestly think we're on different sides, Jerry?"

"As long as you're the speech writer for William Paterno, you are not on my side."

"What do you want me to do?"

"I don't want you to do anything. It has to come from within."

"You want me to quit? Is that it?"

"I want you to do what you think is right."

"How the hell do I know what's right? All I know is that I've been working since college and I'm good at it. I'm one of the best there is, damn it. What else would I do?"

"Come on. There are millions of jobs."

"Not decent speech-writing jobs. Not here in New York. You know that. What do you want me to do, quit Paterno and then get another job in Washington and say good-bye, shake your hand, and hope you'll think I did the right thing?"

"Well, it's interesting to see you've considered it and rejected the idea."

"Jerry, I'm just thinking aloud, for God's sake. You know how I feel about you. You know how upset I've been."

"But not upset enough to show your faith in me."

"If I were in hot water with Paterno, if my job were in jeopardy, would you quit to show your faith in me? Would you, Jerry? Or would you say 'Gee, poor Marcia' and keep right on working."

"Don't shit me, Marcia, and don't shit yourself. You know goddamn well if I offered you a wedding ring you'd quit in a minute. The only reason you're hanging on to your job so tight is that it's the only secure thing you have."

"Well, you've said it, haven't you. You want me to give up the one secure thing in my life just so you can have the pleasure of giving Bill Paterno a good hard kick in the pants. I think you stink, Jerry."

"Jesus, have you twisted things. I may be a lot of things, but I am not vindictive. And I don't use people. I just thought you ought to put things in perspective. You ought to look beyond this primary. How are you going to feel afterward?"

"After what?"

"You really don't understand, do you, Marcia?"

"What? What the hell do you want from me?" Jerry explained softly that he wanted only what I could give. "But what do you want me to give?" I demanded. "Do you want me to go in and resign? Is that the display of faith you need?" He said that faith was nothing you put up for display. "What are you talking about? Are you using some kind of Jesuit secret code, for God's sake? Speak to me. Tell me what you want." He would not. He told me he wanted to take a nap, he was tired, and would I please turn off the lights. If I wanted to read, could I do it in the living room so he wouldn't be disturbed by the rattle of pages turning.

12

Our adversary, Sidney Appel, announced his candidacy for governor of New York from beneath a flowering dogwood. He stood behind a row of microphones which reached toward him, like flowers in different stages of bloom seeking warmth or nourishment from his mouth.

His wife stood at his left. Political strategists hold differing views of a wife's position. Some say she should be on his right to show her importance: "She's my right hand." Others say the left, the wedding-band hand, is better, more clearly associated with marriage. Mrs. Appel wore a blue shirtwaist dress, appropriate for a country wife under a dogwood tree. Her expression was unreadable, although it might have been the late-afternoon Catskill sun in her eyes. Perhaps she was annoyed that, despite her cat-food millions, she was forced into a cotton dress when she could have been draped by Givenchy. Perhaps the cameras made her nervous. Maybe she didn't care. She could have been drugged.

On Appel's right was Senator Maryjo Beinstock, two years into her first term, wearing her usual sensible suit and, quite unsensibly, taking sides very early in the primary. Squinting through her thick glasses, she looked pleased with her decision though, pleased with Appel, with life, and with the television coverage. She was a liberal, a Reform Democrat. She and Paterno were polite to each other, but he had no reason to suspect she would back him. Yet he seemed upset, angry with her.

"Damn Maryjo," he spit out. We were standing in LoBello's office, in front of his color television, watching Appel declare. "Not even a courtesy call. She just marches out there wearing those goddamn eyeglasses of hers." Paterno, just back from an upstate swing, was trying on moods until he could find the right one. He had been pleased at the attention paid to him by the press, chagrined that the mayor of Utica would not endorse him, angered that the crowd at the Albany airport had been so sparse, delighted that the teachers' and the steamfitters' unions had come forth with hefty contributions, irate over Sunday dinner in Syracuse. "Could you believe it? Rare chicken," he had told me. "Disgusting. I almost threw up."

On each side of "the two best supporters a man could hope for" were arrayed Appel's backers and key staff people. His media director had obviously decreed that this was a simple plain-folks event. All of them—from Lowell Drutman, a normally pin-striped congressman, to Phoebe Nemo of the International Ladies Garment Workers Union, who generally preferred made-in-U.S.A. green sateen—were dressed as if about to choose partners for a square dance.

Rowena Hollander, who would head Appel's advance teams, actually wore a red bandanna over her short black hair. While this might have been acceptable on a teenager about to allemande right, it was odd-looking on a Smith alumna who hadn't seen nineteen since the days of the Army-McCarthy hearings.

"Hey, look at old Rowena," Lyle hooted. "Boy, does she look like a jerk."

She had advanced for every major New York Democratic candidate since Harriman, and her decision to take up the veil, so to speak, for Appel was disturbing. I noticed Paterno shift his dark eyes to his jeans-clad advance man, who looked hairy and frenzied, like an electronic guitarist. The young man had come under LoBello's aegis.

"Hey," the advance man said, hooting a little like his patron, "that Rowena's some trip." Paterno closed his bulgy eyes.

Appel pointed his finger at Paterno and demanded, "Do we want government by the weary?" Paterno opened his eyes. "Do we want our lives ruled by the heirs of Tammany Hall? The poet Wystan Hugh Auden once said . . ."

I said, "Peter Messing is doing his speeches."

"You're sure?" Paterno asked. I nodded. "A lot of old Kennedy faces there," he continued. "But none of the really top crew. Did you notice that, Marcia? The big guns are quiet."

"Bill, Peter Messing is heavy armament." Either Mrs. Appel's money or her husband's clout had convinced a lot of smart political operatives that this was a campaign where they could once again, in Peter Messing's words, seek a brighter day or work for a time of decency, of caring, among all peoples of this earth. Messing's speeches could have been written by a pocket calculator, but he traveled in the right circles. He went where the heavies went. I saw familiar faces, people who had been around since Robert Kennedy ran for the Senate in 1964, people who knew their way around New York far better than Lyle LoBello.

Appel's smooth elf face puckered a little. "I'm going to state the facts and I'm going to name names in this campaign . . . starting right now. Let's take our honorable governor, Mr. Lawrence Parker. I'm asking you, ladies and gentlemen, what has this man ever done? Just what has he done? Has he been a meaningful legislator? An executive? Has he ever met a payroll?"

"This is embarrassing," Paterno said. He backed away from the television set and leaned against a wall. LoBello went into reverse and wound up beside him. Paterno was uneasy because he sensed he was next. LoBello whispered to him, pointing with his head toward the door, obviously suggesting that Paterno might be more comfortable being pummeled in the privacy of his own office where the attack might be contained on a tiny black and white TV. But Paterno shook his head, showing the assembled staff that he was tough enough to take whatever glib criticism Appel might fire off.

"And City Council President Willian Paterno. His title says it all. *City* Council. William Paterno sure knows New York City."

William Paterno sure wasn't a cool country boy. He exploded. "That bum! That bastard! Did you hear him?"

"But what Mr. Paterno doesn't seem to understand is

that the five boroughs—as crucial as they are—do not make up a state. Urban specialists are fine, I'm not saying they're not. But why doesn't Mr. Paterno run for mayor? Why, may I ask, is he running for governor of the great and varied State of—"

"That little stinker was born in the Bronx!" Paterno roared. "Born. Raised. Listen to him. Noo Yawk. He ties a goddamn scarf around his neck and everyone's gonna believe he's a hillbilly? Announcing up there with a tree hanging over his head!"

"—but even if we wanted a big-city governor, is William Paterno the man? No. No. And no again. Paterno. Parker. They all come from that same old school: the College of Closed-Door Deals. And let me tell you something, ladies and gentlemen. On this very day you and I are paying dearly for some of those secret deals made by Professor Paterno and Professor Parker. . . ."

The door opened, and one of the fair-haired boys from upstate tiptoed in and tugged at my sleeve. His nearly invisible blond eyebrows were pulled together with concern, so I assumed it must be urgent. I slipped out of the room just as Lyle LoBello began a tight-throated chuckle, attempting to laugh off Sidney Appel. We were outside so I didn't see if Paterno could be persuaded to see the humor.

"You have an important phone call, Ms. Green," the kid said.

"From Jerry? Mr. Morrissey?" I asked, walking down the corridor and talking to the rug. When I tried to give Jerry a light kiss good-bye as I was leaving for work, he had averted his head and mumbled, "Leave me alone."

"Mr. Morrissey? No. It's some woman. It sounded really important."

He led me into a spacious room filled with long tables, probably left from salad days when the hotel had done a big catering business. The tables were loaded with petitions. A telephone, its receiver off the hook, rested on a windowsill.

"You want privacy, Ms. Green?" the kid asked.

"Yes," I said. He left. "Thank you," I called after him. "Hello."

"Darling, how are you?"

"Fine, Aunt Estelle."

"Good. I'm so glad."

"Is everything okay?"

"Yes. Of course. I just wanted to talk to you."

"Could I call you back? Another candidate, Sidney Appel, is declaring. He's—"

"I know who he is. His wife is from a very prominent German-Jewish family. Philip went to Harvard Law School, with a nephew of hers. They're a monied family, you know."

"Yes. Cat food."

"Marcia, they were originally investment bankers, and they happen to be accepted by Our Crowd."

"Their Crowd. Good, I'm really glad. Anyway, Appel is on TV right now."

"I'll only take a minute of your time, Marcia. I know it's your busy season, but you can see it all on the news tonight. They always run films of things like that. What I called to say is this: I know I sometimes have a tendency to be overbearing, and I want to apologize. I know you're going to say it's not necessary, but I want to get it off my chest."

"Okay."

"What's the point of holding things back? Especially with family. You lost your temper and maybe I would lose mine too, if I was in your shoes, not the same way, obviously, but we're of different generations. In any case, I just wanted to say a small 'I'm sorry' and also to thank you for coming to the Leventhals'. It meant a great deal to them."

"I'm glad."

"Lydia Leventhal said you were a dream, a doll. Sweet, polite. Not like the ones who can't look a person in the eye. Chewing gum."

"What ones?"

"Plenty of girls your age. And Butch. He was touched too. I think it was nice for him to have a contemporary there to talk to. Someone near his age."

"Well, I'm glad I could do—"

"Marcia, he's still there."

I peered around the room. It contained only petitions. "Who?"

"Butch. He's staying home for the next week or two, just to help Lydia settle into her new life."

"Very considerate."

"He always was. You might consider giving him a call, you know. I know he's impressed with your important job. He won't go out with just anyone, like secretaries or teachers. Only girls with important careers."

"I don't want to call him, Aunt Estelle."

"You know, I really can't understand your attitude. On one hand you're the modern girl, and then you stand on ceremony. Look, darling, you know and I know that ten–fifteen years ago I never would have suggested the girl calling the boy. But we're living in a different world now."

"It's not that I'm standing on ceremony Aunt Estelle. I told you, I tried to tell you, he wasn't for me. I didn't like him."

"Marcia, are you sure in your own mind that you really didn't like him or was it a reaction against us? You know what I mean. You felt your mother and I were putting on the pressure, so you made up your mind that under no circumstances was Butch Leventhal going to—"

"Aunt Estelle," I said slowly. "I did not like him at all."

"All right. Your tastes are your own. It's just too bad. He's free. Available. Comfortable. His wife was like you, one of those who wouldn't accept alimony. Very independent, she was. And I know he'd like to hear from you. I mean, how often do two intelligent—"

"No, Aunt Estelle."

"Can I ask you something?"

"What?"

"Marcia, I hope you won't take offense. Is it because you had that miscarriage? Is it?"

"What?"

"Because it can happen, darling. It happened to me before Kenny was born. I've never told you that, but it happened. It's nature's way. It doesn't mean there's anything wrong with you. You can still get married and have children."

"Aunt Estelle, I have to go."

"I know. I'm sorry if I upset you ugain. But Marcia, you're thirty-five years old. You still have time to make a life for yourself. Look ahead. Someday you'll be forty. Fifty. What do you want for yourself?"

"Not Butch Leventhal, I thought a moment later, meandering around the petition room. I came to a table with a large oak-tag sign taped to it saying GREENE COUNTY. There were not many petitions on it, but the one I picked up had names like Simon Flood and J. Maureen Turner and Eulalie Benson. Why shouldn't I pick up and move to Greene County, buy a little frame house or a big frame house, depending on the Greene County real estate market, and settle in before I hit forty? Fifty. Get a job with WGRN, the voice of Greene County, as their political analyst or sell mitten clips at the five and ten. Maybe Simon Flood would ask me out. Conversely, maybe Simon Flood would burn a cross on my lawn, but J. Maureen, a hotshot lawyer for the Greene County ACLU, could come running to protect my rights, and Eulalie Benson would invite me over to apologize for Mad Simon and to share her dinner of red-flannel hash. She would tell me how much she admired the Old Testament.

"Do you want to tell me what you're doing in here, Marcia?" Lyle LoBello's voice was calm, but since he flared his nostrils at me, he was either aroused or angry.

"I had a phone call."

"And now? Checking how the petition drive is going?"

"I'll ask you for a hall pass the next time I leave the room."

"A little sarcastic, aren't you?"

"Lyle, come on. Let's forget it. Is Appel finished speaking?"

"Yes. What were you doing here? Don't you think it's important to hear him? Take notes?"

"I'll listen to the news tonight. I don't take notes for something like that."

"Debbie Drake always did." She had been one of Gresham's speech writers. "No matter where she was, she always had a little spiral notebook and a pen. And let me remind you that despite your loyalty to your boyfriend, I'm the one who's in charge."

"So hire Debbie Drake."

"I didn't say that, Marcia."

"You want Bill to sound like he's running in California, hire Debbie. He can go on television and say, 'Hey, I want to share my feelings with you.' Why in God's name she needs a notebook when she writes like that I'll never know."

"That's not funny, Marcia. Now listen, you and I have to talk."

"Okay."

"Not here. After work."

"No, Lyle."

"Hey. Come on. Do you really think I'd try anything?" His nostrils flared again. "Marcia, what happened with us happened a long time ago. All right, I kid about it every now and then, but you know I respect you. I won't get frisky." Frisky was a word he must have picked up from Gresham. It made lust sound snub-nosed. Lyle could no more frisk than he could gambol or romp. "Listen, we're colleagues now. Trust me."

"What's it about, Lyle?"

"Speech-writing. Hey, Marcia, I'm serious. Even if I had ideas, and I don't, I wouldn't mess around because of Morrissey and because you're too important now. Anyway, I go for the young ones. You know that. So come on, have a drink with me. I swear, no male chauvinist passes. I'll let you pick up the check if you want to. Anything."

"You can pay."

"About seven? Meet me in my office, okay?"

I didn't want to call Jerry because I was almost paralyzed by his coldness. Each icy interchange froze something between us. But I began to worry about his back, imagined him screaming in pain, being ignored by all Greenwich Village, so I phoned. "Do you need anything?" I asked, using an aloof Department of Social Services voice.

"No thank you."

"Would you like me to bring you a sandwich for dinner?"

"It's not necessary."

"All right. See you later."

He hung up the phone.

"Marcia!" Lyle seemed delighted to see me, and I realized that half his joy was that our being seen together would be construed as an alliance of one sort or another. He kept smiling as we walked down the dark, shabby corridor of headquarters. At least five people, including Joe Cole and Paterno himself, saw us leaving together. Since I was dragging around a weighty attaché case, a handbag, and a sweater, there was no way I could pretend I was on my way to the Xerox. And it was clear that Lyle was also on his way out because he was wearing a hat—his latest piece of Protestant haberdashery—which seemed to have been made from a soiled raincoat.

Paterno met us as he was leaving the men's room, pushing the door open with his elbow so as not to break sterility, his just-washed hands red and still damp looking.

"Hey, Bill," Lyle crowed, "you caught us! We were just sneaking out of here for a drink."

Joe Cole nipped by us as we waited for the elevator. Lyle put his hand on my shoulder, a gesture that could be interpreted as the boundary of friendship or the door to romance. "Night, Joe," he called out.

Although there were at least two bars and three cocktail lounges within a block radius, Lyle led me on a half-mile sprint through the lazy spring twilight to what he hinted was the chic-est bar in New York, known only to high-ranking U.N. diplomats and high-fashion models. It was a dark place and mirrored, the walls lined with banquettes so thickly upholstered in blood-red wool that they were more suitable for a snooze than a chat. We were the only patrons.

"Hi," he said to me, after the waitress disappeared into the darkness that gave birth to her, carrying our order. "How's it going?"

"How's what going?" I snapped. Each time I looked at Lyle, I saw a familiar face beyond him, like the face of someone I went to high school with. Although I realized after a moment it was my own reflection, it was disconcerting, because the mirror image looked younger and more attractive and might, at any moment, walk over and tell me how happily married she was or recommend a good hairdresser.

"Marcia, take it easy. I gave you my word of honor, didn't I?"

I made myself peer at the bridge of Lyle LoBello's nose, so he would know I was unafraid of eye contact and so that I would not be distracted by the woman in the mirror. Lyle peered at me too, but lower, at my mouth or maybe my chin, and kept talking.

"I promised I'd be a good boy, and I keep my promises."

"What did you want to talk about?" My skirt was pulled up under me. The wool seat irritated the backs of my thighs.

"About us. Listen. . . ."

The waitress seemed to be curtseying before us, acknowledging Lyle's sexuality, but then I realized she was just bending her knees to lower herself as she set the drinks on the table. "One white wine spritzer," she told me. And, turning to Lyle, "And one champagne cocktail for the gentleman." In exchange, she got a quick wink.

"Where was I?" Lyle demanded.

"You wanted to talk," I replied, lowering my head to study my drink. The bubbles seemed unusually large and rose languorously to the surface.

"Look at me," he said. I did, pulling my eyes from the magnetic mole under his eye back to the bridge of his nose. "Tell me the truth. Do I look like a bad guy? Do I, Marcia? Because you're treating me like I was one, and it hurts. It really hurts."

I went back on carbonation patrol, staring at my drink.

"Here I am," he continued, "a virtual stranger in the midst of friends, and instead of making me welcome, you set the tone and I'm treated like I'm an enemy."

"What did I do?" I asked.

"You were snotty at the staff meeting."

"Lyle, for God's sake. I just told you I was leaving early."

"You set everybody off. They were just waiting for a signal from you."

"That's ridiculous."

"It is not. Here I am, trying to run a campaign that your boy friend fucked up and—"

"He did what?"

"You heard me. His contacts upstate are older than whatever his name is, that old guy in the Bible."

"Methuselah."

"Right. Come on, Marcia, what choice did Bill have? I'm not saying this to hurt you. Jerry Morrissey is a very valuable guy. I wouldn't make a move in the city without consulting him. But on a statewide basis? Look, we both know there's a whole generation up there that your boyfriend hasn't even been introduced to. I'm talking about powerful people, Marcia. People who can help Bill."

"Then how come Sidney Appel was able to get such a lineup today?"

"What do you mean?"

"All the old Kennedy people. Maryjo Beinstock. They all came out for Jim Gresham. Why couldn't you get them for Bill?"

"I don't understand you. Maryjo's an ultra-liberal."

"She went for Gresham."

"Jim could make liberal noises."

"So? Why aren't you teaching Bill to make them? What's your value, Lyle? Why are you here? You were supposed to pull in the upstate heavies, and all anyone's seen is one senile county chairman and four or five of your old buddies on the payroll."

He caressed the rim of his glass. "Didn't anyone ever tell you, Marcia, that it doesn't pay to make enemies? Didn't anyone? Because what you are doing here tonight is so fucking stupid that I cannot believe it. Here I am, giving you the opportunity to save yourself, to keep your job, and—"

"Who's going to fire me, you? Do you think Bill would go for that?"

"He'll go for what I say is good for the campaign."

"Crap."

"You shouldn't talk like that. Listen to me, Marcia, you're so goddamn smart. You get canned now, where will you be? Who's going to hire you if I make thumbs down? And what would you do for money? You went off the city payroll, and you haven't been working for the campaign long enough to get unemployment, so what are you gonna do?"

I forced my mind to move from fear to consciousness. I thought, I have been in politics for fifteen years. I said, "Double crap. Let me tell you a couple of things, Lyle. One is that Bill is not going to fire me. He knows damn well if I go he'll wind up with one of your creeps who'll make him sound like a cocaine pusher, and Bill and I have spent too much time working to make him sound like he's a cross between Leonardo da Vinci and Al Smith to throw it away. He speaks my language. Do you understand me?"

"Bullshit, Marcia. And I'm telling you, this is your last warning."

"And two is that you are in no position to be making grandstand plays. You've got to pull this campaign off, and you need all the help you can get."

"From you?"

"From me and wherever else you can get it. Come on, Lyle. Half the support you counted on went to Parker because he's the incumbent."

"You come on, Marcia. A couple of old farts who couldn't even bring in their own election districts went to Parker, that's who. I've brought in a hell of a lot more support than your boyfriend could have."

"And the other half you counted on, the important half, is drifting to Appel. Mrs. Appel's money can buy the best, Lyle. The campaign has hardly started and already—"

"You're a real cunt, Marcia."

"You're interrupting me, Lyle. I was saying you're in big trouble even now. You promised Bill you'd bring in all of Gresham's people."

"I did not."

"All right, most of them. But you forgot one thing. Gresham is dead. D-e-a-d. Thereby out of office. You have no clout anymore, Lyle, Your padrone choked to death on a liver knish, and you are fucked."

"The check," he hissed into the darkness. He turned his head away, but I could hear him breathing heavily. Minutes went by. Then he looked at me again and said, "I guess you don't want to be friends."

"I guess not."

"I don't understand you, Marcia. Here I offer you my hand in friendship, show you I'm willing to let bygones be bygones, and what do I get? A slap in the face. Here I am, busting my chops to run a decent primary fight, and you're sabotaging me at every turn. I can't follow you, Marcia. I've tried to be a friend to you."

"Is that why you called me a cunt?"

"Come on. Even friends get mad. And I've been a gentleman. No one's heard from me what I got from you." The waitress put the check on the table. Lyle grabbed for it and knocked his champagne over, soaking his hand, his shirt cuff, and the check and making a small lake of champagne in the ashtray. "Goddamn it. Give me a napkin." I handed him the tiny square that had been sitting under my wine. "What was I saying?"

"Good night, Lyle."

I tried to telephone Jerry from a phone booth just outside the bar, but I was again reflected darkly and afraid that Lyle would see me on his way out and begin his assault again, so I decided to walk a few blocks to a phone booth. But once outside, away from the spooky loneliness of the bar—the U.N. diplomats and high-fashion models had obviously found a more chic place to toast each other —I felt too tired to risk another confrontation right away. So I kept walking uptown, through the rich, warm spring night, past couples lured outside by starlight, entwined together, kissing each other's ears or biting each other's lips, while pausing for the light to change or waiting for that final rush of blood that would send them hurtling home into bed.

I wound up in front of Eileen's building. The stone urns on either side of the front door were filled with white and purple hyacinths. I inhaled, wanting to put down my attaché case and handbag and bury my face in their scent.

"Yes?" demanded the doorman.

"Ms. Gerrity," I said, before I could decide whether or not to disturb her.

"Anything wrong?" she asked as she opened her apartment door. She wore a long pink robe of some expensive-looking silky fiber. Her white-blond hair was loose on her shoulders.

"I'm sorry. I didn't realize you'd have company. I'll speak to you tomorrow."

"Marcia," she said, opening the door wider, "you're behaving very strangely. Who would be here on a work night? Come on in." I passed by her, feeling slightly shocked by the private Eileen, dressed in an elegant robe, her hair let down.

"Are you expecting someone?"

"Yes. Six men are due any minute to serenade me on the lute. But meanwhile, sit down. Maybe I can spare one. Now, what's happening? Naturally, I'm glad to see you, but it's not like you just to drop in."

"I can't go home. I don't know how to deal with Jerry."

"What do you mean?"

"We had a fight."

She said nothing but swept over to a small brass and glass cart and, from a silver ice bucket, took a handful of cubes and dropped them into a glass.

"Are you sure no one else is coming?" I asked.

"Yes. Why do you keep asking that?"

"Because you're so—so prepared. Your ice bucket is full."

"Of course it's full. I generally have a drink."

"But don't you think most people would just go to the freezer, grab a few cubes, and dump them into a glass?"

"They might, but this is nicer. Now, what happened between you and Golden Boy?"

"Eileen, he's so hurt."

"He should be. Keep talking."

"He really seems to need me now."

"I'm sure he does."

"Are you being sarcastic?"

"No. I'm sure he needs you. Would you like a drink?" I nodded. She poured some white wine over the ice cubes. "How, specifically, did he express his need for you, Marcia?"

"What do you mean?"

"Does he want you to sit at his bedside? Meet his darlin' mother in the Bronx? Run away to—"

"He wants me to quit."

"Classic."

"It's not as simple as it sounds."

"I'm sure it's absolutely laden with ambiguity, Marcia. It's just that on the surface it sounds as if he's using you."

"That's not fair. He's upset, threatened. And I think it's important to him that I show my faith."

"And then what?" she barked. "You show your faith, he'll show his? Don't just let things drift by. Analyze them. What will happen if you threaten to quit your job?"

"I don't know."

"Neither do I. But I have a feeling that Bill is already committed—for better or worse—to Lyle LoBello. He may be starting to regret his decision, but it's a fait accompli. So unless you're big on making fruitless gestures, hang on to your paycheck."

"I hope I can." I told her of my fight with LoBello at the cocktail lounge. She listened, sipping her wine and tapping her bare feet on the floor. The light caught the clear polish on her toes and sent off twinkly sparkles. "Wouldn't it be the ultimate irony if I wound up getting fired because of whom I went to bed with? I mean, here I am, one of the best-known political speech writers in this part of the country, and I get the ax because first I was stupid enough to sleep with Lyle and then besotted enough to move in with Jerry. Wouldn't that be something? Both of them, Lyle and Jerry, know my capabilities—I mean, out of bed. But all the games they're playing have absolutely nothing to do with my writing. It has to do with my sex. I can't believe it."

"Believe it."

"What am I going to do, Eileen?"

"What do you mean? What do you want to do? Quit?"

"No."

"Then go to work. Write your speeches. You'll ride this out. Nothing's going to happen. You saw that tonight. Lyle LoBello's running scared, and he's not going to antagonize Bill by getting rid of another of his old staff, especially someone Bill is really comfortable with. LoBello will let you stay on as long as you don't make a horrendous fuss or cause him any more embarrassment. He has too many problems to worry about to afford a showdown with you."

"But if I stay on, Jerry will view it as an act of faithlessness."

"What is he, the Grand Inquisitor?"

"Come on, Eileen. He needs a friend."

"Friends don't need proof of faith. God, this gets me so angry. He is so incredibly selfish. What kind of faith is he offering you? What will he give you?"

"I'm not asking for anything."

"You sound positively Christian, Marcia. Next you'll be wanting to die for the Immaculate Conception. Now be serious. What is he offering you? Love? Marriage? Would he marry you to show his faith and loyalty?"

"He's not interested in marriage."

"They never are. But you are. Come on, don't shake your head. You can't throw off your background any more than he can his. But you're fighting your inclinations because you're fighting your family. That's self-defeating. Tell them to take a walk if you have to, but at least give yourself the chance to make a real life for yourself."

"What about you, are you interested in a real life?"

Eileen lifted her hair from her shoulders and let it drop again. "I'm not averse to marriage. But I come from a very conventional Irish Catholic background, and for someone like me, marriage is a jail. Wives are chained inside a house until their deaths. Wives are boring. To themselves. To their husbands, God knows. I know intellectually that it doesn't have to be that way, but I'm still afraid of it. Even of having children. Pregnancy is like being imprisoned from within instead of from without. I just hope all these feelings will pass and I'll be able to approach the subject more calmly.

"But calm or not calm, I can understand Jerry Morrissey. Don't you see, he's the other side of the same coin. And marriage is a trap for him too."

"So why aren't you more sympathetic to him?"

"Because he's a man, damn it. Because he can go home to his mother's house and have everyone make a fuss over him, praise him, adore him. He's considered a wonderful, complete human being. I go home and they talk about this girl or that girl I went to high school with, and how many children they have, what their husbands are doing. Nothing I've accomplished—Phi Bete in college, law school, my job—is worth anything to them."

"But Jerry has that too. He's told me that every once in a while his mother lets him know that she really expected more from him. I mean, politicians aren't up to her lofty moral standards. Minimally he should have been a hot shot in the Jesuits or a partner in a Wall Street law firm. Her perfect, brilliant, adorable Gerald is taking orders from some pol. An Italian pol, no less. She lets him know—very subtly—that she's a wee bit disappointed."

"But he just didn't measure up. She still idolizes him. My parents view me as unnatural, denying my nature by refusing to marry and have a thousand children. It's not that they just don't idolize me. It's that they view me as defective." She paused and inhaled deeply. "Understand, Marcia, that my reaction to them is completely irrational."

"If I can't understand that, no one can."

"But I'll tell you what is rational. Time. I'm thirty. I still have a few more years to come to grips with my fears. But you don't have that luxury anymore, not if you want children."

"I'm not even sure I would ever want to marry again."

She set her wineglass on the coffee table and leaned forward toward me. "Well, let's hope you don't want marriage because . . . what was your husband's name?"

"Barry. You know that."

"His last name."

"Plotnick."

"That alone is grounds for divorce in some states. But understand one thing. You will never be Marcia Green Plotnick Green Morrissey."

"You sound very positive."

"I am. Even if some inexplicable transformation occurred and Jerry decided a wife was a brilliant idea, he'd wind up with some soft-spoken, sincere little thing with red hair and thick ankles."

"My ankles aren't thin."

"But they're not thick, Marcia. Nowhere near thick enough." She lifted her glass. "Keep your job."

13

No one was nice to me in June except my family. More precisely, my cousin Barbara was the only one who seemed to care that I was sad and frightened. Everyone else was too busy.

Paterno, to start with, was in a foul mood. The success of Sidney Appel's ads enraged him, so he'd bluster at me. "Did you see his ad last night on Channel Four? Did you, Marcia?" His small fist crashed down on his desk. "What the hell does it mean? It was crazy! Stupid!"

Appel was running hundreds of thousands of dollars of ads, all with his logo: an apple which would split in two. Each half apple would serve as a screen for filmed vignettes of New York life. And a deep Jehovah voice-over would intone, "Sidney Appel knows the State of New York." Or the state of New York. By the middle of the month, Paterno could get cranky simply by passing a fruit stand.

"It's nuts," he'd sputter. "They take out the pits and put in movies of Niagara Falls and kids playing basketball. Does he think anyone's going to vote for that tazia?" But there was a tight edge to his voice when he spoke to me that had never been there before. I was his liaison with his advertising agency. I was his writer. I should have thought to do a split-screen presentation on an artichoke heart. When I handed him a new speech, he did not say thank you.

Three weeks after his television ads began, Appel's recognition factor soared from a pathetic 2.5 percent to 23 percent. It continued rising, as did Paterno's, but in a far more dazzling fashion. On the subways, I began to notice Appel's little elf face more and more; it was superimposed on a Red Delicious which in turn rested on the white background of a campaign button: the button was pinned on a surprisingly large number of lapels.

"And don't give me another one of those damn artsy speeches about New York intelligentsia," Paterno snorted at me. "No one cares about intelligentsia. No one can even pronounce it."

Ms. Green, a memo would begin. *Mr. LoBello has requested you pay further attention to developing new situations that have intense visual appeal and asks that you convey such information to his assistant, Ms. Kimmy Danoff.* As the flow of contributions began to slow, Lyle began demanding I dream up gimmicks that would get Paterno free television time on the news. But Lyle would not deal with me directly, even in writing, so I sent a short memo to Ms. Danoff suggesting Paterno stand on the banks of the polluted East River holding a dead flounder.

Ms. Green: Mr. LoBello suggests that, unfortunately, there is little time for levity in a primary campaign.

"Why go out of your way to antagonize him?" Eileen asked. "Never mind. Don't even bother answering. I don't have time to listen." Nor to look. I sat opposite her desk while she whizzed through piles of yellow papers, not even glancing at me. "I'm no longer a human being," she muttered, her pale hair askew, falling out of the barrettes that held it. She clutched a lawbook, leafed through it, leaned back on her chair, and closed her eyes. "It's never been this hideous," she added.

"I'll speak to you tomorrow," I suggested. "When you have more time. Okay?"

"Tomorrow will be even worse. I have to be in court at nine o'clock." Eileen was spending June in three-piece linen suits, challenging the validity of Appel's petitions. "It's unspeakable. His lawyer is a screamer. 'May it please the court,' " Eileen imitated, shrieking, " 'there is a presumption of regularity here, Your Honor!' Do you know what it's like to have to listen to that? For hours and hours and days and days to that crazy, high-pitched voice. He sounds like a hysterical eunuch. Forget what I said. I should have gotten married. Spend the day talking to a mop. Anything. Anything but this."

"Would you drop into my office when you get the chance?"

"Sure," she said. "Next month. Sorry, Marcia."

Jerry spent the beginning of June in bed. Occasionally he spoke to me. "You look tired."

"I am tired," I began, kneeling to pick up the sections of the *New York Times* he had dropped to the floor. "It's beyond the usual campaign fatigue. There's an aura—"

"I really don't want to hear about auras."

It was a warm evening and he lay without clothes on, covered to his chest with a light blanket. His left arm was lying limply behind his head, and his underarm hair was separated into dark, damp strands. I stroked it with my palm, taking up his sweat.

"Stop it," he snapped. "It's annoying."

"Sorry."

"Where are you going now?"

"Inside. I'm going to watch the news. I'll tell you if anything interesting—"

"I haven't eaten all day."

He turned his head away as though I were saying something excruciatingly boring that he couldn't bear to hear.

"All right, Jerry. What would you like? A sandwich? An egg or something?"

"For dinner? It's six o'clock. I told you if you didn't want to bother, my sister could take me in."

"How about a veal chop?"

"All right." The silver hair at his temples blended into the pillow, so it appeared to be a part of him.

Jerry slept stiffly each night, as though his body were concentrating all its resources on healing itself, so it could escape. Occasionally he would grunt and it would sound more sexual than painful, but when I would reach over to him, he would shake off my touch.

Awake, he wanted neither kisses nor cuddling nor succor of any sort. When I undressed, he'd close his eyes or pick up a newspaper.

On what turned out to be the final night of Jerry's invalidism, we lay in the dark bedroom. Since he did not want to talk, I listened to his breathing, trying to analyze it for signs of sleep or sadness or anger. But it was just inhale, exhale, inhale, over and over, with not even a snort for me to interpret. The evening had cooled, but I did not want to grab more blanket for fear of annoying him, and I did not want to get up and get a nightgown for fear of signaling defeat. Like Jerry, I had begun sleeping naked, perhaps trying to test the depth of his indifference, or maybe hoping that his body would be a heat-seeking object, attracted to my warmth the way I was to his.

Finally he spoke to me. "Come here."

I eased across the bed so as not to jiggle the mattress, feeling how chilly and stiff the sheets were that stretched between us. Pulling close, nearly touching him, I sniffed his body, bitter and pungent from lying in anger, and it made me want him more. I stretched myself along his side, feeling the hot skin of his side and hips and thigh. I was ready to dissolve into him in reconciliation.

But Jerry wanted only a limited merger. "Get on top," he said. "It's easier." I did. I bent over, my tongue peering out in the darkness, searching for his mouth. But he just put his hands on my breasts and rubbed, a routine, impersonal male feel. Then he rolled and squeezed my nipples between his thumb and index finger with the detachment of a biologist noting the responses of a new specimen. "I'm ready," he said a moment later. Slowly I lowered myself onto him and slid down carefully. I wanted to prolong that first moment of entry. And I wanted to move lightly, so the result of the union would be melting pleasure for him, not traction. I moved in easy circles and listened for him to call out in the dark, to groan a deep "oh" or moan "Marcia." But he lay mute and still, letting me pace my own ride. And then, as I began to go faster, back and forth, leaning forward, closer to him and nearer to my goal, he finished unexpectedly in silence, with a sudden gush of hot juice. "Okay," he said, his voice conversational, and I sat on him, stunned as he shrank away. "Thanks. You can get off now." He put his hands on my waist and gave a light shove. "See you tomorrow," he said, as we lay in the dark again, apart.

In the morning, he banged on the bathroom door. "Please get a move on," he called.

My grip on the toothbrush tightened. I yanked open the door. "I thought you'd still be in bed," I managed to say through a foam of toothpaste. "Do you want breakfast before I go?"

"I'm going too," he said. "I need the bathroom. And I'll need some help with my socks and shoes."

"You didn't say you were going to the office," I remarked later, trying to maneuver the sock over his heel without breaking his ankle. "Because Bill is out of town. I didn't mention it because you weren't in a talking mood, but he's on an upstate—"

"I know."

"Oh. I thought if you wanted to speak with him personally, about leaving, that you wouldn't want to make the trip uptown and only find LoBello there. That's why I mentioned it."

"I'm not going to headquarters. I'm meeting Bill in Rochester this afternoon."

"To tell him?"

"No."

"You're staying on?"

"For now."

"Why didn't you tell me?"

"I guess it slipped my mind." He glanced down, at his sock, not at me. "I'll wear the brown loafers."

"When will you be back?"

"How would I know?" While I stood to get his loafers, he filled his pockets with coins, keys, handkerchiefs, a billfold. "Now come on," he said. I stood before his closet, shaking. "No scenes. I mean it, Marcia. This is my affair. Don't keep trying to inject yourself into the middle of my life."

"What's happening?" I whispered.

"Why are you being so melodramatic?" he asked and brushed me aside. "I have a nine o'clock plane to catch. I'll manage my own shoes."

He did manage his loafers, but I had to fetch his suitcase since it was on the floor of his closet, way in the back, under his sneakers and boots. As I handed it to him, his mouth twisted a little in annoyance. Now he had to speak again.

"Thank you," he muttered and then began packing, slapping down precise piles of shirts and underwear, smoothing long ribbons of ties over them. He filled one corner with political mint mouthwash. Another he stuffed with a very social, special-occasion English Fern cologne.

After those days and nights watching him lie in bed naked, magnetic, faintly animal, I was stunned to see his civilized magic again. I had forgotten how seductive he could be in a white shirt and tie. Jerry's panache had remained intact. The stewardess's smile would turn genuine as he boarded the plane. I began to cry.

"I can't believe you're carrying on like this," he said as I followed him to the door, tears pouring down my face. "This isn't the first time I've been away."

"Jerry," I managed to say, "can't we talk straight to each other?"

"See you," he said and marched out the door.

A few minutes later, still weepy, I called my cousin Barbara, telling her it would be nice if we could talk.

"Don't cry, Marcia," she said, pressing a handkerchief into my hand. She had dashed into Manhattan from Long Island without even inquiring what I wanted to talk about. I patted my eyes with her monogram, letting the big D of Drexler absorb most of my sadness. "Why am I saying that?" she asked. "That's stupid. Go ahead. Cry."

"Not here." I glanced around the restaurant where she had suggested we meet. The waiters were all formally dressed. The silverware was etched with a coat of arms. I tucked the handkerchief into my sleeve. I tore my roll in half.

"Don't be silly. Ridiculous, pretentious place. Look at them," she said, motioning her head to the busboys, who wore footmen's uniforms. "They look like Cinderella's mice." She smiled and patted my hand. She turned her eyes away as I coated my roll with butter. "If I ever find out I have a fatal disease, I'm not going to fritter away my last days surrounded by loved ones. I'll lie in bed and have a team of private nurses feed me banana cream pie." Her dark eyes narrowed a little. "Your weight never shows, does it? It never did."

"Of course it shows. But it's all below the waist. If I were a Victorian, with those huge skirts and dark bedrooms, everyone would think I was the most adorable, delicate thing since the invention of the doll. But—"

"But you never got really fat."

"Yes I did."

"Not serious fat, Marcia. Not big-time stuff. I remember, my mother would always give you seconds on the starch. She'd say, 'Have some more noodle kugel, darling.' " Barbara's imitation of her mother's warbling, refined tones was nearly perfect. "And then she'd look at me and shake her head before I got up the nerve to ask for more. She'd say, 'No, Barbara. You've had enough. Marcia needs a little extra. Her shoulder blades stick out.' "

"So did my behind. And you know I can carry ten pounds on each hip. Even Jerry says—" My words choked in my throat. My eyes began to fill again.

"Tell me everything," Barbara said softly. I did, pausing two or three times to sniffle back a potential torrent of tears. "Marcia," she murmured, when I had finally finished delineating my woes.

"What?"

"Do you want to be fair?"

"Fair?" I asked. The waiter came with a platter of cold asparagus. Each spear was the same size, as if one perfect asparagus had been cloned. He gave me six. Barbara got eight but didn't seem to notice.

"What I mean," she said, in her slow, easy voice, "is do you want to have an objective discussion about Jerry or do you want to sit around and attack him?"

"How would you attack him?"

"I'll get out my list."

"Let's make it objective."

"Okay. Well, he's spent the last few weeks being threatened on every level. Really, Mar. First his job. Then his health. On the one hand he knows his back will get better, but on the other he sees himself lying in bed, dependent, for the rest of his life. And then you, his woman—I mean, from what you said, it was obviously upsetting to him that you had had an affair with that Lyle."

"The word 'affair' makes it sound so glamorous. It wasn't."

"But does Jerry know that? Did you ever tell him going to bed with this Lyle was a great big zero? You didn't, did you? So here is Jerry, feeling down and out and probably worried sick that at any moment you're going to run off with this terrible person with biceps."

"Why would he think that?"
"Why wouldn't he? What had you really said to reassure him?"
"He knows how I feel about him. Anyway, Barbara, he could have any woman he wanted. Anyone."
"But he wants you. He's living with you, Mar. God, at his age, on his salary, what's he going to do with hundreds of women? You make such a production about his looks. I can tell you the number of men I've heard about, horrible looking, like turtles, who run around on their wives. You're setting up false—"
"Barbara."
"What?"
"Don't be fair."
"All right. But give me a minute to work up a vicious streak. See, I just close my eyes and imagine my mother's voice." She actually shut her eyes and leaned her head back. Her hands, like a medium's, remained on the table.
Barbara's fingers were devoid of the gems my Aunt Estelle would have loved to have seen her wear. She wore only a thin gold wedding band. However, her handbag, which she had dropped to the floor as she sat down, was probably made from the jowls of a minute Chilean reptile and no doubt cost as much as a decent diamond. And one wall of her room-sized closet was lined with shelves for her handbags.
"Okay," she said, opening her brown eyes, "he doesn't want to get married. Doesn't that strike you as odd?"
"Very good, Barbara."
"Thank you. I am my mother's daughter, you know. Should I go on, or do you know what I'm going to say?"
"That there's something wrong with a man who refuses to even consider a commitment."
"Exactly."
The waiter came and made a slight bow. "Ladies," he said, looking at Barbara. He set down a platter of seafood salad, tiny white bits of lobster and crabmeat, dainty scallops mixed with a minuscule dice of celery, like a mound of pearls and scattered emeralds.
"But to tell you the truth," I said, "I'm not sure marriage is such a great idea either. I mean, we've never really discussed it because I never found it all that appealing."

"You did once," Barbara said, serving me a generous portion of seafood salad.

"Come on. I was just doing what I had been programmed to do, to marry a doctor. If we hadn't been divorced, I'd be following the rest of the programming. I'd probably be out right now, getting my eyelashes tinted."

"That's not fair, Mar. Do I get mine tinted?" She blinked her dark, thick lashes at me. "Anyway, it was more than programming. You and Barry had a lot in common."

"Only sexually." For an instant, a flash of memory blinded my consciousness: Barry and me making love in the warm sea, on our honeymoon. I felt a flush. I crossed my legs and shifted about in the chair. The memory faded.

"And what about you and Jerry? Your dominant theme is his looks. I mean, all I get from you is a feeling that you're enormously attracted to him. But that's enchantment, not love. He may have the best profile in the world, but what good will that be ten years from now?"

"Barbara, come on. I could skip lunch with you and go over to your mother's and get the same argument."

"Marcia, what does he really give you?"

"He cares about me. He's interested in me."

"What else?" she demanded.

"What else is there? He's intelligent. I enjoy his company. We have loads in common. I mean, there's always something to talk about, and I can talk as his equal. There's none of this 'How was your day, dear?' crap."

"Why is that crap? When Philip comes home from school, I always ask him that." Philip taught at New York University Law School. That was in the mornings. He and Barbara tried to spend the afternoons together, unless she had a date with a friend or he had to see one of the Drexler bankers or brokers to decide what to do with his latest million.

"Does Philip ask you the same thing?"

"Yes."

"And what do you say? How do you answer him?"

"I say I had a fine day."

"And did you?"

"Yes, Marcia. I really did. I do. I know that doesn't particularly appeal to you, but it's the truth, I am"—and she raised her thick brows in a mischievous leer—"happily married."

"But how can you make a career out of it? What do you do with yourself all day? I mean it, Barb. I'm not being condescending."

"I know you're not. I'm busy. I read, probably four or five books a week. I spend time with my friends. I work for four different charities. What do you think is more productive, pushing papers in an office all day or raising money for the Israel Museum and working with a cerebral palsy child, teaching her how to put on a coat? Which benefits society more? And then I have the boys and Philip."

"And that's enough?"

"Yes. Why should I go out and open a cookware boutique or something like that and work six days a week selling soufflé dishes to strangers? Why? I don't need the money, God knows." We both smiled. "And what's so intrinsically fascinating about pots and pans—or French lingerie or silver jewelry?"

"Maybe it's stimulating to run a business. Maybe it's important to know you can survive and thrive by yourself. Be your own woman."

"But I am my own woman. I have no doubts about my own competence." She pierced a piece of lobster and held it aloft. "Anyway, it's far more stimulating to go to lunch with a friend and discuss Virginia Woolf than sell omelet pans. And it's a hell of a lot better going to the galleries in Soho than taking some half-assed master's degree in counseling so I can spend the rest of my life listening to obnoxious teenagers. I'd rather spend the time with my own children. They're delightful company. Well, most of the time."

"What are you saying, Barbara? That women shouldn't work? I can't believe you really think that."

"No. I'm just saying that marriage is better."

"It may be if you're working on an assembly line and doing something meaningless and mechanical, although even then you're on your own. But what about me? I have a fascinating, important job. I'm not selling French lingerie. I'm making actual contributions to the way this city is governed."

"Is it enough, Marcia?"

"Is what enough?"

"Your job. It may be wonderful, satisfying, exciting, but what about you as a human being?"

"Why are you setting up a conundrum that's impossible to untangle? It doesn't have to be either-or."

"All I know, Marcia, is that I see women, friends of mine, taking all sorts of jobs—market researchers, administrative assistants—that contribute very little to the well-being of anyone. . . . Wait, let me finish. They work eight–ten hours a day and come back to their children so exhausted they barely have strength to push the kids away. Is that meaningful? Is that being your own woman? Because if it is, I think it's a crock."

"Don't you think your perspective is a little off? I mean, being married to Philip, never having to do all those menial, repetitive jobs like laundry, washing floors, grocery shopping. If I had a choice of staying home and ironing and going out and selling negligees, I'd be up to my ass in nighties. Anyway, we're talking specifics here—or we were. My job is wonderful. Your marriage is wonderful. Maybe we should just be thankful and order dessert."

"I can't have dessert."

"For God's sake, Barbara. What's the difference? You're gorgeous no matter what you weigh."

"No I'm not."

"If you worked, you'd have a better self-image."

"Well, you work. How is your self-image?"

"That's mean, Barbara. That's as mean as when you wouldn't lend me your black evening bag."

"When was that?"

"In tenth grade. When Mickey Singer invited me to his brother's bar mitzvah. Don't you remember?"

"No. But I apologize. For the evening bag and being mean. But try to understand. I'm not spouting anti-feminist propaganda. I'm not wasting my life. I feel I'm doing very important work, at least as important as yours."

"Don't you ever want to break out?"

"Of what, Marcia?"

The waiter returned. "You're paying for lunch?" I asked Barbara.

"Of course."

"Then I'm ordering chocolate cake to make up for the black evening bag. I'm going to eat it slowly."

"You always had a sadistic streak. At least we're even now. But listen, seriously. You know I love you and I'm proud of what you're doing. Nothing can change what you've accomplished. All I'm saying is try not to live just day to day. Look at the rest of your life."

"I'm looking."

"All right. I just have one more thing to say—even if you don't want to hear it. Marriage can work. It can be fun."

"Maybe. At the beginning."

"No. It gets better."

"Better than what?"

"Marcia, I know what Barry did to you. Emotionally, I mean. But to use that one horrible experience as the standard for judging all men is wrong."

"I'm not using him as any standard."

"Yes you are. You equate marriage with Barry, with hurt and humiliation. And that's why you ran around from one man to another afterward. You were escaping from marriage."

"Barbara, be serious."

"I am. You be serious. Then you wound up with Jerry because you can't take promiscuity anymore, but you're still safe. Do you know why?"

"Because he's Irish and a bachelor and therefore won't want to marry me. Is that your analysis?"

"Yes."

"I can't believe what's happening to you. Your genes are taking over. You're sounding more and more like your mother. Next thing you'll be telling me how the Baroness de Rothschild sets her hair."

"She doesn't set it. She wears it short and brushes it back. I met her in Sardinia last summer. She's darling."

"Hot shit, Barbara."

"It's better than selling soufflé dishes, Mar."

14

William Paterno was too swarthy for a red flush, so when he became angry his face purpled, like a giant eggplant. It did so now, even under his television makeup.

"I am not afraid of confrontations," Sidney Appel had just snapped. "You, Mr. Paterno, have mismanaged New York City! And you," he continued, turning his head to Larry Parker, "you, Governor, have mismanaged New York State!"

"That's a lie!" Parker shot out.

"A lie? If the governor wants to talk about lies—"

"Gentlemen," the moderator intervened, his western clean looks and bland television voice working to tranquilize the New York crazies, "this is a debate. I have to remind you that we agreed to a set of rules." He smiled at the camera. His knowledge of New York was negligible, although he had probably been to the top of the Empire State Building.

"That's fine with me," Paterno said magnanimously, much less purple than a moment before. He sat on the last chair on the set, next to Appel. This was unfortunate, because his large head looked huge beside Appel's allover diminutiveness. When they appeared on the monitor together, it looked like a normal man debating Humpty-Dumpty.

"Who the hell asked you, Paterno?" Larry Parker hissed.

His speech writer, standing next to me in the studio, clapped his hand to his forehead and hissed back, "Your mike's on, Governor!" Parker looked confused, as though someone had yelled at him in another language.

The show's producer mouthed an enraged "out" as she stepped over the cables on the floor, pursuing the entourages of the three candidates out of the studio. Her assistant, clutching her clipboard as if afraid one of us might grab it, herded us out the door and said, "God. You people behave like children." She directed us to a waiting room equipped with a set. The debate was live.

". . . in the nursing-home industry?" the moderator was asking. Paterno would be eloquent on this subject, so I flopped onto a segment of the long modular couch that clung to the walls of the room. I stretched my legs in front of me and closed my eyes so I would not have to talk with anyone. Jerry had been gone for three days. He had not called.

"The governor seems to think age is a disease he's immune to," Paterno was saying. He was performing well. I tuned out the television.

The only news I had of Jerry had come two days earlier, when Paterno returned from Rochester. "I saw your friend yesterday."

"How is he?" I had asked, pushing a ball-point pen hard on the paper, trying to force it to give up its ink.

"Fine. Still a little stiff in the old back, but he'll soon be as good as new. You want another pen?"

Jerry never displayed profound emotions in front of other people. I knew what he felt because he told me. So, because much of our recent time together had been spent in ungiving silence, I could not predict how he would behave when he came home. He had given no signals. He might hold me and plant gentle kisses on my eyelids. He might toss me a casual hi. He might not speak at all. Or he might suggest I find a new apartment. I wanted him back. I feared his return.

"Hey, Marcia! Marcia, over here!" I opened my eyes to locate a faintly familiar voice. "Here." The room was full, with about twenty people, some of them standing. It took me a moment to locate a beard behind several pairs of shoulders. It was the governor's speech writer. I waved unencouragingly. "Hey, Marcia, Paterno was well prepared on that one. But don't worry, we'll get him yet."

"Right, Ted." He was a know-nothing from upstate whom I had known in Washington. He had been working for—and subsequently fired by—a congressman from Binghamton who was almost his intellectual equal. I snapped my eyes shut again before he had a chance to come over and chat. I wanted to think about Jerry.

"Excuse me," another voice said. Sensing it was addressing me, I opened my eyes. It was a man I had spotted with the Appel contingent. "Are you Marcia Green?" he asked.

"Yes."

"I'm David Hoffman." Even casually dressed, like the rest of the Appel group, he looked like a man of substance. His jeans were so smooth they must have been dry cleaned. His shirt was a white and brown and gray tattersall, and its sharp-edged collar formed two perfect v's on either side of the neckline of his lightweight beige sweater. Like his posture, controlled and conscious, his clothing seemed well thought out.

"Hi," I said, somewhat nervously. Occasionally my reputation preceded me. Sometimes I ran into men who had heard about my speech-writing abilities. Sometimes I ran into men who heard I was an easy lay. Both types seemed friendly and eager, and I hated the slow agony of discovering their interest.

"I'm really glad to meet you," he said.

"Thank you."

"I'm a friend of Philip Drexler. Your cousin Barbara made me promise I'd introduce myself to you if we ran into each other."

I flashed a smile that would have satisfied even my Aunt Estelle. "I'm glad you came over. Do you want to sit down?" David sat on the segment of couch next to mine. He smiled. His teeth were large and white, but they merely added to his substantial appearance. No one would ever make Bugs Bunny jokes about David Hoffman. "How do you and Cousin Philip know each other?" I asked.

"We went to law school together."

" 'Law school.' Well, you have incredible restraint, not blurting out 'Harvard.' "

He kept smiling. Even on the low couch, David Hoffman managed to look impressive. Most of us had given up, allowing gravity to curve our spines into weary arcs; he sat erect among the slouchers, but not so erect as to seem stiff. "How do you think the debate is going?" he inquired.

"That depends on who your candidate is. You're with Appel?" He nodded. "Well, you might consider being a little nervous, because he's coming across as glib."

"He is glib. In all the years I've known him, he's never uttered a single thoughtful sentence." David Hoffman sounded like what a friend of Philip Drexler's should sound like. My mother would have observed that his voice was cultivated. In any case, it was deep and pleasant.

"May I ask you a question, David?"

"Of course."

"How come you're working for Appel?"

"How come?" He seemed to find the question intriguing.

"Yes. I mean, you look like a solid citizen, a nice, normal person. Not the sort who'd wind up working for a politician."

"Well, I'm not exactly working for him. I'm helping out a little. But I actually came here tonight to see what a television studio looks like, to watch the debate live." He peered at me. "You look like a normal person," he observed. "Aren't you?"

"Yes, but not in your sense. I keep crazy hours, spend most of my day dealing with megalomaniacs and sociopaths. Most people would run from it, screaming."

"But you like it?"

"I love it."

"Well, you don't sound *ab*normal. Besides, you're Barbara Drexler's cousin. She's one of the finest, sanest people I know. How crazy could you be?"

"Just mildly deranged." We smiled again. He was not wearing a wedding band. "But you still didn't answer my question."

"Excellent. You'd make a good lawyer."

"David, it doesn't take three years at Harvard to figure out you don't enjoy talking about Sidney Appel."

"Oh, Sidney. He's my uncle."

"Your uncle? Uncle Sidney? You don't look anything like him." David's face was big and squarish; even sitting, he looked fairly tall and large-boned. He bore no resemblance to an elf.

"He's my uncle by marriage. He married my father's sister."

"Oh! Cat food!" Then I added quickly, "Sorry."

He lowered his head and laughed. "I keep away from cat food. I practice law."

"On your own?"

"No. With a large midtown firm. I specialize in tax."

"And that's more fascinating than cat food?"

"Barbara warned me you'd be snide."

"I thought I was being charming."

"You were. And to answer your question, tax law is much more fascinating than cat food. And frankly, it's paradise compared to a political campaign. My God! Every time I go over to his headquarters, I'm stunned by some new irrationality."

"You were expecting an exercise in Jeffersonian democracy?"

"Well, I was expecting something a little different from what I found. May I ask *you* something, Marcia?"

"Sure."

"Doesn't the boredom bother you? I spent a day traveling around with Sidney, running from place to place, hearing him mouth the same speech over and over again. It's so prepackaged, so routinized."

"Well, it may be boring to the press, because they have to hear the same thing over and over. The candidate can handle it better because his ego is fed by each new audience. But it's not boring for me." I stretched out my legs again, took a deep breath, and began a lengthy explanation of how I worked en route. "You see," I concluded, "if Paterno's gotten a last-minute invitation for a Hellenic Day festival, I can write a zingy speech on how terrific Greeks are while we're riding out to Queens to mend fences or while he's talking to a business group on diddling the capital budget. And if I'm not writing something, I listen to him. Try to figure out what lines get the best response, what lines bomb."

David gazed at me as I spoke. His eyes, which should have been brown to match his outfit, were actually hazel, with dots of yellow and green and gray. They were his best feature. The rest of his face was filled up with an ordinary broad-bridged nose, a large mouth, and a determined-looking chin. He seemed to be about Philip's age, forty, with a network of busy-looking lines around his eyes.

"Listen," I said, "I really didn't mean to make fun of your tax law. I don't even know precisely what it is. What do you do?"

But he didn't have a chance. I heard a shout of "Marcia!"

The two candidates stood outside the waiting room until Paterno, in an artful subway maneuver, elbowed Parker and Appel aside and stood framed in the doorway. "Let's get going," he called. "I want to get back to headquarters."

I stood. David did also. I was about to shake his hand and tell him it had been nice meeting him but Paterno came over, clamped onto my arm, and said, "Come on! Let's get out of here." With his other hand he reached for an upstate staff member who was standing nearby and pulled us both toward the door.

"Bye," I called to David.

Paterno's car careened toward headquarters, barely slowing down when a hubcap flew off from the shock of a large pothole. I stared out the window, trying to figure out why my cousin had never mentioned David Hoffman to me before.

"Well, what do you think, Marcia?" Paterno demanded. "You haven't said a word. Was I awful? If you think I was terrible, tell me."

"You weren't terrible." I turned to him. He was wiping his television makeup off with a large white handkerchief.

"Well?"

"You were fine. You know that."

"Really?"

"Yes. You were very specific, and you have to keep that up. Appel is coming across as superficial, and the more exposure he gets, the more evident that's going to be. So what you've got to do is keep dazzling them with your knowledge, your expertise."

"You're right." He paused. "What about Parker? Do you think he has a shot after tonight? I actually felt ashamed for him, he was such a fool."

"Well, there are still two more debates. He could redeem himself a little. Or maybe there's a big underground stupid vote. But the main thing is . . ."

"What?" Paterno demanded.

"If you or Appel aren't seen as individuals, if you don't make a strong and distinct impression, then people are going to go for Parker just because he's a known quantity."

"But he's a fool." Paterno looked peeved. His mouth pulled tight at the corners. "He honestly doesn't comprehend what's going on."

"That may be, but he's a familiar fool. Anyhow, if you keep up the level of tonight and come across as authoritative—and if Sidney keeps mouthing his slogans—then you have a real shot."

"Just a shot?"

"You know the polls better than I do. Appel's ahead."

"I know, and it's killing me. I'm the best man. No one can do the job I can."

"I know that, Bill. But it's not getting across the way it should."

"Well, why the hell not? I'm pushing myself to the limit, risking a major coronary, running around the whole state tearing my guts out, eating hamburgers in airports—"

"You can't expect me to be objective, Bill."

"What do you mean?"

"I mean the support you were counting on has been going elsewhere. The advice you've been getting has been less than stellar. I think it's been slick and shallow." The upstate aide, a LoBello protégé, turned around from his seat next to the driver and glared at me. "And that kind of superficiality, well . . ." I let my voice trail off and then resumed. "Why bother going on? You know my prejudice. I can't even swear to you that what I'm saying is the objective truth. My loyalty to Jerry may be getting in the way. But don't forget, besides my loyalty to him, I have a very strong loyalty to you. I've always been straight with you, Bill. And I think you've got to consider making some changes."

Paterno nodded. At headquarters, he sloughed off LoBello's pat on the back and retired to his own office. The upstate aide snarled at me and pulled LoBello off for a private conference. I adjourned to my own office to rewrite a speech on the right of public employees to strike and decided I didn't care what they did. I sighed, wondering what my cousin Barbara had told David Hoffman about me. I changed my typewriter ribbon. Then I shrugged, sighed again, and got up. But as I waited for the elevator,

Lyle LoBello sidled up beside me, pushing me as if we were on a rush-hour subway car together.

"You fucker," he hissed. "I'm going to get you for this."

"Go away, Lyle."

The night had become sticky. The air was so thick and stagnant it was almost viscous. And it was hot, like a foretaste of August. I caught an air-conditioned Fifth Avenue bus and worried my way downtown in a finger-numbing chill.

Maybe my fears and sadness were due to some tediously predictable mid-life crisis, the sort that every thirty-five-year-old who reads magazines is susceptible to. Maybe it was some primeval need burgeoning within, forcing me to nest and breed, making me smile at David Hoffman. By Fourteenth Street I thought about Jerry. If he would just come home and shepherd me into bed, I wouldn't spend another moment feeling fearful or sad or the least bit vulnerable.

Back at the apartment, I undressed and lay across the bed musing about him, like a mortal waiting for Zeus to transmogrify into a cloud and come down for a visit. But after a half hour I grew restless. I showered and put on one of Jerry's pajama tops. I looked around the bedroom for some useful employment: washing out pantyhose, trimming toenails, reading the sonnets I had written in tenth grade—with titles like "Silence" and "Song of Seymour"—which were in a shoe box on the top shelf of my closet.

Instead, I called my cousin. "Hi, Barbara."

"Marcia! How are you? Feeling better? Did Jerry get back yet?"

"He's still upstate, but I'm okay. Am I calling too late?"

"No. Philip's in the library working on a law-review article and I was just reading in bed." The library was in their house. "Now tell me, have you heard from Jerry? Has he called?"

"No. Not a word."

"Are you upset, Marcia? Talk to me. You know it makes me crazy when you pull your uncommunicative act, especially on the phone. Anyway, you need to get things off your chest."

"I met your friend," I said softly.

"Who? What friend?"

"Don't 'who' me, Barbara. The cat-food king."

"David? You met David! Oh, I was hoping you would."

"How come you never mentioned him to me?"

"Because I knew you'd go out of your way to avoid him."

"That's ridiculous."

"It is not. Every time I mention introducing you to one of Philip's friends, you look at me as though I've done something disgusting, like throwing up at a formal dinner. Do you think I'd be crazy enough to say, 'Marcia, there's a nice lawyer I want you to meet; he's highly eligible—and Jewish'? You'd never speak to me again."

"Come on, Barb. Isn't it that you were afraid how I'd behave with one of Philip's fancy lawyer friends, that I'd pull down my panties on the first date or do something to besmirch the family name?"

"You are so impossible that I'm not even going to dignify that with a denial."

"Oh, all right. Anyhow, why is he hanging around Appel?"

"Well, David's genuinely interested in politics and this is a wonderful chance to see things up close. And . . ." Barbara paused, then shifted her voice to a confidential pitch. "Promise you won't tell anyone?"

"I promise."

"Well, he's been spending so much time with Sidney Appel, keeping an eye on things, because his father and his other aunt are terrified that Appel is going to fritter away Aunt Marjorie's—Mrs. Appel's—entire legacy or trust fund or whatever. They wanted David to take a leave of absence from his law firm to really watch things, but David said absolutely not. He cannot abide his uncle. Can you keep a secret?"

"What?"

"Appel's a real adulterer. With teenage girls!"

"I've heard."

"You've heard? Really?"

"Sure."

"Well, not only does he run around, but Marjorie Appel knows all about it."

"No kidding. And she's paying for his campaign anyway? Lovely. Your pal David sounds like he comes from a terrific family."

"In fact, the Hoffmans are a fine old German-Jewish family."

"Right. Did he go to prep school, like Philip?"

"I'm not sure. But he went to Harvard, undergraduate and law school. Is that good enough?"

"For my mother."

Barbara's voice grew smooth and teasing. "You liked him, didn't you, Mar?"

"He wasn't bad. But I'm warning you, Barbara, please don't try to push this. I'm still in the same place. Half the bed is mine, the other half is Jerry's."

"Who's talking about beds?"

"David Hoffman is a nice guy and that's that. Okay?"

"Sure. Honestly, the only reason I mentioned you to him at all is that he doesn't know anyone in politics and if he ran into you, it would be a nice experience. I mean, meeting someone intelligent, fun. He's spending a lot more time with his uncle than he wants to, and it's only because his family is absolutely desperate."

"They just don't want Auntie Appel hitting them up for another few million. Your friend is probably protecting his own inheritance."

"Marcia, that may be true, but that doesn't take away from David as a person. He's a marvelous man. Warm, sensitive, cultured."

"Is he married?"

"He was. He's divorced."

"What went wrong?"

"Nothing. Don't be so suspicious. It just wasn't meant to be. He and his wife—his ex-wife—grew up together, had the same background, the same tastes . . ."

"Cat food?"

"Stop it. Everything seemed sweet and nice and right at the beginning, but then they discovered one thing: they were miserably unhappy. So they were divorced, but very amicably. She's remarried and lives in Connecticut with the children."

"How many children did they have before they figured out they were miserably unhappy?"

"Three. And I think it's very unfair of you to be so sarcastic. He's a good friend of ours. I'm not saying you have to love him or even like him, but you could at least be polite."

"I was. I even bordered on charming. You wouldn't have believed it was me talking. Ask him."

"I will." Soon afterward, she wished me good night. I imagined her running down a flight of curving stairs, dashing into the library, and announcing to Philip, "Marcia met David!" Or she may have just called her mother and said, "Guess what? It worked!"

Ascribing such manipulativeness to Barbara may be unfair, but I was never completely sure of her. I always needed her more than I wanted to and trusted her less than perhaps I should. She was, after all, a relation.

Other than my lawyer, who had to drag the facts from me, she was the only person I told about finding Barry getting his licks from Noreen. I confided in her the history of my cold, dead marriage, warmed only by the heat of sex. I said to Barbara, Swear to me you'll never tell anyone, and she said, Of course, of course. And yet it seemed, once the first shock had worn away, my Aunt Estelle was a little too sanguine over my ditching a future doctor and my mother's reflexive disappointment at my failure was too muted.

Sometimes I felt that Barbara was simply a modern-dress version of my Aunt Estelle. Wasn't it wonderful to have a happy husband! And children! The light of your years. And the joys of creating a gracious home, to spend a long afternoon stalking the perfect guest towel.

But Barbara didn't take her mother seriously at all. She'd chuckle, "That woman's pretensions are boundless. Boundless. She goes around telling people about my staff of servants. Can you believe that?" The Drexlers had a cook, a houseman, a couple of maids, a gardener, and a laundress. "And she actually says things like 'sorbet' for 'sherbet.' She'll say, 'What lovely blackberry sorbet.' I can't even look at Philip when she does that because we'll both start laughing."

Barbara seemed to be her own woman. She followed her own interests, not her mother's. She went to the ballet, theater, concerts, lectures. She planted prizewinning azaleas. She read fiction in the south of France, poetry on the window seat of her boudoir. She knew enough about politics to hold her own with me in conversation, and she was astute enough not to fall into the shallow cynicism outsiders often do. She was a pillar of the Embroiderers' Guild, a fellow of the John Donne Society.

And she had done exactly what she was supposed to do.

By those same standards, I had screwed up unforgivably.

But she shared her French antique canopied bed with a bald and nasal Philip. I had Jerry. And that night, he came home.

I heard him as he came in but pretended to be sleeping. I stirred a little as he sat on the edge of the bed, letting a feigned dream sigh escape.

"Marcia, it's me. Jerry. Marcia?" He shook my shoulder gently. I did the standard Hollywood awakening, yawning, blinking my eyes a couple of times, murmuring a little in the back of my throat.

"Jerry?"

"Hi. You awake?"

"Yes." I added a starlet bit, running my tongue over my allegedly dry lips. "What time is it?"

"Late. The plane was supposed to land at ten thirty, but we ran into lousy weather and had to circle for an hour and half the passengers were airsick. And then I couldn't get a cab. I thought we could go out somewhere, have a drink, talk."

"I'm not dressed for anything fancy."

"I can see that." He put his hand under the covers and ran it over my thigh. And that was how I knew things were dandy again.

"Jerry, let's talk."

"Sure," he said, continuing to rub, putting on a little more pressure. "What do you want to talk about?"

"Jerry, your appeal isn't working." I sat up and pulled the cover high across my chest. As I did, I noticed he needed a haircut; a fringe hung over his ears. I brushed it back. The only light in the room came from the moon, but it was sufficient to spotlight Jerry, to play upon the contrast in his hair and bring out the phosphorescence of his pale skin.

"Of course my appeal is working," he said, crooking a finger over the edge of the blanket and pulling it down.

"We have to talk," I said, but I was already taking off his tie, unbuttoning his shirt, pulling off his undershirt, and running my hands over his chest.

"Talk to me," he said, helping me out of his pajama top. "What do you want to say?"

"Kiss me."

Could the Philip Drexlers and David Hoffmans sit in moonlight and shine so that they had to be embraced to contain their brightness? Could they kiss so deeply as to bring tears?

If asked, and even if not, my Aunt Estelle would explain that handsome men couldn't be trusted. Things came too easy to them, you see, so beneath the shining countenance was a soul the size of a cockroach.

My mother would ask, You know the expression beautiful but dumb? Yes. Well, they didn't make it up for nothing.

Barbara told me I had to distinguish between enchantment and love.

Jerry lay on top of me, grinding himself deeper and deeper into me. My arms flailed up and down the mattress, banging down on it, then fluttering, like a bird trying very hard to fly.

And with Jerry propelling me, I could soar.

15

"Please come," my cousin Barbara pleaded. "Really, you haven't been out to the house for ages. It'll be fun." Each July Fourth, Barbara and Philip threw a picnic, a triumph of Americana, a ketchup-covered celebration of their assimilation. A Dixieland jazz band played on the back lawn. Barbara wore a casual summery cotton whipped up by her favorite American couturier. Aunt Estelle went out of her way to make the black faculty members of Philip's law school feel comfortable. My mother squinted in the sunlight. Philip's roommate from Choate wore yellow slacks with splotchy white flowers on them. Uncle Julius wanted to know, "Is that how they dress for casual or is that guy a fairy?"

Hot dogs and hamburgers and steaks sizzled on a brick barbeecue overlooking Long Island Sound. Silvery pails filled with ice were studded with cans of soda and beer and the inevitable sugar-free cola. Frank, the Drexlers' houseman, who had probably been a major war criminal, guarded the vat of corn on the cob. "You vant a corn, madame?" he would demand.

You could bring your racquet and play tennis on their court. Bring your suit and swim in their solar-heated pool. Bring your lotion and sit on the beach that brought their backyard to an end and watch the impudent little waves of the sound lap the sand. Or bring your lover and walk in the woods that stretched over the eastern four acres of Drexlerland, lie on the mossy earth, or stoop to pick wildflowers.

"I have a couple of appearances with Paterno. By the time I'm finished, it'll be too late. Next year, Barbara. Okay?"

"No, it's not okay. Everyone wants to see you."

"Who is everyone?"

"My parents, my in-laws, you know."

"You wouldn't be planning any surprises, would you?"

"What do you mean?"

"I mean, you wouldn't be planning on trotting out any of Philip's friends, would you? Lock us away in a room and give your mother the key?"

"You're certifiably paranoid. Look, of course Philip is going to invite his friends. But that has nothing to do with you. I swear it. Now that you've kissed and made up, you can even bring Jerry."

"You're kidding."

"No. I want you to understand something. I love you the way you are. I only want for you what you want for yourself. I'm not my mother. I'm not your mother. Anyway, I'm dying to see him."

"This is some sort of a ploy."

"Marcia, I swear, I'll hang up on you. Really, I'd like to meet him."

"So would my mother. It would give her a good excuse for having a stroke on your patio and blaming it on me. But it won't work. He's upstate again."

"Well, with or without him, I insist you come and I'm not going to listen to any excuses. Whenever you're finished politicking, just grab a cab or a plane or something and get over here. Okay? Remember, I love you and I'm going to hang up now so you won't be able to give me any arguments."

Certainly no one else gave me arguments. Jerry called late at night on July third, briefly expressed his condolences that I had to spend the holiday with my family, and spent the next fifteen minutes telling me, in fine detail, how the Onondaga air made him horny and how he would like to have me writhing underneath him. I lay on my stomach as he spoke, on top of a heating pad, hoping the codeine I had taken for my menstrual cramps would soon take effect.

"Do you miss me, Jerry?" I was nauseated also.

"So much, sweetheart, I can't begin to tell you. How about you?"

"It's so terrible without you." I inhaled. "Jerry, can I ask you something?"

"What?"

"It's hypothetical. What would you say if I told you I wanted to have a baby, wanted to get—"

"Marcia, come on."

"It's just a question."

"I would tell you what I told you the night you moved in. I don't want to get married. I don't want to have children. Sweetheart, you know how I feel about you and sometimes I'm very tempted, but it wouldn't work."

"Do you think it would be that much of a change from what we have now?"

"Yes. It would change everything. Really it would. Look, I wish I could make you happy. . . ."

"You do, Jerry. Honestly. It was just a question."

"Wait till I get home. You'll see how happy I can make you."

The next day, my handbag filled with enough tampons to see me through menopause, I rented a car and drove up to a park in northern Westchester, where the combined police forces of the county were having their annual Independence Day outing. Many of them were Irish, and of these at least a third looked good enough to be Jerry's distant relatives. They lounged around the softball field waiting for their turn at bat, shirts off, smelling of beer and sweat. I would have liked to have been second base. Instead, I followed Paterno as he shook hands and smiled. He wore a plaid sports shirt opened an extra button's worth to show he was one of the fellas. He chatted with policemen's wives, mostly young and fair women, dressed in aqua pantsuits. He spoke about capital punishment and what a lovely sunny day it was. He rumpled the hair of at least ninety children and afterward found a men's room where he could wash his hands. "There's head lice going around," he confided to me. "It's reaching epidemic proportions."

From there I followed his station wagon, festooned with BILL PATERNO CAN DO IT banners, to another park about ten miles south to meet Lithuanians. Then to the Bronx, for the Italians, where we both relaxed, trusting the food.

"Marcia," Paterno said, holding a fresh fig in his hand and looking at it fondly, "the new polls look good. Appel's falling, plummeting."

"How much ahead are you?"

"We're even now. Neck and neck. By next week I should be ahead." He sighed then, remembering probably that he had two more picnics and a fireworks display that day, and another two hundred thousand hands to shake before the September primary. "Let's get going," he said. "I think we can stop off at the Botanical Gardens before we hit the Zoo. There's an extra half hour we picked up somewhere along the line."

I asked him if he would mind terribly if I left his caravan and visited my relatives on Long Island. Knowing me well enough to realize I was not traitorous, Paterno looked at me as if I were loony. I had never before asked for time off during a campaign.

"Gee," he said.

"It's a shindig at my cousin's house. Philip Drexler. Remember him?" Philip had written a tasteful check for one thousand dollars to the campaign.

"I remember him," Paterno said.

"Well, he's having this big party and a lot of his rich friends will be there and I just thought it would make sense to go up there and smile and tell everyone how terrific you are. Unless you feel you want me at the Zoo. . . ."

"No, that's all right. Go. Go ahead. Have a good time."

I considered it, although by the time I reached my cousin Barbara's house on Peacock Point, a community on the north shore of Long Island for the congenitally rich, I began to feel that shaking hands with baboons at the Bronx Zoo would be preferable to a Shochet-Green-Lindenbaum-Drexler holiday.

"My dear!" Mrs. Drexler said, as I walked up to the front porch. "How beautiful you look. Politics must be wonderful for the complexion. Look, Alfred," she said to her husband, Philip's father, "doesn't Marcia have the most flawless skin you've ever seen?"

"She certainly does. How are you, young lady? It's good to see you. Are you still working for Mr. Paterno?" Mr. Drexler, tall and thin and slightly stooped, looked like an Episcopalian bishop, self-possessed but understated to the point of seediness. He sounded like a bishop too, saying cahn't for can't and clearing his throat whenever he didn't want to respond to a question. His grandfather had discovered copper somewhere in South America. His father had found zinc. Mr. Drexler did not have to find anything. He had houses on two islands and three continents and spent his time writing treatises on the Marranos, the Jews of Spain and Portugal who were forced to convert during the Inquisition. He was a respected Judaic scholar. He was an even more respected philanthropist, giving away at least two percent of his yearly income and keeping a lot of charities happy.

"Yes," I managed to say, "I'm still working for Paterno. We're right in the middle of a campaign now."

But of course Mr. Drexler knew all about the campaign, even though he viewed the Democratic Party as the institutional embodiment of the mob; it was his obligation as a citizen of the Republic to know what was going on. And Mrs. Drexler had heard about it too, although she was generally too busy supervising the making of silk flower arrangements for her houses and attending planning sessions for charity fashion shows to read about the details in the New York papers. "You know I went to Wellesley with Jean Gresham, don't you, dear? She was the governor's mother. Of course she was Jean Willets then. I hear she still hasn't gotten over it."

"She means the shock," Mr. Drexler explained.

"Marcia knows what I mean. Don't you, dear?"

I said I did. We stood on the front porch of the house, a huge Victorian mansion which Barbara once estimated to have thirty-four rooms. It was painted a white so pure and so clean that it seemed nearly sacred. "Do you mind if I sit down?" I asked. The combined assaults of picnics, heat, bare-chested Irishmen, Italian sausage, and my period hit me simultaneously in the head and gut.

"Right here, dear," said Mrs. Drexler, guiding me to a big rattan porch chair. "Alfred," she said to her husband, "go get Marcia a large glass of water. Not too cold and please hurry. She looks faint."

Mr. Drexler looked at me and obviously agreed. He trotted into the house.

I did not like feeling faint in front of the Drexlers. It was another confirmation that the lower classes were weak and deserved to remain lower class. Mrs. Drexler could be bleeding to death, but she'd still spend her Volunteer Wednesday at New York Hospital and attend her college reunion and order fresh potpourri from her herbalist in London. She took out a handkerchief and patted my temples; it was scented with bluebells. "Your time of the month?" she whispered.

"Yes," I whispered back, and then added in a normal voice, "And I was running around Westchester and the Bronx all morning with Paterno."

"My dear! Why?"

"It's July Fourth, Clarisse," Mr. Drexler explained, placing a tall thin glass of water in my hand. "All their people have picnics then. The candidates travel from one to the other, shaking hands and eating ethnic foods. Although after Jimmy Gresham, you'd think they'd have more sense. Feeling better, Marcia?"

"Yes. Thank you." The Drexlers were peering at me, concerned but—unlike my relatives—under control. Mr. Drexler gave me water, not the phone number of Albert Einstein Medical School's top specialist in heat prostration. Mrs. Drexler patted my head; she did not once suggest abandoning her opera subscription for the next six months to care for me, nor did she confide the story of her neighbor's niece, who died from severe menstrual complications.

"Marcia? Marcia?" It was my Aunt Estelle's voice, and soon she followed it out the front door, wearing a flouncy beige dress and an enormous-brimmed hat, so she looked like Scarlett O'Hara's distant relative. "My God! What's wrong with you?"

"She's fine, Estelle," said Mr. Drexler, not looking up. "A little too much heat. We have things under control."

"We'll send her out to you in a few minutes, dear," Mrs. Drexler said to her. It was as if a drill sergeant had bawled, "Dis-missed!" My aunt about-faced, murmuring "Fine, fine," and marched back into her daughter's house. Or her son-in-law's house. And Mrs. Drexler flashed her husband a very brief but meaningful glance and he blinked back in understanding. Then they both smiled back at me. I felt as though I were under the protection of the prince of a major city-state.

"Thank you," I said. "I'll just sit here for a couple of minutes. Then I'll join everybody."

"Of course, dear." And the Drexlers walked toward the party.

I suppose Barbara must have paid extra for it, but at that moment a wonderful cool breeze blew across the porch, stirring the skirt of the pink cotton dress I was wearing, drying up the perspiration. How wonderful to have the Drexlers, even if it meant taking Philip as part of the package. They were polite and nice and restrained. Refined. But still not completely able to leave well enough alone. They gave me about four minutes and then sent Barbara out.

"Oh," she said. "Glad to see you're not dead." She bent over and kissed my cheek. "Want to take a nap or anything? I can file you away in a guest room for a couple of hours."

"No, I'm feeling better. Your in-laws are really nice."

"I know. Remember how panicked I was about meeting them, right after we became engaged? I was afraid they'd snub me or convince Philip that marrying someone from Queens was an act of blatant self-destructiveness. But they were so lovely. And very fond of you, incidentally. By the way, when you're up to it, your mother's out in back."

"How is she?"

"Cheerful and charming."

"Very funny."

"Very true. She's sitting under a crab-apple tree, being romanced by David Hoffman. Isn't that nice?"

"Shit!"

"I swear to you I had nothing to do with it. He found her all by himself, and apparently it was love at first sight."

"Barbara, I don't want any part of this."

"Of course not. What sane person would?" Barbara rose, smoothing the razor pleats of her skirt. "I have to mingle. I'll see you whenever you're ready."

I let several minutes pass, while I made a real effort to recall the usual stable details of my life: Jerry's damp shaving brush leaning against my Q-Tip box, the overflowing garbage cans outside our apartment on Tuesday and Friday mornings, the amount of my paycheck after deductions, the creak of the elevator at campaign headquarters as it wearily pulled its passengers up an exhausting four stories.

But the spell of the house was too powerful. I walked

inside, through the long hall with its dark wood floor, past polished old tables with bowls of puffy white flowers with ruby centers, through the kitchen with its glass-fronted cabinets and fireplace, and stood by the back door, watching the long lawn that sloped and fell until it reached the sandy beach. There were no visible garbage cans here.

Mrs. Innis, the cook, smiled, and said, "Hello, Miss Marcia. Having a nice time?" I told her I was. "Just making some more mayonnaise here," she explained, letting golden dots of oil dribble into a bowl. "Has to be real fresh, this time of year." I agreed.

Outside, clusters of people decorated the lawn in their bright summer clothing. Many of them, I guessed, knowing Barbara and Philip's friends, received paychecks not much larger than mine, and yet they all seemed to belong there; the Drexlers' house was so seductive that all their guests shed their raucous voices and enlarged pores and became upper class for the Fourth of July.

Even my mother. I finally located her under a tree with a dark, twisted trunk. She was sitting in a canvas lawn chair, with one of her sister's old straw hats perched on her head; it was a small, red straw and made her look almost jaunty. Chatting with her, leaning up against the tree, was David Hoffman in white slacks and a navy T-shirt. I'm not certain why, since I stood at a distance and it was just a T-shirt, but I knew it was quite expensive. David's T-shirt was probably worth about four or five of Uncle Julius's alligators. Even though it was ordinary-looking, it was probably a brand immediately recognizable by any fabulously rich Harvard alumnus.

I hovered by the coolness of the house, tempted to see how long she and David could continue to talk. Surely even his good manners had limits. Surely he could not be that enthralled with me or that stupid that he would attempt to gain access through my mother. But my mother's farsightedness paid off. She spotted me and waved with such enthusiasm that other people must have thought I was some marchioness's daughter or at least the child of an orthodontist. "Marcia!" Pale waves of sound reached me over the comfortable laughter of the other guests. "Come join us!" David left the support of the tree and joined in the waving, not as enthusiastic as my mother but certainly more sincere.

I sauntered over, passing out my own waves as I went, to the elder Drexlers, to one of the professors at Philip's law school who was a Democratic state committeeman, to a couple of Barbara's suburban lady friends whom I had met the previous summer at her pool.

"Hi," I said to my mother. I turned to David, who seemed to be waiting for some daughterly show, a kiss or a hand squeeze, before I acknowledged him. But I felt, under the circumstances, a hi was more than sufficient, so I turned to him. "Hello. Did you see the latest polls? Uncle Sidney's getting his ass kicked in."

My mother's wan color grew wanner. David smiled. "Don't use that kind of language in front of your mother," he said. He turned to her. "Does she usually carry on like this, Mrs. Green?"

Her response was a weak "well" and a shrug.

For some reason, David seemed to find this response endearing, because he beamed at her and asked if she minded if we went for a stroll.

"I don't stroll," I told him as we began walking. He grasped my elbow in the traditional gentleman-taking-lady-for-stroll position. "What were you talking to my mother about?"

"Politics. She's very well informed. Is that where you developed your interest in the subject?"

"No." We passed a flower bed covered with light green leaves and pale blue flowers that grew along the ground, upper-class flowers, pallid and indolent. "She usually doesn't talk to me."

David was amused. "You *are* being difficult today. Barbara said that being in the midst of your family seems to make you a little edgy."

"Really? What else did she tell you about me?"

"That you're very intelligent. And pretty. But that I can see with my own eyes."

"You're trying to worm campaign secrets out of me, aren't you? Uncle Sidney sent you down here to get copies of our next press release."

"Do me a favor," David said. "Let's call a moratorium on talking about Uncle Sidney."

"It's that bad?" I asked.

"Awful. Well, for me it is. I spent all yesterday at his

headquarters. You'd probably feel very comfortable there. Not with Sidney, of course, because he's a prize pill, but with the campaign atmosphere. But I'm used to a law firm where things are organized. Anyway, there I was, at headquarters, trying to read something, with three people standing around the desk next to mine screaming about whose job it is to answer the telephone. It's so inefficient."

I nodded. I remembered times when I had screamed at two other people that it was not my job to answer the phone.

David rubbed his chin, as though testing for five-o'clock shadow. "And then," he went on, "at least once an hour someone broke down and cried, and everyone was running around trying to line up someone to sleep with, and when I didn't appear interested they took it as a personal affront, which I suppose it is. . . ." He stared at the Drexlers' clipped lawn.

I stared at his expensive T-shirt and tried to imagine what was under it: tennis-made muscle or thick flesh, the texture of marshmallows. Because of the neckline, I could discern no chest hair and could not have made even an educated guess as to whether any existed. But David began talking again and his voice was more magnetic than his torso.

"Look, I'm sorry to go on like this."

"That's okay, as long as I get a turn to attack law firms."

"Well, of course. They're eminently attackable. But at least they fulfill their purpose. Here I look at what's going on and marvel how the democratic process survives. Nobody cares about the issues."

"Come on, David. Of course they do. They have to appear knowledgeable during a debate. And then if they're elected, they have to have some sort of program or position."

"But everything is appearances." His face was flushed. A woman who cared about him would have told him to wear a hat. "Tell me, does William Paterno really care what happens to this state?"

"Yes. Why are you such a terrible cynic? Because of Uncle Sidney? He's not a typical politician. He's a rich businessman who decided that politics is laughs. And you're upset because you feel obligated to spend time with him, watching him make a bigger jerk of himself than he already is and using your money to do it."

"A, it is not my money, it's my Aunt Marjorie's money, and B, I have watched him behaving like a jerk for the last thirty or forty years, so this campaign is not precisely a novelty, and C, he seems to be doing quite well compared to the other candidates, incidentally, which I suppose might be construed as a judgment of the overall quality—"

"And D," I interrupted, "you can construe until you're blue in the face and still not know your ass from your elbow about politics if you keep hanging around with Sidney Appel."

"Your subtlety overwhelms me, Marcia," he said. We had stopped halfway between a small grove of weeping willows and the narrow dark-yellow beach.

"Then go back to my mother," I suggested. "You can have a nice subtle chat about your latest issue of *Foreign Affairs*. I'm sure she'll bend over backward to behave splendidly."

He beamed at me. "You're cute. So irascible."

"I am not being cute. I am being nasty."

"No you're not. Anyway, before you walk off in a huff, tell me why Uncle Sidney's campaign is atypical."

I did as we sauntered down to the beach. I also explained the differences between the various polls and why there was an excellent chance that Appel's early lead would not only evaporate but was illusory to begin with.

David said "hmmmm" quite a lot and "no kidding" once or twice. On the beach, we passed a line of old-fashioned wooden deck chairs, filled with the bodies of the Drexlers' pale guests. I leaned over to unbuckle my sandals, and David offered me his hand to hold for balance.

We held hands until we found a spot on the sand that was quite isolated. It was a friendly hand-holding. He did not attempt to tickle my palm or kiss my fingertips. We strolled a few steps farther and sat at the water's edge.

David took off his shoes, brown moccasins with white rubber soles, and we let the sound cool our heels. His feet were big but quite ordinary, golden-mean feet, neither calloused nor manicured, with straight toes and neat, even nails. And for the next hour and a half, while I stared at his feet and out at the water, we talked politics. He was knowledgeable about issues, even about personalities, but was almost naïve in his understanding of campaigns. Other than his Uncle Sidney, whom he obviously considered barely worthy of contempt, the only political figure he had ever met was one of his law partners, a former Secretary of Defense.

"I never knew that," he kept saying, or "Really?"

I said "Really?" a couple of times when he explained the economic power wielded by multinational corporations. He represented several. He talked about his work, explaining it took him abroad only three or four times a year.

"*Only* three or four times?"

"Yes."

"What's your favorite country?"

"I don't know. I think England's the only other place I could live, but I get more excited about going to France. What's your favorite?"

"I don't know. I've never been out of the United States, except for my honeymoon in the Caribbean."

"You've never been to Europe?" he demanded.

"I'll just bet you're a Republican, David."

"Wrong. And stop trying to stereotype me."

"I'm not trying to stereotype you."

"Yes you are. What do you think, I go to bed with the *Wall Street Journal*?"

I changed the subject. "Don't you live in the country somewhere? Connecticut or someplace horrendously verdant? I thought I remembered Barbara telling me that."

David grinned. "I see she's supplying a little background. No, I live in Manhattan. My former wife lives in Connecticut. And my children. I have three."

"That's right."

"She's remarried. To a writer. Arthur Abel. Have you ever heard of him?"

"No."

"He's a novelist. He's really a very nice guy and wonderful to my children. Reads poetry to them, takes them riding."

"On horses?"

"Yes, of course. They live on a farm and they have quite a nice setup."

"From writing novels?"

"No. From Lynn, my former wife. She bought the place."

"Mr. Abel has himself a nice deal. If you like kids and horses." David, who had been looking at me, turned his head to look across the sound, toward Connecticut. "Look, David, I'm sorry. I didn't mean to be *that* snide. You miss your kids, don't you?" He nodded. "How often do you see them?"

"Every other weekend and winter vacation and for two weeks in the summer. But now they go to camp with their friends during the summer." He turned to me. "I have tickets to a concert next Wednesday. All Chopin. Would you like to go?"

"I can't, David. Thank you."

"You can't get an evening off?"

"It's not that. We're in the middle of a primary campaign and you're involved with another candidate. It just wouldn't look right to be seen with you."

"You're joking."

"I'm serious."

"Do I look like Mata Hari?" he demanded.

"A little around the eyes. Really, David, it's just not done. But thank you."

"You're welcome. What about after the election? Would you see me then?"

"Didn't Barbara tell you?" I asked.

"That you were involved with someone?"

"That I'm living with someone."

David's light brown eyebrows pulled together, creating a vertical column of skin between his eyes. Then his forehead creased into several horizontal lines. He seemed a little annoyed with me and a lot annoyed with my cousin Barbara. At least that's what I read the lines to mean. But his voice was cool and polite He said, "Barbara didn't mention that."

"I guess she was afraid you'd think I wasn't a virgin."

David erased his lines. "To tell you the truth, I rather assumed you weren't after she told me you had been married for a while."

"Then you've gotten my whole biography."

"Only the highlights." He plowed the wet sand with his toes. "Look, Marcia, I've had a very enjoyable afternoon with you. I don't know what your living arrangements are, but I'd like to see you again, if that's at all possible."

"Well . . ."

"Even if it's just for a friendly evening. But I'll leave that up to you. I'm in the phone book. David C. H-o-f-f-m-a-n, Fourteen East Sixty-seventh. And I promise not to ply you with drink to get Paterno's secrets."

He smiled and I smiled back. And a quarter hour later, when we returned for the barbecue of enough protein to feed Swaziland for six months, my cousin Barbara smiled. So did Philip, Aunt Estelle, Uncle Julius, and Mr. and Mrs. Drexler. And so did my mother.

"Have a nice walk?" she asked sweetly.

16

Jerry was no dope. He knew how to soothe an anxious heart. So I was wooed long distance. From Schenectady he murmured that my hair had the texture of flower petals. "Like cornflowers," he began.

"Cornflowers are blue," I said.

"Don't interrupt a compliment, sweetheart."

From Rome he extolled the enticing curve of my small waist as it flowed into my generous, womanly hips.

From Oswego, he proclaimed I was in perfect balance: a keen mind coupled with a gentle heart.

From all over he told me how he wanted me. He couldn't wait to see me again And I couldn't wait for him.

I sensed a turbulence only Jerry could calm. The Fourth of July feeling would not wear off. I caught myself thinking like a member of my family. I longed for elegance. With Jerry around, I would have no eye for rich fabrics, no nose for bluebelled hankies. He filled all five senses. With him gone, I felt empty.

I grew angry at the dirt and bleakness of headquarters, the squawking voices of the city. I was irate that I had to be exposed to the rank body odors of a summer subway ride. I daydreamed about sitting at the edge of Barbara's pool, wiggling my toes in the water, picking at a bowl of seedless grapes on the brick patio beside me. I could see myself with one of Philip's leather-bound volumes of Henry James, lounging in a hammock between two of the fine Drexler oaks.

"Can't I come upstate for just a day or two?" I asked Jerry.

"Marcia, it's the middle of a campaign."

"But it's awful here. Humid. The air feels filthy. And we could have such a fabulous time."

"You're just tense. Tired. Don't worry. I'll be back soon and I promise you, I'll make you feel better."

I wanted a little gracefulness. I called David C. Hoffman and asked if he still had the second ticket: I would like to listen to Chopin.

"Of course I have it. I'm glad you called. Shall I pick you up?" I suggested we meet at Lincoln Center, by the fountain. "You're not worried about someone catching us, in flagrante, listening to music?"

I answered truthfully. "I've never heard of anyone who would go to hear Chopin during a campaign."

"Then we're safe. Would you prefer dinner before or after?"

"Oh, I don't know. How about after, so I won't feel guilty about leaving too early."

I got a little gracefulness. The pianist played with such fineness that I was drawn out of myself and into a mist of pleasure. I might have been George Sand, listening to an étude I had inspired a few hours earlier.

"Isn't he good?" David asked during intermission.

"Wonderful."

David was a relaxed concertgoer, leaning back in his seat and letting the music flow to him. Unlike Barry, he did not hunch forward, as if panicked that a note might give him the slip. Nor did he grab my hand, blow in my ear, or try to play games with my knee. He listened.

"David, what a pleasure that was," I said, as he held open the door of a taxi. I did not mention that I hadn't been to a concert since my divorce.

"Well, it's a pleasure to go with such a music lover," he answered.

We arrived at an expensive northern Italian restaurant—it had a doorman and a blue canopy in front—and the maître d' was thrilled to see Signor Hoffman again and so obsequious that he nearly licked David's shoes. David ordered a pasta called angel hair first. It was so delicate I hesitated before piercing it with my fork.

Our chatter was breezy. David offered some amusing stories about Harvard's history department, which I had never before considered as a source of humor. I managed one or two sallies about the city's fiscal policies, and David seemed to find them witty enough.

Over the veal, he asked me about being an only child. "I wasn't typical," I said. "No one tried to spoil me. My mother wasn't very demonstrative, so I never felt overwhelmed."

"You were very lucky."

"No. I would have loved to have been spoiled rotten, have millions of presents showered over me, have someone worrying about me all the time, telling me to button my coat and eat my vegetables."

"Eat your vegetables, Marcia," he said, indicating my zucchini. "Don't you think she might have left you alone because she sensed you were enormously competent?"

"Oh come on."

"But you're so self-sufficient. Maybe she felt intimidated by such a strong child. Maybe she felt inadequate."

"David, a ten-year-old kid may be able to dress herself, but she still needs to feel protected, to know there's an adult in charge of her life. It's very frightening to realize that no one's worrying about you." I peered at his plate. "You ate your vegetables first. What a good little boy you must have been."

He smiled a little and shrugged.

"Were you?"

"I guess so. I was one of those solid-citizen types, the kind of child who can always be relied upon to behave, keep busy, and not bother anyone "

"Do you have any brothers or sisters?"

At first he didn't answer. Then he said, "A brother. He's two years younger."

"Oh. Are you close?"

"No." He paused. "You see, he's retarded. He's institutionalized."

"David, I'm sorry."

He looked around the restaurant, almost as if to see if there was an emergency exit for escape. But then he looked straight at me and spoke quickly, much faster than his normal measured pace, as if to rush away from his ingrained propriety, to flee from his world where family flaws are not discussed. "I never even knew about him until after my mother died, when I was nineteen. They never mentioned him. They just threw him away. Oh, it was a nice place they threw him in, but it was like he was some disgusting piece of refuse they wanted to get rid of. They never visited. I only discovered him by accident, when I was talking to one of the lawyers about my mother's estate. He said something about 'your brother' "

"My God. You must have been stunned."

"Shocked. My father denied he existed. It took me two years to get the information from my Aunt Marjorie."

"Did you see him?"

"Yes. I went there; it's in New Jersey. He's badly retarded. He can't feed himself properly or get dressed. But he smiles at me. I mean, there's a trace of humanity there. I go every few months."

"Do you think he remembers you from time to time?"

"No. But I take him things. A hat, one of those wool ones with a big pompon. Candy. He seems to like it."

"I'm sure he does. He must sense you're someone special, someone who really cares about him." He looked away again. "What is it, David? Tell me."

"He looks like me. It's eerie." I nodded. "Anyway, enough happy memories," he said. "Tell me how a nice person like you got into politics." He waved to the waiter and ordered another bottle of wine.

The next night I had to write a speech about bond ratings, so we only had time for drinks at the Plaza. We sat at a table in a dark wood-paneled room, sipping wine and discussing our marriages.

He and Lynn were third cousins. They met when they were twelve at some mutual relative's birthday party. They had the same cultural interests, the same passion for riding, even the same straight brown hair and hazel eyes. They knew they were well suited, and everyone was pleased by the match. He never dated another girl—or woman—until after his divorce.

"Never? Not one?"

"No. When did you meet Barry?"

"When I was almost seventeen. But I had dated other

boys. I mean, nothing much happened except for some intense kissing, but at least I had a vague idea that boys came in different varieties."

"Well, I was amazingly naïve. We both were." As he spoke, I began to sense that they had had more fun on top of their horses than on top of each other.

"Where did you ride?"

"In Central Park or at my family's place in Pennsylvania."

"With high boots and those funny little hats?"

"Sometimes. Have you ever ridden?"

"No. And don't look at me that way. I would never consider it."

"Never? Just to try?"

"Not as long as there are taxis."

I told him about my marriage to Barry, and he nodded with polite interest until I mentioned that the only reason we had lasted as long as we had was because of our sex life. "Really?" he said. His eyes widened. His eyebrows lifted. He seemed fascinated.

"Yes," I said, looking into my wineglass.

I regretted mentioning sex. There was something fastidious about my conversations with David. We were fairly intimate for near strangers, but it was a chaste intimacy. Since the afternoon at the Drexlers', when he held my hand at the beach, he had not attempted to touch me. He was always the gentleman, unfailingly correct. This suited me, although I was starting to sense that he was waiting for a signal from me to initiate something beyond the talk.

When I looked up, I saw his eyes had that moist, unfocused look of people who are thinking about sex. "It's getting late," I said. "And I have a horrendous day tomorrow."

But I agreed to see him again. The following night, most of the staff members were driving up to Rockland County for a Paterno rally. Several people stuck their heads into my office and I told them I already had a ride; I would see them at the rally. I didn't. I saw *Measure for Measure* in Central Park with David. On the way to dinner, we had a fairly heated disagreement about Shakespearean comedy. "Do you have any idea how wrong you are?" I demanded.

"I'm right. I've never been more right."

"Well, at least it's nice to talk to someone who has an opinion about Shakespeare, even if it's wrong."

We had dinner in the outdoor garden of a Czechoslovakian restaurant. I could feel my curls getting tighter in the humidity. I glanced at the strings of colored lightbulbs that looped from tree to tree, then at two cats who meandered around the tables, looking for a friend.

"Watch it, Marcia," David said.

"What?"

"No cat-food comments. I know you're prone to them."

"Just one?"

"No. Come on. Talk to me. Tell me about you and Barbara. Would you like some more noodles?"

"No thank you. I mean, no noodles and no Barbara. If I talk about her then I'll get onto my Aunt Estelle and from there it will be my mother and then my father's death and I don't feel like it tonight. Let's discuss something frivolous—offshore tax shelters or something."

"In a minute. Tell me, how old were you when your father died?"

"Ten. Why do you keep cross-examining me?"

"I'm not cross-examining you. I'm not a litigator. I'm just interested. Tell me about him. What was he like?"

"Very quiet. Undemonstrative."

"Like your mother?"

"No. Look, David, I really would rather not go into it."

"All right."

"The weekend before he died he took me to the Museum of Natural History. I just remembered this. We spent hours looking at the stuffed animals. Mainly the birds. Here he was, this little nebbishy accountant with an absolute passion for birds. And I'd never known it before that day. He'd never given any indication about caring deeply for anything. 'That's a puffin,' I remember him saying. 'It's a sea bird.' And I told him it looked like a penguin and he began to explain the differences between the two, and he was so articulate, so self-confident, like I'd never seen him before and . . . shit, David. Why did I start this?"

I was crying. Not just a couple of tears straying down my cheeks, but a flash flood, so when I put my head down they dripped into my lap.

"Here." David handed me his handkerchief. "I didn't realize, Marcia. I'm sorry."

"No more of this. It's awful. People are staring."

"Don't worry."

I sobbed, then sniffled into his handkerchief for a few minutes.

He reached across the table and patted my hand. "I had no idea it would still be such an emotional topic for you."

"People are going to think you're telling me good-bye, the way you're patting my hand, that you're running off with a tall thin brunette."

"I only bother with tall thin brunettes when I'm desperate. Anyway, how could I even consider one of them when I have you?"

I stuffed his handkerchief into my handbag. Until that minute, I hadn't realized I was doing anything that might jeopardize my status quo. I wasn't cheating on Jerry, I told myself, because David was behaving like a friend. There was no sex. It was like going out for dinner with Barbara or Eileen. He was certainly no threat, no Noreen Ostermann like Barry brought home to our bed. I could imagine David in a tuxedo, in jodhpurs, in tennis shorts, but not naked, sweaty, rolling on top of a sheet. He was too fastidious, too mannerly.

But when we stood on Third Avenue waiting for a cab, he put a hand on the back of my neck and massaged it softly. "Whenever you're ready," he said. "I don't want to put any pressure on you."

I rolled around the bed that night alone, unable to find a part of the mattress tempting enough to seduce me into sleep. I didn't desire David, but I didn't want to tell him good-bye. I could, in my old promiscuous mode, let him take me to bed and keep himself amused; I could remain aloof. It wouldn't be actually cheating on Jerry since we weren't married. Technically there would be no adultery because I was a free woman; Jerry himself had determined there would be no ties. My insomnia mushroomed.

The next morning Paterno demanded an analysis of his performance at the previous night's rally. "You were brilliant, Bill. The best yet." He nodded, concurring with my assessment. Then I disappeared into my office, put my head on the typewriter, and fell asleep. The telephone woke me at noon, when David called to announce he was making me dinner at his apartment.

And that night, Jerry came home. I froze as I heard him

open the door, my hand clenched over a pair of small but genuine pearl earrings Barry had given me for our first anniversary. Only my eyes darted about, like someone psychotic or guilty. I had been caught.

"Marcia," Jerry said, gaping. "What did you do?" I was wearing makeup. He had never seen me in it.

"Don't you like it?" I asked, clutching the earrings even tighter and gazing at the loosened knot of his tie to avoid being flustered by his face.

"Sure. I guess so. You look so different. What made you do it?"

"You're still holding your suitcase," I observed, licking my lips. The gloss tasted like raspberries. Each time I inhaled, I smelled the moisturizing cream made from—the woman at the makeup counter assured me—the essence of almonds. I desperately needed this balm, she confided, because my skin was screaming for lubrication.

Jerry did a shallow knee bend and put his suitcase down in front of his dresser. His skin was darker than usual, glowing from the upstate sun. He needed no almonds.

"Where are you going?" he demanded. He sounded stunned, as if I had metamorphosed into a different species, a tree or a swan. He stepped closer to inspect me. I shut my eyes so he could see my subtle, creative use of three different shades of blue eye shadow, which the saleswoman had told me would bring out the color of my eyes. I used the time to think of a fast lie.

"I'm going to the theater. With Barbara and Philip." I opened my eyes. Jerry closed his briefly.

"With makeup?"

"Why not? I'm thirty-five years old. Anyhow, I need color."

"Blue?"

"I got tired of looking at the same face."

Jerry ran his hand down his chin and over his neck, as if trying to come up with some urbane rejoinder. He could not. "If you're going to the theater, why are you wearing all that makeup? You'll be sitting in the dark."

"I don't know. We'll probably go out for a light supper afterward."

"Oh," he said, in a drawing-room-comedy butler's voice, "madam may be having a light supper after the theater. How divine."

"Come on, Jerry. I've been working every single night. I needed a break. I didn't know you'd be coming back."

"Of course you didn't. And how can an evening with me compare with a night out with the Drexlers. Are they picking you up in the Rolls, my dear?"

"I'm not going to even bother to answer that."

"Of course not. A person of your refined background wouldn't deign to get into a cheap discussion with a peasant."

"Why is it that you can come and go whenever you feel like it, have a night out with the boys two or three times a week if you want to, and I have to stay home, ready for you? Why is that?"

"Marcia, we're being unfair, aren't we? I wouldn't dream of interfering with your social life. Have a wonderful evening with Cousin Barbara. Do give her my love."

"For God's sake, Jerry . . ."

"Au revoir, my pet." He began to undress, slowly, teasingly, letting his tie drift to the floor, opening his shirt buttons with the self-consciousness of a stripper, keeping his eyes on his audience. "Have a rich cultural experience."

By the third button, I was involved in his performance. While I cannot recall my thoughts, I'm sure I considered leaving David to watch his salad wilt and catching the rest of Jerry's show. But something pushed me out of the apartment. I tongued my raspberry lips, whispered a fast good night, and ran on my new high-heeled sandals out of the apartment and down the stairs.

David was waiting for me. "Marcia! Don't you look glamorous! Come in."

He was not as tall as Jerry, but he seemed larger because he was broad-shouldered and big-boned. He wore a yellow cotton shirt with the sleeves rolled up and gray slacks. "I thought you'd be wearing a maroon silk smoking jacket," I said.

"I'll buy one tomorrow." Then, in what was either an example of Ivy League good manners or keen intuition that I was nervous, he asked, "Would you like to wash up after that hot ride uptown?"

"Yes. Please." He led me down a long entrance hall and opened the door of a guest bathroom. "Thanks." He said he'd meet me in the living room.

I was not sure whether "wash up" was upper class-ese for going to the bathroom; my mother had skipped that lesson. But I did anyway, sitting on a cool, sophisticated black toilet seat and studying my surroundings. It was an elegant room, tiled in large squares of black marble and lit by a small bronze fixture. In the sink, in a crystal dish, were tiny spheres of alabaster soap; on the rack, linen guest towels that appeared old and fine and ironed by a maid. I opened the door and continued down the hall toward the living room.

David stood as I came in. "White wine tonight? Or champagne?"

Aunt Estelle had told me never to order the most expensive item on the menu. "White wine will be fine."

I had expected a big apartment, and it was, but only its size conformed to my expectations. The wealthy bachelor look which I had anticipated from my recollection of Doris Day / Rock Hudson movies—long, low couches, dim lighting, and stereo equipment that responded to remote-control instructions—was absent. Instead, David's living room was very much like David: tasteful, pleasant, rich.

"Are you nervous?" he asked.

"No. Actually, yes, but I'm not sure why. Let's not analyze it."

"Okay."

I sat on what I assumed was an antique French chair covered in a white brocade. David sat across from me on a long couch upholstered in a nubby dark-blue silk. To my right was a fireplace with an elaborate beige marble mantel. Between us, a beautifully polished mahogany coffee table; on it was a china basket heaped full of raw vegetables and two bowls beside it, full of thick, tasty-looking sauces. I dipped a carrot into one of them.

"Delicious. You did this all yourself, David?"

"I was hoping you wouldn't ask."

"Okay. I take it back."

"No, I'll confess. There's a store on Madison that does this kind of thing. But I'm fixing the steak myself. And I picked out all the wines. What do you want to start with, Montrachet or Chablis?"

Dinner was like that too, filled with choices between good and better. Beaujolais or Bordeaux with the steak?

Grapefruit ices or chocolate cake for dessert? Or both? Back to the living room for brandy or a cordial—or should we try the terrace?

Initially, our conversation was less personal than on our other nights, as if we had to fulfill a quota of chitchat before our realtionship could move along. We debated the validity of psychohistory. We talked about New York in the twenties, Germany in the thirties, and growing up in the fifties. We even touched on the campaign, at first dispatching Uncle Sidney as if he were a comical villain in a farce. We also dismissed Paterno quickly, because he was too intense, too hungry for the New York that twinkled before us as we sat on the terrace. The city sparkled in the first cool of the evening.

David took a sip of brandy from a snifter worthy of Ronald Colman. "My uncle by marriage is thinking of spending another half million for television time." It was the first time he had trusted me with one of the details of the Appel campaign.

"He's panicked?" I asked casually. "The polls?" Normally, I would be leaning forward to seize each word as it tumbled from David's mouth, grabbing it and sticking it onto my memory so I could hand it over verbatim at the morning staff meeting. But I merely lounged on the wrought-iron chaise, ran my hand over the green-and-white-striped cushion, watched as a cloud floated over the moon, took a sip of orange liqueur, and wiggled my newly pedicured toes.

"He's beyond panic," David remarked coolly. "He's insane. His whole self-image is wrapped up in this campaign, and just because there's been a little slippage he sees the entire State of New York on the verge of rejecting him."

"Good," I said but without my usual primary venom. "The more inadequate he feels, the worse he'll perform. I can't wait for the next debate."

But I could wait. Another debate would mean late nights of rehearsals, of firing questions at Paterno until he became an old smoothie on dairy price supports, Medicaid abortions, and drug-related deaths. It would mean tuna on wet white bread at my desk instead of poached salmon by candlelight.

"Well, I don't mind his making a fool of himself," David

explained. "It's just that I'm fond of my aunt, and when he gets upset he takes it out on her."

"Why did she marry him?"

"Why does anybody marry anybody else? I don't know. I guess he seemed very vital, very alive to her. You see, she was very sheltered. During the thirties, when most of my grandparents' contemporaries were minimally tightening their belts, my family was flourishing. They had invested in a pet-food company as an afterthought, and suddenly, when the rest of their portfolio was reduced to almost nothing, this business was thriving. They didn't object to the income it produced, but they were terribly embarrassed by living off . . . well, basically, living off cat food instead of the quiet commerce they had always been involved in. They were a little nuts, I guess. Very defensive. My father and my Aunt Louisa were older, so Marjorie got the brunt of it. They pulled her out of boarding school and had tutors for her at home. They said they didn't want her to be teased by her classmates."

"That is nuts."

"Very." David adjusted the gold band of his watch. "They supervised her social life to such an extent that she had no real friendships. They even had a fiancé picked out for her. They were just waiting for her eighteenth birthday to announce the engagement."

"And then?"

"They owned some property upstate, and my grandfather hired Sidney to drive them around. Sidney was about twenty—a porter at the local railroad station but a real go-getter. Anyway, Margorie began developing a fondness for mountain air. She was always happy to go upstate with my grandfather. And she started taking long walks; she'd go out to the barn of a farm they owned and meet Sidney. That was in June. By July my grandparents sensed trouble, so they took her off to Europe. And by August she announced she was pregnant and wanted to marry Sidney." David swallowed. I thought briefly how much Jerry would enjoy this story. "Well, it was Sidney Appel or die. She threatened to jump out of her window at the Plaza Athenée if they didn't agree. She was wildly in love."

"And Sidney loved her?"

"No, of course not. But he was delighted to marry her.

And finally my grandfather agreed. So they got married and Sidney kept her quiet and pregnant for the next few years, until my grandparents died. And then he started managing her money. You know the rest."

"Of course. People like us can't be too careful. I'm so wary of fortune hunters."

"Come here," he said, patting his lap. I rose and walked across the terrace. The floor was covered in tile, and I was afraid I'd trip on my new high heels and sprawl over him or splatter over East Sixty-seventh Street. When I reached his lap I sat quickly, as though it were a haven.

David interpreted this as eagerness. He pulled me close and kissed me, first tentatively, tasting and testing me with small, soft kisses. Then he grew more fervent. For a moment I tried to rise. It was partially panic. It was also uneasiness; I was afraid I was too heavy on his lap and he was too polite to say so. But his breaths grew deeper. He seemed as solid as he looked and held me firmly on his lap.

I sensed it was my turn. With clinical coolness I licked his lips and put my tongue in his mouth; he tasted sweet. I snuggled closer. David bit my tongue between his big front teeth. I began thawing and pulled back in surprise before I could melt into his lap.

"I don't think this is a good idea." My voice was hoarse.

"Let's go inside."

"David, no."

He stood, taking me with him. "It's much more comfortable in there."

"I didn't bring anything," I whispered as he led me through the living room. I had decided that bringing my diaphragm to David's would make my sleeping with him a fait accompli. I had deliberately left it behind.

"Don't worry. I have something inside." I closed my eyes, hoping he understood me and meant a condom. "Come on, Marcia." He led me along another long hallway, this one carpeted by a dark Oriental rug that glinted red and blue under somber lights.

His bedroom was dark, its blackness barely pierced by the low light in the hallway. He held me by the wrist and guided me into the room until I banged against the edge of the bed.

"Let me undress you," he said.

"No."

"No?"

"Yes." He did it smoothly, fondling me as he took off my dress and slip. For a while, he fumbled over the hooks of my bra but finally flung it across the room in triumph.

He left my underpants on while he undressed, interrupting himself occasionally to run his hand through my hair or to bend and kiss me so as not to lose me in the dark. He whispered my name. Then he helped me lie on the bed and drew off my pants. I reached out for him and found his chest. It was hairless and appropriately solid. I drew my hand down to his belly, where a patch of soft hair began, and then lower still, where the hair grew stiffer. Then I said, "Oh, my God!"

David Hoffman had the biggest penis in the world. I had never seen—or, more accurately, felt—anything that could compare to it. I caressed the head of it and then moved on down slowly, as if to see whether he was pulling some sort of bizarre trick in the dark. He was not. He covered my hand with his and pressed it against him, as if showing off its astounding size again, its unyielding stoniness.

"Oh, my God," I echoed.

"Kiss me, Marcia." I was not sure where he wanted the kiss, but I put my mouth on his. We held each other, kissing for a long time, before he reached for my breasts and behind. His touch grew harder then, grabbing at me, and I tried to pull away once or twice. But I was back before he could even begin to coax me.

His hand slid between my legs, and while he had almost no expertise, I was so excited by the thought of him that I didn't even bother to show him what I liked. Then he rammed a finger inside me, then two, then three.

"You're ready," he said, climbing on top of me.

"I'm not. I'm not." I braced my hands against his chest and tried to push him off. I slithered back and forth, trying to wiggle my way out. I was afraid he would damage me. I knew he wasn't wearing a condom. I was scared I was committing an act that would split me off from the life I had established. "David, wait."

He didn't, of course, and I suppose I really didn't want him to. He was probably accustomed to these protests, to writhings and cries of no that meant yes. I screamed as he entered. It kept hurting. And he held onto me so tight, squeezed my flesh so hard, that that hurt too. And then the pain turned to pleasure. David had taken me over.

He was not an adept lover. He moved arrhythmically. He did nothing more than the average teenage boy would. There were no studied sexual techniques to remind me that this was a meeting of minds as well as bodies. But feeling him was enough. I let go. I screamed. I scratched him and bit him and wept. I came over and over, more than I had ever done in my life.

And finally he did too, with a long deep groan, as though he too were in pain. He grasped my arms and I could feel the curve of his short nails pressing on my skin.

A moment later, David C. Hoffman of Harvard returned to me, civilized as ever. "Are you all right?" he asked gently.

I was so sore I could not pull up my knees to curl into a ball to give myself some comfort. "I think so."

"Can I get you anything?"

"David, we forgot. . . ."

"Oh, God. I'm sorry. I got carried away. Is it a bad time of the month for you?"

He stroked my eyebrow over and over. Every once in a while he'd brush my forehead with a kiss. "I'm not sure," I replied.

17

“How do you like your bath water?” David called. He was an excellent host.

“Hot, please.” As the water whooshed into the tub, I pushed myself into a sitting position on the bed. David returned from the bathroom and offered me a large towel, as if assuming my modesty was so great that I would not permit him to see me undraped. “Thank you.” I put the towel over my arm and walked, very gingerly, into the bathroom. My insides hurt; my legs felt spongy and I could not keep them together. I thought I must look like a wishbone. “Oh, boy,” I muttered. I left the bathroom door open a few inches. David, the gentleman, remained in the bedroom.

I lay back in the steamy water that filled the claw-footed tub. “Tomorrow I’ll go out and get you some nice bath oil,” David said as I lathered up with a big cake of soap. It had a manly, spicy smell, like oranges and cloves. I covered myself with suds, even the bottoms of my feet. The apartment in the Village had no tub, only a stall shower, and I luxuriated in the bath, washing off the odor of sex and replacing it with the well-bred scent of expensive soap. I felt guilty for not feeling guilty, but that lasted for just a moment. I got out of the bath and wrapped myself up in the blue towel, thick and lush enough to absorb a year of after-bath moisture. I sniffed the lightly perfumed skin of my arm.

"I'd like to ask you something," David called.

"Hmm?"

"What are your living arrangements?"

I clenched the towel tight around me. "Well," I began.

"Is that a rude question?"

"No. Of course not." I mused that David probably didn't comprehend what rudeness really was. To him it was just a concept. And he seemed bred to emit waves of light courtesies to obscure any dark emotion he might feel. "You knew I was living with someone."

"Yes." His voice was soft and courtly.

"Well, he's away. Out of town. The apartment is his, the lease is in his name, but I'm staying in it until I can find another place—or until he gets back to the city."

"Oh. Can I ask what he does?"

"He's involved in politics. I'd rather not discuss it anymore. Okay?"

"Of course."

I returned to the bedroom somewhat more surefooted than when I had left it. David had put on a brown bathrobe.

"I didn't mean to seem intrusive," he said, "but I wanted to know. I couldn't figure out whether you'd be offended, but I said to hell with it."

"It's okay, David." He was holding my bra, and I reached for it.

"Oh, here. Sorry."

"You don't want to keep it as a souvenir?"

"I'd rather keep you." He walked toward me and I watched, hoping his bathrobe would part, so I could see inside. But it was well-cut; it stayed closed. "Please sleep here tonight," he said, folding his arms around me. "We'll get up extra early and have breakfast at the Regency. Fresh-squeezed orange juice."

"I can't, David."

"Croissants."

"I have a lot of paper work at home. Really, I can't stay."

"At least promise me another night tomorrow." I swallowed and nearly let my hand drift up and reach inside his robe. "I'll come up with a place that has a real old-fashioned orchestra and we'll waltz up a storm."

"I don't know how to waltz."

"Of course you do. Everybody does."

It wasn't until the taxi whizzed by Washington Square Park, two minutes from the apartment, that I began thinking of Jerry. He would understand that I couldn't waltz. Instead of trying to dance in too-high heels, or growing tense trying to recall an apt quote from *The Tempest,* I could sit in a cheap restaurant in Little Italy with Jerry, sucking in linguini and swapping Carmine DeSapio stories. I could gaze upon a face that made me want to purr with pleasure instead of one so ordinary that, ten minutes after I left, I could not recall it. I could relax.

Perhaps the episode in the dark was an aberration. I had had much too much to drink. I was seduced by the richness of his apartment, by his solicitousness, by his being just the sort of man my family insisted I should want.

As the cab turned onto my block, I dipped my pinky into my lip gloss and smeared on a thick coating, so Jerry might believe I came straight home, loyal and loving after an evening of theater with the Drexlers.

My hand shook as I paid the driver. The night had brought out the worst in me. Even in my bleakest days I had been reasonably honest. Suddenly I had become a sneak. I had lied to Jerry. I had lied to Paterno, missing a rally I should have attended and petting his ego to cover up. I had even lied to David, telling him that Jerry was not merely past tense but absent.

I was greatly relieved to find the apartment dark. I had worried that Jerry might be up, willing to forgive and forget, especially after his celibate upstate nights. If he was deep in sleep, I could slip into bed without any confrontation. If he stirred, reached out for me, I could develop a headache. A stomachache. But Jerry was not there.

My insides ached. I fell asleep and wakened an hour or two later. I probably had a dream about David. At least I assumed it, because I woke aroused, wanting him. I turned over and then stiffened, realizing where I was. But Jerry still hadn't come in. I tried to wait for him, but I gave in to my need to dream.

I awoke again, in that blue-gray hour just before dawn.

Jerry was standing silently at the foot of the bed. I had been pulled into consciousness by the smell of liquor, as if someone were holding an open bottle of scotch under my nose.

"Jerry, are you all right?"

"Yes. Fine." He spoke clearly, showing no signs of being even tipsy. "I have to get a couple of hours' sleep. No conversations." His voice was husky. His words were clipped. I turned on the light and he turned his back to me. "Please turn that off." He was so remote. He was not cranky, angry or hurt. It seemed like another Jerry, as though the alcohol had permeated his cells, manipulated his genes, turning him into a remarkably familiar but new individual.

"I know how annoyed you are, Jerry. I mean, you came home to see me and I rushed out on you." He would not look at me. "I'm really sorry." The back of his shirt was wrinkled and translucent with perspiration. "Look, I know it's been tough with us. I mean, we keep sniping and making up and then sniping again, but once the campaign is over we'll be able to relax."

Jerry marched to the bathroom, closed the door, and threw up.

"Are you all right?" I called.

"Let me be."

We awoke the same moment the next morning, curled in each other's arms. We opened our eyes, stared for a moment, and then jerked apart. "I'll shower first," he said. "I have to get in early."

The day was as awkward as the night. Lyle LoBello was rumored to be in Troy, convincing a senile industrialist that his money was better invested in Paterno than in negotiable securities. Jerry took over. "You're fifteen minutes late," he announced as I dashed into the staff meeting, climbing over feet and knees until I found an empty chair.

"Sorry." There was nothing unusual about the content of the exchange. When we had begun living together, Jerry and I agreed that he would continue to treat me like any other member of the City Hall staff. But his tone was icy, as though he were talking to a young volunteer who had just made some stupid, irreparable error. I opened my notebook. When I looked up, I saw he was flipping through a file of papers and computer printouts. He seemed to have forgotten me.

But a vein on his temple throbbed, one of his silent stress signals, and every minute or so he'd run his fingers over it. "All right," he said, looking up, "you've heard the bad news. Now the good news." I peered around the room for some clue of what had gone on, but while most of the staff looked appropriately morose, I could get no clear feeling of what had gone on. Joe Cole, sitting beside me, had his lips compressed into a severe pout. I glanced at Eileen. She looked upset too. She gave me a fast blink and turned back to Jerry, who had begun speaking again.

"I have a copy of tomorrow's *Daily News* poll." Metal chairs squealed as people shifted expectantly. Jerry had announced good news. "We finally made it. We're four points ahead of Appel!"

Cheers. Hey! Fabulous! No shit! Wonderful! About time! Wow!

"He's got thirty-two points, we've got thirty-six, Parker's got nineteen, and the rest are undecided. Now that's damn good. Appel will be running scared, and the more he shows himself, it seems to me, the deeper he'll bury himself." Jerry didn't even glance at me as he said this, although it was my theory, one that I had expounded to him weeks earlier, when Appel began to seem vulnerable. "Now, what we have to do is take an aggressive position." Jerry's legs were slightly apart, as though he were standing firm, prepared for a fight. "We can't sit around and wait for Appel to mouth off some more on humane balance sheets or whatever the hell he talks about. Right?"

LoBello's contingent, sitting in the first two rows, were nodding in agreement. Jerry was playing to them, smiling and wooing them. Their heads followed him as he strode across the front of the room.

"We have to decide what themes in this campaign are working, which are solid and worth stressing, and which are bullshit. Okay? Are you with me?" They were. Even a little redhead, reputed to be LoBello's newest lady, was with Jerry. Her head was tilted to one side, taking him in. He flashed her a fast grin, nearly thoughtless, but one that would repeat itself in her mind throughout the day.

The men in the front rows sat up straighter, listening to

him. Jerry didn't have to swagger like LoBello; just walking was enough. And when he talked, his easy voice and slightly rough Bronx accent caught them up. He was the cool Yankee third baseman who would inevitably be Most Valuable Player. They sensed that now. Jerry was back in the game.

"All right. I'm going to call each of you into my office today, and I want your straight opinions on what stays and what goes. Now I said straight. This is a fight, a real battling primary, and there's no time for personalities and tender feelings. We only have time to win."

It was sophomoric. Yet as he walked from the room I had—as I sensed the other staff members had—a deep urge to cheer him as he departed, to throw confetti and roll up my sleeves and work all night. I forgot I was to waltz.

In my office, I wrote three speeches in two hours. I reviewed the ad agency's work and finished a rough draft of an article for the op-ed page of the *Times* that would be submitted in Paterno's name. I worked unceasingly, waiting for the phone to ring and summon me to Jerry's office. It finally did.

"Hello," I snapped, trying to sound annoyed at being interrupted.

"Marcia? Is that you?" It was my mother.

"Yes. How are you, Mom?"

"Fine. Fine, thank you." She was using her aristocratic voice, which meant she was probably calling from my Aunt Estelle's house. "And you, Marcia?"

"Fine, thanks. A little rushed right now." I did not want Jerry to get a busy signal.

"Well, I don't want to disturb you. I just wondered if you knew David Hoffman's address."

"What?"

"David Hoffman's address. There are seven David Hoffmans in the Manhattan phone book." I couldn't speak. "I want to send him a thank-you note," she continued.

"What for?" I managed to say.

"Oh, we were discussing politics at Barbara's home and he suggested I read a certain book by a writer he had gone to Harvard with. It was delivered today, from a Manhattan bookstore. And I was going to take it out of the library."

"Oh."

"And he sent a lovely note on his calling card. It's an engraved card with just his name on it, nothing else, and it says, 'I enjoyed our talk. David Hoffman.' Very thoughtful."

"He said he lives in the East Sixties."

"Oh. I assumed he'd live in that area. By the way, has he—"

I didn't let her finish. "Look, I have a meeting right now in Jerry's office. Can I speak to you tomorrow?"

"If you have time." Still upper class, she hung up gently, on her best behavior for David's calling card. I slammed down my receiver, angry that David was now disrupting my days as well as my nights.

The phone remained inactive for the rest of the afternoon, and by five thirty I knew things were going to be awkward with Jerry. My walk down the corridor to his office felt slow, as if I were plodding through fog. Yet everyone else seemed to be rushing about, energized by Jerry's pep talk. Aides crossed my paths, carrying new leaflets or piles of mimeographed press releases, murmuring " 'scuse me." Or they raced from one office to another, bringing tidings of joy.

"What is it?" Jerry demanded as I stuck my head into his office. He was sitting with his feet on the desk, talking to one of the kids who was doing negative research on Parker. His upstate tan was still glowing but his hair was mussed, as if he had been running his fingers through it all day.

With a very dry mouth I asked, "What time do you think you'll be getting to me?"

"What? I don't have to speak with you." He spoke to his fingernails, not to me.

"I see. All right."

"I'll be working late," he said.

"Maybe I'll call my mother. Invite her to the city."

"Fine."

"Or maybe I'll go out to Queens."

"Okay. Look, I'm busy right now, Marcia." The aide, a Puerto Rican kid from Brooklyn, about nineteen or twenty years old, was trying to act disinterested, but his eyes kept darting from Jerry to me.

"If we go to a movie, I may sleep over at her apartment."

"Okay. See you tomorrow then."

I wanted to shout, what's happening here? A relationship like ours just doesn't fade out. This isn't natural. We should fight and curse. Crockery should be thrown, faces slapped. Hearts should break. And then we should make up.

"You keep getting prettier," David said, two hours later. We sat at a small round table with a long pink tablecloth in a large and elegant dining room of a very grand hotel. His fingers ran over the top of my hand lightly. "That black is such a beautiful contrast with your skin and hair."

David's airy touch erased a day of Jerry. I stared at his big hands, his thick fingers, and was suddenly so overcome by lust for him that I was certain the orchestra could feel the vibrations of my need across the room. I didn't want dinner. I didn't want to waltz. I only wanted to climb onto David's lap like the night before, to rub against him until I felt him rising into me.

"What are you drinking tonight?" he asked. "White wine?" I nodded. He raised one hand and a waiter appeared. A few moments later he leaned forward and asked, "Marcia, is anything wrong? You're so quiet."

I made myself look at him. His face was simply the face of David C. Hoffman. Large-featured and pleasant with nice hazel eyes. His mouth was open slightly, and I wondered, If I put my tongue between his teeth, would he bite down on it, hard, the way he had done the night before? But he smiled pleasantly, as if what had gone on in his bedroom had happened in another world to other people. This world was one of violins and silver candelabra. He had admired my dress. I wanted him naked.

"Marcia?"

"Did you have a haircut?" I asked.

"Yes. Why? Don't you like it? Is it too short?"

"No. No, it's fine. You just looked a little different, and I couldn't figure out why for a minute."

"I caught myself in the mirror this morning and realized I looked too scruffy for you. So I had it trimmed. You're sure it's okay?"

"It's fine, David. You look very nice."

We drank wine and listened to the orchestra warm up with Cole Porter. We ordered dinner. We danced to Rodgers and Hart. David, of course, danced elegantly, taking me along with him, holding me close enough to guide me but not close enough. Once, when I glanced up and saw my hand completely enclosed in his, I experienced another flush of arousal and started to trip, but he whirled me out of it, around the floor, back to the table.

We ate, but I forget what. We discussed in which musical direction George Gershwin would have gone if he had lived. David told me I had porcelain skin. I thanked him.

"More wine?" he asked. I shook my head.

He told me about his children. He said the worst part of the whole divorce had not been losing Lynn; it had been the first few months when he had come home from work to a silent apartment.

He asked, "Have you ever thought about having children?"

Within three minutes my eyes filled with tears as I told him about my miscarriage. Then I mused, "I'm afraid they'd interfere with my career, or at least cause complications. And I'm afraid that I might wind up like my mother, having a child and then not knowing what to do with it, fearing it because it brings responsibilities I couldn't manage, or loathing it. What would happen if I had a child who was as remote as my mother? Could I love it?"

"Do you really believe that could happen?"

"No, I guess not. But it's safer for me, at this stage in my life, to think that way than to melt and go goo-goo every time I see a baby carriage pass by. Sometimes when I see a baby, I wonder whether—you know, when I was pregnant, if it was a boy or a girl. . . ."

"Marcia."

"No more, David. I can't take it. Every time I talk to you I wind up crying."

"And every time I talk to you I find myself saying things I've never said to anyone else. About my brother. How it was losing the children. I don't want this to sound negative, but you bring out the worst in me. No, wait. That sounds terrible."

"I bring out the honesty in you. And most of it's fine and dandy, but some of it isn't. And that's the part you can't acknowledge, so you engage in this cover-up, this barrage of politeness."

"Well, perhaps. You may be right." He glanced away from me, across the room to the orchestra, and began humming "Swinging on a Star" with them. "Want to dance again?" he asked.

"No." He hummed another bar. Then I cut him off. "I want to talk with you, David."

"I know what you're going to say, that I'm embarrassed by opening up to you and that's why I started humming."

"No."

"Well?" I said nothing. David signaled the waiter. "I'll just have another cup of coffee while I wait. Would you like one?"

"You sent my mother a book," I said.

"Yes. *The Seeds of Destruction*, about the Wagner administration. Have you read it? It's very good, scholarly and readable. It was written by a friend of mine."

"I don't want a book report. You know what's bothering me."

"That I sent your mother a book?"

"Come on, David."

"I see. You're objecting because I'm acting as if the way to your heart is through your mother, and that's a major error because you're still rebelling against parental authority. Right?"

"I don't find you amusing."

"You're being silly. She's a lonely woman and I had a nice talk with her. I gather she's not terribly well off and couldn't go out and buy the book herself, so I sent it to her."

"Didn't you ever hear of public libraries?"

"Don't be so mean. It's not like you."

"It is like me. Don't you realize that if she thinks you're even mildly interested in me she'll start putting on all sorts of pressure? And my aunt and then Barbara. I just want to be alone with you. I don't want my whole damn family along. And you went out of your way to encourage her—"

"Marcia, if you want to feud with your mother, that's

your concern. But I liked her. The book is between her and me, all right?"

"No. It's not all right. It concerns me." He turned his attention to his coffee. "You're tuning me out. I'm bringing up something unpleasant so you're making believe you can't hear me."

"What would you like, Marcia? To have a screaming fight about your mother right here?"

"I bet that's what you really expect from me, isn't it? Barbara's low-class cousin who keeps forgetting her manners."

David slapped his credit card down on the silver plate without checking the bill. "What I expect from you is the honesty you're going on about. Honesty about yourself. Don't manufacture crises, Marcia. Don't try to work up a fight just to make sure we keep our distance."

"But it's all right for you to hum."

"I admitted it. I apologize."

"You behave like you cornered the goddamn etiquette market, do you know that? 'Can I get you anything?' That's what you said. Don't stare at me so blankly. Afterward. Last night. Like the whole thing was something casual and you were offering me an after-dinner mint."

"Did I behave casually? Did I? As though it were the sort of ho-hum thing I go through every night with a different partner? Is that the impression you got?" I didn't answer. "Is it?"

"No."

"Then cut the shit, Marcia. And don't stare at me. I know all the words you know. Don't try to pigeonhole me, make me into some damned upper-class fop. I'm a human being, and believe me, my feelings go as deep as yours. I may not be as proficient at expressing myself as some of your friends are, but I'm trying."

"David—"

"Just listen. If you think we're going too fast, fine. Tell me. If something's bothering you, let me know. But don't pick unnecessary fights. I don't want nonsense about books or dinner mints obfuscating—"

"Obfuscating?"

"Please let me finish."

"I want to sleep at your apartment tonight."
"Let's go."
"Don't you want to finish?"
"We will."

18

Jerry and Paterno stood in the corridor of headquarters rocking with laughter. Paterno punched Jerry's arm in masculine fellowship and said, "You are one mean, conniving bastard." They threw back their heads again and laughed. Then Paterno, still chortling, ambled back to his office.

"I see you two are friends again," I said. I stood at the door to the ladies' room. Jerry hadn't seen me. "How nice."

"We're coming along."

"I'm so glad."

"Are you being sarcastic?"

"You wanted me to quit working for him, remember? He was such a no-good son-of-a-bitch that you swore you'd never have anything to do with him again, and you all but told me—"

"I expect you to have those two speeches on my desk by noon."

That was our only confrontation. We hardly saw each other. Jerry's romance of Paterno was so intense that it made it easy for me to cheat. The moment Lyle LoBello was out of sight, Jerry was in Paterno's office, cajoling, charming, flattering. His success was increasingly evident; LoBello began to be dispatched to the same upstate cities that Jerry had been banished to.

My evenings were mine. After Jerry drove an exhausted

Paterno home to Queens, he would evaporate. I sensed the stress of re-establishing his position was enormous, and he was temporarily regressing to an easier phase of his life—drinking and telling stories with the boys. Jerry would float into the apartment about two or three in the morning, gliding across the bedroom, sliding under the blanket with great finesse, taking pains not to touch me.

I usually returned to the apartment by midnight or one, but I could never drift right off to sleep. Part of me waited for Jerry, for a final scene. The other part was alert, stimulated by David, by glamorous evenings with his law partners and clients.

They were all so rich. They spent hundreds of dollars a week on theater tickets, concert tickets, ballet tickets. I had never before seen a play up close enough to watch the actors' expressions. They spent thousands a month on clothes and food.

"David," said Mrs. Millar, wife of the Mr. Millar who owned fifty-one percent of the company which owned fifty-two percent of Central America. "Marcia is such a find! She's been telling me all about Queens. Fascinating! I can't believe how abysmal my ignorance was." Neither could I. "She's so bright!" Mrs. Millar's ruby and diamond earrings flamed in the candlelight. Mr. Millar smiled at me, his teeth black from caviar.

"That woman!" I said later.

"The worst. But he's one of the firm's biggest clients. You were very brave."

"Can you believe she's lived in this city all her life and never heard of the Board of Estimate?"

But most of them were like David: intelligent, kind, and cultured. Some were even fun. One of his partners' wives was an associate professor of political science at City College, and we spent three hours at a dinner party in passionate conversation, ignoring the eight other guests and the host and hostess, hooting over each other's tales of Capitol Hill idiocies. "I can't tell you how much I enjoyed this," she said at the end of the evening. She lowered her voice. "Especially after that bovine creature."

I matched my tone to hers. "Who was that?"

"David's ex-wife. Exquisitely boring human being. Could go on for hours about adverbial clauses in Lytton Strachey. It was like being beaten with brass knuckles."

But most nights I spent alone with David, usually winding up at his apartment. Once, though, when Jerry accompanied Paterno on a three-day upstate swing, I asked David to Greenwich Village for dinner. I wanted to allay any suspicions he had about what he had called my "living arrangements."

He finished a second helping of strawberry mousse. "Wonderful. And it's such a nice apartment."

"What did you expect? A slum?"

"Yes. Although I must say, for riffraff, you're quite a good cook."

David intimidated me. He was always correct. He never had to glance at anyone to see which fork to pick up. He always had read the book or seen the movie under discussion, and—though he was no intellectual exhibitionist like Barry—he would make an intelligent remark that would leave the company nodding at his perspicacity. Maître d's fawned on him, doormen bowed, even taxi drivers were courteous.

"Do you have enough pillows?" he asked. We were lying on his bed, fully dressed, watching Katharine Hepburn enchant Spencer Tracy.

"Look at her," I said. "Just at the way she holds her head. Perfection. It's too depressing."

He pushed a button on the remote-control switch and turned off the television. "Why do you feel so inadequate?"

"I don't. Can I have Katharine Hepburn back?"

"What am I supposed to feel? Secure?"

"Why not? That first night I met you, at the debate, you had such presence. You just sat there with your eyes closed in the middle of all that chaos. Everyone else was wringing their hands, and you were completely self-possessed. If you're comfortable in that kind of high-powered situation, I don't see why you can't be comfortable anywhere. But you're always worrying about your dress or that you don't have nail polish or something silly."

"It's not silly. If those women didn't care about clothes they wouldn't spent a fortune on them. And I keep wearing the same two dresses over and over."

"But they don't care what you wear."

"How do you know?"

"Why should they care? You're smart, pretty, good

company. Do you think they'd overlook all your good qualities to criticize your clothes?"

"I just feel that everybody's waiting for me to gag on the fish course. Look, do I demand you feel comfortable in a TV studio? It's not your world. So why should I relax in somebody's house on Sutton Place?"

"I thought your mother gave you fish lessons."

"No. Fish *stew* lessons. Fish lessons were graduate work." I propped myself on my elbow. "Do you want to see something I learned on my own?"

"Would it be acceptable on Sutton Place?"

"Definitely not." I climbed off the bed and took off my dress, watching David grow under his well-tailored navy slacks. His hand reached out and felt for the lamp. "Would you mind keeping the light on?"

"You don't mind?" he asked.

"I want to see you." I dropped my clothes to the floor and stood watching as David eased off his slacks and undershorts. I climbed on top of him, straddling him. I leaned forward and put my mouth to his ear. "Give me a riding lesson," I whispered.

He did.

There were three Davids. There was urbane David, delighting his hostesses with bright conversation, impressing his partners with his breathtaking grasp of the United Kingdom Tax Treaty.

There was my friend David who told me about his life. His marriage had been so bleak that mine seemed idyllic in comparison. He and Lynn, who had everything in common, had nothing in common. Their evenings alone had been bleak silences dotted with "Have you finished the *New Yorker?*" or "Cousin Joan had a baby girl." Their sex life was joyless.

"She would only do it in the dark," he explained.

"Did you ever tell her that you might like a light on?" He shook his head. "Did you ever ask why she liked the dark? Was it modesty? Fear of seeing you? Maybe she just got worked up by the anonymity of the darkness."

"She didn't get worked up."

"But you never spoke to her about it, David?"

"No."

Their honeymoon had been difficult, and Lynn appeared

to dread his advances. Even a passing stroke of the hand could cause her to stiffen. For his part, he thought sex overrated.

"You? You thought sex overrated? I can't believe it!" I announced. We were lying together on the chaise on his terrace, naked.

"I was . . . I don't know. I thought something was wrong with me, that my needs were uncivilized. But fairly soon my desires seemed to fade away. Not just for Lynn, but in general. This may sound odd—"

"What?"

"I became numb."

"You never thought it might be different with someone else?"

David rubbed his jaw thoughtfully. "How could I let myself think of someone else?"

"Well . . ."

"My mother was dead. My father was—well, my father. Lynn was the only one who cared about me."

"How did she care about you? In what way?"

Lynn Hoffman had three affairs. She confessed all three times and apologized twice. The third time she told David to speak to her lawyer.

"What did you do when she told you?"

"Do? The first time?" I nodded. He looked away from me as he spoke. "I told her I was terribly hurt and disappointed."

"How?"

"How? I can't remember. But it had been with her yoga instructor, and he—"

"David, did you yell? Scream? Carry on?"

"You keep wanting me to behave with great excesses of emotion. I'm not that way. I wasn't raised to carry on."

"But she was your wife. She had an affair and then had the vindictiveness to tell you about it. I don't know. I told you what happened to me, how I caught Barry with someone. I didn't say, 'Oh, Barry. I expected more from a man of your caliber.' I can't understand your acceptance of her. Your passivity. Don't look like I've said something hideous and boorish. Talk about it."

"You make it sound as though her adultery was my fault. What should I have done? Gone after her guru with a shotgun? Slapped her around?"

"I'll bet that's what she wanted. Some indication you were passionate about her."

"Oh, come on. Marcia. She knew I cared about her."

Another night, we sat across from each other at a booth in a restaurant in Chinatown. "Do you know what the worst of it is?" David asked. "That I didn't put up a custody fight. I had a decent chance of winning. She was quite public about it, carrying on with Arthur at some writers' conference while we were still married. And there were the two other times. But everyone—my father, my aunts and uncles, my friends, even my own lawyer—advised against it, that it would be traumatic for the children. So I caved in."

"Is she a good mother, though?"

"Yes, in a way. She's very sincere and serious. She buys every child-care book that's published, and if she reads 'Children thrive on affection' she'll walk over and pat their heads."

Later I asked, "Did you have any affairs when you were married?"

"No."

"Not even after she . . ."

"Especially not then." David felt inadequate. It was not until more than a year after his divorce that he slept with his second woman, a secretary to a lawyer he had been working with in Zurich. Since his German was poor and her English worse, they hadn't much to say, although he knew her name was Gerda. He postponed his departure a week. He discovered he was adequate.

That was the third David, my lover. He intrigued me much more than the other two. He was neither sophisticated nor imaginative, but he was wildly eager. He'd grab and hold me so tight, whispering my name, that I knew for certain that it was me and only me he wanted; a reasonable facsimile would not do. And I lusted for him. My greed for David was nearly boundless. Sometimes I became irritable when urbane David or David my friend intruded. I wanted to shoo them off, so my lover would be free to throw me on the bed. I dreamed of his body, not his mind, not his character. Even when we were finished and I was satisfied to the point of near paralysis, my imagination pulled him inside me again and again.

"David," I said late one night, "Lynn was the biggest jerk who ever lived."

He eased the pillow out from under my hips, fluffed it, and placed it under my head. "Do you want to hear something odd?" I nodded. "Lynn made a pass at me about a year ago." Although the lights were dim, I could tell he was blushing. "I was up in Connecticut, waiting for the children to get their things together. They're never ready. I was sitting at the kitchen table, having a cup of coffee with Lynn, chatting. We're reasonably amicable. Well, all of a sudden, I felt something. It was her hand on the inside of my thigh, very high up. And she said, in a low, seductive voice that sounded nothing like her, 'I'm taking a seminar at Hunter.' "

"What did you say?"

"I said 'oh' or some such thing. And then she said, 'I'll be in town every Thursday, David. We could have lunch.' "

"Did you?"

"Of course not. Besides, I was seeing someone else."

David had had several romances after Zurich, but the most serious was an eight-month-long affair with a woman he had met while riding in Central Park.

"Claudia was marvelous," he told me one evening. She was ten years older than he, and married. "Beautiful. A great sense of humor."

"What did she do?"

"Do? Nothing much. Some charity work, some painting. She had a studio, but she really just dabbled, although I think she got a lot of pleasure from it."

"Were you in love with her?"

"I don't know. I think I could have been, but all the sneaking around took the edge off for me." He paused. "Marcia, don't look away."

"What?"

"I don't like this pussyfooting around we're doing either, not telling Barbara and Philip we're seeing each other, not—"

"David, I'm in the middle of a campaign. It's not easy. Your goddamn uncle is spending quintuple the money we are. I'm doing sixteen hours of work in eight so I can be with you. I'm frazzled. I wake up in the morning so exhausted that I fall asleep in the subway going to work. Please, I have enough on my mind right now."

But we were caught. David was spotted first.

"David! How marvelous to see you!" We were strolling up Fifth Avenue, hand in hand, on the way back to his apartment after an organ recital at St. Patrick's. We both wheeled around. "David!" the voice said again.

"Mrs. Drexler!" he responded. "How good to see you." And there they were, Alfred and Clarisse Drexler, walking down the avenue with a huge fuzzy dog on a leash. "I hadn't heard that you were in town."

"Heel, Boris," she said. "We just flew in for the week. We wanted to . . . oh, my—well, goodness, it's Marcia, isn't it?"

"Hello, Mrs. Drexler, Mr. Drexler." I recalled my mother's saying that refined people say "hello," never "hi." I smiled. "It's so nice to see you."

"It's good to see you again," Mr. Drexler said. "You too, David. You're looking fit as ever. But I didn't realize you two . . ."

His wife cut him off expertly. "How is your campaign going, Marcia?"

"Pretty well, thanks." David's hand held mine tightly. Mrs. Drexler was eyeing the hand-holding. "We've pulled ahead in the polls, and we're getting a pretty good press."

"Marcia's been writing some nasty speeches about my uncle and they've been very effective." The three of them smiled. I gathered Sidney Appel's displeasure pleased them all enormously.

We chatted for a few more minutes about the campaign. David would not let go of my hand. Then Mr. Drexler launched into a dissertation on economic conditions in the town in France where they owned a villa. I couldn't grasp the name of the town because Mr. Drexler's accent was so perfect it sounded like Lmmm. But David knew Lmmm well because he had visited the Drexlers there several times. Mr. Drexler then related his caretaker's analysis of the inflationary spiral—in French. David nodded. "Not bad for a peasant," Mr. Drexler remarked.

David answered him by quoting Montaigne—in French. It must have been a witty remark for the Drexler's laughed. And we left each other with genteel good-byes—in English—and warm hope-to-see-you-soons.

"All right, what's wrong?" David asked, as I pulled my hand from his.

" 'Not bad for a peasant.' My God, what condescension."

"He wasn't being—"

"What does he think I am, for God's sake? I'm a peasant. And so is his daughter-in-law, and so are fifty percent of his grandsons. And four generations ago, no one was inviting the Drexlers to tea. A peasant! I'm every goddamn bit as intelligent as he is."

"Who's saying you're not?"

"You. Making all kinds of references in French, just to put me in my place. And all that upper-class crap. 'Ooh, David, so too too marvelous to see you.' 'Oh, my dear Mrs. Drexler.' Let me tell you something, David. You and I are not a match made in heaven. I cannot begin to tell you how wrong we are for each other, and if it weren't for the sex business you'd realize it too."

"Do you realize you've been blowing up at me on the average of every four days?"

"I have not."

"You have. You relax with me, have a wonderful time, but the minute you sense how close we're getting, you pull away and start behaving like a lunatic."

"I don't behave like a lunatic."

"You most certainly do. What do you think, I plotted with Alfred Drexler to speak French to point out the deficiencies of your education? It happens that the conversation had nothing whatsoever to do with you, and if you'll forgive me, I wasn't thinking about you at all when I was talking to the Drexlers."

"You're always the gentleman, aren't you? So polite."

"It's a hereditary trait of the upper classes, my dear. Like the Hapsburg jaw. Now listen to me. You're just upset that your secret's out."

"Well, you wouldn't let go of my hand. Of course it's out. Mrs. Drexler is going to run right back to her apartment and call Barbara and demand to know all the details and Barbara will say *"What?"* and by tomorrow I'll be receiving an entire delegation of my family. They won't leave me alone. I'll never be able to be natural with you again. You don't know them."

"I do know them and I'm glad it's happening. I don't like carrying on this back-street romance. There's no need for it. We're both free and clear."

"David, we've had so much fun."

"I know."

"But it can't stay that way. They become hysterical at the thought of me being single, working, and enjoying my life—managing by myself. They're going to put horrendous pressure on me to entice you or seduce you or whatever, and I can't take that."

"Well, you've already enticed me and seduced me beyond my wildest imaginings. You know how I feel about you."

"David, please."

We turned the corner to Sixty-seventh Street. "Come on, you can't pretend this is some lighthearted flirtation. We're two adults who mesh beautifully together, and I want it to continue and to grow. I don't want to have to go slinking about, avoiding Barbara and Philip. They're good friends of mine. And of yours, for goodness' sake."

"Why can't it wait until after the campaign is over, when I can think clearly?"

"You really feel so pressured?"

We stepped into the elevator. The operator, a tiny Irishman with long tufts of white hair sticking out of his ears, greeted us. I didn't speak until we were in David's living room.

"I do feel pressured."

"Why?"

"Because you're so perfect. You're exactly what they want for me."

"What's wrong with that? I admire their taste."

"What's wrong is that you are always wonderful, always polite. I open up to you, I feel so much for you, then all of a sudden I pull back and ask myself: Is he really here, with me, listening to me, or is this some man who's enduring my blabbing on and on because he can't be discourteous, because—"

"Marcia, stop that."

"I'm sorry. I don't want to hurt you—"

"You know how I feel about you. Don't you think it hurts me when you imply that I'm some externally correct robot, some automaton? You called me passive, about the way I behaved with Lynn—"

"David, let me explain."

"No. You're right. I was passive. I was covering up a

great deal of fury with a few polite objections. I was afraid to make waves. But don't you understand? That's why I need you so much. You're such an iconoclast. At first, at the TV studio, I thought you were pleasant, clever, but no more than a sassy street kid. Then, at the Drexlers' Fourth of July party, I realized you were a great deal more.

"You keep testing people, Marcia. You poke away at pretensions. You never accept any givens until you can prove them real. And if you sniff out a phony . . ."

"I don't know," I said, sitting on the edge of his couch.

"I know. That's why you have so many problems with your family. Yes, they're pretentious. They posture. Yet underneath you know there's something real, something valuable."

"You've read too many oversentimental chicken-soup novels. I don't know any such thing."

"You do. And it's terribly difficult to resolve all the contradictions facing you. But enough about that. Think of me. Indulge my selfishness. I need you. Please look at me. I need you to bring me out. I need you to help me recognize that someone with whom I haven't quite felt comfortable for ten or fifteen years is a jerk. Remember when you said, after the dinner party with that criminal lawyer, that he was a big jerk?"

"Of course he was a jerk. He kept talking in Latin phrases all night. Who the hell does he think he is, the Pope? And the way he kept sucking and licking that monster cigar, like it was—"

"But you saw that right away. I've known it subliminally for ages, but because of his background, his credentials, I never allowed myself to think it. But you helped me see it. Marcia, I need you to help me find my way past my own pretensions, past my own defenses. All right? And please, don't feel pressured."

"But David, it's overwhelming. Look, I want to feel we can just be ourselves, and that if anything happens, it will happen for the right reasons, because you like what I do to your defenses or because I trust you or love you in bed or whatever—not because I've been strong-armed by my family into being cowed by your pedigree or credit rating. Okay? Do you understand?"

He paced in front of the fireplace. Then he turned to me. "Yes. I guess so. In any case, no more pressure. I understand you're tired, feeling overwhelmed. Do you want me to call your mother and tell her I think you're horribly déclassé?"

"I think she knows."

"Good. Now I want to make love to you. Where will it be? Here? The bedroom? Kitchen? A closet?"

Afterward, I fell asleep on a couch in the small office he had set up in a spare bedroom. At midnight, he woke me. "Are you going back to your apartment tonight?" I shook my head and tried to wrap the short afghan he had covered me with under my feet. "Come, Marcia." He led me into his bedroom. I fell right back to sleep.

"Marcia," he called, sometime later.

"What time is it?"

"Two. I've been up thinking. Listen to me. You'll go back to sleep in a minute. Remember you said you were under pressure. Well, I'm under pressure too."

"Okay."

"I'm spending huge chunks of time away from my firm, having other attorneys service my clients, trying to play watchdog for my uncle's campaign expenditures, trying to help preserve my aunt's sanity—and her solvency. I can't spend an hour at my own office without some relative calling, intimating that I'm letting the family down by not spending every moment sniffing around Appel headquarters. Suddenly I'm supposed to be an auditor and a politician and keeper of the Hoffman honor, whatever that is. So try to understand that this is not the greatest time for me either."

"I understand. Come here. Hug me."

"No. Hear me out. Despite all the pressure, I still have to live the rest of my life. I can't ignore you or put you off until after some election. I care about you now."

"I care about you too, David. You know that."

"But I'm not willing to set an arbitrary time limit on my feelings."

"Okay, David."

"Good. I'm glad you understand. So I'll just say it once. With all the pressure, I care about you very much. In every way. Not only here in bed. I've never been able to talk to anyone the way I can to you. And I have so much fun with you."

"Me too. It's just that—"

"I love you very much, Marcia. I want to marry you. I understand you may not be able to answer me now, or even consider it, but I wanted to let you know." He paused, perhaps waiting for me to say something, but I could think of nothing. After several silent seconds, he bent over and kissed me. "I know that's a lot for this hour. Go back to sleep."

I pulled up close to him. Surprisingly, I fell asleep a moment later. The next morning I woke still tired and nauseated, aching. "I have a virus," I told David.

"Stay here, then. Rest. I'll come home around one and check up on you."

But I dragged myself to headquarters and spent a half hour with Paterno—before he began the day's personal appearances—rehearsing a speech attacking Appel's plan to restructure the Metropolitan Transportation Authority.

"My voice," said Paterno, rubbing his Adam's apple. "So strained. You sound awful too."

"Just fatigue, I think, or a mild virus."

"Do me a favor then. Move your chair back a little. I can't afford to come down with anything. You look pale. I'll tell them to send you in some tea. Tea and lemon, that's the thing. No sugar. Sidney Appel's going to have a heart attack when he hears this speech, the way I make fun of him while sounding serious."

I spent the morning in my office. My electric typewriter had jammed so I was working on a recalcitrant manual which lacked an operable "q." Around eleven thirty someone knocked on my door but I kept typing, thinking that all the important staff members had my extension number. I half feared it was Jerry, ready for a showdown. I had muttered something to him about spending the night at my Aunt Estelle's, but by now he must be seeing through my subterfuges.

The banging continued. "Come in," I finally called.

The door opened and in poked the head of a volunteer. It was a typical volunteer face: young, slightly overweight, earnest, and Jewish. "Excuse me, I hate to bother you," she said.

"Yes?"

"There's a woman out front who wants to make a contribution. I wasn't sure . . ."

"I'm Marcia Green, the speech writer. Finance is the next door down."

"I know, Ms. Green. She specifically asked for you. I tried to explain to her, but she was very insistent." The volunteer's voice was soft.

"All right," I said, rising. "What did she say her name was?"

"She didn't." I marched down the hall, the volunteer beside me. "Whoever she is," the girl continued, "she's a real goddamn pain in the ass, throwing her weight around like she was the fucking Queen of Sheba."

Aunt Estelle stood right in the center of the reception area, forcing everyone else to detour around her. "I know. I know. You're busy. I came to give a check to your candidate and take you out to lunch, but it has to be soon because I'm meeting my decorator at one thirty to look at sconces." Staff members, volunteers, messengers passing through the hall stared at her, at her summer black dress and summer black shoes and summer black straw hat. And white gloves and pearls. She was formidable, like the head of a Matrons for Eisenhower committee who had somehow kept her job through the decades. "Marcia, get me a pen and I'll make you out a check."

"Aunt Estelle," I whispered, "you can't just come in here like this."

"You're finally wearing some makeup and you look very, very nice," she announced. "I am glad to see you're using a light hand with it, not those hideous dark colors."

I guided her toward my office, ostensibly to give her a pen but really to get her away before she began to berate me in front of six or seven political operatives for wearing shoes with no stockings in Manhattan or to proclaim the advantages of sober Semites over the besotted Irish. As I held her silky, fleshy arm and steered her down the corridor, she was saying, "Such a fine person he is. And brilliant. *Law Review* at Harvard with Philip. Did he tell you that?"

"Who?" I asked.

"Don't get cute with me, Marcia," she snapped. "I came into the city early today because it's obvious someone has to talk to you and you've got your mother and even Barbara walking around on tiptoes and bending over backward not to interfere with your liberation, so it's fallen on me to be honest with you. And believe me, I'm not afraid to do it."

"I know you're not," I began, and would have finished quite sharply, except I saw Jerry walking down the hall toward us. I smiled and murmured "hi" while opening my office door and nearly shoving my aunt inside. He smiled vaguely at both of us and kept walking.

"Did you see that man?" she demanded. "Did you? He looks like Tyrone Power. With a little Victor Mature thrown in. And those eyes. Blue. What we used to call . . ."

"Aunt Estelle . . ."

". . . bedroom eyes. Did you see how he smiled at me?"

"That was Jerry Morrissey, Aunt Estelle."

"That's the one you've been—"

"Yes."

"Handsome," she said. "Very nice-looking. But no character in his expression." She peered around my office. "This is where you work, in such ugliness?"

"It's temporary. We just rent it for a few months, for the primary. My office in City Hall is much nicer."

"How old is he?"

"David?"

"The other one."

"Forty-seven."

"He looks fifty. Now go wash up and I'll take you out to lunch. Barbara told me the name of a lovely restaurant a few blocks away and told me to put it on her charge there. They specialize in fine salads."

"Aunt Estelle, I'm sorry, but I can't go to lunch. I feel awful. I have a ton of work."

"You just don't want to discuss it."

"What? That I'm seeing David Hoffman? There's nothing to discuss."

"He's a wonderful boy."

"He's no boy."

"Marcia, I hope you're not making it too easy for him. Don't get angry with me. For years you've been going out of your way to mingle with all sorts of shkotzim just so you could show how independent you are. You're thirty-five years old—"

"And no spring chicken, right?"

"You're thirty-five years old and that's too old to be

rebelling against your family. Working in a place like this. That man. What has he ever given you besides a face full of sunshine? And now with David—"

"Do you honestly think before I make a decision about anything—a man, my career—that I sit down and think, 'How can I manipulate this situation to hurt my family?' Yes, I want to be independent. I want to find some decent values, and I won't find them deluding myself that I'm an aristocrat. I want to find out—"

"And how do you find your values? Living with someone who only wants one thing? Is that values? I call that rebellion. But that doesn't matter. Forget us. We're not important anymore. What's important is you. Your future. Do you want emptiness, or do you want the things David Hoffman can give you?"

"You never let up, do you?"

"Someone has to be honest. Listen to me, darling. David is no fly-by-nighter. He'll always be there for you. He's one of your own kind."

19

My family decided to love me. My aunt called me every day to check on my well-being. "Your virus better? You're still wearing makeup, aren't you? Five minutes each morning. That's all it takes, and what a difference it can make in your life." She lowered her voice and told me that David had confided in Philip that I was very intelligent.

In the beginning of August, my Uncle Julius telephoned the office. "Sweetheart!" he bellowed. "How's my girl?"

Had my aunt been near him, she would have ordered him to lower his voice. "You needn't speak so vociferously, Julius," she would murmur, like a queen giving the king a tiny royal reminder.

"Fine, Uncle Julius. It's good to hear from you."

"Listen, dollface, you know this is August and it's the middle of my busy season. I mean, some of those ladies on the beach are suddenly realizing that in a few months they're going to need a fur to keep them warm." My uncle pronounced "fur" as "fuh."

"Right, Uncle Julius. I remember." The air conditioner had resigned its cooling function and seemed willing only to blow hot wet air into my office. My skin was glossy with perspiration.

"So before I get too swamped, I just thought I'd ask you if you want a garment. I have right here—I'm standing in the back of the workroom, you understand—I got a lovely garment, a sheared beaver that wouldn't overwhelm you."

"It's really such a bad time for me now, Uncle Julius."

"Sure. How many people have the foresight to think of fur when it's ninety-eight degrees? But come November and you're shivering—"

"I mean, I really hadn't budgeted for it. But I appreciate your call."

"Sweetheart, would I call my own niece soliciting business? This is a gift, sweetheart, from me and Aunt Estelle. Look, you're going around in good company now. You have to make the right appearances. You'll come out for dinner one night and we'll take a drive over to the store and I'll show you what I have in mind. I'll fit you myself. People think you can just walk in and buy a garment off the rack, like it was a cheap dress or something."

"Uncle Julius—"

"I know. You don't have to say anything. No thanks necessary. We're family. Just call Aunt Estelle and make a date for dinner."

David sat at the edge of the bathtub and laughed. "Sheared beaver. It sounds like something in a men's magazine."

"It probably looks like it too. It makes me so mad." But I was calm, lying back in the cool water.

"Don't get upset."

"Never," I said, "never in all those years when I really needed Uncle Julius, when my mother was desperate, did he do anything. A one-hundred-dollar bill every year. And suddenly he's handing out sheared beaver so I'll look furry enough to impress you."

"Of course. Get out of the water. You've been in for a half hour and you're starting to look chilled." He handed me a towel. "He's clever, your uncle. First you snare me with sheared beaver, and once I'm hooked I'll spend the rest of my life buying mink and sable from him."

"You know, sometimes you talk like a born politician. How devious you are. But I think you're right."

"Take the beaver. You'll get your sable at Bergdorf's."

"If you're trying to buy me, I'd prefer to deal in cash."

"All right. Are you ready to negotiate?"

"No. I told you, David—"

"I know. No pressure. Would you make me an omelet for dinner?"

My mother called at least once a week with what appeared to be an agenda for a mother-daughter chat. It began with an inquiry into my health and my work and then proceeded into several well-thought-out observations on the state of the world, the nation, and the region, clearly garnered, in page order, from the "Week in Review" section of the Sunday *Times*. Then she'd ask, "How is David Hoffman?"

"Fine."

"Just fine?"

"How else should he be?"

Once she said, "You know his father, Leo Hoffman, is a very sick man. A heart condition."

"I've heard."

"Is David an only child?" she asked coolly, trying to be subtle. I told her I wasn't sure and ended the conversation.

David hated his father. It was not merely profound dislike of a cold parent whose only expressions of interest were "Your jacket is too big" or "You ride like a ranch hand." His father had isolated him from his brother and his mother and not allowed him anything in compensation.

David's mother was forty when he was born, and he said she never got over her surprise. Eleanor Cutler Hoffman had been a sculptor of minor repute. She was a charmer, a great hostess, also quite beautiful, with green eyes and thick pale brown hair.

"She always treated me like a guest," David explained, stretching out his legs on his coffee table. "I would come into her studio to see her, about five in the afternoon, and she'd always sit up straight and say 'David?', as if I'd dropped in unexpectedly but she was thrilled to see me. She'd give me tea and we'd talk. I only saw her for an hour, but it was the highlight of my day. She was always so pleased when I came through the door."

Leo Hoffman joined them occasionally and would tell his wife—in front of David—that she coddled him too much. "He's a boy, Eleanor, not a suitor. Don't ruin him."

David said, "He tried to get her to agree to send me to boarding school in England when I was nine, but she wouldn't go along. Then he held out for prep school and she almost agreed, but I kicked up such a fuss that she finally convinced him to let me stay home and go to school in Manhattan. You see, she really liked me. When I got older, she stopped giving me tea and offered me a cocktail every afternoon. There I was, a fifteen-year-old boy, drinking whiskey and soda and discussing Nevelson. But it all seemed very natural. We'd laugh, have a great time. She was always so delighted with whatever I said."

His parents traveled a lot. David believed his father encouraged his mother to spend her winters in Boca Raton and her springs in Europe to keep them apart.

"You really think your father was that venomous? Or was it just that he didn't care?"

"I think he was venomous. I can't prove it. But I always felt his feelings were a lot stronger than indifference. I think he saw me as a rival."

"I think you're being unfair to him. He didn't threaten your mother with bodily harm if she didn't go to Europe. She went because she wanted to go. Don't overromanticize her. She knew that traveling meant being away from you."

"She loved me."

"I'm sure she did. Why shouldn't she? But if she had really wanted to spend more than an hour a day with you, you know damned well she could have managed it."

"And your mother was so much better?"

"David, this isn't a contest. My mother stayed with me because she didn't have enough money to get to Manhattan, much less Europe. All I'm saying is that maybe you're putting too much blame on your father."

"This is a useless discussion. She's dead."

When David was in his freshman year of college, his mother discovered she had cancer. She announced it to him on Thanksgiving day. "The doctors are very hopeful," she told him, patting his hand. By Christmas, he saw the doctors were wrong.

"My father hired private nurses, had an army of doctors. But he was in charge of everything. And he wouldn't let me come home. He said it would interfere with my schooling and that it was too great a strain for her. She called me, though, once a week, but wouldn't agree to see me. She said, 'David, your father asked me not to and I must defer to him. He's the one who will be around, the one you will have to deal with.' She said she was feeling fine, getting the best possible care, and I should go ahead with my plans, go to Italy that summer. 'I'll be here when you get back,' she said. I kept trying to change her mind but she refused to defy my father—and I could see the conversations were painful for her. Fatiguing."

David's eyes were filmed with tears, but he continued to speak.

"I saw her just twice, right before and after I went to Italy. I was so stunned the first time. She was so thin and so weak. She hardly had any strength in her hand. And then when I came back, it was as if she was barely there. I wanted to stay there, just stay. But my father insisted I get back up to school. And then she stopped calling two weeks after the beginning of the term. I kept waiting and didn't hear from her. I called my father and asked him what was happening. He said, "Your mother is very ill." I said I knew that and wanted to see her. He said she was in a hospital, but he wouldn't tell me where. He said she was comatose and wouldn't recognize me anyway. I waited six more weeks, and then my Aunt Marjorie—not my father—called to tell me when the funeral was."

I pulled him next to me, holding him, kissing him, wiping his tears away with my fingers.

"And do you know what the irony of it is?" he whispered. "I always did everything my father wanted of me. I did well socially, academically, professionally. Even during those six weeks, I kept studying as though nothing were happening, as though she were just away for the winter. I got all A's that semester. And my father congratulated me, said it showed great forbearance. He said, 'I'm proud of you, David.' " He stared at the rug for a moment. "I'm going inside for a little while. I feel like being alone. Excuse me."

I met my cousin Barbara for lunch the next day. "Tell me about David's father," I demanded. "What's he like?"

"Well, I only met him a couple of times. He seems nice. He has a kind of old-fashioned courtesy and a real dignity. I liked him."

We sat at a table at Tavern on the Green, a restaurant surrounded by the moist leafiness of Central Park. Barbara leaned back in her chair. Her heavy, dark hair was pinned up on her head, but stray curls fell along her temples and the back of her neck. It looked artless, but she had just come from the hairdresser.

"We have been here over fifteen minutes," she said, "and all you've done is make polite conversation. Now come on, I want to know absolutely everything."

"What would you like to know?"

"I want to know every minuscule detail about you and David. Really, I think you owe it to me. First of all you met him at my house and . . . never mind. Just talk. I'm going to sit back and sip sangria and you're going to fill me in."

"Okay. I went out with him the Wednesday night after your party. We went to hear Claudio Arrau play Chopin. It was a very nice evening."

"Marcia, please. I'm leaving tomorrow and I'll be gone the rest of the summer. How can I go abroad with a clear head if I don't know what's happening?"

Every once in a while, the spirit of Aunt Estelle possessed Barbara and would speak through my cousin's mouth: a word like "abroad" would emerge, a signal that the transfer of souls was complete. "Abroad" was one of those words that my aunt decided demonstrated delicacy of breeding. My Aunt Estelle believed that if you said "sofa" for "couch" and "purse" for "pocketbook," people would immediately recognize you as gentry. My cousin Barbara had been worked over by her mother for too many years simply to go to Europe.

"What's happening is that we're seeing a lot of each other."

"I know that. He told Philip that."

"What else did he tell Philip?"

"Well, he implied that the two of you are quite serious."

"We are and we aren't."

"What does that mean?"

"It means I care about him very, very much. He's the finest person I've ever known."

"So? What's holding you back?" I didn't answer her. She leaned forward and mouthed, Sex? Then she said, "Stop laughing. How am I supposed to know what's going on with you two?"

"Look, without going into detail, everything is fine. He's wonderful. He's bright and he's charming and—"

"Then what in the world is wrong?"

"I don't know. Everything is happening so fast. I feel very pressured: by David, by your mother, by the fact that I'm thirty-five."

"But if you're so happy with him, why not relax and enjoy it?"

"I'm trying to. But everyone keeps talking marriage and—"

"Marcia?" she said, putting down her glass. "Has he actually proposed?"

"If you tell anyone, Barbara, and I mean anyone . . ."

"I swear. Oh, my God, this is fabulous."

"I don't know that it's fabulous. I don't want to get swallowed up."

"What are you doing, involving yourself in some Kierkegaardian snit over marriage? Do it!"

"No, I can't just do it. I don't know if I could handle the whole package, being a lawyer's wife, dealing with a whole different class of people, with his children—"

"They're adorable."

"They may be. Everything about David is terrific, so why not his children? But I don't want to become his wife just because there's no reason not to. Do you understand me?"

"I understand that you're frightened."

"I'm cautious."

"Do you love him?'

"I don't know. I wish I could just say 'whoopee' and collapse in his arms. But I can't. I know I love aspects of him. His intelligence, his decency, his polish. He's so at ease all the time. He always does the right thing. Even when he's angry or tired, he's still courteous. But that's unnerving too. He's like a magnificently oiled machine that always works."

"I think you're just a little intimidatd by his background," Barbara said. "May I ask you something? Do you love him—well, sexually? I don't want you to think I'm a voyeur or anything."

"Sexually most of all."

"Imagine. David Hoffman. It just goes to show that you never really know your friends."

"But you know your cousin, so take my word for it. He makes my teeth curl. But is that enough to make a marriage?"

"Well, added to his other qualities. Anyway, Mar, be a little selfish. Aren't you tired of running from pillar to post? Wouldn't you like to indulge yourself, to buy expensive clothes, travel . . . ?"

"Let's order lunch. Paterno was acting more irrationally than usual this morning. There's a meeting in his office at two thirty."

"You're upset with me. You think I'm mercenary, don't you?"

"No." The waitress came and took our order. Barbara described the salad she wanted in lush green detail, and even though it wasn't on the menu, the woman promised Barbara she'd convince the chef to prepare it.

"You do think I'm mercenary," she insisted. "It's because you think there's something intrinsically wrong with letting a man pay for things."

"Barbara, come on."

"But on the other hand, you'd also like nothing more than a nice duplex on Central Park West and three in help."

"I'd rather have a penthouse on Park. I don't like the West Side. It's full of reformers and out-of-towners and old ladies who look like Grandma Yetta. Feh. Hey, Barb, remember the engagement party your mother made for the Drexlers, when Grandma took out her teeth and put them on the salad plate?"

"God, I repressed that. I wanted to die."

"Remember your father-in-law? He didn't even look away. He just acted as though it was the sort of thing that happened at most of the dinner parties he went to."

"He's wonderful. And Philip is just like him. But the West Side. You know David and Lynn lived there?"

"He told me." I poured some more sangria. "Tell me about Lynn."

"Well, she was intelligent. She had a master's in English from Harvard. She wasn't particularly pretty—but *very* big on top." She paused. "Frankly, I couldn't stand her. So tedious. I mean, her family had as much money as David's, so she should have had some flair. But you'd go to their house for dinner and the food would taste like hay. And they had a cook. But Lynn would say—after we choked down four horrid courses—'Can you believe that everything we served tonight was made from soy flour?' And of course you could."

"What would have attracted David to her?"

"I'm not sure. I think it was simply the fact that she was there. They got married very young, when they were about twenty. They're distant cousins and I think childhood sweethearts. And he tried to make it work. I mean, he was loyal, considerate. He seemed genuinely proud of her intellectual attainments. And she was the mother of his children, and that counted a lot with David. He's a fabulous father." The waitress came with the salad and presented it to Barbara. "Aren't you wonderful!" Barbara said to her. "Just what I wanted. Thank you."

"Do you always eat salads for lunch?" I asked.

"Always. It's my curse. Anyway, Lynn. She was studious, dull, and not very much at ease socially. I mean, David travels in pretty high-powered circles and there was Lynn, with those awful handmade leather sandals that wrapped around her legs. She got them at some halfway house for the mentally ill. I really don't see how he stood her. She was always going around sprinkling wheat germ on the children or inviting socialists to dinner."

"Maybe she was all he had at the time."

"Maybe, but he's such a catch. You don't know how lucky you are."

"Your mother already told me."

"At length, I'm sure. Anyway, what about the other one? Don't look blank. Jerry."

"What about him?"

"How did he take it, your moving out?"

"I didn't move out."

"What? Are you insane? If David finds out—"

"I'm just using the apartment a couple of nights a week. We hardly see each other. Even at work, we're so busy that we don't have time to talk. He thinks I've developed a sudden affection for my mother. And he goes out every night, comes in at all hours."

"Marcia, move out of there. Please. It's not right."

"I will. Really, Barb. I promise you. It's over. It just died, and I never noticed its going."

I realized how dead it was that afternoon. I sat on a chair in Paterno's office with the rest of the City Hall staff, about a foot away from Jerry. I stared at his profile, the clean cut of his jaw, his remarkable nose. I looked down at the hand draped casually in his lap. And I felt nothing except admiration for the God who had created such a man. And a little sadness.

"Jerry," I said, tapping his arm just before Paterno came into the room. "I'd like to talk. It's—"

But Paterno came barreling in. "You want to know what happened? I'll tell you what happened. Goddamn it, Morrissey, let me do the talking. Seven this morning I'm home, having breakfast, and the phone rings. Hello. Who is it? Richard Black of the *Daily News*, and Richard Black wants to know what's with my campaign coordinator, Mr. LoBello. And I say, he's upstate, in Watertown, I think. Can I help you, Richard Black? Can Morrissey help you? What would make you happy? Well, he says, I just want to know what you think about LoBello's going over to Larry Parker." No one moved except Jerry, who had obviously heard the news before. He shifted around uneasily in his chair. "So I said to Richard Black, Well, we just weren't happy with the results Mr. LoBello was getting. He's not what he was cracked up to be, so we had to let him go.

"Now listen, Black's still working on the story, and it won't be out until tomorrow. So before that, I want you all to go through your files, each one of you. Is there anything missing? Has that bastard stolen anything? I don't want any nasty surprises."

Jerry rose. "It goes without saying that we tell everyone he was fired last Friday." He cleared his throat. "I don't have to say that, bottom line, this is all for the best. LoBello's full of hot air; he's perfect for a windbag like Parker. They'll fizzle out together. All right, now. Any comments? Suggestions? Questions?" No one spoke. Jerry jerked his head around the room. He appeared more ill at ease than I'd ever seen him, hands stuffed deep in his pockets, his legs stiff as he paced the office. "Okay. Let's get to work. We're still in business."

Eileen raced out, as if late for a court appearance. Joe Cole and the economic affairs expert put their heads together and emitted the low grumble of male talk. As I walked toward Jerry, he joined them and hustled them out of the room. I turned to Paterno.

"I'm sorry, Bill."

"Thanks." The glow of fury had left his face and his skin looked ashen. "I appreciate it."

"I hesitated to say anything before, but . . ."

"What?" he demanded.

"LoBello might have Xeroxed a lot of our stuff. If he did, we won't find anything missing."

"Oh, shit." He rubbed his hands over his face. "Why didn't I think of that? It's so goddamn obvious. Sorry about the language," he muttered.

"Okay."

"Tell me what you think. Are we better off without him? Forget what Morrissey said. The truth."

"The truth is Appel's spending it as fast as they can print it and Parker's got the advantage of incumbency. Plus LoBello. Lyle's an arrogant ineffectual peacock ninety-five percent of the time, but the other five percent he can be dynamite. You know that. You can't just forget about him. So, the truth is, I think you're in trouble."

Paterno exhaled slowly. "I do too. Every day things get worse. I can feel it fading." He put his hand on my shoulder. "Remember the beginning of the campaign, Marcia?" I nodded. "Things aren't turning out the way we thought they would, are they?"

20

The last week of August was almost unbearable. The temperature soared. The homicide rate actually decreased because people were too enervated to kill. Dogs whimpered as they walked on the searing pavement. On the fifth day of over one-hundred-degree weather, David came home from his office, his face flushed and damp, and knocked a spinach souffle across the kitchen counter. "How can you expect me to eat anything hot?" he shouted. "How?"

He apologized almost immediately. "I'm sorry. The heat got me. Just walking those few blocks." He bent over and inhaled the souffle. "It smells wonderful."

He smiled. David had been well trained. "You didn't have to fuss with dinner. You've been working so hard."

"It's okay," I replied, arranging pieces of roast chicken on a platter.

"I can't get over the heat," he said pleasantly. "Do you know, I just realized—walking home—that I've never been in the city in August before. I had no idea. . . ."

I had spent every August in either New York or Washington. "Is it cooler on the Riviera?" I screamed. "Go ahead! Leave! Go where it's cool. You can talk French with your goddamn cool friends. You can eat cold food until you choke on it, for all I care. Good-bye. Have fun in Cannes." I thought I had energy to shriek for another five minutes. Instead, I swooned. Feeling helpless and very foolish, I found myself slumping to the floor. David saw me and caught me in time. "I'm all right," I said.

"Are you sure?" He looked frightened.

"My air conditioner broke down completely. And I couldn't get the window open. Oh, David, it's like working in Hell."

At headquarters, the stench of mildew grew so strong that I held my breath as I rushed through the corridor. The hotel management, aware of our short-term lease, claimed they could not stanch the march of the rot; it was a "structural problem," they explained ominously. And they felt bad about the air conditioners, but the machines could not tolerate such humidity.

One evening, when I was working late, rehearsing Paterno for his final debate, I glanced up from my notes to look at him. His face was glossy with perspiration. His nostrils were quivering and his teeth were clenched together, like a child trying hard not to cry.

"What's the matter, Bill?"

"Nothing."

"Come on," I insisted.

"You know the Medicaid speech I was supposed to give in Hempstead, for the senior citizens? Well, you know who the audience was?"

"Who?"

"One senior citizen. I'm in this big hall, up on the stage with a podium and microphone, and there's only this one real old guy, sitting in the second row. So I ask Jill, the advance man—lady, woman, whatever—I ask her, 'What's wrong?' And she looks blank, and the guy, my audience, says, 'Who'd come out on a day like today to hear a politician?' So I asked him, 'How come you're here?' And he says, 'I'm a reporter *Mister* Paterno.' Just like that, '*Mister*.' And then he takes out a pad and pencil and kind of licks the point of the pencil and gives me this look, like it's my fault it's a hundred and three degrees and on account of me he's risking a major stroke. So I gave the speech, standing right up there, and when I'm finished this guy just flips his pad shut and walks off."

"Bill, it must have been awful."

"Terrible. Then Jill starts crying, trying to explain it's not her fault that half of Nassau County has dropped dead from prickly heat or something and the other half doesn't have the energy to walk out the front door. I mean, they're scheduling me for ten-twelve hours a day, Marcia. It's killing. I go out to Suffolk County, to that shopping center in Huntington for a rally, and it's a rally for eight people. Two thousand 'Paterno can do it' buttons and eight people. Do you know what that feels like?"

The combination of heat and humidity finally wore out the building itself. Half the ceiling in Joe Cole's office crumpled, and a chunk of plaster grazed his head. He refused to go to a doctor. "But you have a bump the size of an egg," I said.

"It's a small egg."

"You really ought to have it checked."

"I ought to have my head examined for working here. Crazy place. Pigsty. It's going to collapse before election day. You'll see. We'll all be buried."

"Better now than then," I said.

"Yeah, Did you see the last poll? Appel's moving up again."

"Do you think he has a shot?"

"Marcia, he's buying so much TV time that they hardly have room for regular programs."

"But his ads are so slick."

"But they're so good." He rubbed a patch of scalp near the bump. "Well"—he sighed—"at least I don't have to run out and buy a suit for a victory party."

I tried to seek refuge with Eileen. I stepped into her office and closed the door quietly behind me. "Oh. I didn't hear you come in," she said.

She looked almost ill. Thin to begin with, Eileen had lost even more weight. In a sleeveless blue cotton dress, she looked like a tall frail child. The two bones of her forearm shone through her skin. Her hair seemed so pale it looked white.

"Eileen, are you all right?" She nodded. "Are you sure? Have you been taking care of yourself?"

"I'm okay," she muttered.

"Look, why don't we go somewhere cool and get a drink," I suggested. "It's been ages. I'm sorry I haven't had time to talk, but things have been happening so fast."

"I can't talk now," she said, rising from her desk. She moved with her usual vigor, standing on tiptoe and searching through her bookshelves.

"Hey, it's been all summer. I know you're busy. I'm busy. But it will do us both good to take a half-hour break. Anyway, I need your advice. It's really important."

"I can't talk. I have a brief due. And compliance papers for financial disclosure. Please." She picked up a sheaf of papers from one of the shelves and leafed through them so rapidly I thought she would shred them. "Some other time," she said, not looking up.

"Maybe early next week. We'll have a long lunch."

"No. I can't. I'm sorry."

"Eileen, you're putting too much pressure on yourself."

Her voice rose to a pitch higher than I had ever heard it. "I have meetings. Obligations. Please! I have to work!"

The Friday before Labor Day weekend, I walked into Jerry's office. "We should talk," I said.

"I'm busy now." He collected the pencils and pens on his desk and put them into a coffee mug.

"Please. There's not that much to say. You know that as well as I do. It's been so painful and awkward—"

"I have to go. I'm having drinks with a guy from *Newsday*."

"Jerry, why can't we be honest? Come on, we were such—"

"I'll talk to you when there's time. I've got to go now." I watched as he stood. He took a deep breath to compose himself, hooked his jacket over his index finger, and—with the grace of a Barrymore moving upstage—strode out of his office.

Two hours later he retained his matinee-idol stance as he slouched against the wall of his office, handing out small smiles to the volunteers as they trooped in to watch Lawrence Parker on television. The governor had called a news conference for six thirty in the evening; he would be carried live on almost every news show in the state.

Paterno paced up and down the room. "I don't get this," he said to me. "What's he doing?"

I rubbed my hands nervously. "I don't know."

Jerry grinned at one of the college kids. She blushed.

"Ladies and gentlemen of the Empire State of New York," Parker began. "I want to talk to you." There were titters in the office. Most of the staff and the volunteers sat on the floor or leaned against walls in imitation of Jerry. Many followed his cue and snickered at Parker's oafish countenance, his thick features, his liver-spotted temples, his slow, mechanical delivery of inanities.

"This is a very, very important thing I have to say." The titters became laughs.

Parker went on. "I am going to talk about the thing no man wants to discuss, a problem that when it's talked about at all, is talked about in whispers. But it's my problem and I want to tell you, my friends of the State of New York."

"Morrissey," Paterno said in a hushed voice, "what do you think it is?"

"I don't know." Jerry traced the outline of his upper lip with two fingers. "He's always had a girl friend. And his wife. Never heard anything funny about him. It's probably something stupid."

"I believe in honesty," Parker was saying.

"Marcia?" Paterno asked.

"LoBello's making a move."

"Stop it," Jerry called from across the room. "They're in third place. They know they're dead."

"The problem is," Parker announced, and then paused for a deep breath of courage, "prostate!"

"Jesus!" Jerry said.

"Later this evening, at exactly nine o'clock, I will be entering University Hospital in Buffalo where doctors Herbert Ungerleider and Nicholas Peterson will, tomorrow morning early, perform a prostatectomy."

"Did you see how he pronounced that?" I demanded of Paterno. "He's rehearsed—"

"So what?" Jerry interrupted.

"Now, why am I telling you this?" Parker continued. "I could have had my press secretary announce that I was tired or tell you I had a bad cold. Ha! How many times have you heard that one during a campaign?" Parker rubbed the bottom of his nose with the back of his hand. "I could have said I couldn't campaign because of the press of state business. You know. I'm sure you've heard that one too, over the years of voting you have partaken in."

"Can you believe this?" Paterno said. "Who let him do this? Disgrazia."

"It's just as though he was formally pulling out," Jerry observed.

"But too many men have trouble upon urination *not* to talk about it. Too many men are ashamed to pay a visit to their doctor, and believe you me, they pay for it in the end." The younger staff members and the volunteers hooted or rolled on the rug in silent laughter.

"And you know, ladies and gentlemen, what the bottom line is," Parker proclaimed. He was nearing the end of the five minutes the television stations would grant before cutting him off. "The bottom line is that we lose good men, good citizens, to diseases they don't have to die from if they just saw a urologist or even a regular doctor.

"Today I went to church and prayed. And now, as I leave here and go home to my lovely wife, Gertrude, and pack and then go to the hospital, I ask that you pray for me too. I won't see you again probably before the election, so I thank you now for your support. And I only hope my speaking out has not offended you. I hope it can help other men, so they won't try and keep secrets from everybody. Thank you and have a good evening."

"Idiot," said Jerry.

"Fesso," said Paterno.

I faced Paterno. "This is going to get Parker more attention than if he outspent Appel and outthought you. I'm telling you, Bill, it's brilliant. It's a typical LoBello grandstand play, taking a liability and turning it around."

Jerry's voice was stronger than mine. "Parker's canceled himself out, Bill. It's only you and Appel now."

Paterno glanced from Jerry to me and back to Jerry again. He looked disgusted with both of us. Then he cleared his throat and announced, "I'm going to my sister's for dinner. She's making veal."

A half hour later, as I was getting ready to leave my office, the telephone rang. It was my mother.

"Are you all right, Mom?"

"Yes."

"How are you managing in all this heat?"

"Not very well. The elevator's been broken for a few days." My mother lived on the sixth floor. "It's so hard climbing the stairs."

"Don't climb them, for God's sake. This heat is killing. Listen, I'll make a few calls and get you a room at a hotel. Someplace with air conditioning and—"

"I can't afford things like that."

"I'll pay for it."

"No. thank you." She was being neither noble nor manipulative. She didn't like taking anything from me. Since I had started working for Flaherty in Washington, I had sent her money from each paycheck I received. She said thank you the first time and never mentioned it again. "I'll manage." My cousin Barbara explained my mother to me by saying she was proud, that she did not want to concede her need. I might have accepted this, but at least once a month my mother would allude broadly to her poverty. "There are mice all over this building. I wish I could afford to move," she'd tell me. Or "I had to stop buying coffee. Do you know what they want for a pound?" Each time I offered to help, she'd refuse brusquely. "I'll get by." I often felt that my father and I let her down, he by dying broke and me by not marrying someone who would set her up in lavish style. Alone, I could only ameliorate her poverty, not cure it.

"I tried to call you last night," she said. "I heard there was a blackout in Greenwich Village. No one answered."

"I wasn't around." Then I paused. "Look, Mom. Don't call me there anymore." Her answer was silence. "I'm not living there anymore. Well, I have some stuff there, but I've moved."

"Oh. You hadn't mentioned you were planning on moving."

"I'm staying uptown."

Again she said nothing, as though my telling her I had moved out of Jerry's apartment was just a tidbit of ho-hum news in an otherwise scintillating day.

"I've moved in with David Hoffman."

"What?" she whispered. "Why did you do that?"

"What do you mean? We've been seeing a lot of each other and—"

"How could you do anything so stupid?" she hissed.

"What's wrong with you? Why are you talking to me like that?"

"You're ruining it for yourself again. You're taking a good thing and just throwing it away. Moving in with him. Do you know what he must think of you?"

"I know damned well what he thinks of me," I yelled.

"You don't care, do you? You don't care if Barbara gets everything and you wind up with nothing."

Only one thing made the last week of August tolerable. "I love you," David whispered from the bed. I reached into a jar, took a gob of cream that smelled of spearmint and rubbed it between my hands, then massaged it into the back of his neck and his shoulders.

"I know," I whispered back, even though we were alone in his apartment. "How does this feel?" I ran the heel of my hand along his spine.

"Wonderful. But lower, near the small of my back. Oh, Marcia. Paradise."

While everything else fell apart, my life with David came together. One night when we were taking a shower together, he had shampooed my hair. Several nights later, announcing that he needed pampering, I had clipped his fingernails. We began to coddle each other doing the small favors for each other that parents do for children. I scooped his soft-boiled egg from the shell. David read me bedtime stories, a chapter of the Lord of the Rings trilogy each night. Interspersed between bouts of rough adult sex, we nurtured each other, as if trying to fill in the blanks of our younger lives.

"The back of the legs. Press a little harder. Wonderful," David whispered. "It's better than being fanned by six Nubian slaves with palm fronds." He turned his head to look at me. "Are you all right? Not too tired?"

"I'm fine."

"No more dizziness?"

I rubbed some more cream between my hands and massaged his calves. "David?"

"Hmm?"

"I'm pregnant."

21

The red needles on the gauges of David's Italian sports car quivered in response to the slightest change in the engine's mood. So did I. David, on the other hand, was in high gear, singing the score of *Oklahoma* and watching the dead turnpike scenery whiz by as we sped to his father's country house in Pennsylvania. Finally, he finished with a booming rendition of the title song and then lifted his hand from the gearshift to my leg. "Ready to talk?"

"I'm still a little queasy. Give me five more minutes."

The night before, right after I told him I was pregnant, I had frozen with terror at the audacity of sharing my secret with him.

"Marcia," he said, "are you sure? Have you been to a doctor? Is everything all right? Please, talk to me." I tried to get up and walk from the bed, but David grabbed onto my arm. "Are you sure?" he demanded. I nodded. "Please, Marcia. Don't do this to me. Tell me what's happening."

My mouth was dry, I licked my lips. "I went to the doctor."

"Well? What did he say?"

"She."

"Excuse me. What did she say? Marcia, don't make me interrogate you."

"She said I was definitely pregnant."

"And?"

"And what?"

"Are you all right? Is everything going well?"

"Yes. Everything's fine. She said I have to have that amniocentesis and there's a slightly increased chance of a miscarriage because I've already had one, but that was statistics and everything looks fine. Could you let go of my arm?"

He didn't. "What are you planning on doing?"

"What do you mean?"

"Don't be coy. Please, not at a time like this. You know I want to marry you, that I love you."

"David, I'm so confused right now."

"Please, just listen to me. I may not have any real rights in this matter, no legal rights, but I want this baby. Marcia, I don't care if you don't want pressure or if you're confused. Right now I'm just asking you, please, please, don't have an—"

"David!" I yanked my arm out of his hand.

"You want an abortion?" he whispered.

"No. No. I want this baby too. You don't know how much. I'm not sure about anything else right now, but I know I want it." I stood. "David, I'm going to sleep in one of your kids' rooms. I need time to think."

"No. Sleep here. I promise you, not another word. We'll talk about it tomorrow, on the way to High Oaks." He pointed to the bed. "Come on. You know you can't sleep without me anymore."

It was true. We'd sleep so near each other that we often wound up sharing a pillow. We nestled so close that several times we woke in the middle of the night in the middle of sex so pure and ardent that it seemed like the middle of a perfect dream. I lay down beside him.

The car crossed the border from New Jersey to Pennsylvania. "You know, I was shocked when I saw this car. Really, I pictured you with something solid and conservative, like the biggest Buick ever invented." I glanced out the window at the trees heavy with the shadowy dark-green leaves of the end of summer. "Is High Oaks pretty?" I asked.

"Are you going to marry me?"

"If I like High Oaks. Do you think your father—"

"Marcia!"

"I want to marry you."

High Oaks was a huge stone farmhouse set in the middle of acres of fields and forest. "Nice, isn't it?" David observed, as we came to the end of the mile-long tree-lined drive that led to the house.

"Don't give me understatement. It's magnificent! I love it."

"Unfortunately, my father is part of the package."

Leo Hoffman walked to the car to meet us, taking the slow, mincing steps of the old and sick who are afraid of tripping. "David," he said. They shook hands. "A new car, isn't it?"

"I've had it for about six months."

"I see." There was little resemblance between father and son. While David was large-featured and big-boned, Leo Hoffman was small and thin to the point of delicacy. "And this must be Marcia," he said. David put his arm around me. His father shook my hand. "How nice of you to come."

"Thank you for inviting me."

Leo Hoffman must have been heavier at one time because his face was full of excess tissue: floppy jowls and under-eye bags and a shaky wattle hung from him. Had he been younger, the extra flesh might have made him look unappealing and decadent, but at eighty-five he merely looked very old and wasted.

"Let me help you inside, Father." David offered his arm and his father—hesitantly, I thought—took it. Even the walk from the car to the living room exhausted him; he breathed with difficulty and his ravaged heart did not beat hard enough to propel him smoothly. I walked behind them.

David treated his father politely, as if the older man were the parent of a remote acquaintance of his. His father was courteous too, although he shied away from his son, as if afraid of him. Later, we had tea. When David tapped his father's shoulder to ask if he wanted one of the small sandwiches, the old man recoiled, as if he expected a slap across the face.

"Your father's actually scared of you," I said later. We were in David's room, dressing for dinner. The housekeeper had put my suitcase in another bedroom, and David had picked it up and carried it into his.

"Well, it must be difficult for him. He's completely dependent on me. I manage everything for him. He really can't do anything except just hang on. His heart is so bad."

"Aren't you ever tempted to scream 'boo'?"

"Stop that." But he laughed. "No. There's no score to even. He's old and dying and helpless. What does he have? He bullied his sisters for so many years that they avoid him. He never remarried. I'm the only one who really bothers with him, and he knows I do it out of duty, not out of love. He's afraid I'll stop even that some day."

"No. He fears you, David."

"He fears himself. He fears his disinterest in me and his abandonment of my brother coming back to haunt him now." He zipped up my dress. "You wore this that day at the Drexlers', remember?"

"I remember." I kissed him lightly.

"Look, I know this isn't going to be a great weekend for you, especially since it's your only vacation all summer, but I promised him I'd come. He sleeps most of the time, so we can go off by ourselves."

"This kid of ours is going to have two terrific grandparents." David sat on the edge of the bed, watching me put on my makeup. "I mean, it's really not fair. What ever happened to all that Jewish warmth and love? My mother would rather be kicked to death than touch me. And your father." I turned to him. "Do I have too much blusher?"

"You look fine." He stretched out on the bed. "You know, neither of us conforms to stereotype, but at least you have the feeling of belonging to a community. You're part of the Eastern European cultural tradition, the Yiddish humor, the food . . ."

"The insecurities, the nagging, the impossible goals . . ."

"Marcia, listen. I was never even certain what being Jewish meant. My parents certainly never discussed it. Until law school, when I became friendly with Philip Drexler, I thought of being Jewish as a minor social liability, like having a lisp or an alcoholic parent. Philip is such a proselytizer. He really converted me."

"You think of yourself as a Jew?"

"Of course."

"That's interesting, because one of your attractions for me is that you're so—I don't know—so un-Jewish. It's like marrying a Protestant without the guilt. You're so American. You belong here."

"So do you."

"No. I think like an ethnic. I belong in New York, on a certain block in Queens with people who got off the same boat as my grandparents did. But with you, I can escape that. I can move out of the old neighborhood and feel decent about it. I'm not deserting anyone; no one will throw rocks at me in the new place. Do you understand?"

"I think so. But you shouldn't cast off your background. It's a niche, not a pigeonhole. That's why I like your family, your Aunt Estelle—"

"David, come on."

"At least she's human."

Leo Hoffman sat at the dinner table gazing at a platter of vegetables the maid held in front of him. "Let me see," he said slowly. "Green beans tonight? Or broiled tomatoes?" The platter was silver and, from the arch of the woman's back, looked heavy. "You know, Marcia," he explained as she stood before him, "we grow our own vegetables here, and some of our own fruit too. Raspberries and strawberries. Oh, and plums—Burbank and Green Gage." The woman's shoulder muscles twitched slightly. I hoped she would drop the vegetables onto his lap. "We haven't had much luck with figs, though. There's a great deal of wind in this valley and the trees are so fragile. And in the fall we have our apples. Four different varieties. McIntosh, Paragon, Wealthy, and McCoun. I think I'll just skip the vegetables tonight, June."

For a while we ate in silence. Then David said, "The tomatoes are good, Father."

"We've had a fine crop, David. A fine crop."

I glanced across the table at David, hoping to exchange smiles. But he sat stiffly, clutching his fork so tight that his knuckles showed white. He barely ate. There was no pleasure for him when his father was around.

As we rose from the table, David said to his father, "The children did well at camp this summer."

"Good. Fine children. When are they coming home?"

"They're in Canada with Lynn and Arthur, fishing. They're spending next weekend with us. Marcia hasn't met them yet."

"Fine children. Both of them." David had two sons and a daughter.

The next morning, when David went riding, his father took me for a walk around the house. "Over here we have the original chimney of High Oaks. It was built in 1784, you know. See? The stonework is not as sophisticated as on the right wing. That was completed in 1856 or 1857. No, that's the left wing you're looking at. It's the right wing as we're facing the house."

Leo Hoffman's hand was dehydrated into a claw, and he clutched my arm for support. I murmured "hmms" and "how interesting" as we walked. He told me about the lichen of Pennsylvania and why the forsythia was a highly overrated shrub. "Does your family live in the country?" he asked, as we approached the front door again. I suspected he already knew the answer.

"No. My father's been dead for twenty-five years. My mother lives in an apartment building in Queens."

"I see." I helped him onto his chair in the living room, a large wing chair that emphasized his diminutiveness. "I hear my son has asked you to marry him."

"Yes. And I've agreed to."

"I see." He sat absolutely still. "I hope it works," he said finally. Then, although it was just ten thirty, he excused himself for his afternoon nap.

I walked alone through the woods of High Oaks, past groves of wildflowers, white and lacy, tall and proud and yellow, down to the stables, where I waited for David. I ran my hand over a rough wooden fence in a proprietary gesture. My child would spend summers here, making wildflower bouquets. Winter vacations. I imagined a small red-cheeked child, screeching with delight, throwing half-formed snowballs at David and me. I grabbed the fence.

"Anything wrong?" David asked as he rode up.

"No. I was just hanging around, feeling overwhelmed." David seemed to ride well. At least his posture was good, he didn't fall off, and both he and the horse seemed content. "Do you ride well?"

"Yes. Why are you overwhelmed?"

"All this upward mobility."

"You'll get used to it."

"I know. That's the amazing thing, how fast I'm adjusting to all this. Having a maid make the bed." I watched him get off the horse. "The only problem with that is we can't get right back into bed and mess it up again."

"Are you in the mood for messing up beds?"

He was patting the horse's nose, still paying a little more attention to it than me. "Yes." I put my arms around his waist and hugged him. "David, I want you so much."

We did not make it back to the house to mess up the bed again. Halfway through the woods, David asked, "Do you think we could manage standing up?"

For a man who once surrounded himself with darkness, David had learned to love the light. We undressed in a patch of sunshine. When we kissed and I closed my eyes, I sensed his were open. He watched me as I climbed on a rock, and, when our heights were equalized and we began making love, he said softly, "Let's watch each other." We were so close I could only see his eyes, but they reflected the entire forest, gleaming green and gold and brown.

"Can we have another rendezvous in the woods?" I asked, as we drove home late on Labor Day. "Even after we're married?"

"Just pick your rock. I'll be there."

As we entered the Lincoln Tunnel to Manhattan he said, "We have to make wedding plans. And honeymoon plans. Where would you like to go?"

"France. What did you think I'd say, Niagara Falls? I want to stay in fabulous hotels and gorge myself and go to museums and make love twice a day. Okay? Or do you want to go someplace more exotic?"

"I was considering Miami Beach."

"David, don't even kid about that."

As an afterthought, I had him drop me at the Greenwich Village apartment, so I could pick up some clothes and leave Jerry a final check for my share of the rent. I walked up the stairs slowly. I knew Jerry would not be in. He had murmured something about going on an upstate swing with Paterno. Still, I was nervous and mildly nauseated, although I wasn't sure whether it was pregnancy or anxiety. On the last flight of stairs I began to pant and sweat.

Perspire, my mother would have it, if she would have it at all. Sweating, I unlocked the door and discovered Jerry.

"Just let me rest a second," I muttered. "Oh, boy. Coronary time. How are you?" I plopped down on the couch, breathing heavily.

Jerry leaned against the wall in the hallway, facing the living room. His own suitcase stood next to him but, unlike me, he was not windblown and gritty from a two-hour ride in an Italian convertible. Nor did he appear sick to his stomach. Instead, Jerry looked cool, as if he had just sipped an iced julep in an evening breeze. He wore a new shirt, a white and blue and green plaid, and it was opened enough to show the top of his flower of chest hair. "You were gone this weekend," he said.

"Yes. To Bucks County. Pennsylvania. Jerry, I have something to tell you."

"Please. I want to talk to you."

"Fine." I paused. "Actually, Jerry, it's not so easy. I don't know how to say . . ." I felt my eyes filling with tears. He looked so splendid, so secure, and I didn't want to see him hurt, watch him crumple.

"Marcia, I'm leaving," he burst out. "I've been going crazy all summer, trying to find a way to tell you, not to hurt you. You can have the apartment. It's all yours. I'll help you with the rent for the next few months."

"Jerry—"

"You've got to hear me out. I'm leaving. I'm leaving the apartment. Leaving you. I'm sorry. Jesus Christ, I don't know how to explain it to you. It was that night I came in and you were all dressed up, with makeup, going to the theater." The night I first made love with David. "You were acting so strange, so charged up."

"I wasn't."

"You were. You ran out of the apartment, like you weren't even thinking about me. I knew that since the beginning of the summer things hadn't been right. I didn't know what was happening. I knew part of it was my fault. We had been fighting. But you were so different that night, not even saying hello properly. And not looking at me, not caring—"

"Jerry, please listen to me. I can save us both a lot of time, a lot of ill will."

"No. Let me finish. I didn't know what was happening to us. So I took a long walk. I went uptown and wound up at Eileen's. I decided to talk with her. I knew how close you two were, so I thought maybe she could help me understand why you were behaving the way you were."

"Jerry, Eileen was the wrong person to ask. I hadn't confided in her. And she's always been antagonistic toward you. I don't know why. She says it's because you're too much alike."

"Marcia, listen to me."

"I'm listening. What did she say, that you were wasting my time?"

"Marcia, we made love that night and we fell in love."

"Who?"

"Eileen. Me and Eileen."

"Oh, my God."

"Marcia, you know there's been someone else. Does it really matter who? I mean, I haven't been home a whole night all summer. You knew I was with someone. We just started talking that night, sitting in her apartment—"

"You were drunk."

"Eileen said you would say that. But I understand. I know what this is doing to you and I swear to you, both of us are sick about it. Eileen's been wanting to tell you for over a month, but I begged her not to. It was my job. But we feel awful." He took a step toward me but stopped. "And there's one more thing."

"What is it?" I managed to say. The air of the apartment was thick from heat and dust. My throat felt tight and I wanted to escape uptown to David's, where the air was clean.

"We got married." The living room was quiet, but the clock in the kitchen whirred noisily. "We weren't going to, but we want to . . ."

"What, Jerry?"

"I don't want to hurt you."

"Go ahead."

"We want to have a family." He sat on the couch beside me. After a weekend of David's horsey smell, the scent of his cologne seemed almost feminine. "Marcia, if there's anything I can do . . ."

I rose from the couch.

"Well . . ." Jerry reached up and touched the back of my

hand, offering sympathy. He wore a thin gold wedding band. When he saw me staring at it, he pulled his hand away.

"Marcia, both of us are so sorry."

"Don't let it spoil your honeymoon."

"Please. Try not to be bitter. You're a wonderful person. You deserve someone who can really make you happy. You'll find someone someday, sweetheart. I'm sure you will."

22

Jerry Morrissey caught me napping the day before the primary. He cleared his throat so vehemently that my body reacted violently, jerking about in my desk chair before I even opened my eyes.

"Oh," I said, rather stupidly. "What do you want?"

"You were sleeping."

"Yes. What is it?"

"I need three speeches for tomorrow. A victory speech and two concessions: one if Parker wins, one if it's Appel. In the Parker one, pledge our support. Make it fairly friendly. Appel's can be short, okay but noncommittal."

"Okay." I covered my mouth as I yawned. "Excuse me."

"Don't you think you could wait till after the primary to get your rest?"

"Do you have any complaints about my work? Do you? Because if not, there's no reason for you to be criticizing me just because I shut my eyes for five minutes."

I was tired. Each lunch hour I met David and we hiked around a square-mile area of the East Side, searching for a new cooperative apartment. "What's wrong with yours?" I had inquired. "It's not exactly material for *Tenement Monthly*."

"It's too small. Look, we'll need a bedroom for us . . ."

"I can just strap a mattress onto my back."

". . . one for the baby, three for my children, for when they visit, then possibly an office for each of us. And what if we have another child? If we can find two adjoining apartments, it might even pay to tear down a few walls and renovate."

"David, that sounds like an awful lot of money."

"Well, I have an awful lot of money."

We found a huge apartment on Park Avenue, terribly run down from two generations of neglect but potentially grand, with dark wood walls and high ceilings. And bedrooms. Bedrooms for pre-existing Hoffmans and future Hoffmans.

I met David's children the weekend after Labor Day. I half expected they'd be the missing kink in David's character I'd been searching for—small, hazel-eyed psychopaths or unregenerate snobs. But they were pleasant and polite. The two older children, Dan and Jim, had David's pale brown hair and mouths full of metal braces. They were too embarrassed to hug and kiss their father, but they let David ruffle their hair and they gave him frequent manly slaps on the back. Seven-year-old Bonnie barely climbed off his lap all weekend. I was afraid she would be resentful, but she was very affectionate with me too, holding my hand as we walked along Madison Avenue. I took her for a haircut and then out for a hot fudge sundae. "My mother doesn't let me eat anything with sugar," she confided, after taking her last lick of the spoon.

"You should have told me that before, Bonnie."

"Are you kidding?"

They were bright and friendly and put their napkins on their laps without being reminded. All three of them kissed me good-bye.

"Whom do you have in mind as a decorator?" David asked.

"The one who did my mother's apartment. You can get a couch and two chairs in the same fabric for just five hundred—"

"Why don't you ask Barbara who helped her?"

A woman who looked like Queen Victoria arrived and surveyed the new apartment. She found it had potential. She spoke through her nose, mainly to David. "I know your aunt. Louisa Patterson. She is your aunt, isn't she, Mr. Hoffman?" David nodded. "And you, my dear," she said, finally turning to me. "Have you any thoughts on the living room?"

"I think a marquetried bombé would be perfect over there, in that corner."

"Yes. Yes, it might just do."

Later, David demanded, "Where in God's name did you come up with a marquetried bombé?"

"Are you kidding? I spent an hour and a half in the Forty-second Street Library this afternoon. She scares me, David."

"Me too."

Jerry pulled a rickety bridge chair up to my desk. He tested it with his hand before sitting on it. "I'd like to talk to you seriously," he said.

"All right."

"This isn't working out, the three of us here. Eileen hides in her office all day. It's painful for her to see you. I feel funny, uncomfortable."

"I know you do."

"I thought you'd understand." He pulled his perfect dark eyebrows together in thought. "Wouldn't it be better," he said gently, "if you left? I mean, you wouldn't have to feel awkward."

"What are you talking about?" I boomed at him. "I don't feel awkward at all."

"Marcia, don't try to shout me down. Of course you do. We all do. It's an unnatural situation. Listen, we all made mistakes. Wouldn't it be better for you to start someplace fresh, someplace where you'll feel more at ease? You've had loads of job offers over the years. Eileen says—"

"Jerry, listen to me. I am staying here. If your wife feels she has to hide in her office, that's her problem. What does she think I'll do, spring for her jugular? And if she can't take hiding in her office, let her move her ass and find herself another job. She's a lawyer, for God's sake. There are jobs all over the city where she could do a full day's work without feeling ashamed. And as far as you go—well, I think we can manage. We had a lovely time together, and hopefully pretty soon we'll be able to remember that and forget the bitterness."

"Marcia—"

"I like this job. I like Paterno. I am staying. This is the

second time you've asked me to quit work, to screw up my career on your behalf. If I didn't do it before, Jerry, can you think why I would possibly consider doing it now?"

Jerry crossed his legs and rubbed the cleft in his chin. He was about to deal his big card. "Marcia, I happen to know for a fact that Bill approved a month's leave for you starting the week after the primary. Now that's not just because you're tired. You're planning on job hunting anyway. So why not let me help you, make some calls."

"Jerry, I will tell you something that really doesn't concern you. The Sunday afternoon after the election, I am getting married. The following morning my husband and I will be getting on an airplane and flying to France, where we will spend four weeks on our honeymoon. Then I will come back to work, and by that time I'm sure we can begin to enjoy a pleasant working relationship."

"You're bullshitting me," he whispered. "Where did you find someone so fast? Where?"

He called out "Where?" again as I stomped out of my office and down to Paterno's. "Excuse me, Bill," I said.

Paterno lifted his big head from his hands. "Didn't hear you come in."

"How are you doing?"

"Fine. It'll all be over tomorrow, one way or another. How are you doing?"

"Fine. I just have those three speeches to do, the victory and the other ones."

"Where would you put your money?"

"On you, Bill. Win or lose."

"Thanks."

"Can we talk?" He nodded. "Jerry was just in to see me. He mentioned something about how awkward things are, with the two of them and me. . . ."

"That Morrissey. I don't get him. He's a good-looking fella. Why does he have to keep picking people on my staff? Can't he look outside?"

"Well, he won't be looking anymore," I observed. Paterno agreed, looking away from me in embarrassment. "Bill, he suggested that because things were so—well, uncomfortable, for Eileen and for him, that I resign."

"He *what*?"

"I just wanted to make sure that it wasn't coming from you, that—"

"Are you kidding? That son-of-a-bitch. Let me tell you something, Marcia. That wife of his, that Eileen, is no shrinking violet, and she can learn to handle things or get out. So can he and so can you. I'm a city official, not a producer of some damned soap opera, and the three of you can either put your personal lives behind you or get the hell out. All of you. I mean it."

"Okay, Bill."

"Hey, why am I yelling at you?"

"Maybe it feels good."

"Listen, this whole thing isn't your fault. I don't know whose fault it is. Crazy, carrying on in the middle of a campaign, like it was spring fever. Who has time for that? Your boyfriend, that's who, that crazy Morrissey. . . . Oh, sorry."

"That's okay. Listen, I'll see you tomorrow night, at the victory party."

"Marcia, come on. You've been straight with me for too long. Don't start changing now."

"Then I'll see you tomorrow night."

"And after that? No matter where?"

"As long as you need a speech writer."

The polls closed a nine o'clock. By ten, the ballroom of the Hotel Knickerbocker was pulsating with a badly amplified three-piece band and shouted conversations. A limp Paterno banner hung from the empty stage. Balloons hung in a net from the ceiling, waiting to be released in case of victory.

Volunteers from the boroughs and the suburbs milled around, their smiles still as wide as Paterno's was on the campaign buttons on their lapels. They peered up at the balloons, gazed in awe at the TV correspondents, and sipped their free drinks. Some of them dashed around purposefully, jotting down telephone numbers, knowing this was their last chance for a big romance.

By ten thirty, the returns began coming in. I stood beside Joe Cole, in front of one of the four television sets in the ballroom, each tuned to a different station. "Look at Westchester County," he said. "Twenty-eight percent for us. Just twenty-eight percent. Shit, that LoBello must be grinning from ear to ear. We counted on at least forty."

"My God, Queens," I replied. "His home borough." Paterno was pulling in only thirty-eight percent of the vote.

Brooklyn's returns were, surprisingly, more favorable to Paterno. He received a clear majority. He also did well in Manhattan. But each time the camera switched to the tote board, the results became, as the anchorman suggested, fairly inevitable. Governor Parker was being re-elected. Paterno was losing. Uncle Sidney was being humiliated. "At least Appel is getting his," Cole said. "Do you know how much he spent, what it cost him per vote? He could have just gone out and bought each voter a color TV or a vacuum or something and they'd still be screaming 'Yeah, Sidney!' Je-sus, if I had his wife's money, I wouldn't waste it in politics." I agreed with him.

At eleven, I saw Eileen Gerrity Morrissey on the other side of the ballroom. I walked toward her. For a moment, she looked to each side of her, trying to find a friend or an exit, but finally she stood motionless, waiting for me. "I don't know what to say," she said quietly.

"Well, there's not a lot to be said. I just don't want any more pressure on me about quitting. I'm here and I'm staying here. Understood?"

"Yes." She chewed the inside of her cheek nervously. "Well, I hear you're engaged. I guess congratulations are in order." I didn't answer. "Marcia," she said then, "I'm so sorry. I can imagine what you must think of me."

"Then I don't have to tell you," I responded, and crossed back across the ballroom, to watch the television set with Joe Cole.

The anchorman, who had perfect, even teeth, all the same size, returned after a commercial. "I have with me here in the studio Midge Bashian, the Albany correspondent of the *New York Times*. Midge, what's happening here? The polls predicted the governor would go down to ignominious defeat. And as we can see, with sixty-three percent of the vote counted, we have him as the projected winner. What happened? What went wrong?"

"Well," Midge began, shaking her head back and forth until she found the right camera to address, "it looks like the Democratic voters of New York State gave their hearts to their ailing governor. I think his speech before he entered the hospital, its unusually direct and unashamed appeal to the emotions of his constituency, served Larry Parker well. He showed himself as a man with a problem, and people responded." Midge would probably not be asked to return as a guest commentator. Her teeth were spotted and crooked, pushing for room in a tight mouth. "As opposed to him"—the camera went back to the spiffy newscaster—"Sidney Appel looked like a media creation, too studied, too perfect. Shades of the 1968 Nixon." He nodded on-camera as she spoke off. An excellent television arrangement. "And William Paterno was perceived as, if we can say such a thing, too smart for his own good. This is a year of simplicity."

She was right about Appel, and perhaps about Paterno too. In a year of simplicity, the simp had won. No doubt, politicians in Utah and South Carolina would soon be running on a prostate platform.

"Thanks again to Midge Bashian of the *Times*. Fine analysis, Midge. And now I think we're going to switch to Paterno headquarters. Betty-Jean, are you ready?"

She was, but Paterno wasn't. He could not be coaxed from his room in the hotel until eleven thirty. He stood before the cameras dry-eyed. He read my concession speech in a clear, calm voice. He repeated to two TV correspondents that yes, he would be proud to support the nominee of the Democratic Party and no, he hadn't meant to disparage Governor Parker's abilities, but everyone says things in the heat of a campaign that might be misinterpreted. And maybe he would consider running for mayor in three years' time, but first he wanted to get home and get a good night's sleep.

And when the television lights turned off and the reporters shuffled away, Paterno put his hands over his face and cried. Joe Cole patted his shoulder; Jerry put his arm around him; Eileen said he'd done a fine job; the women's affairs coordinator said his mother would have been proud.

I reached him a minute later. "I'm so sorry, Bill. You were the best man. You should have won."

"I know," he murmured.

David waited up for me. "I saw you on TV! You looked beautiful. But upset. You were talking to a black man and you both looked upset."

"We were watching the returns," I said softly, taking off

my shoes and curling up beside him on the couch. "It was enough to make anyone upset. David, it's such a sad loss. Paterno's a bright, decent man. He would have been a terrific governor. He deserved to win."

"I know."

"It's all so uncontrollable. Who would have believed Gresham would choke to death? Who would have thought Sidney Appel would decide he was a politician? Can I tell you something? I have it in for your uncle. If it hadn't been for him running around and obscuring the issues with all his goddamned money, we could have won." I rubbed my hands over my face. "You know, experience doesn't make losing easier. It's harder, the older I get. I try so hard, I've become so professional at it, but it's still completely out of my hands. I did fabulous work this summer. Parker's speech writer is a goon. And look what happened."

"I'm sorry he lost. Really. I voted for him today."

"For Paterno? Did you? Honestly?"

"Honestly. He deserved to win. But don't be too hard on Sidney. He's responsible for us meeting each other. If he hadn't run, I'd be working late tonight, staring out the window and wondering what my blind date for Saturday night would be like."

"A beast."

"Of course. Here, let me help you up. You're starting to get that overtired, hypnotized stare. Come on, right to bed."

I slept even closer to him than usual that night, my face pressed against his chest, thinking exactly where I'd be if it weren't for Uncle Sidney.

The next night I wondered where I would be if it weren't for my Aunt Estelle. "Darling," she said, "wasn't I right? Look at him sitting there. Such a person. So fine. I told you. . . ."

I tried to catch David's eye, but he was deep in conversation with Barbara and Philip, sitting on a corner of my aunt's titanic sectional couch, their three heads bent together as though sharing rich, exclusive secrets.

My mother cooed, "May I see your ring again?" I held out my left hand. David had bought me a diamond engagement ring large enough to please my aunt and my mother combined. "Oh," she said, "it's very fine looking. David has such classic taste." I had picked it out. "Do you know what jeweler he used?" she asked, her voice so hushed and reverent it was nearly a whisper.

"We went to Cartier's."

"Shh, Marcia," my aunt said. "Not so loud. He'll think we're talking about the ring."

"Well, of course we're talking about the ring. I'm standing here with my left hand out and the two of you are—"

"Marcia," my mother explained, "it's not considered in good taste to discuss jewelry."

"Then why are we discussing jewelry?"

"Don't get temperamental, Marcia," my aunt said. Then she turned to my mother. "Pre-wedding jitters. They all get them."

I marched across the room. David made a place for me on the couch. "Marcia," Barbara said, "we're talking about the wedding. High Oaks should be beautiful this time of year."

"We're going to be married in the rose garden. And the rabbi—your father-in-law recommended him—turns out to be this guy I went to high school with. We were in the same plane geometry class. I mean, David and I walked into his study for an interview with him, and there's Sandy Langer. But now he's Sandford and has a mustache and a doctorate in Judaic studies. Isn't that unbelievable?"

"Yes," Barbara agreed. "Who's the caterer?"

"I don't know."

"You don't know?" Barbara looked surprised, but her expression lost none of its unfailing good humor. Her face, however, although tanned and glowing from her biweekly facial, had grown rounder over the summer. By marrying Philip, she had traded up her love of Mallomars for *milles feuilles,* but her month in Europe meant an annual gain of fifteen pounds. When she had walked through the door that evening, her mother had squeezed her full chin and remarked, "No dessert for you tonight, darling." A mere glint from Philip's icy stare had caused an immediate amendment. "You were never so crazy about blueberry crumb cake, so I bought a gorgeous melon. Cranshaw. You'll love it."

Barbara turned to David. "Who's the caterer?"

"Sara Asher," he answered.

"Oh, she's marvelous. Her lemon mousse cake! Everybody's dying to get her, but she's so booked! How did you manage it?"

"I don't know. My aunt made the arrangements."

"What's your first course?" she asked me.

"I don't know." I glanced at David. "Have we decided?"

Barbara interjected, "Marcia, you're getting *married*, for goodness' sake." She took Philip's hand. "When we got married we went over every single hors d'oeuvre. We knew exactly what we were getting, down to the filling of the last quiche." David sensed I was about to say something; he pressed his leg against mine to signal not to. "Do I dare ask?" she said.

"What?"

"Have you bought a dress yet?"

"No. I will. Yesterday was election day. Today was chaos. But we're going tomorrow night. The stores are open late."

"Where?"

"I don't know, Barbara. Someplace horribly expensive, all right?"

"What's wrong with you?"

"Nothing. I'm going for a walk." I looked at David. "Alone."

"Not alone," he said.

He followed me out the wide front door that my Uncle Julius had paid the builder extra for thirty years before.

"What's the matter, Marcia?" He circled his arm around me and pulled me close, so my cheek rubbed against the cashmere of his sweater.

"This isn't going to work."

"What isn't going to work?"

"Us. I can't be what I'm supposed to be. I don't want to have to deal with arrogant, disgusting decorators and worry that I won't know which caterer is chic and which designer dress I should buy. I came in the house tonight and you saw what happened. My mother runs up to me and says 'Marcia!' like she just discovered me and kisses me. Plants a kiss right there, on my cheek. And it only took an eighty-million-carat diamond ring from Cartier's to get that kind of warmth from her. And my cousin. Did you hear her? Have I told Paterno I'm going to quit? That was the first thing she asked, like my old life is over and now I can spend all my time taking Chinese cooking courses. And your wonderful friend Philip. The only thing he's ever spoken to me about is politics, and suddenly he's asking me about our honeymoon plans, the new apartment. Not a word about the election. It's as if nothing I've done is worth anything. Excuse me. One thing. Hooking you. That justifies the thirty-five years of sweat and tears they put into me. Well, let me tell you something. I don't want any part of it."

David said nothing. I walked up the block silently then, and he followed. We passed the Leventhal house next door where, presumably, Lydia Leventhal was learning to live alone. We continued to the end of the street.

"I know what you're going to say," I said to him. "That I'm tired, cranky from the pregnancy, and all that. Depressed over the election. You don't have to say it."

"I wasn't going to." David leaned against a parked car.

"What were you going to say then? That I shouldn't be rude to my cousin? That I should ask my mother what wine the Baroness serves with the meat course, just to humor her?"

"No. They're your relatives. You can treat them however you wish."

"Well?"

"Well, as you've been saying, you're thirty-five years old. I'm not going to try to tell you what you should feel, how you should behave." I pulled my eyes from his stare and examined the sidewalk. "You say it isn't going to work," he added.

"David." I looked up at him.

"What is it?"

"I love you. I love you very much."

"Come here." I leaned against him. He put his hand on the back of my head and smoothed my hair. "It's okay now. Stop shaking. You've said it, Marcia. It's out."

"David, I've never said 'I love you' before. Not just to you. To anyone. Did you know that? You're the first person I've ever truly loved. And you're the first person who ever truly loved me."

"But you say it won't work."

"They get to me. They undermine me."

"Stop that. They can't do anything to you unless you let

them. Think about it, Marcia. In all the time we've been together, have we ever discussed caterers?"

"No."

"Have we ever spent more than one second more than we had to with that dreadful decorator?" I shook my head. "And have I ever even hinted that I'd rather you spent your time making wonton soup or whatever instead of writing? Have I? Marcia, they have very little to do with us. We have everything to do with each other."

My arms wrapped around him. "I really love you. You don't know."

"I do know," he said. "And I also know you're going to make me a wonderful wife. And do you want to know something else? I'm going to be a superb husband. You and I are going to be very, very happy."

"I know, David."

He kissed me. "I know you know."